An Earl's Sacrifice

The Clandestine Sapphire Society
Book 3

Kathy L Wheeler

ARE YOU SIGNED UP FOR DRAGONBLADE'S BLOG?

You'll get the latest news and information on exclusive giveaways, exclusive excerpts, coming releases, sales, free books, cover reveals and more.

Check out our complete list of authors, too!

No spam, no junk. That's a promise!

Sign Up Here

www.dragonbladepublishing.com

Dearest Reader;

Thank you for your support of a small press. At Dragonblade Publishing, we strive to bring you the highest quality Historical Romance from some of the best authors in the business. Without your support, there is no 'us', so we sincerely hope you adore these stories and find some new favorite authors along the way.

Happy Reading!

CEO, Dragonblade Publishing

Additional Dragonblade books by Author Kathy L Wheeler

The Clandestine Sapphire Society

A Silent Accord (Book 1)
A Daring Pursuit (Book 2)
An Earl's Sacrifice (Book 3)

PART ONE

CHAPTER ONE

11:00 A.M. Tuesday, 28 May 1844
London, St George's Cathedral

LUCIUS OSHEA NEVER cared much for his father, the current Earl of Pender. Now, he outright hated him. Enough to kill him. St. George's was packed to standing room only. His bride at one and twenty to his one and thirty was obscene. And the Duke of Rathbourne was behind this entire farce. There were so many candles burning, Lucius was tempted to knock over one or two and set the place ablaze.

His bride—he couldn't recall her name and couldn't force himself to care—was wearing ice blue. Fitting, as it went with the blood congealing in his veins. A veil of stark white lace covered her face. Clearly, Brussels. He'd once lauded a piece for Docia upon his return from his Grand Tour. This trend of the Queen's in covering the bride's face was one of which he gladly approved at the moment. It saved him from having to see her. He envisioned terrified, tear-filled eyes. Why, they'd never even met!

The bishop's deep resonance jarred Lucius from his dark and seething resentments. *"Wilt thou have this Woman to thy wedded wife, to live together after God's ordinance in the holy estate of Matrimony? Wilt thou love her—"*

And that was just about enough of that. He would *not* love her. He would *not* comfort her. He absolutely would *not* keep her in sickness, nor health. The minute he could escape this catastrophe and ditch his *bride* to Cornwall, Lucius Oshea, Viscount Perlsea, future Earl of Pender, was finished. His father and the duke could hang. There would be no heirs, not from his seed, by God, he promised himself.

"Lord Perlsea?"

Lucius flinched.

"Your vow, sir." The bishop's low timbre grated through him.

"I will," he gritted out. Thank God Docia had stayed in Northumberland.

The tedium continued with Lucius dutifully reciting the ring vow in a flat tone devoid of inflection. His soon-to-be-wife's fingers shook with a violence he had to steady in order to slide the gold band into place.

"You may lift the veil, sir."

It was a wonder no one called Lucius out on the grinding of his teeth. He gripped the softness of her veil with whitened knuckles. He forced himself to unbend and loosened his hold, then lifted.

Light brown streaks within the blondish, goldish hair swept from her face in a bun set at the crown of her head, encircled with a diamond-studded tiara. Widened eyes of moss green stared up at him. God, she was so young. For a long moment, he was caught in that unblinking stare. Rather than frightened, she appeared stunned at the inevitability of this lifelong prison sentence of which they were now destined and unable to curtail for the remainder of their lives.

Her plump, pink lips firmed, revealing she had no desire for this match any more than he.

Excellent. That should alleviate his cause when he abandoned her in the wilds of Cornwall without a problem.

But she was so, so young. He hardened his stance. The duke was likely counting on her innocence swaying him to her favor, and Lucius would allow that to *never* happen.

Never. He was in love with Docia Hale. It was she to whom his heart belonged.

Regardless, Lucius took his new wife's arm and faced the

standing congregation. Together, they took the long walk to the open doors at the back of St. George's. Upon reaching the stone steps just outside, a chaotic crowd of onlookers let out a roar of *huzzahs*. The entire scene reminded him of some outrageous farcical he'd witnessed at a production of *The Vampire* he'd seen at the Theater Royale some years past.

Quickly, however, Lucius felt the weight of the spectacle shift as a knot of commoners gathered near the base of the church steps, pressed together like eager spectators at a boxing match. Their faces, flushed and animated, betrayed a range of emotions—from open delight at witnessing a noble wedding to sharp-eyed curiosity, trying to catch any hint of discord between a reluctant bride and groom. Some of the younger men stood with arms crossed and sly grins slashing their faces. Instinct had him tugging his bride tightly to his side.

The most worrisome members of the throng were the gossip-hungry wolves that lingered just beyond the boundaries of propriety. Ink-stained fingers clutched their notebooks and pencils, poised to capture his expression and hoping for any awkward exchanges between the wedding party. Men in flat caps and threadbare coats lurked beyond the church gate, pretending to be loiterers, but quietly jotted down details that would soon appear in the pages of the *London Times* and the *Intelligencer*. Some whispered to their compatriots of what Lucius could only imagine. The significance of his marriage did not escape him.

A caricaturist, seated on a wooden crate nearby, scratched away on a pad in his lap. In a matter of seconds, he held up an exaggerated portrait of Lucius that showed him with drooping shoulders and wearing a scowl.

The air hummed with murmurs and snickers, punctuated by the sharp clatter of horse hooves as carriages began to pull away from the church. An underlying tension vibrated through the crowd with a mix of curiosity, envy, and joy at another's misfortune. Everyone seemed to be waiting for something to go wrong, hoping for some misstep or a statement ready to be taken out of context.

Raindrops splattered on the cobblestones, and the onlookers shuffled, pulling collars higher, adjusting shawls, though none looked eager to leave. A low rumble spread through the horde, like ripples on a pond.

"He didn't even look at her, did you see?"

"Poor girl. She looks ready to faint."

"Two years? I wager not even one before it's a tell-all scandal."

Every word was like the nick of a dirk, pricking his skin.

The clanging bell of a passing hansom cab briefly drowned out the whispers, but only for a moment. The scent of wet stone and fresh flowers mingled with the damp air, creating a heavy oppressiveness. With most of the aristocracy crowded at his and his viscountess's backs, there was no barrier to keep the onlookers from pressing forward like waves lapping at the shore, craning necks to catch every detail.

The thought jarred Lucius from a dark vortex threatening to pull him under. He glanced at his bride. Her face was pale but composed, but then, she was a duke's daughter, so of course she remained composed. He gripped her arm with a tension born of both duty and frustration, then ushered her quickly down the stone steps, sweeping her toward his waiting carriage.

The gaze of the crowd pressed in on him, judging, dissecting, waiting for cracks to appear. These people weren't here to celebrate; they were here to witness his downfall. He caught the eye of one man, who quickly pulled down his low-crowned hat. With a snarky grin, the man signaled the caricaturist, then handed him a coin.

With a shake of his head, Lucius gave a curt nod to his driver, then fought his way through the cluster even as the crowd squeezed tighter, murmuring louder and louder. Cheers and jeers filled the air with deafening zeal. Bartlett swung the door open just as someone in the back shouted, "Here's to your first fight!" drawing another wave of laughter from the throng.

His shoulders stiffened, his grip on his bride tightening for a heartbeat before he assisted her into the carriage. The door slammed shut behind them, muffling the sound of the crowd's amusement.

Outside, the noise of whispers and laughter continued, carried on the wind like a curse, as the carriage wheels turned.

"Welcome to the life of a duke's daughter," she said lightly. Her gaze was on the crowd beyond the window.

He wished he could smile, but the bitterness was too ingrained. "And the son of a notorious earl," he rejoined with a bark of bitter laughter.

Friday, 1 June 1844
Cornwall, Perlsea Keep

MEREDITH JEPHSON-OSHEA, LADY Perlsea to Lucius Oshea's Viscount Perlsea, found herself stunned that her new husband hadn't bothered to just run her over with the carriage in his haste to depart Cornwall. Bridal night?

No, thank heavens.

She glanced down at the gold band weighing down the fourth finger of her left hand. How tempting to rip it off and toss it over the cliffs and into the sea below. It appeared, unfortunately, to be the only protection afforded her, watching the dust stir beneath the flying hooves of her new husband's destrier.

She hadn't even had time to find a new maid, having left her other one behind. The cheeky girl seemed more loyal to the duke than to Meredith.

This was her third day at Perlsea Keep. A monstrously unkept castle that hadn't seen a mistress in some twenty years, she'd venture. Disrepair was evident everywhere. From the crumbling stone stairs that led below, of which she had no desire to see, to rotted planks in the sitting room, parlor, morning room, and dining hall.

She'd ventured into the unused portion of the castle and nearly ran screaming, but for one interesting chamber that kept drawing her back—three times already. An ancient library that seemed to hold heavy, untold secrets that sent delicious shivers over her skin. Such fanciful notions would run amok given half the chance. But even a ghostly atmosphere was more entertaining than sitting about moping over missing her friends.

For the life of her, Meredith couldn't fathom why she just didn't take the carriage and rush back to London. But, oddly, she found the gusting winds and wilds of Cornwall embracing.

Meredith stole down an old stairwell before the housekeeper could warn her yet again of the dangers of this unused tower of the Keep.

A rash of raw fury engulfed her. Lord Perlsea hadn't even had the consideration to see that her chamber had been properly prepared. Thankfully, he had left the footman behind along with the carriage and had ridden his stallion off the grounds without a backward glance. Her new husband was not the only person she was angry with. Her own father topped that short list, followed by the Earl of Pender, placing the viscount at number three.

Desolation swept through her at the bleak future that lay ahead.

She entered the drawing room, wandered to the windows, and gazed out at the rocky coastline. Her husband was a horrible man. All her good works with her friends, Geneva, Abra, and Hannah to set things right with the world's injustices just when plans were finally making headway were for naught now.

Still, the desire to return to London lagged. There must be something she could do from Cornwall. Unfortunately, Geneva was the one talented with the pen. Meredith was no simple miss herself. Perhaps she could no longer assist with the publishing and distribution of their pamphlets on education for the masses and women's equality for economic futures now, but she'd find a way to extoll her own resourcefulness.

She was not one for self-pity and she steeled her spine, reinforcing it with pure resentment. She turned slowly, surveying the condition of her surroundings. A duke's daughter shouldn't have to live like this.

Slowly, the ideas churned through her. This might be the ideal place to start—readying this dilapidated keep that was unfit for a woman of her station. If her husband didn't like it, then he could voice his displeasure.

To. Her. Face.

She went to the desk and whipped out a piece of yellowed foolscap, found an inkwell that wasn't completely dried out and a pen. Fury had her fingers trembling so violently she could hardly manage to write. But write, she did.

Greetings, Lord Perlsea.

The condition of Perlsea Keep in which you've apparently seen fit to imprison me,

All right, a slight exaggeration…

is in horrendous shape. I shall do my best as the <u>daughter</u> of one of the most powerful men in England <u>and your wife</u>, to restore it to his former glory. Damn the costs.

Regards, Your wife, Lady Perlsea.

Whether he answered or not was up to him… the scoundrel. She dropped the pen, then rang for Mrs. Verity.

"Yer ladyship?" Mrs. Verity wore a snarl on her lean face. It went with her pointed nose and hair drawn back so tightly no creases marred her forehead. The butler didn't appear any less severe, though rather than the thin whip of Mrs. Verity, Meredith considered him portly. The estate's abhorrent condition told Meredith everything she needed to know about her husband and his libertine father, the earl.

Meredith handed her the missive. "Please see that this is posted." She took a seat near the fire and ticked off her questions. "What is the population of Perlsea Keep? How many maids? We require more fuel for the fires. What is the state of the kitchens?" She lobbed the questions, one after another until the poor woman's expression shifted from scowling to wonder to... joy? "Who is the steward? *Is* there a steward?"

"Nay, milady. He done left not long after Lord Pender's last visit." Her eyes narrowed toward the heavens—in this instance, on the plaster that threatened to fall on their heads. "Some ten years past, it were. Mr. Oshea was last 'ere p'rhaps a year or so ago."

Meredith gasped. "Ten years since there's been a proper steward? That's deplorable." She drummed her fingers on the arm of her chair. "And Mr. Oshea—"

"Lord Pender's brother."

"—didn't see fit to hire another?"

"Course, he did, yer ladyship. We've 'ad one every year, but they flee on account the Keep's haunted."

Meredith raised her brows at that bit of nonsense, but her thoughts strayed to the deserted tower. "Then why haven't you and Mr. Verity vacated the place?"

"On account of Lady Pender, ma'am. Couple of generations back. 'Twas in 'er family, ye see. The ghosts don't scare me or Mr. Verity. Nothin' scares that old codger."

Meredith pinched the bridge of her nose. "I shall have a look at the household ledgers, then. They are up to date, are they not?"

"Aye. I reckon. I don't read or write meself. That's Mr. Verity's responsibility."

"You don't read? But this is 1844," she sputtered.

And just like that, the joy was wiped from the woman's face and replaced with her ferocious scowl. "Ye callin' me stupid—"

"Certainly not." Meredith inhaled deeply. The effect was immediate in calming her. "Mrs. Verity, please forgive me. In no way do I believe you of less intelligence. The fact of the matter is, the Keep is in dire need of... updating," she said carefully. "I must have some way of determining the normal expenses and income for its existence."

"Ah. That's easy. The expenses are minimal. The income comes from the mines."

"The mines?"

"The tin mines. More'n 'alf the townfolk works the mines. The child'en too."

"And the mines belong to Perlsea?"

"Yessum."

How was this possible? "But, there hasn't been a steward, er, regularly for ten years."

"That's jes' 'ow it is."

"Who's in charge of the mines?"

That scowl reappeared even more fierce. "Basil Thornfield. Runs it with an iron fist, 'e does."

"I see." Which Meredith certainly did not see. "I shall endeavor to speak to the man then."

6 June 1844

LUCIUS LIFTED HIS pounding head from his pillow. His valet, Graham, stood in the door. "What the devil do you want?"

"I've brought coffee. The Turkish variety. 'Tis stronger."

"I told you not to disturb me."

"So you did. But you've a letter."

Lucius jerked the pillow from beneath his head, fell against the mattress, and covered his face with it. "What day is it?"

"Sixth. June."

Christ. He'd been in a drunken stupor for nearly a week. He groaned.

"It's from your wife."

"I refuse to be married. Burn it."

"I'll just leave it here on the tray for you." The door latched on his exit. Twenty minutes dragged by before Lucius forced his arse from the bed. With a snort of disgust, he stuffed the note in the bottom drawer of the bedside table without breaking the seal. "Gone from sight, removed from memory," he growled to the room at large. Then staggered out of his bedchamber in search of the brandy.

5 October 1844

THE COPPER KETTLE tea shop was a hub of social activity for this hour of the late morn. China clinked in delicate tings, and the fragrance of freshly baked pastries filled the air, causing Meredith's stomach to an embarrassing rumble. But here she sat, nursing her second cup of tea, watching as the Widow Elspeth Trelawney bustled about the packed tea shop, filling cups, listening and nodding to the various disgruntled ailments and complaints of husbands, and mischievous pranks of children and livestock alike from a shop full of women.

After six months of living in the area, Meredith was no closer to learning more about the villagers other than their names. From her small table at the windows, she recognized some of the more prominent members of the community: Mrs. Agatha Mordaunt sat with her cronies, Mrs. Vera Thims and Miss Bernice Oppy who huddled together like hens in the barnyard, pecking at the dirt for food. There were a couple of older men whose names escaped her and a couple of other shop owners who'd popped in for a mid-morning break.

The calm atmosphere should not have frustrated her so. But her attempts to forge a bond with the locals were failing abysmally. She'd been unable to interest one individual in learning to read or attempt basic mathematics that could drastically improve their lives. Education for children? Ha. All that resulted in was blatant hostility and a cut direct when she ventured into town. Something that would never have been tolerated in London.

Mr. Basil Thornfield had paid his respects to her at Perlsea Keep within the first three months of her arrival. The man was respectful, and quick to let her know he was acquainted with her father. If he'd thought to impress her with that tidbit, it did not. She'd rarely seen Papa throughout the course of her life. But at least the man had reached out. She wouldn't consider the meeting completely useless, however, as he'd offered to assist her in locating a steward.

The bell over the door jingled and a tall man entered. His worn coat was ill-fitting and his hat in severe need of brushing. He carried a satchel under one arm and stopped.

The chatter in the shop leveled off to silence as all eyes fell on the stranger.

A short but heavy beard covered the bottom half of his face. His dark green eyes surveyed the small, bustling shop. His gaze paused at her then moved over her shoulder. She glanced in that direction to see there was only one empty table.

There was something regal about him but for his tattered garb. A second son, she supposed. England's class structure could use a recalibration in her estimation. And highly unlikely.

Meredith turned her gaze back out the window. Not even a warm scone could entice her. She missed her friends. Letters, while nice, were not enough. Abra's stepmother, Lady Woodbridge, was trying to wrangle a betrothal for Abra to a horrid marquess. Hannah was busy with the Season's events. And Geneva... Ah, Geneva. Geneva was the most unpretentious, down-to-earth, yet ambitious woman Meredith had ever known. Even during their days at Miss Greensley's School of Comportment for Young Women of Quality, Geneva hadn't allowed her humble background to silence her against those who treated her as unimportant.

The friend who grew up on Berwick Street never hesitated to take up the fight against those who said hurtful things to their friend, Lady Abra Washington, Lord Woodbridge's daughter whose mother was of Jamaican heritage and shy Hannah who struggled with stuttering unless around people she knew well and with whom she was comfortable.

"Lady Perlsea?"

Startled from her musings, Meredith's head snapped around. "Er, good morning, Mrs. Thims. Would you care to sit?"

"Oh—" The woman was in or near her fiftieth year. Her slight frame looked frail enough to blow away in a stout Cornish wind. She wore her gray hair in a bun at her nape and her blue eyes appeared worried. "Um, thank you," she said, tentatively taking the chair across. She leaned in—huddled, rather—and lowered her voice. "It's my daughter. Derwa. Her husband is in trouble."

"What sort of trouble?"

"At the mine. Mr. Thornfield forced him to sign a paper admittin' to something he didn't do."

"Then why did he sign?"

Tears filled her soft blue eyes. "He... he couldn't read, milady." She took a handkerchief from her reticule and dabbed at her cheeks. "Ruby's my cousin and she thought ye'd be able t'help."

"Ruby?"

"Verity. She's the housekeeper at the Keep."

"Oh, yes, of course." Meredith cleared her throat. "Do you have a copy of what he signed?"

"No, milady."

Meredith glanced about their surroundings, giving herself a moment to think. "What is your son-in-law's name?"

Her fear was palpable. "Bray Cardy." Her trembling whisper was so low, Meredith had to lean in to hear.

Meredith clasped her hand over the older woman's and spoke low, too. "Perhaps we should talk someplace less frequented. Is it possible for you to visit your cousin at the castle? Later. Tomorrow afternoon?"

With a sharp nod, Mrs. Thims rose and went to the door. The door flew back, nearly knocking her over, and Basil Thornfield entered.

"Oh, my pardons, Mrs. Thims," he said with a condescending curl of his thin lips. He held the door for her, and she skirted past him with her head down. The conceited brute didn't even notice. "Ah, Lady Perlsea." He strode in Meredith's direction and sat down without so much as an invitation.

With a haughty look down the bridge of her nose, she donned Papa's most pompous façade for her own. "Please, feel free to join me, Mr. Thornfield."

To her greatest satisfaction, two red flags dotted his sallow cheeks. "Er, thank you, madam." Of course, it never took such an insufferable prig long to overcome their discomfort.

The Widow Elspeth appeared at the tableside. "Would you care for more tea, Lady Perlsea?"

"No, thank you, Mrs. Trelawney. I shan't be staying much longer."

She started to walk away, but Mr. Thornfield stopped her. "I'll gladly take a pot, m'dear."

Mrs. Trelawney visibly bristled at the too-familiar address, only nodding, then gliding away.

Meredith gathered her gloves and reticule. "As I said, I must be on my way, sir."

Disappointment, then irritation, fleeted his narrow features. "I have information regarding the matter of your steward we spoke of."

A conversation which had taken place over three months prior. She'd hoped he'd forgotten. She didn't trust the man as far as she could toss him.

"I fear Mr. Underhill has been detained for an indeterminate time. However, I would be honored to step in and assist you until he has arrived to take up his duties."

"That won't be nec—"

"Surely, you don't wish to be bogged down with the mundane duties of household accounts and the hiring of servants. Such tasks require a firm hand." His presumptions outweighed his audacity, momentarily stealing her ability to respond.

"I'm sorry?"

"With my position in handling the mines, I've vast experience in these matters."

She gave her own condescending smile, recalling Mrs. Verity's assertions regarding Mr. Thornfield. How he ran the mines with an iron fist. She disliked the images that thought brought forth. "I wouldn't dream of imposing on you, Mr. Thornfield."

He shook his head. "It's nothing. Nothing at all."

"No, it isn't," she said firmly. "I've someone—"

"I can begin right away," he interrupted.

A familiar tightness banded her chest. "No." She slapped her hand on the table, causing her delicate cup to jump.

Startled, his gaze flew to hers.

She smiled again. "As I was saying. I've already someone in mind."

"B-but," he sputtered, "I've corresponded with the duke and he's approved my suggestion."

Meredith clucked her tongue. "Oh, that is a shame, Mr. Thornfield, but my father does not rule *my* household." She rose from the table and adjusted her bonnet. "Thank you for your concerns."

He reached for her arm but Meredith stepped back. "But—"

"Lady Perlsea?"

Meredith turned and looked up and up and up to the tall man who'd entered the shop earlier. "I'm Mr. Ashcroft."

"Yes?"

"The steward you were expecting, ma'am."

Meredith's smile froze on her face. It seemed every eye and ear in The Copper Kettle was trained on her, Mr. Thornfield, and now this Mr. Ashcroft. Mischievousness sparked his expression. As if he held in his mirth with some effort. Compared to Mr. Thornfield, however, he appeared the lesser evil of the two. "Of course, Mr. Ashcroft. I've been expecting you. Come along." She turned to Mr. Thornfield. "Good day, sir."

The rendezvous with Mrs. Thims never took place. Mr.

Cardy's position as a hewer had turned out to be a fatal one. The winch he'd been operating to lift a heavy load of rocks had snapped, burying him beneath falling debris, crushing him instantly.

PART TWO

CHAPTER TWO

Cornwall, May 1847

MEREDITH GLANCED AT her watch pin. Heavens, she was almost late. No one knew of the time she spent in this ruined portion of the Keep. She started to shut the old journal and stopped as the words on the page seemed to leap off.

2 July 1758. Preparations for tonight's gathering are set. The Keep appears to be the most logical place to convene. The need for confidentiality is vital and will remain secure within these ancient walls.

Folded within the pages, she found a missive and read it over.

The chamber I've chosen will serve our purposes well, tucked away from the main thoroughfares of the Keep. Use the entrance closest to the sea. Here you'll be admitted and guided to a familiar facade, a safeguard against the curious and the unworthy. Only those who understand the true nature of our work shall be allowed...

The rest of the text was illegible. A sudden crash startled her. Meredith's heart seized then pounded furiously against her ribcage until she realized a clap of thunder roared outside. Rain slashed the windows and blew in through the broken glass of one.

With a hand splayed against her chest, Meredith took a deep breath. She blinked against shadows, stretched and distorted against the walls in grotesque forms cast by the flickering lamplight. A sharp burst of laughter erupted with the release of that breath and a silent chastisement of the cold fingers that had seemed to curl about the nape of her neck. She shook off the absurdity with another inhale, this one a tad unsteady.

Blast, she must hurry. The Literary Society was due to meet in less than a half hour.

She pulled the door to behind her because it wouldn't latch. The wood was warped beyond repair, hence the broken window. The words from the old journal stuck with her though as she rushed down the stairs. *Confidentiality? Secret chamber?* Is that what the author meant?

There would be time to ponder later. She strode down the hall to the steward's office off the servant's portion of the kitchens and rapped on the door.

"Enter." Mr. Ashcroft sat behind a heavy desk that now sported a high shine thanks to her own efforts. Thin gold spectacles rested on the bridge of his nose.

"The ladies are due in twenty minutes," she said in a rush. What a hellish day. The undertaking of the Keep's main library restoration had been a tedious process. And while she met with the women regularly, tonight was especially important to her. She was to debut all her hard work. Prove to them Perlsea Keep *was not* haunted, as the villagers were so determined to believe.

The years of neglect in rotting wood, warped shelves, grimy windows, and tattered curtains had all been replaced. If it hadn't been for Mr. Wren of Wren's Carpentry who'd taken on the task of rebuilding those bookcases and Marigold Tremayne who'd completed the final touches today with new curtains, Meredith would have been sorely disappointed. She couldn't wait to invite the women into their new meeting place.

"And hello to you, too," Mr. Ashcroft teased.

"Apologies, sir. Did you receive the latest London papers in today's post?"

"Yes, yes. And there is quite the notice, I must say."

The sudden gleam in his eye stopped her momentarily. "Oh?"

He held out a stack of broadsheets. "Indeed, Lady Pender."

Meredith hurried over and reached for the stack, halting mid-poise. "What did you call me?"

"Lady Pender. It appears the late earl has met his reward." He met her gaze. "You didn't know? I would have thought you'd received notice. You are now a countess."

Meredith stumbled into a chair before the desk. "No. I… had no notion."

He lowered the stack and read from the top one.

"Sudden Demise of the Earl of Pender—It is with deep regret that we report the death of Damien Alexander Oshea, 7th Earl of Pender, who passed away under tragic circumstances on the grounds of his Northumberland estate, Stonemare, at the age of 54. The earl was found fatally stabbed, and an investigation into this grievous act is currently underway.

The Earl of Pender inherited his title in 1810 at the tender age of 17, following the death of his father. Throughout his tenure, the 7th Earl of Pender was known for his strong-willed nature and his dedication to the management of his extensive estates, though his life was often shadowed by personal and public difficulties."

That brought Meredith's head up. She snorted. "Dedication to the management of his estates," she choked out, thinking of all the work she'd endured over the past three years. And she wasn't close to completing the tasks she'd undertaken.

Mr. Ashcroft cleared his throat and continued. *"His untimely death marks a significant moment in the history of the Pender family, whose influence has been felt throughout England for generations. The circumstances of his death have shocked the local community, and authorities are diligently pursuing all leads in the investigation.*

"The Earl is survived by his sons, Noah James Oshea and Viscount Perlsea, Lucius Alexander Oshea, who now inherits the title and responsibilities as the 8th Earl of Pender. Further

announcements regarding the funeral will be made at a later date. The family requests that their privacy be respected during this period of mourning."

Meredith snatched the broadsheet from his hand. "When the devil was this printed?" She scanned the page and found the date: 31 Mar 1847. "March? That was two and a half months ago. Good heavens. And no one thought to notify me?" She read through the notice again. "He… he was murdered…" The paper crumpled in her fist, white spots dotting her vision.

A minute later, the paper was replaced by a glass of brandy. She met the steady gaze of Mr. Ashcroft. "Drink this. You've still the literary group to meet with in—" He flipped out his watch. "—ten minutes."

"I-I don't think—"

"You can, and you shall. You've much to show for since you've been at Perlsea. They trust you. They are learning to read because of you. You've created a school for their children, much to Mr. Thornfield's abject horror and to my great delight. The man is a menace."

Whatever divine intervention brought him to her doorstep, she couldn't be more grateful. A small smile pierced her. "He still hasn't forgiven me for hiring you."

"True. But he also resents your interference when it comes to the children working the mines," he said grimly. "Now, drink up. You are the Countess of Pender, the Duke of Rathbourne's daughter. I have every faith in your ability to carry forward. It's evident you are bringing the work and the community together."

Meredith sipped the brandy through a constricted throat. Her eyes burned at the confidence he instilled in her. "Yes," she whispered. "I can't let them down. But when word gets out, things will change."

"Perhaps, but if you act the same, the change will be minimal."

She nodded slowly. "How wise you are." Meredith handed over the empty glass. "Thank you."

CHAPTER THREE

The Literary Society
Or as one envisioned

"Y OU'VE WORKED WONDERS with the library." The ribbons in Marigold Tremayne's gray-streaked coiffure fluttered as did her delicate veined hand, though her eyes darted about as if she feared apparitions from the past would waver from the walls similar to that of haze or shimmer above the flames of an outdoor fire.

Meredith suppressed a shiver hating to admit the similar feeling not an hour ago. She pushed aside the discomfort and surveyed the finished product of her efforts, smiling at her company. The dark woodwork gleamed in the newly installed gas-powered sconces. Elegant moldings added a warm ambience to the room along with the upholstery in floral patterns of purples, greens, and white. All which complemented the deep undertones of the carpets. "I'm quite pleased with the end result," she said with a gracious nod.

"Aren't you frightened, my lady?" Mrs. Penrose whispered.

Meredith quashed her inclination to dismiss their fears and spoke gently. "No, Mrs. Penrose. I've been here almost three years now. I've no need to be frightened." Her own lingering unease faded, leaving only a soft awareness of the folly of fear, that the unknown menace was no more than a figment of her mind's darker wanderings.

"But all those men who've disappeared through the years..." Mrs. Penrose's voice trailed away, and she glanced about too. She was speaking of the many stewards who had up and left the Keep without a word. Long before Meredith had arrived and had had the good sense to employ Mr. Ashcroft.

They were also a closed-mouth group, having refused to expound on their thoughts regarding those missing stewards. That said much for the close-knit community of the Penhalwick village.

The Widow Elspeth wrinkled her brow, piercing Meredith with her shrewd and all-knowing gaze. "You do seem a little pale, dear."

Up until tonight's meeting, the small group of four had grown to an impressive number of eight—well, nine including herself—and usually met in a back room of The Copper Kettle. The two absent members were even more superstitious, but Meredith knew the battle she faced was uphill.

With a deep breath, she took her chair and straightened the broadsheets she held. "I'm fine," she murmured. "Now, what shall we read tonight?" Most of the members were illiterate, but Meredith had hopes by way of sparking their curiosity with some of the more outrageous antics only London gossip could provide. She glanced through a couple of papers and stopped. "Ah, here is an interesting article."

She shook out the paper and cleared her throat and read,

"Education: A Quest of Superiority?

"In the quest of superiority in education, 'tis crucial we recognize the vital roles of educators. Instructors are not merely conveyors of information; they are the future of this great country. Mentors, guides, and inspirers of young minds. I implore you to support the quality of education as it can only be as strong as the caliber from those of whom they learn. 'Tis with this conviction that the entire British populist advocate for greater training across the board..."

Her voice trailed at the utter stillness filling her ears. She looked up and found six pairs of eyes on her. Er, five. Megan Penrose was only fourteen, and she was watching her mother's reaction.

"Is something wrong?" Meredith asked.

"Someone really wrote that?" Elowen Coldwater, a lovely young woman nearing the age of twenty, was just the young mind Meredith and her friends were trying to reach. One always eager to learn. It was the age group in which she, Geneva, Abra, and Hannah had fallen into having completed their education at Miss Greensley's School. When the four of them had had the epiphany of women's importance and contribution to the world order. Things were blatantly unfair, and that was when they'd come up with their new secret club: The Clandestine Sapphire Society. Oh, how they'd laughed themselves sick.

Then Geneva came up with the notion of a pamphlet on *Promoting Social Justice and Equality*. But the article had been returned to Geneva's flat in Berwick Street with *Reject* scribbled across the page. Two weeks later, she'd been contacted by *The Chartist Movement*, a group that worked ideas such as allowing all men over twenty-one the privilege to vote regardless of property or ownership of wealth. The measure failed but Meredith and her friends remained hopeful despite the odds. The wealthy and nobles were powerful beyond the bounds of fairness.

Bright interest lit Elowen's eyes. The caveat, however, lay in the fact that her parents had been in the area for generations. Her father, a fisherman for many years, found there was more blunt to be made working in the mines. Her mother, a mild, never-stir-the-waves woman accepting of her lot in life, also worked in the mines. Theirs was a calm, resilient family accustomed to hardship and… loss.

"And the newspaper *published* it?"

Meredith grinned and handed Elowen the broadsheet.

Elowen found the article and put her nose to the paper. Her lips moved as she reread the bit. She glanced up, eyes sparkling. "It's signed by—" She looked down. "The Cland… clande…"

Frustration marred her pretty face.

"The Clandestine Sapphire Society." Agnes Tremayne was the daughter of Marigold Tremayne. Meredith had hired her as her lady's maid... er, in training. She beamed with pride. Meredith had been teaching her to read over the last couple of years and, to Meredith's delight, she'd made great gains.

"Clint... sting... Sapphire?"

Meredith nodded encouragingly. "Society." She couldn't very well announce to the group she was a proud, prominent, and charter member of the CSS. "I, um, suspect it's a consortium of bluestockings who wish to keep their identities secret."

"Oooh, look at this." Excitement colored Elowen's tone anew. "It says here that the Earl of Pender was murdered!"

Another, more deafening silence crashed over Meredith.

"My goodness," the Widow Elspeth said with a small smile. I do believe that elevates our hostess from viscountess to countess."

"Oh, cor," Agnes breathed, eyes dancing, learning she was lady's maid to a countess now.

Groaning, Meredith closed her eyes, then snapped them open. "Yes, it's true. I only just learned of the situation myself before you all arrived."

Miss Clara Lovelace tsked. "No one bothered to tell you?" The spinster owned the local apothecary and had certain ideals of right and wrong. But didn't everyone?

"I'm sure there is a very good reason why my, er, husband has not yet let me know. It all happened so suddenly," Meredith hedged. "Why, he's probably on his way to Perlsea this very moment."

$$\text{\scriptsize ❖ ✦ ══════ ✖ ══════ ✦ ❖}$$

CHAPTER FOUR

St. Petroc's Church
The Vestry Hall

MEREDITH ENTERED THE church with Mr. Ashcroft and with a keen sense of satisfaction rippling through her. Along with reading and arithmetic, in the last year or so she'd introduced subjects of other interests that included music and watercolor painting. The children's ages ranged from five to twelve, at which time many began their work at the mines.

She'd done her utmost, appealing to Mr. Thornfield to push back on putting the children to work at such a young age.

All to no avail.

The man was a cruel taskmaster. In the three years since she'd been in Penhalwick she'd seen more than a few injuries as the mines ran all hours of the day and night. She didn't know the specifics, but she'd seen firsthand the havoc it wreaked on the families. Elowen's mother, Anwen worked as a Bal Maiden. The work was grueling—breaking, sorting, and cleaning the ore, readying it for transport—and was paid considerably less than the men.

Meredith had offered Anwen a position at the Keep, but she was superstitious in the sense that if she wasn't near her husband he would perish beneath the ground. In other words, she believed she was of sorts his guardian angel.

Mr. Ashcroft's and Meredith's steps echoed through the church halls as they made their way to the makeshift schoolroom. Miss Carroway was already leading the children in their morning ritual of the opening hymn.

"I thought to offer Miss Coldwater, Elowen, a position at the Keep," Meredith said.

He flashed a smile in her direction. "I was wondering when you might get around to that. In what position? Your secretary?"

Heat infused her face. It was exactly what she'd been thinking. "What of it? She would make a perfectly acceptable assistant."

"No reason," he said. They reached the door, and he peered in, then spoke barely above a whisper. "No Tommy Trenwith this morning. That child is trouble. You mark my words."

Meredith's lips firmed. "That's the third time this week," she bit out in a responding whisper.

"Some children are just not cut out for the schoolroom."

"He's only ten. I had an agreement with his mother." She spun on her heel. "If she refuses to make him attend, then the extra I'm paying her shall cease at once. You mark that in your ledgers, sir." She escaped Vestry Hall through a side door and marched to the stables for her carriage.

"Lady Perlsea, I m-mean Lady P-Pender." The stableman, Jago, tended to stutter when she appeared. For whatever reason, she turned the gruff old man into a mass of nerves even after three years.

"I must speak with Mrs. Trenwith," she said grimly.

"Ye drivin' yerself?" The shock in his voice had a sharp burst of laughter erupting from her.

"I'm not helpless."

"Er, o' course n-not, yer ladyship." He handed her up to the driver's seat.

"Thank you, Jago. I'll return soon."

The run out to the Trenwiths' was less fruitful. Mrs. Trenwith was there and her wrath spelled trouble for the ten-year-old truant. "I tol' him time and again. Why, I'll whip him into a frenzy. It's that Thornfield. He don' care none. He tol' Samuel ain't no need for educatin' when Tommy's jes' destined for the mines."

"Oh, he did, did he? We'll just see about that." Meredith had just about had it with Basil Thornfield's interference when it came to educating the children. She'd relinquished her arguments on the long hours for the miners, but she refused to let him dictate Meredith's agreement regarding the children's ability to read and basic mathematic skills necessary to bettering their futures. Especially for a child of only ten.

She snapped the reins a little harder than intended and sent the team jerking into motion. It took less than ten minutes to reach the mine's office, a building constructed of rough-hewn stone.

Like many of the homes in the area, the structure was designed to withstand Cornwall's harsh weather conditions. It was relatively modest in size. The single-story building was topped by a slightly pitched slate roof designed to drain rainwater more efficiently.

Meredith jumped from the box to the ground, jarring her teeth. She stormed the entrance to the office marked by a heavy oak door, darkened with age. Iron bands reinforced the door, giving it not just a formidable appearance but also a conveyance of secrets. Shuddering, she reached for the iron lever and pressed—

A low rumble, like thunder, shook the wooden planks on which she stood. The handle vibrated beneath her fingers. Unease slithered through her and the sound reverberated, seeming to echo against the hills. She dropped her hand and stepped from beneath the portico to glance at a darkening gray sky. Heavy clouds hung low. Yet no lightning streaked the sky, though a drop of rain hit her nose.

A loud boom pierced the air, and she ducked. *England was under attack.* But her thoughts shook loose, and common sense returned—

The mine. Meredith didn't hesitate. She ran for the opening where all chaos had broken out.

Inside, screams bounded against the stone walls, raising the hair on her nape. Dust billowed out from a shaft to her left.

"Rocks. Move the rocks. *Hurry.*"

She couldn't discern who bellowed out the commands, but men and women, even children, ran for that section.

Meredith's hand shot out and she snagged a soot-faced Anwen. "What is it?" she demanded.

"One of the child'en," she huffed out. "They ran into the unused shaft."

Meredith, unheedful of her own safety, dashed after her.

Samuel Trenwith's muscles bulged with sheer strength, tearing through the fallen debris. Women stood on the peripherals holding oil lamps and candles, but Meredith could barely see through the thick dust.

"A beam fell," Samuel yelled. "I 'ear 'im. 'ang on, boy, 'ang—" His voice cut as if he'd entered the church. "God in 'eav'n," he breathed and tore through the pile of rocks with herculean force.

"NEVER" HADN'T TURN out to be quite as long as one would like. It had been three years since Lucius Oshea's—Viscount Perlsea, and now the current Earl of Pender—nuptials to the Duke of Rathbourne's daughter. Lucius had rarely thought of his bride since leaving her in the care of the Veritys three years ago. He didn't bother recalling her name. A minor detail. In the event he was required to address her… well, he would deal with that when the time came. His fury hadn't subsided one iota since having left Northumberland.

The ride from Northumberland to Cornwall was hellish. He hadn't bothered with the train, instead deciding the hard ride would do him good. His arse ached. It wouldn't be easy to demand an annulment. The whole ride south he'd been plagued with doubts. The picture of his young wife kept floating through his mind. How terrified she must have been when he tore out of

Cornwall without a backward look.

The castle itself had been in horrid disrepair, and he hadn't given a second thought to it since. She'd never written a second note to the one Lucius had secreted away.

Looking back, it was a wonder the duke hadn't called Lucius out for deserting her as he had. Then, again…

The closer he drew to Penhalwick and Perlsea Keep, the more agitated he became. The steed beneath him reflected his mood.

He glanced up at the darkening sky. The Cornish weather wasn't any more pleasant than that of Northumberland. Warmer perhaps. He was another few hour's ride from the Keep and a storm was brewing. Well, so be it.

He was ready to unleash the ire that simmered just under the surface of his skin, and he let it flow.

Like during the midst of a pre-drink gathering for his father's funeral, how the Duke of Rathbourne had announced to all and sundry that Lucius's wife was with child. It made no sense for his wife to announce an illicit expectancy. Even someone as young and naïve as his wife should realize the danger of bandying such tales about. The revelation had been stunning to Lucius since she and he had never consummated their forced marriage.

The stranglehold on Lucius was asphyxiating.

He'd never been close to his father. From the time Lucius and Noah were children, it was their Uncle Lysander to whom they'd turned. The control Lucius had thought he'd wielded over his own life had turned out to be nothing short of farcical. His and Miss Docia Hale's romance had blossomed. Their dreams to marry shattered when Lucius one afternoon in London had happened upon his father, the Earl of Pender and the Duke of Rathbourne sharing a bottle of port. The ring Lucius had purchased for his future bride burned a hole in his waistcoat pocket.

White's bustled with activity considering the thick carpets beneath his feet. There was a quiet efficiency about the hall as Lucius made his way to an intimate room with a fire blazing in the large hearth at one end. He would miss the quiet nights here once he and Docia married. She loved the spotlight, but she always feared being away from Chaston Manor long in the event her missing father returned unexpectedly.

"Ah, Perlsea. If it isn't my long-lost heir."

Lucius glanced up and saw his father seated in one of three winged-backed chairs before the fire. "Hello, Father." In another, sat the smug Duke of Rathbourne. Theirs was an odd pairing Lucius hadn't thought to encounter. His father was sloshed. Not an unusual state by any means.

"What brings you here?"

A glass of brandy was poured and handed to Lucius. "I've news," he said, unable to keep the grin from his face.

His father nodded. "You're in love."

"I've just purchased the ring."

"And who might the lucky chit be?" the duke inquired. But his nonchalance set Lucius's teeth on edge.

"Viscount Chaston's daughter, Miss Docia Hale." Pride filled Lucius at just saying her name.

A roar of laughter shook the duke while the earl just shook his head, a small bitter smile creasing his face.

"'Tis good you have the ring, son," Rathbourne said. "But I'm afraid you have the wrong bride in mind."

With an indignant huff, Lucius threw back the entirety of his brandy and slammed the glass on a low table between them and stood. He glared at his father. "I should have known you couldn't be happy for me."

"There's much you don't know about me," the earl responded. "Nor about yourself, it appears. I've been remiss in keeping you apprised."

A chill stole up Lucius's spine then gripped him about the throat. His feet had grown roots in the span of seconds.

"My dearest heir, I suppose I'd forgotten to mention the fact you're already betrothed."

"Oh?" Lucius spoke through a clenched jaw. "I believe I would remember something of that nature."

The duke narrowed his beady eyes on him. "Don't see why," he said. "You were thirteen when the betrothal agreements were signed. To *the joy of my life, my daughter—" The rest of his words were drowned out by the blood rushing Lucius's ears.*

A mile or so outside Penhalwick a large explosion echoed in the hills, startling him from the awful memories. Lucius put his head down and urged his mount faster.

He breached the hills under darkening skies that finally had their fill and let loose, unleashing their tears in winded fury, tearing at his coat. The sight before him was an uproar of traffic. Droves of folk unmindful of the slashing rain, heading in the direction of the mines. He paused a moment then turned his horse to follow.

Crowds gathered outside the mine's opening. A woman from the back shoved her way through the throng screaming. It took a moment to discern any sense of her incoherence. But she reached the epicenter screeching, "Tommy. Tommy. Tommy." She threw herself on the ground next to a woman whose face was streaked black.

Her fine bonnet was an incongruous spot of color. Her frock was soaked by rain. She lifted a pain-filled face to the distraught woman. The rain washed some of the muddied soot away, exposing a fine-boned profile. Familiar profile. Her eyes found his over the gathering cluster.

Moss-green eyes he hadn't seen in three years.

CHAPTER FIVE

L ucius spotted her carriage parked before the office mine and kicked his horse into motion. He slid from the saddle and the crowd parted a pathway to his wife. What the hell was she thinking? Before he reached her, a man a half foot shorter than his own height of six-two barred his way. Despite the lack of height, he carried himself with an imposing demeanor. Lean and wiry in build, his frame suggested he was more accustomed to administrative work rather than physical labor.

"Might I be of service, sir?" The man's narrow face with its high, pronounced cheekbones and pointed chin went with the cold, steely-gray eyes. Their piercing quality aggravated Lucius.

"Why is my wife sitting on the ground with mud on her face?"

A harsh laugh erupted from his thin-lipped mouth. "My good man, how amusing you are." There was a spectral quality to his sallow skin that sharpened his features. "That is Lady Perlsea, excuse me, Lady *Pender* as I've been corrected. Her husband abandoned her over three years ago and hasn't been seen since."

"Is that so?" Lucius said.

Another man with thick facial hair, and who appeared as tall as Lucius, breached the barrier of people and hurried to her. Pulled her to her feet and pressed her head into his well-developed shoulder. The muscles in Lucius's abdomen coiled into a tight knot of ice-hot rage.

"And who might that be?" he gritted out.

The specter looked over his shoulder. "That would be the steward of Perlsea Keep." A smirk, devoid of genuine emotion gave Lucius the impression he took pleasure in others' discomfort. The man eyed him with his beady hawklike gaze and shrugged. "Or so they say." After a second, he let out a resigned sigh. "Duty calls." He turned and made his way to the heart of the spectacle.

For a moment, Lucius was at a loss. He strolled back to his horse and mounted. The ride to Perlsea Keep took him through the village where nary a soul hovered.

He'd come to demand an annulment and his wife had just handed him the ammunition he required.

Hadn't she?

"COME. YOU'LL CATCH your death." Mr. Ashcroft guided Meredith from the wailing Mrs. Trenwith. "I think we may be in for a rough patch."

"You saw him too?"

He gave a sharp nod.

"Be that as it may, I-I can't leave. Not yet." She broke away, but he held her arm, keeping her from the woman.

Mr. Trenwith picked up their young son amid his wife's anguished cries. The pain in his face was indescribably heartbreaking. Their other two children, Sarah and Jacob, stood off to the side. Silent tears mingled with the rain coursing down young Sarah's cheeks.

"Bring the carriage, Mr. Ashcroft. I refuse to allow the family to walk."

His hesitation was minute, but then he said, "Of course, my lady."

Meredith strode to Sarah and Jacob, her mind sluggish but for one thought: this was the second death within three years. Bray

Cardy had perished before she'd been able to speak with Mrs. Thims about the document Mr. Thornfield had forced him to sign.

The mine conditions required better and more frequent supervision, she thought with a surge of fury.

Sick with the tragic events of this day, Meredith took Sarah's hand silently promising to ease the family's path using whatever power she possessed in her role as benefactor of Perlsea.

And, with her elusive husband's return, she had every intention of following through on that very promise.

CHAPTER SIX

Mr. Ashcroft stopped at the portico. He started to jump down and Meredith touched his arm. "Don't bother, sir. I'm saturated through. I'll manage."

"Hurry, then," he said. "I shall see you tomorrow." He helped her down without letting go of the reins but waited until she was under the portico before driving off. She knew he would drop the carriage at the stables before making his own dash for the steward's cottage on the far side of the grounds.

Meredith was met at the door by a surprisingly efficient Mr. Verity. The number of times he'd opened the door for her could be recounted on one hand in the three years she'd been in residence. "Have Agnes fill the tub with hot water," she told him, stripping off her spencer, gloves, and bonnet.

The portly man cleared his throat. "Mayhap you would care to change first, milady."

She started for the stairs. "Of course, I'm going to change. I'm freezing."

"Er, you've a… er, the, ah, master is waiting in the library, milady."

"What?" Blast. How could she have forgotten—easily, of course. Her own misfortunes were nothing compared to what the Trenwiths were facing now with the horrifically tragic event they'd just endured.

With a squelching spin of her half-boots, Meredith changed direction and stormed her favorite chamber.

Lucius Oshea, Viscount Perlsea, *Earl* Pender stood at the windows with his back to her, his hands in the pockets of his finely cut trousers.

"Well, if it isn't the specter of my long-lost husband," she said.

He turned slowly. Unperturbed. Unrepentant. Unwelcome. The depth of his gray eyes swirled with seething fury.

Meredith caught herself from stepping back, instead straightening her shoulders, though her skin rose in gooseflesh, not all due to the chill. "I see your memory has returned. Two-fold. One, that you have a wife, and two, that you were able to find your way back to Perlsea Keep. Was it a sudden aberration?" she asked in a speculative tone. The fire failed in warming her and she stepped closer, rubbing her palms over her upper arms.

His eyes narrowed but he didn't speak. He went to the corner cabinet where she kept the decanter of brandy and poured out two glasses. He strolled over and handed her one. With an indication of his head, he said, "What a handsome alteration you've affected."

"What else was I to do?" she muttered. "Lest you forget, it has been three years."

"So it has." He shook his head, his expression one of abject disgust. "A countess wallowing in the mud with the locals no less. Hugging a man who was *not* her husband, I might add. For all of God and sundry to witness."

Suddenly, she was no longer cold. Her skin burned from the inside out. A raging fever that, if bottled, could heat the entire castle. A hate so intense, it seemed to rise from her body and tint the air with a steaming red haze. The contents of her brandy sloshed the sides of the glass, nearly spilling over. She gripped it with both hands to steady it, stared down into the amber contents too furious to speak momentarily. Slowly, she raised it to her lips and took a cautious sip. Liquid fire singed all the way down. She took another.

Meredith lifted her eyes to his cold, cold, cold ones. "How

dare you?" she gritted out in a harsh whisper.

"Who is he?" How good he was at banking his anger, she noted with a surreal detachment.

"The steward, of course. He's been here almost from the moment of your desertion," she bit out, wishing she could manage the same sense of detachment. "Do you know how it felt to learn that my father-in-law had been murdered? From a London broadsheet?" Her voice sounded almost shrill. With an inhalation through her nose, she let it out slowly and tried again. "The townspeople have been kind enough to inform me that I am now countess to the Earl of Pender."

His flinch was minute, but it was a crack in the calm façade he presented. "I came here to inform you that I will be petitioning for an annulment."

Shock rendered her speechless and she stared at him, quite aware her mouth hung open yet with an inability to close it. A second later, the statement hit her with an unexpected bout of hilarity and her laughter erupted. "On what grounds?"

"Your lover. He *is* the one who fathered the child you carry, I take it." His hand came up and flattened against the lapel over his heart—rock. Rock she envisioned as his heart.

A chill iced away the fire in her blood even as outrage at this bunk had her sputtering. She slammed her glass down on a low table and rubbed her arms again. Then confusion hit. "Mr. Ashcroft is *not* my lover. He is our steward. I have no lover, and I am *not* with child. Who on earth would say such a thing?"

"Your father. He announced the thrilling occasion the night before my father's services. Regardless," he went on, reaching inside his frockcoat. "It changes nothing. I wish to apply for an annulment."

Again, she laughed at the absurdity. "Any child I bear will be considered yours, my lord. It would also negate any fact that our union was unconsummated. Besides that, Rathbourne will never allow it. He will kill you first." Meredith moved to the settee and sat. Her teeth chattered.

SHOCK PULSED TO Lucius at her words. He pulled his hand away from the drafted letter he'd had every intention of presenting her and ran a hand through his too-long hair; looked at this slip of girl he'd met only once before—on the day of their nuptials. She was right. If she was with child, it wouldn't matter who had sired it. He would be considered the father.

Long locks of her gold-burnished hair hung in tatters, gleaming in the fire's glow, her skin dewy from the rain. He shrugged out of his coat and dropped it around her shoulders. "Why were you sitting in the mud?"

She stared into the blaze and shivered. "I'd just carried a ten-year-old child from the mine." The husky resonance was nothing of what he remembered all those years ago, standing before the bishop. "I watched his father dig him out from the rubble with his bare hands. I've never seen such fierce determination in my life," she whispered.

He waited for, yet knew, the words to follow.

"Dead," she choked out. "His little chest… crushed." She dropped her face in her hands and silent sobs shook her slight frame.

Lucius couldn't remember a time he'd been affected by a woman's tears.

Docia never cried. Women of the night never cried. He and his cronies laughed about the debutantes who'd tried and failed to manipulate them into marriage shackles with such antics. But this display was not an antic. "You must get warm," he said gruffly, shoving a handkerchief in her hand. A hand so delicate, it could break if he looked at it too harshly. "I shouldn't have kept you so long."

His countess didn't raise her head, just nodded and stood where his coat slid off slender shoulders, exposing the letter he'd brought for her to sign. She started toward the doors but turned back, her glistening eyes reflecting the firelight. "There is a reason our fathers wanted this union. They planned it for years. Do you ever wonder why?"

At the door, she clasped the knob. "By the way, your chamber…" she fluttered out a hand. "Has not been updated. I had no reason to expect you, you see." With that, she left on silent steps, leaving him with the conundrum of a very pointed, very good question.

Why *had* their fathers wanted this union so badly? The deal had been struck when he was but thirteen and she… five. It was curious and the question deserved an answer.

CHAPTER SEVEN

L UCIUS WOKE AT the ridiculous hour of eight.
In the morning.

In a cold and dusty chamber.

He supposed he should feel fortunate that the linens had been changed, but that was the extent of the hospitality he'd been afforded. Lucius had no illusions that his task in securing an annulment would be easy and had arranged for his valet, Graham, to follow with his trunk and services. Two days, he figured, with the deluge of rain. He shucked the coverlets and padded on bare feet to a basin filled with—of course—icy water.

He dashed his face and shivered. The infernal rain hadn't let up a bit. He grabbed a towel and heard a clank. "What the devil?" He snatched up his trousers and shrugged into them. It seemed to be coming from the adjoining door, but it was locked. Throwing a shirt over his head, he eased the main door open and peered down the hall. Lighted sconces showcased dark wood freshly polished. Something he hadn't noticed the night before. The annoying and incongruous sound echoed through the halls that sounded suspiciously like… water flowing through… pipes!

But the only other door along this corridor was the countess's chamber. He backed into his room and cocked his head to one side. The sound seemed to be coming through the sitting room. He moved through the hall to his wife's sitting chamber. From there he moved to his sitting room and eased the door open. Correction. What *used to be* his sitting room had been converted to an elaborate bathing chamber.

His body quivered with anticipation. He stepped inside, taking in the copper tub and clay pipes that rose through the stone floor. The modest-sized room still retained its small hearth. A fire blazed in the grate on the far end of the room. The other end held a full-length mirror framed in gold leaf. A folding screen with a floral pattern of soft spring colors allowed privacy for changing.

A wood cabinet with intricate carvings that reminded him of the crown moldings in the newly remodeled library, obviously built by the same individual, took up another wall.

He took in the total ambience she'd created. A world of mollifying luxury and in this one confined space. Steam wafted off water scented with mint and lavender, enticing the self-centered arse he was.

He dropped his trousers, stripped off his shirt, and stepped into pure, heated bliss.

MEREDITH PULLED HER wrap about her and glanced out the window. The rain was relentless and didn't appear as if it would stop anytime soon. The heavy onslaught mirrored her heart. It was difficult to swallow past the constriction in her throat. She hadn't slept a wink the entire night. The sudden appearance of her absent husband hadn't helped matters. She was at a loss as to what to do to ease the Trenwiths' sorrow. Or, perhaps it was her own she wished to ease. Tommy had been an inquisitive child, always sneaking off. He'd been most impatient to follow his father and his brother to work in the mines. Something that was beyond her understanding.

Her vision blurred. The unnecessary loss of life was like a knife in her soul. The depth of Elise Trenwith's grief was unfathomable. Meredith went to the escritoire and dashed off a note for Agnes to relay to Mrs. Verity. She would deliver a basket herself. And while she was at it, she would pay a little visit to that horrid Mr. Thornfield.

After ringing for tea, she went through her sitting room to the bathing chamber where the steamy air seeped beneath her skin and clouded her vision. She retrieved a towel from the cabinet, then released her wrap and dropped it to the floor. She went to the tub—

"Good morning, m'dear." The low, husky resonance held the growl of sleep and startled her so completely, she tripped, sending her towel flying from her arm and floating through the air to land with a plop in the tub. And she nearly followed. "How utterly modest of you," he said without an ounce of remorse. In fact, the smile she heard in his voice infuriated her.

"That is *my* bath, you cur."

"Is it?" He shifted, gripping the sides of the tub and made to stand. The towel hung on his… his—

"No!" She backed away. "I'll return later." She snatched up her wrap and struggled into it, muttering, "I vow, I've never known a man of the aristocracy to rise before noon."

His voice reached through the steam. "It's a first for me to be sure. By the bye, my dear, what lovely breasts you have—"

She slammed the door, cutting him off. Oh, the blasted blackguard. Heat infused her body from her toes up, hardening her nipples, flaming her face. She stomped through *her* sitting room to *her* bedchamber, startling poor Agnes. "Where's the tea?" Meredith demanded.

"I sent for it, milady. It hasn't come yet."

"Did Mrs. Verity receive my note?"

"Of course, ma'am, er, milady, but I had to read it to her on account she, um, well, she said she didn't have her glasses."

Good heavens, Meredith had forgotten the woman's stubbornness in learning to read. "Fine. I've a basket to deliver," she snapped. "I'll wear the brown habit."

"But your bath, milady—"

"Has been invaded. My dress, if you please."

LUCIUS GRINNED AND reveled in the water's warmth. What an inventive little thing his wife was proving to be. And with such a luscious body—then the thought of her head on the shoulder of her "steward" invaded his mirth. A likely story indeed, he decided. That Mr. Ashcroft mirrored her platonic musings was highly unlikely.

Ashcroft was a man of an eligible age, near Lucius's own of four and thirty, he'd guess. A fact that raised his doubt regarding *her* explanations. He would never raise another man's son as his own.

Lucius gripped the sides of the oversized copper tub and came to his feet, sloshing water over the sides with a sudden urge to visit Perlsea Keep's newest steward. Just to discern the man's true reasons for being in Cornwall; to defend Pender—his— property. *The Keep*. It was the *Keep* he was determined to defend. It was a surety that Ashcroft wouldn't have Perlsea's best interests at heart.

Again, the image of his wife's head against the man's shoulder stabbed through him. No. It definitely wasn't the Keep's interests in which Ashcroft was thinking.

Without Graham's attention about, it took Lucius but ten minutes to dress and head down to the morning room. "Bartlett." He greeted the footman he'd left behind three years prior.

"My lord."

"I see you didn't abandon her ladyship and dash back to London."

Bartlett grinned. "No, sir. 'Tis been a challenging yet rewarding position. I thank you for the opportunity."

Lucius eyed him, gauging his sincerity. "Opportunity, eh?"

"Oh, yes. Lady Perlsea—er, pardon, my lord—Lady Pender has worked wonders in her time here."

With a stiff jaw, Lucius inquired, "Is there coffee?" He took a chair at the head of the table. A steaming brew was poured and placed before him. "Do tell."

"Ah, well. She's started a school for the village children. And made remarkable improvements in the Keep—er, apologies, my lord, I didn't mean…"

"No, no. The place was in abhorrent condition. Go on."

"The kitchens have been improved, along with the new bathing chamber. Saves the servants time in hauling heated water. The library, of course. And, the new steward. Well, he's not new any longer, I s'pose. Mr. Ashcroft has worked to keep the workmen from trampling the grounds."

"He's the one hiring the servants? From what I recall, only the Veritys had been in residence."

"No, sir," he hedged. "Her ladyship handles the hiring."

Lucius's gut tightened. "What else does this Mr…"

"Ashcroft. He don't operate like a regular steward. Oh, don't get me wrong, my lord. He gets things done, he does, but…" Bartlett's voice lowered as if he feared the walls had ears. Though in this monstrosity, it wouldn't surprise him. "He don't talk like an ordinary chap. Too posh."

"Too posh," Lucius repeated slowly. "And just where does the posh chap reside?"

Bartlett's brow furrowed as if the question confused him. "Why, in the steward's cottage, of course."

"Yes, of course," Lucius murmured. "And his office?"

"Off the kitchens, sir. Her ladyship affected changes there as well."

"I believe I'll pay the man a visit after I break my fast. How's the cook?"

"Smashing, my lord. I'll bring you a plate. Lady Pender instructed the kitchens not to bother with a sidebar as it was just…" Bartlett's ears turned red. "I'll, um, hurry back, sir."

By the time Lucius finished eating, he was spoiling for a fight. And he had a pretty decent idea of where to locate one. He strode through the halls and down a flight of stairs where he found the man in question sitting behind a weathered oak desk that had been polished to a shine. Prominent scratches and worn edges spoke of its age. The top was cluttered with ledgers, estate maps, and stacks of London broadsheets that should have been tossed out long ago.

His wife hadn't quite managed to rid the room of its musty odor, but Lucius sensed a purpose that spoke of something deeper than this man of business projected.

Without so much as a knock, Lucius entered.

The man leaned back in his chair with an assurance that upset the equilibrium. "Ah, Lord Pender. I anticipated a visit from you, just not first thing." His manner was indeed "posh" as Bartlett had said. Only the wired-framed spectacles detracted from the air of nobility.

Lucius leaned a shoulder against the wall, crossing his arms over his chest. "You held my wife in your embrace for all the village to see," he said. "How did you expect me to react?"

"She'd just learned one of her students had been crushed in a mining incident. She was distraught." His unspoken accusation that Lucius hadn't been there rankled and prickled him with more than a little culpability. "We've spent the last few years attempting to build a trust among the Cornish people your father and grandfather have long since neglected," he accused him mildly.

It was a poison-tipped spear that struck at Lucius's guilt. He straightened from the wall, his hands squeezed into fists. He set them at his lower back. "You overstep yourself, Mr. Ashcroft," he said softly. "I could call you out over such a statement."

"Don't be daft," Ashcroft said. "One of us would die and the other would hang. At the least, be transported."

"Your conduct with my wife is unacceptable." he bit out. The gall of this… this *lesser* was infuriating.

Ashcroft pushed his spectacles farther up on his nose, leaned forward in his chair, and clasped his hands on the desk in front of him. "*My* conduct…" Seemingly reluctantly, he added, "my lord?" A glint of annoyance flashed in dark-green eyes. "I was merely assisting Lady Pender in a moment of distress. Surely, you would not fault me for offering comfort after such a harrowing event."

Heat infused Lucius's face. The man was taunting him. "It's not the assistance I question, but the manner in which it was given. Taking… unnecessary… liberties is what I object to."

A tic next to Ashcroft's mouth was the only indication Lucius had breached the man's calm facade. "Liberties…" Again, that slight hesitation… "my lord?"

Lucius thought Ashcroft might choke on the address and Lucius took great satisfaction in the notion.

"I hardly think helping Lady Pender to her feet constitutes a liberty," he said blandly, clearly recovering his verve. "Your wife was in shock. Not to mention, exhausted from carrying that poor child from the mine. *Someone* had to act, and *I* was there."

Lucius unclasped his hands, leaned forward, and planted them on the edge of the desk. Pure venom snaked his veins, releasing through a voice he hardly recognized as his own. "From what I understand, you've availed yourself of a great deal since you arrived at Perlsea Keep. I, however, question whether your intentions are as noble as you are attempting to claim."

He met Lucius's gaze without flinching. "My only intention, *sir*, is to serve this estate and its people, most importantly Lady Pender." Ashcroft unclasped his hands and placed them on the arms of his chair and eyed Lucius with a hooded gaze reminiscent of one of Lucius's father's cronies he'd encountered at White's. "I fear I cannot help your feelings of inferiority." He lifted a shoulder as if the matter had been settled. "If that makes you uncomfortable, perhaps you should consider the fact that you've been absent for so long, leaving a woman to face such challenges on her own."

The delivery of his jab hit again with that vicious prick of the poisoned-tipped point. An absence for three years *was* inexcusable, but the scoundrel had overstepped. Lucius jerked straight, his hand knocking one of the piles on the desk askew. He caught up one of the ledgers before it could hit the floor. "Mind your place,

Ashcroft. You are steward here, not a confidant or protector to Lady Pender."

Behind the desk, Ashcroft came to his feet. His demeanor remained calm, but defiance glinted in his sharpened eyes. "You, *my lord*, are the Earl of Pender. Perhaps it would serve us both well to remember our roles and focus on what truly matters—the welfare of this estate and its people. Lady Pender requires support, not suspicion, and certainly not conflict."

Lucius eyed him, his suspicions not relieved by Ashcroft's words. "My wife and my property are none of your concern. I have every right to turn you out."

"But?"

"But I shall refrain for the time being. Rest assured, I shall be keeping a close eye on you. Make no mistake—any impropriety or misstep, and you will answer for it. At the end of my pistol."

Ashcroft gave a slight bow, though Lucius detected the trace of steel in his gaze. "As you wish, my lord. I have nothing to hide."

The fact that he hadn't emphasized, or mocked, Lucius's address for the first time in this little tête-à-tête set his teeth on edge.

Oh, yes. The man's reasons for being in Cornwall ran deep. And Lucius would learn the truth of the matter.

He turned sharply on his heel to leave, his mind a tumult of emotions—fury, and jealousy, of all things, and an unshakable sense of unease.

Ashcroft's calmness irked. His measured responses only deepened Lucius's suspicions. They also showed a glaring difference between them. And Lucius did not like the end of the stick he'd landed on. Nor was he comfortable with the man's assertions that he was only there to tend the estate and assist Lucius's own wife.

A deepened resolve stole through him, making him more determined than ever to uncover the truth behind the man's presence at Perlsea Keep.

He reached for the door and realized he still held the ledger. He glanced down at the neat hand, detailing the estate's finances and operations. But it appeared… disorganized—something that immediately struck Lucius as odd. He paused, then slowly turned back to Ashcroft.

"These ledgers," he said, waving the one book he held. "I assume they contain the most recent accounts for the estate?"

Ashcroft nodded, but Lucius detected a flicker of hesitation in his eyes. "Yes. I've been working to bring the records up to date. The previous stewards left much to be desired in terms of accuracy."

Easily confirmable with a note to Uncle Sander.

Lucius quickly looked over the entries, his brow furrowing. The discrepancies nearly jumped off the page. Figures that didn't quite add up, expenses that seemed inflated, and revenues that appeared suspiciously low. His pulse accelerated, though he kept his expression carefully neutral.

"Interesting," he murmured. He set that book down and picked up another. "There seem to be several… anomalies here. Would you care to explain?"

For the first time since entering the steward's office, Ashcroft's composure wavered, just slightly. He quickly rallied. "As I mentioned, the records were in disarray when I took over—"

"Three years ago."

"Yes, well, I've been working diligently to correct the errors, but it's a slow process. As I'm sure you can imagine."

Lucius closed the ledger with a decisive snap. "A slow process, indeed. One that could easily be mistaken for incompetence—or worse."

Ashcroft stiffened and a flash of something darker crossed his face. It was gone before Lucius could blink. "I assure you, *my lord,* any discrepancies are purely the result of poor bookkeeping by my predecessors. I intend to have everything in order soon."

Lucius let the silence stretch between them. More than anything, he wanted to rattle Ashcroft, see if the man revealed more under pressure. He was sadly disappointed. "I expect a full and thorough report on these discrepancies by the end of the week," Lucius finally said, tossing the ledger atop the disorganized piles. "And if I find that these *errors* are anything more than simple mistakes, well, that is just one more thing you have to answer for."

Ashcroft inclined his head, though his dark-green eyes, nearly black, could have iced the Sahara. "Of course, *my lord*. You'll have the report as requested."

Somehow that last mocking address reassured Lucius. He shot the man a last hard look, then left.

He pounded up the stairs to the main level, his mind racing. The glaring errors only confirmed his suspicions—Ashcroft was hiding something. But what was it and why?

Lucius would uncover the truth, and he knew the first place to start. He took the grand stairs to the family level and stormed to his wife's chamber, ignoring the frisson of anticipation that rippled over his skin. He tapped once, lightly, not expecting an answer—he didn't receive one—and he flung the door back, startling a young woman sitting on a cushioned bench carved out for a nook in the window. She clutched a worn tome to her chest. "Where is your mistress?"

She flinched beneath his bark and quickly came to her feet. Large brown eyes blinked back at him as if she hadn't understood the question.

"Speak up, child. Does she know you spend your time lolling about reading while she is away?"

Despite her modest appearance, an inner spark lit her eyes. She looked at the book she held then met his gaze squarely. "Certainly, sir. She taught me to read and gave me the book 'erself. Said I should take every oppor… opportu…"

"Opportunity?"

"Aye. Opportunity—" She repeated the word slowly as if savoring it, storing it to memory. "Lest I forget what I learnt."

"I, er, see." Apparently the school his wife had started began in her own sitting chamber. Her cheeks flushed with determination, her eyes glinted with indignation, and Lucius realized it wasn't just a school in the village that his countess had established—it was a cause, one she had brought into the very heart of her daily life. Such effort that didn't appear for show or public accolades; it was a private, genuine conviction. His chest tightened with more guilt, yet lined with reluctant admiration. It was a selflessness he hadn't expected and knocked him off balance. How had he so profoundly misjudged her? He cleared his throat. "My apologies for interrupting your studies then. But I am looking for my wife."

"Yer wife," she breathed. "Ye're the earl… Ye don' look much like a shadow t' me," she said, obviously gaining more confidence as she spoke.

"Do you know where—shadow?" The term confused him. He shook his head. "I don't understand."

Two red flags flared high on her cheeks, but her slight frame straightened to her modest height. The light from the window touched her, showing just how young she was. Perhaps fifteen or sixteen. "Um, I, um…"

Resigned to his fate, he might as well know the whole of it. The people of this community belonged to him. "Just spit it out. I am just a man as you can see, not a figment of your imagination."

A grin split her face making her look younger than her years, if that was possible. "They referred to you as the, er, Shadow of Pender."

"The shadow. Hmm. I take it there are more references?"

The red grew more pronounced, and she dropped her eyes. "The Absent Lord."

Lucius let out a long sigh then shoved his fingers through his hair. "I see I've much to make up for."

Her eyes snapped to his and what he saw there banded his chest with iron, stealing his breath… *hope?* "So, you're staying?"

"We shall see," he relented. "Perhaps you can inform your mistress that I wish to speak with her."

"Oh, aye. O' course. But she's not 'ere."

He frowned. "Where might she be?"

"She took a basket to the Trenwiths."

"Alone?"

She gave him one of those impish grins. "This is Cornwall, sir, not London."

Right. "Thank you, er…"

"Agnes. Agnes Tremayne. She's wearing her brown riding habit."

"Riding habit? In this weather?" Outrage started to take hold.

"Oh, no, milord. The footman, Bartlett, 'e accompanied 'er."

Lucius glanced at the window where the rain still lashed the windows. "That carriage is not made for—" Good God, she could be stranded with a broken axel, or worse, a broken neck. He didn't even finish his sentence, just tore out of her chamber. "Verity! My greatcoat."

The portly butler appeared, and Lucius snatched it from him and took off out the huge old door and ran for the stables.

"I require my horse. What is your name, sir?"

"Quill Prys, yer lordship."

"Are you familiar with the Trenwiths, Prys?"

"Aye."

"I require their direction."

"That I can 'elp with, milord. Take the road south. Go past St. Petroc till ye cross the river. Turn on the old minin' path. It runs alongside the mines. Trenwiths' cottage is one o' the 'omes afore the road bends t' the 'ills. Can't miss it."

One could hope. It took Prys less than ten minutes to bring Lucius's horse around and with a short wave, he was off.

The directions turned out to be quite specific. He found the old mining path easy enough until he came to the fork…

CHAPTER EIGHT

"I HATE TO force you out in this weather, Bartlett, but I just feel a visit with the Trenwiths is too important to put off." Meredith smoothed her skirts as Bartlett set the basket at her feet.

"'Tis my pleasure to serve you, milady." His climb on the box shook the carriage and they were off.

The trek into the village took almost an hour. Meredith hadn't any idea where her errant husband had disappeared, but with his accusations burning her ears, she'd opted not to inform Mr. Ashcroft of her plans. The realization hit hard; she'd become too dependent on the man.

The chances were great that her husband would not be long at Perlsea Keep. She wouldn't mind giving him his cursed annulment, except her father would kill him. He'd threatened her with that very fate. The memories rushed her…

"What, Papa?" Meredith looked in the entryway mirror and adjusted her hat. An adorable poke bonnet of cream with streaming blue ribbons she'd tied under her chin.

Her father strode past her. "Come into the study. We must speak."

The dictatorial cur. All he did was demand: Do this, don't do that. Oh, the day she clamored not to be under his all too pressing thumb. If she thought it wouldn't get her killed, she'd accept the first offer to come forth. With an annoyed sigh, she clutched her gloves and followed.

"I don't wish to be late."

He speared her with a glower. "You'd better not be meeting with that harlot from Berwick Street. I've warned you before."

"I'm meeting Lady Hannah, Papa." She didn't add that Geneva and Abra would happen along, as that would have her confined to her bedchamber for the rest of her days.

"You're to marry this Tuesday. Everything is in place."

"No." The word slipped out and he was in front of her before Meredith blinked, his massive hand gripping her by the throat.

"I see it has slipped your mind that you were to marry Pender's heir. He's a comely enough fellow. You could do worse." He pressed briefly cutting off her oxygen then just as suddenly released her and shoved her back.

She gasped out a small cough. "W-when?"

"Tuesday morning. St. George's has been secured."

"But today is Saturday. What of m-my dress… the flowers… my… my friends," she whispered.

"Everything has been taken care of. The dressmaker will be here Monday for your final fitting. You may be excused. To your chamber. I'll send a note with your regrets to Lady Hannah. I've much to do."

A rut in the road rattled Meredith's head from that horrid day and she glanced out the window. Bartlett turned the carriage onto the path leading to the Trenwiths' cottage. Thank heavens for the gravel. It saved the carriage from sinking into the mud, but the uneven ground made the ride rough. Small primroses and stalks of heather grew alongside and over the landscape but were beaten down with the rains. He drew the conveyance up to the door and assisted her trembling body down before taking the basket. He held an umbrella over them and ushered her to the door.

It opened before she reached it. "Hello, Sarah. Might I come in for a moment? I won't stay long."

"O' course, milady." Sarah's frame was slight, smaller than Megan Penrose, though they were near enough the same age. Dark blonde hair escaped its tie at her nape. Her large blue eyes, brimming with sadness, reached into Meredith's chest and ripped out her heart.

Sarah stood back and Meredith retrieved the basket from Bartlett. "Wait inside the carriage. I shan't be long." She crossed the threshold into a humble but warm and cared for home. The main room was small and dominated by a rough wooden table surrounded by several mismatched chairs set off to one side in a makeshift kitchen.

A large stone hearth took up one wall, where a low fire burned. Flickering shadows danced across the room. Above the hearth, simple iron hooks held a few cooking pots, while a small cupboard near the table contained a meager collection of crockery. The scent of peat smoke and something faintly herbal filled the air.

The floors were of uneven flagstone, topped with a few scattered rugs woven from coarse wool. The one window was small and covered by thin, threadbare curtains, allowing limited light. With the pounding rain outside, it turned the inside into a dim shadowy cave. Wood shelving along the walls held simple belongings—a chipped teapot and small mementos likely passed down through generations.

Meredith's heart broke.

"Papa and Jacob are at the mine working," Sarah said softly. "Mama has taken to her bed."

"Working, but…"

"They won't get paid otherwise." The words weren't spoken in anger or resentment but of hopeless resignation.

"I see." It was an outrage. Meredith found a small plate on the shelf and pulled out a fresh scone and set it on the table, then guided Sarah to one of the mismatched chairs and gently pushed her into it. Meredith took the chair next to her. "Eat," she commanded the girl.

Sarah broke off a small piece of the scone and nibbled.

"Did Mr. Thornfield happen to pay your papa a visit?" Meredith was careful to keep her tone light, fully aware of the anger simmering within.

Sarah pinched off another bit and crumbled it between her fingers, all thought of eating clearly obliterated. "Oh, yes." Her eyes glistened with tears. "He told Papa accidents happen and that he and Jacob were needed. He said if they didn't come in, they might as well stay home and not come back at all."

"Oh, Sarah. I'm so sorry," Meredith whispered, her own tears threatening. She covered Sarah's hand with her own. With a small squeeze, Meredith stood. "I believe the basket contains enough provisions for your family to last a couple of days."

"Oh, milady, you shouldn't have. Mama…"

"Of course, I should. I only wish I could do more." And she would, starting with a meeting with that oily rogue, Mr. Thornfield. "I won't stay, dear. Please, accept my condolences for your loss. Tommy… he was an adventurous child. I know you'll miss him." Meredith squeezed her hand again at a loss for more words. Sarah was much too young for such heartache.

"Thank you, milady."

Meredith nodded and went to the door, shocked to see the rain had abated. She didn't wait for Bartlett to come for her. Instead, he emerged just as she reached the carriage. "Take me to the mine office."

"Ma'am?"

"I wish to speak with Mr. Thornfield. Immediately."

"But—"

Meredith stopped and pierced him with a glare. "Am I mumbling my words, Bartlett?"

"No, milady."

"Excellent." She entered the carriage and dropped onto the seat setting the conveyance shaking with her fury.

The ride was short because the stone building was visible from the split in the path. Bartlett pulled to a stop. Again, the carriage shook with his descent and the putting out of the steps before the door opened.

His forehead creased with worry. "Lady Pender, are you certain about this?"

She considered him for a long moment then asked, "Would you question your lordship for taking action?"

"No, milady. But…"

"No buts, Bartlett. I've been handling matters for Penhalwick for three years. I shall handle this as well." She held out her hand for his assistance.

"Of course, milady, but—" He leaned in, lowering his voice. "Mr. Thornfield is a dangerous man. And, Mr. Ashcroft has been about to assist you."

It was true, she had never confronted Mr. Thornfield before. But she was a countess. She represented these people and as such her word was law. Her husband—she couldn't bear thinking of his name—would be on his way back to London within days, if she had anything to say about it… hmm. Perhaps it wouldn't hurt to help him along.

"Lady Pender?" Mr. Thornfield's condescending tone reached through her momentary musing. "What a lovely surprise." His gravelly voice had softened, but the false air of courtesy was blatantly apparent.

She stepped down from the carriage. "I'd like a word, sir."

"Certainly." He came forward and offered her his arm.

With no option, she took it aware, and thankful, of Bartlett right on her heels. Mr. Thornfield led her inside a large room with rough wooden benches and chairs along two walls. A large noticeboard was posted and Meredith caught what appeared to be work schedules, safety warnings, announcements, and such. But before they reached what she assumed was his office, a list of names brought her to an abrupt stop. She read through the list and her mouth fell open. She jerked her hand from the vile man and turned to him. "Is this a list of those who have been…" She couldn't bring herself to voice the actual words because at the end of the list was T. Trenwith.

"'Tis a list of those who have been injured and disciplined."

"Tommy Trenwith? He was not an employee of yours, sir," she said coldly. "He was a child who snuck into the mine under *your* watch. His blood is on *your* hands."

With a sharp glance about, he took her arm a little forcefully and pulled her past a small desk manned by a clerk, who stared at her open-mouthed, and into his office and shut the door in Bartlett's face.

Seething, Meredith took in the relatively spacious room. The size reflected what the man clearly thought of himself. Walls bare of artwork hosted crudely drawn maps pinned on dark paneling. Heavy curtains were drawn to block out the chilled morning, yet Meredith shivered from the inside out. Several oil lamps about the room burned brightly. He led her to one of two wood chairs, no cushioning. She refused to sit.

"I realize as a woman of quality that the interworking intricacies of mining and miners is quite beyond your comprehension." He offered up another one of those oily smiles. "Quite understandable, Lady Pender, as such things fall outside a woman's knowledge." His words, laced with a patronizing undertone, set her teeth on edge. He drew out his sentences as if she hadn't a brain. As if she were unable to grasp the gravity of a situation. *Any* situation.

The hint of smugness in his tone grated on her. The audacity that he thought he could bend her to his will easily steeled her resolve. She had grown up dealing with a powerful father, learning from the best. She was not one manipulated so simply as he obviously believed.

He moved behind a massive desk, laden down with ledgers and account books. A document that appeared legal in nature was in the prominent space with a pen lying across it. She took in the stack of correspondence, some opened, some unopened, attempting to pull her thoughts together. Because he was right about one thing: she had no notion of the inner workings of the mining business.

The one thing she did know was people. She leveled a glare on him that seethed her disapproval. "As I understand it, Mr. Trenwith and his son, Jacob, were"—*forced*—"encouraged to return to work today."

Mr. Thornfield let out a condescending sigh. "Such tactics are necessary for disciplinary purposes, my lady. If the miners don't see examples of misconduct, how am I expected to keep things running on schedules? There are obligations to be met."

"But Mr. Trenwith just lost his ten-year-old son, sir." His lack of compassion was as shocking as it was insulting.

His thin lips curved in a disdainful smile that sickened her. "All the more reason for him to maintain his sense of consistency." He let out a huff of barely concealed impatience. "If the miners aren't aware of the consequences of the dangers, they would not understand the reasons for the rules, my lady."

"There have been at least two deaths since I've come to Penhalwick, Mr. Thornfield. And, I reiterate, the second one is that of a ten-year-old child. You have his name posted on a board just outside this office. Not to mention the list of those injured, which I suspect is a great many."

His lips tightened.

Perhaps there was *some* compassion in him. She pressed on but softened her tone. "Mr. Thornfield, please, the Trenwiths have just lost their child. I believe it appropriate for Mr. Trenwith to be with his wife at this trying time. I am of the belief that unless properly dealt with, such devastation takes a toll on a person. Which can raise the chance of more haphazard mistakes to take place."

He stared at her as if he'd just reached the gates of Hades and she was Cerberus. An image she rather liked, reinforcing her backbone. She tilted her head, giving the meaning behind her words time to sink in.

It was a slow process and started with his ears turning an unbecoming shade of scarlet. So, no compassion then. "You," he sputtered, seemingly at a loss for words. With a sharp inhalation, he spoke in a low, menacing timbre. "What exactly is it you are proposing, Lady Pender?" Gone was the patronizing undertone. His voice had hardened, the tempered patience disappearing, revealing a more menacing aspect of what she suspected was his true nature as he attempted to regain control.

She came to her feet, ditching her own efforts at appealing to a sympathy that did not exist; she sliced him with her own tone of glacial fury. "I insist you give the Trenwiths three days to process their grief for the loss of their son and brother."

"This is outrageous, madam. *I* run this mine, not you, and I will run it as I see fit." He slammed his hands flat on his desk, sending some of the correspondence fluttering to the floor.

She waited. Easy enough for someone who had suffered through enough of Papa's tantrums.

"Impossible." He sputtered. "This mine cannot operate without employees. That is what we pay them for." He swooped the letters from the floor.

"Then you leave me with no alternative. I shall be contacting the mining authorities to oversee the safety measures you say you have installed. I suspect they are quite insufficient."

He laughed. A robust sound that reverberated against the walls.

"The fact that Tommy Trenwith entered the mine under your watch clearly shows you have violated the Mine Acts of 1842, sir. You've lost two individuals in the three years I have been in residence at Perlsea Keep and that is unacceptable."

"What of it? Considering the dangers involved, madam, two losses is an extremely conservative number."

"I disagree. That is two people too many in my estimation. How glib you are when speaking of two lives. Two families. Well, I won't stand for it. I insist you give the Trenwiths three days to process their grief. I will not say so again."

The smile he turned on her turned her stomach. "I suspect your husband would have much to say about this. But alas, he is nowhere to be found, is he?"

Obviously, he hadn't heard the Absent Lord had returned. She smiled, her own lips tipping in condescension. "You are quite correct, Mr. Thornfield. My husband will have plenty to say about your actions. And I shall see that you are replaced."

He snorted.

"My wife is quite correct, Thornfield."

Startled, Meredith's gaze flew to the door.

Pender leaned casually against the doorframe, his arms crossed over his broad chest, but the tension in his posture was unmistakable. His gray eyes, dark and calculating, pinned Thornfield with an intensity that sent a palpable chill through the room and through Meredith. There was no grand gesture of entry—no dramatic step forward—but the quiet power in his stance spoke volumes.

The moment stretched, heavy and silent. Meredith's gaze moved back to Mr. Thornfield's startled expression. His sallow complexion paled.

"Ah, Pender. You've arrived."

His brows lifted and the faintest shadow of a smile crossed his lips.

Anyone watching could sense the controlled anger simmering beneath his calm facade. She shivered.

"We meet again, Mr. Thornfield." Pender's voice was smooth, low, yet razor-sharp. The very sound of it seemed to suck the air from the room. "It seems you were about to enlighten my wife on how you intend to rectify the disaster you've overseen."

Meredith frowned. "Again?"

Thornfield's earlier smugness vanished as Pender stepped forward, his boots making no noise against the flagged-stone floor, yet each step seemed weighted. He made no move to sit, simply loomed over Thornfield's desk. His gaze flicked over the ledgers and the legal document still prominently placed, then slowly raised back to Thornfield's now flushed face.

"I trust," Pender went on as if he hadn't paused, his voice as cold as the North Sea, "you did not intend to challenge Lady Pender's very reasonable request." His emphasis on "reasonable" was a deliberate mockery of Thornfield's earlier arrogance.

Inwardly, Meredith cheered. Outwardly, her confidence boosted.

Thornfield's mouth gaped like that of a beached fish, but

Pender raised a hand, silencing him before he could manage a single word.

The fear flickering in Mr. Thornfield's eyes was most satisfying, but it wasn't enough. Two individuals had perished, and Meredith was out for blood. Watching her husband now sent a surge of foreboding through her.

It was difficult to believe Pender had returned, not just to claim his estate, but to right the wrongs and neglect his family had wrought.

"You speak of discipline, Thornfield," Pender said, his tone measured. "Perhaps it's time you experienced some yourself." His gaze hardened, and Meredith decided it was time for her to intervene.

Mr. Thornfield's days in power were numbered, she thought, but they still needed him. "So, you see, Mr. Thornfield, his lordship has plenty to say. I'm sure you'll be thrilled to have some of the heavy load lifted from your shoulders."

Pender turned his glare on her, but she wisely ignored it, giving him a bright smile. One of approval.

His lips tightened. A deliberate calm she was quite certain he manufactured at will spoke, his voice softening, though still firm. "The Trenwith family will receive their time, as my wife has insisted." The subtle undercurrent of respect in his tone was undeniable, acknowledging her strength in the face of Mr. Thornfield's contempt.

She let out a small, relieved sigh.

Pender straightened and turned his full attention back to Mr. Thornfield, whose attempt at bluster had fully disintegrated. "You have until the end of the day to grant the Trenwiths their leave and address the safety concerns at the mine my wife has requested. Failure to comply will not be tolerated, and rest assured, I will make the necessary arrangements for a new agent should you prove incapable of the task."

The threat was implicit, and Pender had made no effort to soften the blow.

"That's enough, *dear*," she said through clenched teeth. "I'm certain Mr. Thornfield understands—" She spared the odious man a smug glare. "—his place."

She took her husband's arm that resembled more a shaft of forged steel, recently taken from the fire, and did her best to steer him out of the stuffy confines.

But he was not quite willing to leave, stopping at the clerk's desk with specific instructions regarding the Trenwiths. He turned back to Mr. Thornfield one last time. "I'm certain nothing untoward will happen to the men under your watchful eye. Am I right, Thornfield?"

"Of-of course, my lord."

Before they reached the door leading outside, a crash sounded from behind that had Meredith hunching her shoulders.

Bartlett held the door open for her, but it was her husband who handed her inside. "We'll talk once we reach the Keep."

"I'm sure we will," she muttered as the door clattered shut and the skies opened up with another round of battering rain.

Lucius hunched in the saddle, his cloak heavy with the unrelenting deluge. The steady clop of his horse's hooves in the saturated mud and the creak of the carriage ahead seemed to be the only sounds in the world, save for the persistent downpour. His body still vibrated with the force of his outrage.

It stuck in his craw having heard Thornfield speaking so to a woman—not just any woman, but the Countess of Pender, *his wife*. His gloved hands tightened on the reins. She truly cared for these people, as he so recently realized. She'd spent the last three years living among, helping, supporting the community. Her actions, though reckless today—and he'd certainly be speaking up on that—showed the depths of her commitment. His leaving now could put her in peril. No, leaving now was out of the question... for now.

Not to mention the questions surrounding Ashcroft.

With his father dead and Lucius at the helm, he had an innate interest in the tin mines. His own family profiting from them made that a given. The land was nothing more than a challenge, he told himself, the remnants of a birthright he hadn't wanted. Yet, the sensation that he couldn't abandon it was… new.

Like it or not, Perlsea was his.

Groaning, Lucius followed the carriage through the village and past the church through to the path leading up to the Keep unable to stem the pelting thoughts laden with guilt. The land, the title, the people—it had all felt so foreign to him. He could blame his father, but ultimately the fault lay on his own shoulders. Uncle Sander and Noah had taken the burdens Lucius had ignored, preferring the benefits but not the responsibility.

But now, despite the rain and mud, despite the cold seeping into his bones, there was something familiar that whispered to him that he belonged here, that this was where his life had been leading him, no matter how far he had tried to run. *Chosen to run,* he silently amended.

Was it possible that his slip of a wife was at the center of that pull?

The turn his life had taken did not sit well. He'd learned what he'd come to Perlsea for. The temptation to disappear was but a breath away. All he had to do was depart, leave his wife to her follies. Hell, he couldn't even recall her name!

But glancing at the darkened outline of his countess's carriage, he knew he couldn't deny it—he had begun to stake a claim, not just on the land but on her. The thought hit him like the cold rain on his face. His request for an annulment was waning, his purpose changing.

Agnes.

Ashcroft.

Thornfield.

Purpose… An interesting concept. For him, leastways. Purpose.

The dark silhouette of the carriage was barely visible through the sheets of rain. His wife was in there, sheltered from the storm, but he sensed the tempest raging within her just as fiercely as it did in him. She had every reason to hate him, to wish him to the devil, to stand against him as she had done since his return.

And, oh, how he was tempted.

His gaze moved past the carriage to the shadow of the Keep easing into view. The imposing structure didn't look so horrid from this angle. Seeming to watch over Penhalwick like an avenging angel of sorts. *Or was it her?*

Did he really think he had what it took to oversee the people of this land? Be accepted? Be a… husband?

These were the questions that had plagued him from almost the moment he'd arrived, and in that instant, he knew he would not be leaving. He would not be abandoning these people, this land, or his wife.

The thought brought a grim smile even as the cold rain trickled down the back of his neck.

For whatever reason, it was time to face the fact that he, Lucius Oshea, was the Earl of Pender. The affairs of the title and all its holdings were *his* responsibility. Not his uncle's nor his brother's.

And what of Docia?

Docia. The most shocking revelation of all. That he'd barely spared her a thought.

CHAPTER NINE

T HE LIBRARY'S USUAL warmth failed in penetrating Meredith's chilled skin. She stood before the fireplace, her wet cloak discarded over a chair as the flames and her temper crackled. The glow from the hearth cast sharp shadows in the low-lit room. The door flew back and her husband stormed in, his own coat dripping water onto her new carpets, his boots squelching with every step. His expression was as dark as the battering torrent outside.

"*What* in God's name were you thinking?" he demanded, his voice hard and low, but the fury beneath was unmistakable.

She bristled with outrage. Meredith turned, facing him, her eyes narrowing. "You've a lot of nerve, sir. I did what needed to be done. Someone must stand up to that fool."

"*Someone*, yes. But not you!" He stepped closer, his hand tightening into a fist at his side. "You had no business facing a man like him on your own. Do you even understand the sort of man he is? The danger he poses?"

Her jaw set and she lifted her chin. "I understand far better than you think." The audacity of his outrage, after leaving her to navigate this mess in the first place, was almost as infuriating as his sudden, *supposed*, concern for her safety. She'd laugh in his face had she the capability. But she was too cold and too angry. "Let me make one thing clear to you, *my lord*. I do not require *your* permission to do what I know is right."

"That's not the point," he shot back. He shoved a hand

through his hair, his frustration obviously boiling over. "You shouldn't have confronted him. And certainly not alone. I'm here. *I* should have handled Thornfield, not you."

"You were too busy stealing my bath." Meredith's vision hazed with a red fog. "How dare you think you can just sweep in here after three years and handle something you know nothing about. You're deluding yourself," she scoffed. "The Keep, the village, the *mines*—all left in ruin because you couldn't be bothered. I'm the one who's been dealing with matters—" She ticked off one finger. "Gaining the women's trust—" She ticked off a second. "Teaching the children to read—" A third. *"Hiring a steward* while you—" She was so angry the words refused to come. She drew in a deep breath through her nose that went far in resetting her temper.

"I know I wasn't here," he bit out in a tone sharp and cutting. "Don't you think I know I left you to face all of this alone? But damn it, I'm here *now*."

Meredith stepped toward him, her voice low but trembling with rage. "I'm not some delicate flower that needs sheltering, Lord Pender. I've had to fend for myself long before *you* decided to show up." She swept up her cloak and strode to the door. "It is my greatest desire to see you crawl back under the rock from which you emerged."

"Perhaps I shall do exactly that."

She grabbed the knob and turned it, stopping short of opening the door. She looked over her shoulder, giving him her harshest Duke of Rathbourne glare. "You're dripping water all over my new rugs. *That* never happened before you arrived either."

THE DOOR SHUT hard behind his countess. Well. That hadn't gone quite as he'd planned. Lucius dropped his gaze to his feet, to the water seeping into her precious rug. Squelching his way in the offending boots to the hearth, he tugged them off where the floor was stone, disgusted with himself that he even spared a thought for her overpriced floor coverings.

With no care for his sopping stockings, he trudged to the cabinet and poured out a measure of brandy and threw it back. *You're my wife!* he'd wanted to shout. *I have every right to care whether you live or die. I care what happens to you, whether you want me to or not.*

Unfortunately, and rightly so, her jab at his sudden appearance, his sudden interest in her well-being, no doubt rang as absolute absurdity.

Hell, if he had any sense at all, he would jump on his horse first thing in the morning. But that was beyond reach now that he'd taken Thornfield to task. Giving the man the upper hand now was out of the question.

Lucius poured another couple of fingers of brandy then moved to the settee before the fire and sat down. Yes, he would see the matter of Thornfield through then leave her to her Mr. Ashcroft. But the thought left a bitter taste in his mouth the brandy couldn't mask.

She'd made such a timely exit, he hadn't even said all he'd intended.

Lucius slammed his half-empty glass on a low table and rose. He snatched up his boots and stalked out the door only to find his valet had finally made it to the wilds of England's southwestern coast.

CHAPTER TEN

Three Days Later

LUCIUS'S COUNTESS, IT turned out, was as elusive as the blasted sun.

For. Three. Days.

Upon entering the morning room, he'd find she'd just finished breaking her fast. At the noon hour, he'd learned she and that crackpot, Ashcroft, had departed to Vestry Hall. Which, upon further investigation, turned out to be a large room at the church that was currently being used as a school for the village children. At the dinner hour, she claimed fatigue. Ha. No more likely than the moon falling from the sky. If one ever happened to see the moon in this godforsaken corner in the bleakest realm of civility. He deserved it, he supposed, after consigning her to this same fate for three blasted years.

Lucius meandered down to Ashcroft's office—in actuality, he justified—it was Pender's property, Pender's affairs, and therefore, Pender's office.

He tapped at the closed door even knowing Ashcroft was not in, then entered. It irritated him that he felt like a trespasser. Almost nothing on the desk had changed. The stacks of ledgers and the correspondence may have shifted a tad but other than that all appeared exactly the same. He moved behind the desk for a different view and *voilá...*

Fingers somewhat unsteady, Lucius lifted a crude sketch that, upon closer inspection, appeared to be of Perlsea Keep's exterior. Ashcroft was the steward, so that was to be expected, he supposed. But it was the various areas circled and marked that sent a chill snaking up Lucius's spine. He started to set the drawing back but a hastily scribbled list of names were scratched out on another scrap of paper. Taking that up, he read…

Reginald Ormsby – Surrey

Evan Blackwell – London

? Terrence Radcliffe – Hampshire

x Alfred Featherstone – Derbyshire

George Copley – Yorkshire

x James Bancroft – Oxfordshire

x Charles Whittingham – Gloucestershire

x Francis Aldridge – Somerset

One or two of the names even seemed familiar but Lucius couldn't have said why. He located a clean piece of paper and jotted down the names, then laid the map back atop and left, closing the door softly behind him. He made his way to the Keep's study.

A study that looked to be the next major project in this renovation project of his wife's. Every piece of furniture was covered with large sheets of canvas. The shelves were devoid of books and the curtains… well, there were no curtains. Mullioned windows exposed the gray skies beyond, and with no fire in the grate, the cold infiltrated the chamber. The walls had been scraped of their paper and, glancing up, he saw that the ceiling was in the same condition as the walls.

He'd no idea of her plans, but it was obvious the environment was not conducive to working in. Lucius backed out of the chamber and went to the library where there was at least a desk. The overhead light was low, and it took a moment to locate the valve to raise the brightness. He moved behind the desk, took the chair, then set the paper he still held on the flat surface and stared at the list of names.

The two he recognized were Alred Featherstone and Francis

Alderidge, but for the life of him, he could not recall why he would have known them. He certainly couldn't picture their faces.

Lucius tapped the blunt end of an index finger on the polished mahogany. His brother and uncle would surely know. A fact that pricked Lucius with guilt. He was now the earl and as earl he was responsible for the title, the lands, the entailment, the people. All of it, and out of petty fury—perhaps not petty, as he had every right to his anger with his father and Rathbourne for stealing his and Meredith's right in choosing their own paths—but Lucius had thus far failed miserably in his duties.

Admitting so allowed a sense of rightness to filter through him. He may have turned up when the candles were stubs, but he was here now, and moving forward he would learn what he should have been learning at his father's knee. He located a pen, inkwell, and a sheet of vellum and penned a note to his uncle. He started to slip the paper with the list of names within the missive but changed his mind. Whatever reason Ashcroft was looking into these individuals, Lucius decided to do the same.

But where to start? He wouldn't mind another glance at that map of the estate but a quick look at the clock over the mantel and not having pinpointed his wife's schedule negated that task momentarily. It was time to speak with Agnes again. The girl had been a fount of information before.

Why was no one where they were supposed to be?

The bathing room was devoid of steam, nor was his wife in their "shared sitting room." He tapped at her bedchamber door, but there was no answer there either. He stole inside instead and meandered about.

An escritoire was situated before a long skinny window. He lifted the top and noted a stack of correspondence. Oddly, the one atop was from none other than Miss Geneva Wimbley. They'd met briefly when she'd appeared in Northumberland for his father's funeral services. Miss Wimbley was not the sort of woman he imagined his wife to befriend… but then what did he really know of his wife?

He started to close the desk but caught sight of a small pamphlet. Across the front in large, blocked lettering was:

Women and the Need for Economic Equality: A Plan for England's Future

What the devil? He picked up the saddle-stitched booklet and fanned the pages. There must at least twenty. The paper was thin and uncoated, rough to the touch. Most shocking, if anything could be more shocking, was the listed author: The Clandestine Sapphire Society. This was beyond propriety's sake, going through his wife's personal papers, but this was too curious to resist. Lucius stuffed the pamphlet in the breast pocket of his waistcoat and shut the escritoire, nearly forgetting his original mission.

He trotted down to the kitchens to speak with Mrs. Verity and found her supervising the pantries. "Mrs. Verity, when is my wife expected back? I thought to share dinner with her." *For once.*

She stammered about before giving him an answer. "I believe, er, um, well, ye see, she don't have no regular time, yer lordship."

"Oh, and why might that be? Surely, the children's lessons don't go beyond evening time."

"Oh, no, sir." Her gaze avoided his before she finally said, almost defiantly, "Sometimes she takes tea at The Copper Kettle."

"I see. And, her maid?"

"Oh, Agnes? Her ladyship typically takes her along. She 'elps 'er out. Gel's taken to readin' 'erself. Too much, if anyone cares t' know my opinion."

Lucius stifled a grin. "And, Mr. Ashcroft?"

"Well, 'e's a drivin' 'er, aint' 'e?"

"Quite right." Lucius went to the door then turned back. "What do you know of a Mr. Ornsby?"

"That cantankerous old coot? Didn't do an 'onest day's work in all 'is time 'ere."

"What kind of work?"

Her mouth dropped, exposing a couple of missing teeth, before she snapped her jaw shut and narrowed her eyes on him.

He froze under the sudden intensity. A creeping sense of unease prickled at the back of his neck.

"Ornsby was the steward after yer mama married that earl of 'ers. Don' know 'ow 'e kept the position long as 'e did. Ten years, I reckon. Last I'd seen o' 'im must a been, oh, 1824 or so."

Lucius had expected something more vague, more elusive, like a groundskeeper. Instead, her answer left him grasping for a response. He felt his footing slip, like missing the bottom step on a staircase. His unease increased. "What of Mr. Blackwell or Radcliffe."

Her thin lips twisted in another sign of disgust. "Stewards, too. Din't last more than a year at most." A momentary flustered silence followed, the weight of her stare making him shift his stance. "Matter o' fact, there were another five or six and countin'."

That was odd… "All stewards?" he asked.

"Aye."

The kitchen, warm and fragrant with the scent of stewing vegetables, suddenly felt too small, too close, too hot. The prickling at his neck tingled.

She turned, muttering something under her breath to the effect of "none of 'em ever worked as 'ard as old Aldridge did durin' his twenty-year stint with the family."

Stunned, Lucius pushed his fingers through his hair. "They just… walked off the job?"

"Daresay they din't give so much as a word o' notice."

THE REPORTS THORNFIELD sent over left Lucius with a sense of incompletion. He leaned back in his chair, staring at the notes he'd scribbled. There were too many inconsistencies for his comfort. It was possible the man had forgotten to include the ledgers regarding the mine's profits. But more likely it was deliberate neglect of sending them over in the first place.

A delay tactic to be sure. He needed that ledger.

Another disturbing aspect was the report on the working conditions in the mine. There was nothing to suggest that notices had been posted on more dangerous areas. That would obviously require a visit. He'd just have to keep the man at his side to assure Lucius's own safety. And, what of funds allocated to the miners' well-being? Absolutely nothing.

Tommy Trenwith's death had not been his imagination. That certainly required investigation. In all actuality, the stack of papers that had arrived via Thornfield's secretary were useless. As tempting as it was to toss them in the fire, they would serve as rope for the man to hang himself, Lucius decided.

Lucius rose from the desk. It appeared Thornfield required another face-to-face visit. What did it say about Lucius that he was spoiling for the confrontation? Plenty. If anything, perhaps a release of pent-up frustration as an image of his wife's heart-shaped face floated before him.

Within minutes he was taking the trek down the hill through a mist that coated the heavy marine air. Thankfully the rain held off. The vast view from Perlsea to the village could be considered breathtaking. Not a term Lucius habitually used. The rugged Cornish landscape sloped gently toward the village, nestled in the valley below.

The sea air carried a freshness easily forgotten after a long stay in London and he drew in a deep breath along with a rare appreciation. Once he reached Penhalwick, he rode past stone cottages and down narrow streets that formed a cluster at the center which culminated at St. Petroc's. Its stone bell tower stood as a silent guardian over the village itself. Moments later, children spilled from the vestry, marking the end of the school day.

He watched for his wife, but she didn't appear, and he moved on, the worn path taking him around the church. The village sported a variety of shops, the busiest of which looked to be The Copper Kettle, a veritable hub of the small, picturesque community. People strolled about, some hurrying into the apothecary and the general store, Penhalwick Provisions as the swinging wood sign above indicated. Lucius kicked his mount into a trot more than curious for an idea of Thornfield's direction over his workers.

On the outskirts of the village, Lucius could see the entrance to the mine, a dark scar in the otherwise peaceful landscape. Smoke and dust rising faintly from its top was a stark reminder of the labor taking place inside. He wondered how deep beneath the ground the mines went. A shudder skittered over him. The farther from the village he went, the rockier the old mining path grew. It was lined with twisted trees and tall grass, and in its own way, was picturesque.

Based on the schedule Thornfield had provided, the first shift changed at six in the evening. Lucius pulled his horse to a stop before the office and dropped to the ground. The yard bustled with activity. Those about took note of him, and slowly the chatter slowed then stopped, leaving only the rustling of the trees in a soft breeze that was unique to Cornwall. With a sharp nod to the workers, he tied off the reins of his horse and entered the stone structure.

Oddly, inside where the same sense of chaos should have transpired, Lucius found the outer room unusually silent but for an altercation that bounded against the walls. Several clerks handling paperwork were doing their utmost to ignore the shouting coming from the open door behind them.

Thornfield's office and Thornfield in quite the altercation.

"I've been telling you for weeks, Thornfield! That support beam in Tunnel Four is barely holding. If we don't reinforce it now, we're risking another collapse. Are you trying to bury these men alive?"

Something Lucius wouldn't mind knowing himself. He

moved to the door and leaned a shoulder against the frame. The two were so intent on one another, neither noticed him.

Thornfield's hand clenched in a tight fist. "We've quotas to meet, Trevorrow. Delays are unacceptable. If you're too soft to push your men, I can think of at least two others willing to step in your place,"—he snapped his fingers—"like that."

Trevorrow's face tightened into one of sheer disbelief. "Your disregard for safety boggles one's mind."

"Get out. This mine's been running fine for years without your complaints."

"If another collapse happens, the blood'll be on *your* hands, you bastard. You think the men will keep quiet forever?"

"They will if they know what's good for them," Thornfield bit out through a stiffened jaw. "I said get out. You're fired."

But Trevorrow wasn't finished. "They're still talkin' about little Tommy's accident. That boy should've never been in the mine in the first place. Where was that goon of yours? Wasn't he placed there to ensure no unauthorized persons crossed the threshold?"

"*I said get out.*" Thornfield's shout rattled the windows, sent the flames in the lighting flickering wildly.

Trevorrow slapped his hat against his thigh and spun. Then froze.

"Good afternoon, gentlemen." Lucius straightened from the door jamb and entered the office. "What an enlightening conversation."

Thornfield's face shifted to a mask of fury. "How might I be of service, my lord? Were my reports not sufficient enough for you?"

"Funny you should ask, Thornfield." Lucius acknowledged Trevorrow with an incline of his head. "Return to work, sir. I require a word with your superior." Though he nearly choked on the word.

With a sharp nod, Trevorrow stormed out, his anger still evident.

Lucius closed the door with a sharp, controlled latch. "You failed in providing the ledgers that corresponded to your reports. In particular, those showing the actual income compared to the ore sold. I'd also like a look at the contract you signed with my father."

The man's sallow complexion blanched to the color of bleached stone.

Lucius strolled across the room and dropped into one of the tall, uncomfortable chairs. "Take your time pulling the information together. I'm in no hurry."

Thornfield went to the door and barked out an order to one of the clerks then returned to his chair behind the desk.

"I expect Trevorrow will retain his position as foreman."

"The man showed an abhorrence of disrespect," Thornfield bit out through clenched teeth.

"It's been my experience that respect is earned." Lucius studied his gloved knuckles. "Respect begets respect per se."

A muscle ticced in Thornfield's cheek. "As I said, there are quotas to be met," he ground out.

"I take it you keep accident reports."

"Of course."

"I'd like the full list of those as well. In fact, I would like to see them going back as far as 1824."

"1824," Thornfield repeated slowly.

The thought seized Lucius that perhaps Rathbourne and his own father had devised some scheme between them. "Yes. 1824." He also had his doubts that the man's contract was in the general files. "The contract now—if you please."

Thornfield stared at Lucius for a long time, then removed one of the maps on the wall, exposing an old safe. Very old. He took a key from his waistcoat and slipped it in the lock. It took but a few minutes for him to retrieve the document and hand it to Lucius.

"Thank you." Lucius stood. "I'll take my leave as soon as I have the ledgers."

With a nod, Thornfield marched to the door and barked another order.

Seconds later, ledgers in hand, Lucius went to the door. He pushed it closed for one last bit of privacy, spearing the man with a cool look. "I recommend, sir, that every precaution be taken to prevent any untoward mishaps among your workforce. I hope I am making myself clear?" He glanced down at the stack he held, then back up. "Until tomorrow then, Thornfield."

CHAPTER ELEVEN

T HE DIMLY LIT backroom of The Copper Kettle was quiet, save for the soft clink of teacups against saucers. Meredith sat at the head of the table with her hands folded in front of her, Agnes on one side of her, Elowen, her new secretary on the other. Meredith focused on the small notepad open before her.

Marigold Tremayne, Agnes's mother, of Marigold's Haberdashery, Edith Kevern who worked for her husband at the Crooked Anchor, and Mrs. Wren the woodworker's wife, sat around the table, each appearing anxious, yet determined.

Derwa Cardy was also in attendance, but almost three years after losing her husband, the young widow was still too despondent for Meredith's liking, and her heart went out to her. When Derwa spoke at all, the words were rarely above a whisper.

The Widow Elspeth, Mrs. Trelawney, moved in and out of the room, her footsteps a mere whisper on the wood planks while her eyes remained vigilant for signs of unwelcome visitors in the main tearoom. She kept the door to the back room slightly ajar, of which Meredith was grateful as it gave the two of them the opportunity to react in the event of anything untoward happening.

Sadly, the village men had not been convinced—were, in fact, suspicious—of the practices Meredith chose to share with her small audience. Practices she, Geneva, Hannah, and Abra had come up when they'd created their pamphlet *Women and the Need for Economic Equality: A Plan for England's Future.*

With a slight nod to the women, Meredith said, "We'll begin with today's lesson on managing the price for your goods." She glanced at Mrs. Wren whose brows furrowed. Meredith went on to clarify her meaning. "This includes charging for different services," she said facing Mrs. Wren, "Mr. Wren's woodworking services. Take, for example, refinishing a piece of furniture versus building a new piece." She turned to Marigold. "Your haberdashery is doing well, but at our last meeting you mentioned a worry of underpricing your fabrics."

Lastly, Meredith faced the much too quiet Derwa. Her eyes were lowered, as if she found the contents of her empty teacup more worthy of her attention. "Derwa?"

The young woman started, and her gaze flew to Meredith's. "You offer sewing services. I suspect you are not paid nearly what you are worth."

Her eyes lowered again, and she didn't speak.

Marigold fidgeted in her seat. "Aye, my lady. Mr. Tremayne constantly berates me for my low prices, but I fear losing customers."

"A perfectly normal reaction, my dear." Meredith smiled. "Try to think of it like this: People value what they pay for. If you raise your prices, even slightly, others may deem your goods more valuable than you expect."

Comprehension lit her eyes. "Oh." She drew the word out.

Satisfaction rippled through Meredith. "Let us start with the importance of maintaining proper records. Numbers will not lie to you. In this lesson I'll show you how to track the overall health of your business."

Mrs. Kevern, who had been quietly sipping her tea until now, spoke up. "It's not the market I worry about, my lady." Bitterness edged her tone. "It's the contract my husband signed."

"Contract?" Meredith's brows raised. "I'm sorry, I don't understand."

"The one with Thornfield for 'is work in the mines. I didn't understand what it all meant—Mr. Thornfield read it to us 'imself, but I can't 'elp feelin' as if we've been 'oodwinked."

The temperature of Meredith's blood spiked. "You are an extremely wise woman, Mrs. Kevern. Contracts like those are often written for the express purpose *to* confuse. I can certainly read through it and answer any questions you may have. I suspect Mr. Ashcroft would also be able and willing to assist."

For the next two hours, she pointed out the importance of using a ledger for income and expenses, saving receipts for purchases. She threw out questions on managing inventory, filing important paperwork, and budgeting. A sense of fulfillment crept through her with their questions, their engagement. Even Derwa's.

Meredith took a breath in a moment of silence, broken only by the sound of a fire crackling in the hearth at the other end of the room. The women looked at one another, a mix of fear yet determination on their faces.

Meredith glanced at the notes Elowen had been taking and nodded at her then gathered up her own notes. "Shall we meet again tomorrow? Bring whatever questions and notes you have." Meredith continued, "Any documents your husbands have signed you wish for me to look through, any terms you think your husbands might not fully understand. I'm happy to read through them for you."

Marigold shifted in her seat. She leaned forward and lowered her voice. "But what if someone catches wind of our doings?"

"We'll be cautious," Meredith assured her. "If need be, we shall change our meeting time. But we won't stop."

Derwa shot a nervous look toward the door. "And Thornfield?" she whispered. "He's got his claws in 'alf the men in this village already."

Meredith's jaw clenched. "I'll deal with him when the time comes. He gave the Trenwiths the time they needed to grieve for their son, didn't he?" she said, thankful she had that triumph on her side to assure them with.

Each nodded slowly and Meredith let out a small, relieved breath.

Elspeth stole into the room holding a fresh pot of tea. She set it on the table with a knowing look. "'Twas a brave thing you did, Lady Pender, facing that man. Not a soul in Penhalwick has stopped talking about it." She faced the women. "We've got to be careful, aye, but we can't let fear stop us from learning what we need to protect ourselves."

Meredith barely restrained herself from jumping up and hugging the elderly widow, instead inclining her head, agreeing. "This is the reason we've agreed to meet in secret," she said quietly, but firmly. "The knowledge I'm here to impart isn't just to help your businesses. It's to help assure you understand that the decisions you make assure you and your families are not taken advantage of by the likes of Thornfield."

The door creaked slightly. Elspeth poked her head in and spoke, her voice low. "Thornfield's in the village, my lady. You should all depart before he notices too many women coming and going."

Meredith quickly gathered the stack of ledgers and papers she'd brought and tucked them into her satchel. The women stood, each glancing at the door, their confidence reduced to apprehension. They exchanged hurried thanks before slipping out the back, one by one, into the growing dusk. Heavens. She hadn't realized just how late it had grown.

As Derwa turned to leave, she hesitated, looking back at Meredith. "Do you think... do you think I can really raise the rates on my sewing, Lady Pender?"

Meredith's eyes softened. "Absolutely, Derwa. With your husband gone—" Derwa flinched, but Meredith pressed on. "You've a child to raise. It's imperative you are able to feed your daughter. And keep her safe. Women have had little enough choices as it is, but with work and with one step at a time, things *will* change."

With a nod and a tiny smile, Derwa disappeared into the misty twilight.

Meredith and Agnes remained behind a moment longer.

"Milady?" Agnes's voice broke through Meredith's quiet satisfaction.

"Yes, Agnes?"

"He—Thornfield—he won't hurt my mum, will he?"

"No. Absolutely not," Meredith assured her. She knew Thornfield would eventually catch onto her interference—no, not interference—her help. She was helping these women help themselves—and when the time came and Thornfield learned of her involvement, there would be consequences. But she would be ready, she vowed. Tonight's meeting only reinforced her beliefs of the importance of women being informed. She was also surprised to find her thoughts turning to Pender. "Not only will I not allow it, but I don't believe my husband will either." At least she hoped that was the case.

For now, the lessons would continue. They had to if the villagers had any hopes at all.

Once she'd ascertained the women had made it safely out the back, Meredith took her haversack and went into the main tearoom. She quickly indicated Agnes take a chair at an empty table and then with as much nonchalance as she could muster strolled up to the counter. She flashed a quick glance at Elspeth just as the door jangled. The hair on her nape lifted even as apprehension prickled her skin. She didn't have to turn to know pure evil stood behind her. It filled the air like a poisoned fog. "I require four of your delectable lemon tarts, Mrs. Trelawney."

"Of course, dear. I'll be just a moment."

"Lady Pender." Mr. Thornfield growled like a troll beneath a bridge. "'Tis a bit late for a woman out alone, I daresay."

Slowly, she turned, facing him. "Ah, but I'm not alone. Not only is my maid with me, my carriage remains at the ready." She tilted her head toward the windows where Bartlett sat atop said conveyance. She lifted her bag. "I've been assisting Mrs. Trelawney with some small bookkeeping matters." Not that it was any of his concern.

Mrs. Trelawney reappeared with a small box. "Here you are,

my lady. Mind you get right on home. I vow the skies are about to wring out their wrath."

Meredith took the box. "Certainly. Thank you, madam." It was with great relief when she and Agnes exited the teashop.

Bartlett took her haversack and the box of tarts and assisted them into the carriage, then set the box on the floor inside. "We best hurry, my lady. Appears we're in for a brutal bout."

Minutes later, the vehicle set in motion, allowing Meredith to take her first deep breath in several hours.

Halfway up the incline to Perlsea, the tempest let loose.

LUCIUS LEANED BACK in his chair and rubbed his eyes with his thumb and forefinger. Nothing overt stood out in Thornfield's employment contract. It read as standard to his untrained eye. Based on the man's reaction when Lucius had demanded to see it though, he knew he was missing something vitally important. The question was, what?

He dropped his hand and studied the page again and tapped No. 2 of Article II and reread. *In addition to said salary, The Agent shall be entitled to a modest percentage of the net profits derived from the mine's operations, the sum of which shall be no more than 5% of said profits, paid annually upon the closing of the accounts at year's end.*

That one point alone opened endless possibilities for misdeeds. Profits. Yes, he was definitely missing something.

Not safety. Not the well-being of the community. This contract spelled greed in the basic sense of the word. He set it aside and drew the ledger in front of him.

He pulled another page labeled Ore Production Report and, with his index finger, ran down the column of Total Ore Mined in tons for the first quarter: 50, 55, 60. The next column listed Processed Ore: 45, 50, 55. He moved to the next, Ore Sold: 35, 40, 42. According to his own skill in mathematics—while not genius level, he'd certainly excelled well enough at Oxford to spot a missing amount of 15 tons. That even included a waste amount of 5 which didn't seem too excessive. A certain amount of waste was to be expected.

Tugging over another report, this one of Sales and Income, indicated the volume of ore mined did not match up to the ore sold. Lucius pressed his lips together. This was embezzlement, pure and simple.

He grabbed Thornfield's employment contract again and reread the terms in Article III. *No. 1. the right to terminate this Agreement forthwith should The Agent be found guilty of negligence, fraud, or any act that may bring disrepute or loss upon the estate.*

A tap at the door startled Lucius. "Enter."

The butler, Verity, entered and announced dinner which sent a resounding ungentlemanly noise from his stomach.

"Thank you. Will my wife be joining me?"

"I'm not certain, sir. As I understand it, she took late tea at The Copper Kettle."

"With Mr. Ashcroft I suppose."

"Oh, no, my lord. Mr. Ashcroft returned around thirty minutes after four. He sent the carriage back for Lady Pender."

Lucius glanced at the windows. Branches tapped the glass in a howling wind he hadn't noticed, having been so engrossed. He dropped his pen and pushed from the desk. "Are you telling me Lady Pender hasn't returned?"

"Oh, no, my lord. She's arrived and is in the process of changing out of her wet garments."

The tension he hadn't realized was gripping his chest released. He nodded. "I'll be right there."

Meredith had managed to avoid him for three days straight and he was damned tired of it. She had one last opportunity.

Twenty minutes later, her choice had been made clear.

A place set for her at the far end of the table remained stubbornly vacant. He sipped at his wine, waiting. And waiting. He suspected he could have waited until hell had frozen and he would still be waiting.

With stoic resolve he ate through the four-course meal. Alone.

Dessert was finally presented in royal fashion… on a small gold platter in the form of a single lemon tart.

In this unlikely, less than formal household, Mrs. Verity set the plate carefully and proudly before him. "Her ladyship picked it out 'erself, milord."

Fury infiltrated his already boiling blood. Such was his anger that his fingers trembled with an urge to take up the dish and dash it against the wall. Unfortunately, an earl who was attempting to bury the offenses of his sire and his own failings made that option untenable and he choked down the entire thing in two bites.

But once again, the temptation to desert this godforsaken village, its unpredictable weather, hit him in the chest with the force of a medieval anvil. Instead, he snatched up his wine and downed the contents then requested the bottle. Shoving back his chair, Lucius made it out the door and to the top of the stairs without encountering so much as a single soul.

Shockingly, someone pounded the oak door that echoed through the foyer. But Lucius had no interest in visitors. "Tell them we're unavailable," he barked at Verity from the balcony.

"Aye, my lord." Verity pulled back the heavy door.

Without so much as a *how do you do*, a powerful voice roared through the vestibule. "Where the hell is my daughter?"

"Oh, for God's sake," Lucius muttered. He had no desire in dealing with the Duke of Rathbourne at this time. But he knew one person who should—and would, by God. He stalked down the corridor to his wife's chamber, burst in without knocking, startling her maid who, once again, sat near the windows with an oil lamp burning and, surprise, a book in her hands. "Where's your mistress?" he demanded.

"Um, dinner?"

He breathed in through his nose, fearing the unleashing of his temper. "Try once more, Agnes. I wish the truth."

Her eyes widened. "She likes to spend time in the old library."

"What old library?"

"I'm not sure. She doesn't allow me to accompany her. Said 'twas too dangerous." She hugged the tome to her chest. "I-I'm sure it's not. I think she just wanted, er, to be alone…" her voice ended in a whisper.

Alone. With Ashcroft. Lucius would bet his life that was what she meant. He turned on his heel and found the servant stairs. He was in no frame of mind to deal with Rathbourne. It was *the duke's* fault Lucius was married to a cuckold, and he might kill the bastard.

He made his way to Ashcroft's office but when he threw back the door, it was black as night. So, he was right. They *were* together. Fury fueled him. He'd find the blasted library Agnes referred to before heading to the steward's cottage. He turned the valve on the wall for the gas lighting. The same map sat on the desk but it was shifted to one side where Ashcroft had begun another sketch. This one of the Keep itself. Lucius picked up the crude drawing and studied it.

With the map in hand, he positioned himself to match the markings, giving him his bearings in relation to the kitchens, the vestibule, the masters' suites. He hadn't thought much of the Keep's layout before.

As a child, he could only recall visiting Perlsea once. It had been a few years before his mother's death. She'd insisted they visit the home of her birth. Noah couldn't have been but two, maybe three at the time, and wouldn't have remembered it at all.

But Lucius, three years older than his brother, could well recall her dismay at the gross deterioration. Papa's disdain at the tears she'd shed. She'd insisted Lucius look after his younger brother due to the dangers surrounding them. From his recollections, their stay had been quite brief.

In one instance, Noah had gotten away from Lucius and he'd been frantic to find him, catching the little tyke before his brother could make it to the top of an old, crumbling stairwell. Oh, how he'd scolded his brother for the fright he'd given Lucius. He'd hugged Noah until he struggled and cried, until Lucius had finally been forced to free him. He shook away the memories and his vision cleared enough for him to focus back on the map.

Noting the three towers, he ascertained the path to each then lowered the lights. He stepped out of the steward's office into the low-lit hall and closed the door behind him. A sturdy wooden utility cabinet tucked into an alcove provided a taper and matches. Then, studying the crude sketch a moment longer, Lucius set out with grim reluctance. He located, and entered, an ancient narrow, dimly-lit stone corridor off the kitchens.

The faint smell of smoke and old wood had seeped into the walls. He followed the map into the farthest tower and into a less-traveled section of the Keep with a moment of sad relief that his mother hadn't lived to witness such decay. The path then veered from the well-maintained areas and ended at the foot of a narrow stairway. Cold seeped through his frockcoat from the harsh Cornish night, and a faint smell of dampness seemed to penetrate the rough stone to settle in his bones. Old sconces with cracked glass that had long since lost their candles lined the walls on both sides. He avoided the rotted handrails. That way lay trouble. The stairwell was steep but only went up one level. With his shoulder against a door swelled shut, he shoved. Hard. And stumbled into a widened hall.

The candle he managed to hold onto flickered violent shadows against the ceiling, casting ominous shades about him. The farther he moved into the forgotten wing, the heavier the air grew. And cold.

Cobwebs gathered in corners, and the corridor seemed to close in. Floors creaked underfoot, and the temperature had dropped to a distinct chill. Such atmosphere could give credence to rumors of the Keep being haunted. A shiver snaked up his spine.

Surely, she wasn't here in this dilapidated tower. Lucius

stopped, listening for any tell-tale signs.

Laughter? Low murmurs? Or worse… Ashcroft's voice. Resentment was a boulder lodged in his gullet, and he cut off the thought.

Nothing. Relief crept over him, taking him aback with the force of its sudden release. There was nothing. He started to turn back the way he'd come when the most ungenteel curse word hit his ear. Quiet relief shifted abruptly to outrage. New determination soared through him, and he quickly spun about, stalking through another long-forgotten hallway, stepping over pieces of fallen plaster and creases in ill-fitted rugs.

He rounded the corner where light spilled into the corridor. He blew out his candle and set it on a hall table. Then, on stealthy steps, forced himself to move through a double-door entrance into a room that hadn't been touched in years, bracing himself for a fight he couldn't avoid. Glancing about, Lucius found his wife standing on a rickety chair, reaching for something on the top shelf of a rotting bookcase.

The effect was dizzying. The smell of must and decay saturated the air. It was impossible to see through the windows. The thick coat of grime, even that of an elusive sun in the height of the day, couldn't have penetrated, let alone eight o'clock in the evening, highlighted wooden shelves that didn't appear strong enough to hold the line of cracked, leather-bound books stacked there.

Lucius felt as if he'd stepped back in time. Even his wife's dowdy frock of dark gray looked as if it belonged to that of another time.

It took a moment to register that Ashcroft was nowhere in sight. He nearly staggered beneath the unbidden rush coursing through him. He sauntered forward, stopping short of touching distance. But, oh, how his fingers tingled with want. "Might I be of some assistance?" His voice groused in a low husky resonance he barely recognized as his own.

She let out a yelp, her arms flailing about haphazardly.

Lucius jumped forward and caught her before she could hit the floor, but the move knocked him off balance. He twisted, securing her in his hold but landing hard into the bookcase. The shelves collapsed under his weight. Plaster showered their heads from the ceiling, and to his dismay, the bookcase teetered dangerously before falling away from them in a crash that reverberated through the wood planked floor.

She lay sprawled atop him, her head tucked into his shoulder. With one arm wrapped about her waist, Lucius cupped her head, doing his best to protect her from the raining debris. A board dug into his lower back, and he let out a groan.

"Good heavens," she breathed. She scrambled off him, which did nothing to alleviate the pain from that cursed board digging into his back. "Are you dead?"

"Not from lack of trying," he retorted. "Help me sit up."

He half expected her to shun his request, considering the animosity between them, but she moved to his side and slipped an arm beneath his shoulders. "Of course."

A huge miscalculation on his part. The move brought her face too close to his. The subtle scent of violets made him flinch, reminding him of the bath he'd stolen from her three days ago. He closed his eyes, but it didn't block the fragrance. The request was a ridiculous one on many levels. To his amazement, she was stronger than she appeared. He tightened the muscles in his stomach and gritted through a sharp stab of pain to help with the process. He opened his eyes to see her lips puckered after her efforts. Just a whisper's breadth and he could capture them with his own.

But as quickly as she'd shifted to assist him, her arm fell away and she leaned back, kneeling.

The sense of loss was too shocking to be believed. It couldn't be fathomed. His insides trembled from the… the… fall. *It was the fall,* he assured himself.

With care, he slid from sitting on the broken wood to the cold floor. He looked into her face but the wonder he saw there was not directed on him. Instead, her focus was over his shoulder. He tried to turn, but that proved an impossible feat, stealing the breath from him.

"Oh, my." In a graceful sweep, she rose from her position on the floor.

"Damn it, what?" he demanded.

"It's a hidden room. There was mention of something, but I never dreamed," she breathed.

The breathy tone feathered his skin in another bout of awareness of which he was wholly unprepared. "Wait, what do you mean 'mention'? I don't understand."

Her slippers whispered over the floor. One bookcase remained standing, and she went over and removed a couple of books to one concealed behind those. She opened it and thumbed through a few pages, then returned to his side and handed it to him.

Lucius looked down at the open page.

2 July 1758. Preparations for tonight's gathering are set. The Keep appears to be the most logical place to convene. The need for confidentiality is vital and will remain secure within these ancient walls.

"There's another note too," she said. Her excitement reflected the light from an oil lamp on a table that enhanced her moss-green eyes. "An invitation of sorts. But no signature."

He couldn't pull his gaze away from her. "What?"

She snapped her fingers nearly catching his nose.

He blinked.

"It's an invitation with no signature," she said slowly, enunciating carefully.

He glanced back down at the journal, surprised he still held it. "Who, er, penned it?"

Her excitement reasserted itself. "It took me a while to find it, but I did. It was the Marquess of Aylesbury." Her melodic tone echoed through the chamber. He lifted his gaze and watched as her steps once again whispered over the bare wood planks.

"He was my grandfather. My mother's father." Lucius's side throbbed, but he loathed to bring an end to this unexpected amicability. "My brother and I never met him. He was already ancient by the time Noah and I were born." Slowly, he worked himself around, doing his damnedest not to breathe too deeply.

The fallen bookcase had, indeed, exposed a hidden chamber that reeked of dust and age. More cobwebs draped so thickly in the corners that he suspected them of acting as insulation. The heavy air was proof to its having been untouched in decades. Rough stone walls were partially covered by faded and worn tapestries. Scenes that might have once depicted vibrant colors now only hinted at their former beauty.

His countess stepped over the threshold onto a floor of flagstone that was uneven and cracked in places. "Stop," he barked, terrified that something more dire could topple. "It's too unstable."

"But—"

He gentled his tone. "No. If anything untoward happened, I—" He closed his eyes, hating to admit the obvious. Then opened them and said firmly, "If something happens, I can't help you. In fact, I believe I require *your* help."

He followed her gaze to the bookcase that had been halted by a heavily built table. From his position on the floor, he could only see a portion of it and that was littered with papers though some had fluttered to the floor in the aftermath.

She glanced over her shoulder at him, revealing the stubborn glint in her eye he was beginning to recognize, but after a long pause, her shoulders fell and she walked back over to him. "All right. How do you propose we get you out of here? And, with the light."

"Help me to my feet."

"Of course." It was a struggle but once he was upright, she handed him the oil lamp and he was able to shuffle from the dank room using the wall. With her assistance, she led him out. She took him from the tower via a different path than from the one he'd initially followed. They reached a wide, main stairway for this dilapidated tower, and with gritted teeth, Lucius handed the lamp back to her, preparing himself for a painful journey down.

Clearly, *thankfully*, he hadn't snapped his blasted spine. But he wagered it was bruised enough that riding his horse anytime soon was out of the realm of possibility. "I've a quick question for you, my lady."

The lamp's light gave her face a spectral quality that sent a shiver over his aching body. "What?" she said with some impatience.

"Did you invite your father to Perlsea?"

"Heavens, no. I haven't spoken to him since…"

Even in the low light, he detected the dark flush that colored her pale skin. An indication of long suppressed fury, he suspected.

A smile touched him in spite of the pain. "Since our wedding?"

"Yes," she bit out.

"Interesting," he murmured.

She gave him a disdainful sniff. "I don't know why that should interest you."

"Ah. I suppose in all the excitement I forgot to mention he's stormed the Keep."

"Your sense of humor leaves much to be desired."

"I thought as much. In any event, where do you propose to house him?"

His wife's expression was one of shock, disbelief, dismay. "You aren't jesting."

"I'm afraid not," he said grimly. "The question is why is he suddenly on our doorstep?"

"Why, indeed. Did you say anything to him?" Her full lips pressed into a tight line and her nostrils flared. "The fact that he's arrived without prior word is especially troubling. I've been here three years, and he's never visited. Not once."

"How odd. No, I said nothing to him. In fact, I have no desire to speak to the man. I do, however, have an urge to wrap my fingers about his neck."

She shot him a black look. "That is not amusing."

"Nor is it intended to be. There is only one man I detest more, and he's dead now. Why is Rathbourne here?"

"I-I don't know." She plopped down on the top step and looked up at him.

He wished he could do the same but feared if he did, rising again would be impossible.

"You said he told you I was with child." Her voice grew contemplative.

"What of it? You've since convinced me otherwise."

"Well, that's a relief," she said with a bite of sarcasm he decided to take on the chin. "Could he somehow have learned you were here to secure an annulment?" Worry filled her darkened eyes. "If that is the case, I fear your life is in danger, sir."

He grinned, but no humor accompanied the feeling. "Then we shall just have to convince him otherwise, won't we?" Another, irritating thought had his grin fading. "Perhaps your Mr. Ashcroft notified him?"

CHAPTER TWELVE

"Just what are you getting at, sir?" Annoyance rippled through Meredith, followed quickly by the most outrageous notion imaginable. She came to her feet, gaping at him. "Are you suggesting Mr. Ashcroft is trying to *seduce* me?"

His tightened jaw told her those were his exact thoughts.

She pressed the heel of her hand to the bridge of her nose. "Lord Pender," she bit out. "Mr. Ashcroft is nothing but what he seems. Perlsea Keep's latest steward. A much needed and revered steward in my opinion. Not only has he been instrumental in me meeting my aspirations for this community, but never once in the entire three years past has he hinted at such a ludicrous notion. A more looming threat, sir, is my father's unexplained visit. He is well renowned for his controlling nature. If you are concerned at all, then take my words to heart. Rathbourne is the one who poses the danger. A danger, I might add, to you. And me. The work I'm trying to accomplish in the village—"

"And, what work is that, *Lady* Pender?"

Fury, fast and sudden, tore through her. "I'll have you know, there wasn't a single program for educating the children in this godforsaken hovel." She poked him in the chest with her index finger, then pulled back quickly at his narrowed eyes. But that didn't deter her tirade. "Hardly any of the women are literate. Yet they are expected to assist their husbands in their businesses, run their own shops. And do *not* get me started on the inhumane treatment and dangers the miners must face day after day under that blackguard Thornfield." She was so angry she could hardly catch her breath.

He grasped her fist and he brought the tip of her finger to his lips.

Stunned silent by this unprecedented action, she could only stare, her eyes drawn to the lips that singed her skin.

"So, this evening you were…"

Meredith tried tugging her hand from him, but he held fast.

"Answer me."

His voice seemed deeper than before. Inviting. Impossible to resist.

She drew in a trembling breath. "While Mr. Ashcroft holds school at Vestry Hall, I meet with some of the women in the village. I'm attempting to teach them practices for helping them with their businesses."

"Their businesses," he repeated slowly.

The fight went out of her and her shoulders fell as if he hadn't spoken. "The men do not trust me." It took a second inhalation for her blood to cool and reason to set in. "What possible purpose would Mr. Ashcroft have for inviting my father to Perlsea?"

"Exactly what I intend to learn." His thumb caressed the heel of her hand in a mesmerizing rhythm that held her enthralled. "In the meantime, we must deal with the fact that the duke is here. What do you propose we do? You know him better than I."

His words penetrated and she winced. "As much as I hate admitting it, we must not let him see the true state of our marriage."

He grinned, that in the low light appeared sinister. "I was hoping you would say that."

"On. The. Surface." She punctuated her words with a stomp on his foot, initiating an immediate release of her hand.

"Hmm." That sounded ominous amid the low grunt he attempted to hide. "All right. Well, the first thing we require is getting me down these blasted stairs and to my bedchamber."

She frowned, wondering how she could have forgotten. "I'll

get Bartlett. He should be able to help."

"No. I can make it... with your help. I don't want anyone learning about this chamber."

"You won't encounter any argument from me. I love knowing I have my own refuge no other is aware of."

"Except me."

She scowled. "Yes. Except you." Her brows furrowed. "But why should it matter if anyone else knows?"

He glanced over his shoulder into the gloom, his expression shielded from her. "I'm not sure. The journal you found, the hidden room, perhaps?" He turned back to her. "I find there are too many unanswered questions for my comfort. From Thornfield's power over the miners to Ashcroft's appearance to the fact that we had no choices in our life's partner, to name a few."

"Oh." The sense of dejection trickling through her hurt. *He* could hurt her. "Yes, I-I see what you mean." She steeled her tone. "Except for Mr. Ashcroft. I refuse to believe he is other than he's presented himself. A traveling scholar turned land steward."

RESENTMENT TINGED WITH envy peppered Lucius. "That certainly explains his lack of attention to detail when it comes to the estate's accounting ledgers," he muttered.

"What are you talking about?"

"Nothing," he said through a clenched jaw. The topic was now a matter between him and Ashcroft. *Contentious as it may be.*

To his irritation, the silence between them thickened. Her defense of Ashcroft stung. Left Lucius dangling with unresolved emotions he couldn't expound on as they made their way painstakingly down the stairs. The walls loomed around them, casting long shadows from the oil lamp she managed to keep steady. If he so much as mentioned having found that list of names which he now suspected were the previous stewards of

Perlsea Keep, it might send her running straight to the man. Whether to warn him or to demand answers was the question he had. And Lucius didn't like either option.

They reached the lower level and he balanced himself, using the wall for support. She guided him to a heavy door, but with a warm hand on his arm, she stepped in front of him to peer on the other side before allowing him through.

The large, cavernous room they stepped into swept him back to a time long forgotten. Low-lit sconces showed he'd entered the family level just inside the portrait gallery he remembered from his youth. How proud his mother had beamed when talking of each one of her ancestors whose portraits still lined the walls, now coated in thick layers of dust. Of course, he couldn't recall a single name, just the feelings she'd projected. Wistfulness, despair, all intermingling with a trace of sadness and inevitability that rained over him.

He recalled with great clarity being distracted with his three-year-old brother screeching, then laughing at his own echoes that ricocheted around and throughout the hall. Mama's small smiles had squeezed his heart to near bursting at the time. But when she'd scooped up a giggling Noah and swung him around with pure joy, Lucius remembered staring, astonished by the spontaneity he'd never witnessed from her before or since that day.

Christ, he hadn't thought of that, of *her*, in years. He'd no idea where his father had disappeared at the time. There were no recollections of him except upon arriving at the Keep. Then their sudden departure under a cloud of his usual abruptness.

"Are you in much pain?" she asked, startling away his memories. How did his wife's voice sound so… so musical? Docia's voice had never seeped into his skin in such a fashion.

His breaths seemed weighted and echoed back just as Noah's childish laughs had all those years ago. "I'll live," he growled, again stunned by the unexpected waves of nostalgia nearly drowning him.

The rest of the way to his chamber was made in a hush he

was unequipped to break, just their footsteps on the flagstones beneath them.

Upon arriving, he found his door slightly ajar, as if Graham had anticipated his return.

His wife pushed open the door and snapped, "Your master requires your immediate assistance."

Lucius scowled. "I'm not dead," he muttered.

Graham rushed forward and stopped short, his brows lifted. Lucius glanced down at his attire now completely covered in grime then groaned.

"My lady," Graham acknowledged with an incline of his head. "Might I enquire what's happened?"

She opened her mouth to respond, but Lucius cut her off. "We discovered the dungeons. Quite a perilous descent," he said using Graham's aversion to dark dank spaces, particularly those underground, to stem any questions. The man had an irrational fear of being buried alive. Though why, Lucius couldn't imagine.

His wife's—he really should learn her name—moss-green eyes shot to him, while she did her utmost to stifle a quirk of her mouth yet not quite succeeding.

"Er, yes. The dungeons," she said.

A delicate shudder quivered over his valet. "I'll take over from here, my lady."

"Be careful. He's hurt his back. It's a wonder he didn't tumble down the stairs. Er, back down the stairs," she clarified quickly.

Lucius rolled his eyes. "Perhaps you shouldn't keep your father waiting," he said pointedly.

"Good heavens, you're right," she said in a breathless rush. She spun for the door, but Lucius snagged her hand before she could move out of reach, and tugged her into him. Swallowing the sharp twinge from the sudden move, he tilted her chin up and brushed his lips over hers. "Give him my regrets, *darling*."

Her free hand flew to her mouth, her eyes widened.

For a brief moment, she hesitated, and he thought perhaps he saw his own thoughts reflecting back as the silence blared between them. Thoughts filled with unspoken doubts and too many complications to currently voice. Something in him softened and he squeezed her hand. "Go," he said, gently.

"Take care of him," she murmured to Graham. With a sharp nod and without another word, she slipped out.

The second she fled the chamber, the dull ache in Lucius's back raged to the forefront. He took a step, and a sharp burst of pain stabbed him with the edge of a dull spoon, digging into his skin.

"What the devil happened?" Graham demanded hurrying to assist him.

"I fell, as Lady Pender said," he grunted out. "Now, blast it, she's forced to deal with Rathbourne. Patch me up. I don't wish to leave her to that cur on her own. He's up to something and I have every intention of learning what he's about."

Graham edged him to the bed. "Would that I was a genie, my lord. Can you lift your arms?" It took the man twenty minutes to divest Lucius of his clothes. "Lie down."

With a great and pain-filled effort Lucius did as directed.

"It's inflamed. You require a liniment. I daresay you'll be indisposed for several days."

Again, Lucius grunted. "We'll see."

Graham could be a dictatorial arse, many times blurring the line between servant and master. But in this instance, Lucius found he didn't have the energy to argue his cause. He rested his head on folded arms and thought of the underlying strength his wife possessed. His own surprise, well… surprised him. Not just the fact she'd been able to assist him physically. It was her confession of helping the village women, finding ways that strengthened her—*their*—position within the community that struck him. Backbone and perseverance in the face of adversity. Like teaching her lady's maid to read.

No one had ever challenged him thus.

He closed his eyes and remembered the pamphlet he'd pilfered from her escritoire. "Give me that booklet from the chest of drawers," he said gruffly.

"This one?" Lucius opened his eyes to see Graham holding out the pamphlet with the block lettering. His brows lifted. "The Clandestine Sapphire Society?"

"Yes. And bring the light closer."

With a shrug, Graham did as he was bade then turned for the door. "I'll return shortly."

Lucius read through the material in short order. Clearly, it had been written for an unsophisticated audience. The tone within spoke volumes to him. He recognized portions that were definitely reminiscent of his wife. And perhaps Miss Wimbley who'd appeared in Northumberland for Father's services. Though he hadn't spent much time with her, she'd certainly made an impression on his younger brother, Julius.

In the quiet of Lucius's chamber, other things began to coalesce in his head that drowned out some of his physical discomfort. The words in the booklet he'd just read, the frank conversation with his wife earlier that night.

Rather than complaints, she chose to respond with actions. Had she deserted the community after his own desertion three years ago? No. It likely hadn't even occurred to her. A realization he hadn't even considered pounded through his veins—his Aunt Vera was cut from the same strip of fabric. It wasn't something that should even matter but somehow it did. He suspected his wife was loyal to the nth degree. Something he couldn't claim for himself, leaving him with the untenable feeling of... shame. He shut his eyes against that thought. For now, leastways, to concentrate on things within his control.

Did her actions, her assistance in the community, make her naïve? An easy mark for the likes of Ashcroft, Thornfield, the *duke*? Her work with the women she spoke about stopped him cold. God knew how the men would react once they learned of the matter. A streak of protectiveness toward her rushed through him and left him stunned.

His thoughts gravitated to how intimate their situation had

just shifted. How close her lips had been to his. The liberty he'd taken in stealing that most unsatisfying kiss before she escaped his chamber. How soft her hand had been, even tightened into a fist, its soft skin beneath his palm while her finger had jabbed his torso. She was a conundrum.

But he warned himself on capitulating so soon, so completely. It had been her idea to show her father there was no contention between them. And, after the enlightenments he'd been awarded that evening, he was more than happy to play.

Such was his last thought as exhaustion overtook him.

— ◆ —————— ◆ —

CHAPTER THIRTEEN

MEREDITH HURRIED DOWN the grand staircase. "Verity!"

The portly butler appeared in an instant. "My lady?"

"Where did you stash His Grace?"

"The library, my lady. But—"

Ignoring the butler, she didn't hesitate, and rushed in. "Papa, I had no notion you were coming for a visit. What are you thinking, traveling to the wilds of Cornwall in such weather?"

Her father, the Duke of Rathbourne sat at the desk, holding a stack of papers she didn't remember being there. As she'd told Pender, she hadn't seen her father since her wedding day.

Though he was in his mid-to-late fifties, the arrogance and self-assurance surrounded him like an impenetrable fog. His face was marked by the passing of the last three years, shocking her, though rather than softening as one might expect, his features had grown more severe.

He waved a few pages in the air, his piercing gaze spearing her from across the chamber with a judgment that had her wanting to tear out of the library and take refuge in her chamber. "What the devil is—" He rose from the desk, and though he was not particularly tall, his presence filled the room in a towering effect—similar to the crumbling ramshackle she'd vacated this very evening. Her father's bearing of rigid dignity showed he was not a man to cross.

How well she knew as she'd grown up under his pressing thumb. He raked a narrowed, critical look over her. "Is this how you greet your guests? Dressed as the wife of one of those vile miners? And what the devil is that in your hair?" he demanded in that deliberate, measured cadence that dripped with condescension, iced with the familiar sense of superiority.

Meredith put a hand to her hair, feeling bits of plaster then glanced down at her dress that had apparently acted as a magnet to every dust particle that had flown up in rebellion at being disturbed in that forgotten room. "Oh, dear," she murmured. "Sorry, Papa. I… we…"

"I have no interest in what misadventures you participate in." He dropped the pages on the desk and moved around it, his shoulders squared, his chest puffed out. His lips curled into a smug smirk. "Where is that libertine husband of yours? He should be here to greet me. I would have a word with him."

To Papa, others existed merely to serve his ambitions and entertain his whims. But she understood him like no other and squared her own shoulders, steeled her spine. She returned his gaze with a fiery one of her own. "How interesting you know he's in Cornwall, Papa, when I hadn't heard one word from you in over three years."

His ears turned a particularly harsh shade of scarlet. The sight had her stomach curling but to relent now—no matter the consequences—could not be borne, and she held her stance, her ground, her head up.

Insufferable as he was, there was no denying the weight of his influence or the sharpness of his mind—qualities that made him both a formidable foe and a dangerous man. But she was his only child, a product of a personality so strong and unyielding in its force that it seemed to bend fate to its will.

His fists clenched at his sides, but he didn't move any closer. "I would speak with your husband."

Meredith's lips curled in an imitation of his though not as smug. "He was injured and is unavailable tonight. Is there some way I might be of service?"

He scowled and she knew for the moment she'd scored a

small victory. "I'll speak with your husband tomorrow then."

With a sharp nod, she moved across the chamber to the bell cord and pulled. "Have you eaten?"

"I could use a bite."

Again, Verity's appearance was instantaneous. "The duke requires a meal. Also, please have Mrs. Verity ready the Rose Room for His Grace." It was the farthest one from her side of the Keep she could think of.

"Very good, my lady." Verity left and Meredith meandered to the desk to see what had had her father so enthralled.

To her astonishment, she caught the title page of the legal document and stifled a gasp. She glanced quickly at her father.

He watched her with keen eyes that missed nothing. "What are you mixed up in, Meredith?"

She straightened the papers then saw the ledger. "Um, nothing, Papa. Pender must have been working in here. I hadn't realized…" It was the truth, leastways. "I'll just remove these for him to his study." And, that was not the truth.

"Avail yourself of the brandy, Papa. I'm a mess as you can see, and I'd like to see how my husband is faring."

"I asked you a question, child." He spoke mildly but the underlying threat was there and it infuriated her.

Meredith gathered the papers to her chest avoiding his eyes. It never took much to ignite her father's temper. Her body trembled—fear or anger—she couldn't say. "I'm not certain what he was looking for, Papa. I'll let him know of your interest in the matter." With that she managed her escape, dashing up the stairs, wondering why she was so frightened.

MEREDITH REACHED HER chamber, the papers still clutched to her chest, her insides quavering, and fell back against the door. She took a moment to gather her wits, moved through her sitting room to the bathing chamber. She tapped lightly on the adjoining door. Bother that. Without awaiting a response, she entered.

Graham looked up from where he stood at the side of the bed, holding a brown jar. "He's sleeping,"

She wrinkled her nose. "The odor is… strong."

"It's a liniment I create. One of lavender and arnica."

"It smells more than lavender and arnica. But it's not horrible," she hedged.

"You've a keen sense of smell," he said, smiling. "It contains rosemary and witch hazel as well."

"What is it supposed to do?"

"I've known it to be effective in reducing bruising and inflammation." Her gaze fell to his patient. "His lordship will be uncomfortable for several days."

"Yes, I imagine he will." She glanced about the chamber, cringing at the condition. "If you haven't supped, I can remain with him for a time."

Graham inclined his perfectly coiffured head. "Thank you, my lady."

After his departure, Meredith crept to the bedside and studied this man she'd been married to for over three years yet hadn't laid eyes on since before the past week. He lay on his stomach with his head resting on his folded arms. The firelight bathed his bared back in a golden hue that beckoned her touch, but she clenched her fingers into a fist. A candle burned on a scarred table near the windows and she moved there—away from temptation.

The curtains' frayed edges sent a ripple of guilt through her, but she squelched the feeling. If the blasted man had let her know of his plans for coming to Cornwall, she would have been happy in having his suite prepared in proper order for him. Honestly, three years? The same went for her father's sudden appearance, only double, she thought scowling, a small snort escaping.

Meredith glanced down at the stack of papers she held then took a chair at the table and spread them out. She began with the employment contract she learned belonged to Basil Thornfield.

The entire agreement was all of two and a half pages. There were a few scratched notations next to Articles II and III, regarding the modest profit clause and termination policy, but those proved illegible.

Her gaze darted to the slumbering figure. Was Pender considering kicking the man to the curb? Thornfield was an abomination, and he deserved it in her opinion. Setting the contract aside, she pulled the ledger in front of her and attempted to decipher a table of numbers that made no sense. Not to her. But what was it her husband had seen when he looked at these columns?

Meredith found it ironic that had Papa not brought it up, she likely wouldn't have given the documents a second thought. But his questions had not only been pointed but had been directed to her in an accusing manner that raised the hairs on her nape.

"What are you doing?" Pender's voice, groggy and gravelly, startled her from her contemplations and her eyes flew to the bed.

"Reading," she said, guarded and unsure of the approach to take. "How do you feel?"

"As if my horse dragged me from the village up the hill to the Keep with a rope tied about my waist." He slowly rolled from his stomach to his back. "Reading what?"

"Mr. Thornfield's employment agreement for one. It's dated over ten years ago and is signed by Thornfield and both our fathers. Do you require help?"

"I'd like to sit up."

Meredith admired the lack of hesitation on his part when it came to requiring assistance. She rose from the table and went to the bed and slipped her arm around his shoulders and was instantly inundated with a masculine scent that nearly felled her to her knees. His skin was smooth and warm to her touch. It had to have hurt but his only response was a quick, sharp intake in his otherwise stoic demeanor as he tried to find a more comfortable position. At which point she hurried to stuff a few pillows at his back.

"Thank you." The husky words came out in a warm breath, grazing her cheek. "Tell me you didn't greet your father dressed like that." There was a smile in his voice that shifted her off axis.

"Like what?" she said, masking her confusion with irritation. She looked down at her gown and couldn't believe she hadn't thought to clean up before seeing to Pender. "Oh." Doubly vexed. "I'd forgotten." Again.

"I'm flattered."

"Flattered?"

"I cannot think of a single woman of my acquaintance who has not given thought to her appearance before wishing to see me."

"You flatter yourself." Annoyed, she rolled her eyes and changed the subject. "You left some papers on the desk in the library. Papa was reading through them when I arrived. He only stopped when he caught sight of my, er, dust-covered frock."

"It's not just your frock, my dear." His hand came up and he brushed his fingers over her cheek and held them out for her to see. A futile measure since all rational thought seemed to have fled along with her ability to breathe.

She lifted her gaze to his. Gray eyes turned black with swirling emotions she couldn't—refused to—decipher. This was the closest they'd been except for that moment in her hidden library when he'd quite literally saved her life earlier that evening. "He was quite appalled." Her voice was a mere whisper.

"You read them as well… and what is *your* take, Lady Pender?" His eyes locked on her lips and her stomach took a dangerous dive.

Meredith touched the tip of her tongue to her top lip shocked by his interest in her opinion. "I… I believe he is up to something vile. And his contract by our fathers has offered him a way to accomplish that deed, whatever it is." By the time she'd uttered this statement, her heart was pounding. Fueled by anger? Or compelled by wanton urges? "I-I suspect it is a matter of degree." She straightened her spine before she did something ridiculous like cup his chin and touch his lips with hers.

"Yes. I thought the same."

An initial jolt of pleasure infused Meredith, and she smoothed the coverlets next to him. She squelched the sudden joy. He'd not secured her trust of him… yet.

"What of the ledger?"

She let out a sigh and went to move away, but he snatched her wrist, staying her. She looked down at the connection then raised her eyes to his.

An impish grin on his face in the shadows was but a mere flash of white teeth. He tugged and she stumbled to sitting on the mattress. He lifted her hand and touched the gold band on her finger. An instant heat seemed to burn her skin from that circlet of gold.

"My lord?"

"Say my name," he demanded.

It was if her face caught fire, and no amount of water could douse it. Her eyes shot to his. "I don't wish to say your name."

"Why not?"

She narrowed her eyes on him. "Say *my* name," she retorted.

A laugh burst from him, booming against the walls. Then he winced. "At the moment, I not only cannot remember your name, I can barely recall my own."

The words floated over her, landing softly on her shoulders. Similar to that of an ermine wrap on a cold night, easing her discomfort, drawing her own laughter. "I, um, can't remember yours either," she confessed.

"It's Lucius," he said with an incline of his head.

"My pleasure meeting you… Lucius. I'm… Meredith." The chamber seemed to shrink as if they were the only two in the world. He still held her wrist within one warm hand.

It felt like a new beginning.

He traced her knuckles with his thumb in a motion that held her enthralled.

Meredith shook her head and tugged at her hand, but his hold tightened. Not enough to hurt her, but his power was evident. "What happened to your request for an annulment?" she said softly.

"Perhaps I'm no longer thinking along those lines."

"I see." She cleared her throat. "Perhaps once you decide we'll talk."

"Perhaps we'll do more than talk." His hold loosened and she pulled her hand away.

Casually. She didn't wish to let him know his effect on her. Thank heavens for just the one candle and the dying fire. She rose from beside him and strolled to the table and blew out the single flame. "Get some rest, my lord. Based on those documents you've acquired, you're going to need it."

She made it back to the door, had her hand on the handle, turned it.

"Meredith." Her name was a growl that filled the room.

She glanced over her shoulder to the shadows that hid him.

"It's—" There was a long pause. "—It's a nice name."

Not a whisper could escape her constricted throat. Shaking her head, again, she stole away.

CHAPTER FOURTEEN

MEREDITH. WELSH. *GREAT Ruler*, he thought. The name suited her though it was primarily a man's name. But Rathbourne had no heir, so perhaps that was his reasoning behind bestowing such a grand title on his only child. She was certainly adept at making exits.

He pressed his lips together. Rathbourne had no business going through Lucius's paperwork in Lucius's home, in his library, on his desk. Duke or not. Such behavior was unacceptable.

Slowly, he moved his legs to the side of the bed, then breathing hard and using the bedside table for stability, he pulled himself to his feet. The chamber was growing dark with the dying fire but there was a candle near the window where Meredith had left the documents. He had questions, though he doubted Rathbourne would supply any satisfactory answers.

The door opened and Graham entered carrying a tray with tea, brandy, and something that smelled warm and delectable. "What the devil are you doing up?" Graham strode over and set the tray on the table. He relighted the candle before turning and planting his hands on his slender hips. "You chased her out, didn't you?"

Lucius turned a scowl on him. "You always think the worst of me."

"I like her. You've changed since you've been here."

Lucius snorted. "How would you know? You've been here

less than a day."

"And, already things have taken an interesting turn," Graham retorted.

The pipes clanked alerting Lucius as to his wife's current activities. How tempting to steal through the adjourning door to the bathing chamber and… "Bah. Never mind that." Undecided where he was directing the actual statement, he asked, "Where has my wife placed her high and mighty, over-the-top, bombastic blackguard?"

"The Rose Chamber."

"Where the devil is that?"

"In another wing. He has the servants running about like mice in a corn maze."

Lucius shook his head and pulled the ledger in front of him. "Do mice run about in a corn maze?"

Graham didn't bother answering, busying himself with pouring Lucius a cup of tea. "Brandy, my lord?"

"Not right now," he said absently, studying the numbers he'd gone over earlier.

"See what I mean? You've already cut back on your imbibing. Astonishing."

Lucius looked up at his valet. "What?"

"Nothing, my lord. If you have any care in the slightest for my peace of mind, please, eat something."

He snagged a scone and bit into it and munched slowly, running an index finger down the columns of the April monthly expense report. He then pulled the March report. "I need paper," he barked out. "Quickly."

A few minutes crept by before Graham located what he needed.

With some impatience, Lucius snatched the paper from his hand. In the next instance, an inkwell and pen were set before him. He went back through the reports and listed the payment due to Perlsea, then listed the royalties for each month, The difference in the two by over £100 was disturbing and would require more in depth investigation. Starting with Meredith's favorite steward, Mr. Ashcroft.

That was a task for the next day. In the meantime, there were other questionable withdrawals for Thornfield's "personal account."

The more Lucius studied and compared the reports the angrier and more disgusted he became. He threw down his pen and came to his feet, ignoring a sharp twinge.

"Sir, your back," Graham said.

"To the devil with my back. Go to bed, Graham. I'll see you tomorrow. Early."

"How early?" he asked narrowing his eyes.

"I don't know. Eight."

He gasped.

"Eight-fifteen then. Good night."

Graham slipped out of the chamber, leaving Lucius wondering if he'd heard the man's muttering correctly. Something to the tune of, "Just as I said, interesting."

THE NEXT MORNING, Lucius crawled from his bed, donned his wrap, and decided to make use of Meredith's favorite bathing chamber before she could protest. One glance out the windows showed another glum day, though the rain hadn't yet descended. He didn't linger and by the time he returned to his chamber, Graham was already present, laying out his salve along with Lucius's clothes for the day.

"Did you break your fast?" Lucius asked him.

"Yes."

"Are the servants still in a tizzy?" Lucius found the thought gratifying.

"Yes."

"Is that all you have to say?"

"Yes."

"What do you know of Ashcroft's schedule?"

"Nothing."

"Nothing?"

"He rises early. Certainly, earlier than your typical time." He cleared his throat. "He departs for the church at eight. Typically with Lady Pender."

"I thought you didn't know his schedule."

"My brain has ceased functioning. In case you haven't noticed, it's barely eight."

"I didn't sleep much."

Graham grunted.

The pipes clanked. "I must hurry. I wish to speak with Ashcroft before Lady Pender makes an appearance."

After that, Lucius was stuffed in his clothes fairly quickly and out the door. The bruising on his back would slow him down, but he wanted those reports.

By the time he made it down to the steward's office, Ashcroft was seated at his desk, his brows furrowed, lifting papers and searching about.

Lucius started to lean against the doorframe but the quick stab in his back negated the nonchalant stance. He folded his arms over his chest. "Looking for something?"

Ashcroft's hand stilled midair. He slowly met Lucius's gaze. "I've misplaced a couple of papers," he said with a wise bit of wariness.

"Oh?"

He leaned back in his chair and the legs creaked. "I take it you've been in my office?"

Lucius didn't bother denying the accusation. It was true after all. "A list of names, perhaps. A map?"

Ashcroft's hand hit the desk with a *thunk*. His expression turned hard. "Lady Pender hired *me* to look after her estate."

"You mean my estate, don't you?" Lucius growled.

He tipped his head. "Of course, *Lord* Pender."

It took concerted effort for Lucius to ignore the temptation of defending his own title, but he persevered. "Who are the individuals on the list?"

Lips clamped shut, Ashcroft went about straightening other papers strewn about his desk.

"A couple of your predecessors, perhaps?"

Ashcroft stopped and glared at Lucius, then slammed both hands flat on the desk and stood. "They were *all* predecessors, my lord. All."

The gut punch was visceral. "And the map?"

Ashcroft's expression shifted to blank, but his eyes flickered with tension. "I'm merely conducting an inventory of the estate's history. It's nothing more than a precaution."

Lucius scoffed. "Precaution for what?" He took a step closer. "It looks to me as if you're preparing for something much more sinister."

"Or making sure I don't end up with a similar fate," he shot back.

"Similar fate. The devil you say. You believe them dead?"

"Yes," he bit out.

"You sent for Rathbourne, didn't you?" Lucius accused him.

The shock on Ashcroft's face rendered the man momentarily speechless. His face may have even paled. "The *duke*? Is here?"

"He arrived last night. Neither Lady Pender nor I were expecting him."

Again, his mouth compressed.

"You know him then?"

"Many years ago," Ashcroft admitted. "The blackguard is rotten to the core."

Lucius couldn't agree more but he was not yet ready to take the steward at face value. For one thing, the beard he wore disguised a good portion of his facial features. Ashcroft moved to the door, took a greatcoat from a hook behind, and snatched his hat from a shelf above. "I must get to Vestry Hall. I've a class to conduct."

"Not so fast, sir. I'll have the Keep's income and expense ledgers for last year."

He jammed his hat on his head. "Help yourself, my *lord*. You seem to have a knack for finding what you need without *my* permission." With that, he stalked from the office with an exit reminiscently, and irritatingly, similar to that of Meredith's.

Scowling, Lucius found what he was searching for in a matter of minutes and wished for nothing more than to dash up the stairs to his chamber, and but for the limitations of the soreness in his lower back he would have. Instead, he made his way to the dining hall as if he'd reached his dotage, stopping short of crossing the threshold.

"Ah, Pender," Rathbourne boomed. "I thought you to be on your deathbed. But I see my daughter's tendencies toward exaggerations have only increased with time."

Annoyance simmered just under Lucius's skin, but he managed to keep from rolling his eyes. He'd seen the obnoxious cur less than a month ago at his father's services when he had made the trek to Northumberland with the rest of the *ton's* curiosity seekers when he'd delivered the shocking revelation—lie—that Meredith was with child. Lucius sauntered into the chamber and ordered coffee.

"Your Grace." Lucius inclined his head, then took his place at the head of the table. He set the ledger aside and placed his elbows on the hard surface and studied the duke with a critical eye.

While Rathbourne was only of medium build, he exuded a presence that commanded attention. His sharp, angular features were cold, and the calculating glint he could bestow at will granted him the air of authority. A quiet confidence conveyed his unmistakable power.

Despite the early hour, his clothing was impeccable, his perfectly tailored dark frockcoat, made from the finest wool indemnified elegance. Beneath his coat, he wore a crisp white waistcoat with subtle brocade detailing. It was a touch of refinement without being ostentatious. His silk cravat of deep burgundy was tied in a precise, understated knot of course. Admittedly, the look showcased his effect of controlled power and impeccable taste. Meredith's father was a man who knew how to wield his influence without a need to flash his wealth.

A surprising morning sun filtered through the windows, casting a pale light over the dining hall, but the atmosphere was far from warm. "Did you sleep well?" Lucius asked him.

"This monstrosity you call a castle is abhorrent." His voice remained pleasant, but the undercurrent of tension thrummed.

Lucius smiled, but humor did not filter through him. "I disagree. My wife is handling the Keep's renovation admirably. But, that is neither here nor there. She and the money involved are my responsibility not yours." He nodded at a footman he didn't recognize who'd set a plate of eggs, kippers, and bacon before him, then waved him from the room. "I'm more interested in your reasons behind announcing my wife was with child in Northumberland last month when clearly she was not."

The duke snapped the newspaper he'd been reading. Not out of anger, though there was a slight tightening about his fingers and mouth that gratified Lucius.

Rathbourne picked up his cup of tea, his gaze flicking over Lucius, then sipped. With meticulous precision, he set it back down then dabbed his mouth with his serviette. "It's a rare thing these days—peace and quiet, without interruptions, don't you agree? It allows one to reflect on certain... responsibilities." His light tone, almost conversational, contained an edge beneath the calm exterior.

Lucius tensed but said nothing, his jaw tightening.

The duke took another bite, chewing slowly before continuing. "And yet, three years have passed. No heir. No assurances for the future. One might begin to wonder if the terms of the arrangement are... at risk."

Lucius's blood boiled at the implication. "The terms," he said evenly, though his voice held a sharp edge, "are no one's concern but mine and my wife's."

Rathbourne set down his toast and met Lucius's gaze, his expression calm but calculating. "Your wife is my daughter, and as such, her welfare—and by extension, yours—are concerns of mine, whether you like it or not."

"And yet, you saw fit to spread a falsehood about her," Lucius shot back, his voice low with tightly coiled anger. "A lie that could have damaged her reputation had it not been contained."

"Contained?" The duke raised an eyebrow, his expression faintly amused. "If anything, it brought attention to the matter. A necessary attention, I might add. The future of both our estates depends on vigilance, Pender. On careful stewardship. I trust you see that."

Lucius leaned forward, his eyes narrowing. "What I see, Your Grace, is a man who enjoys interfering where he has no right."

The duke's smile didn't reach his eyes. "Interfering?" He picked up his tea, swirling it lazily before taking a sip. "Call it what you will, but I've lived long enough to know that in matters of legacy, hesitation is costly. Time has a way of... slipping through one's fingers."

"What exactly are you implying?" Lucius's voice was dangerously soft, his knuckles white where they gripped the armrests of his chair. He forced his fingers to loosen, flexing them.

"Implying?" Rathbourne set his cup down with a deliberate clink then lifted a shoulder. "Merely observing. And offering a reminder that those who fail to act—who fail to secure what is rightfully theirs—often find themselves... left behind."

The room hummed with tension, and Lucius's chest burned with the effort it took to keep his composure. "A curious observation," he said at last, his voice icy. "Though I suspect it's not the only reason for this conversation."

The duke inclined his head slightly, a shadow of a smirk playing on his lips. "Perhaps not. Your reputation precedes you, Pender," the duke said with a condescending turn of his lips. "The late nights, the imbibing. The debauchery. Well, you are your father's son." He waved out a beringed hand. "But as I said, time waits for no man. I trust you'll remember that."

A chill skittered up Lucius's spine. Meredith was his wife. His delectable wife. She no longer belonged to the duke in any legal sense of the word. He reclined, his mind racing. Rathbourne said much without truly saying anything, yet his words left Lucius with the distinct impression that something was being carefully maneuvered just out of sight.

Whatever game the duke was playing, Lucius knew one thing for certain: it was far from over.

With a deep breath the picture became a little more clear. This interview had nothing to do with his and Meredith's marriage and everything to do with something the duke deliberately skirted. Lucius had a sudden desire to read the actual betrothal agreement the duke and his father had signed nearly twenty years ago. He loathed acknowledging anything emerging as a truth from Rathbourne, but the man was right about one thing: Lucius had spent the last three years avoiding his wife. His duty to her. Drinking and cavorting. Not his proudest moment.

"What is that you have?"

The duke's question jarred Lucius's attention and he glanced at the ledgers next to his plate. He'd nearly forgotten them. "Perlsea Keep's household expenses. Nothing of import." He laid his hand atop them as if to make sure they wouldn't migrate across the expanse of the table within distance of Rathbourne's prying eyes.

The duke's reptilian gaze narrowed slightly, but he tapped his lips with his serviette once more. With an incline of his head, he rose from his chair. "I believe I should like to visit the mines today. After a quick visit with my daughter."

"Of course," Lucius said and watched as the duke made his exit, hoping Meredith had made it out of the Keep before Rathbourne could locate her, even if it required a ride to the village with Ashcroft. Better yet, Lucius would drive her himself.

Rising from the table, Lucius snatched up the ledgers and

slipped out the servants' entrance and up the back set of stairs, wincing through the twinges still plaguing him.

He went straight to Meredith's chamber to find the room empty, the bed made, and no sign of her maid, Agnes. The disappointment that struck his sternum left him momentarily stunned. He made his way back down the hall to his own room and lowered to a chair before the fire to review the ledgers he still held.

CHAPTER FIFTEEN

MEREDITH AND AGNES entered The Copper Kettle's backroom to a somber group where Derwa Cardy, Mrs. Wren, Mrs. Kevern, and Marigold Tremayne sat huddled. Their low chatter slowed to silence and four pairs of wide eyes turned to her. She set her satchel on the table. "Is something amiss?"

It was Marigold who took up the torch. "We hear tell the Duke of Rathbourne has arrived in Penhalwick."

Meredith looked at each woman in turn. "It's true. But that shouldn't change anything," she assured them.

The silence shrieked against the blue floral papered walls. In the excruciating moment that passed, Elowen entered and some of the tension eased.

Marigold nodded. "Iff'n you say so, ma'am."

"What exactly is the concern?" Meredith asked, taking her chair.

The women exchanged uncertain glances, their apprehension palpable. Mrs. Wren shifted in her chair. "When men like the duke come around, it ain't for nothing good. Henry says there's been talk at the mine—things bein' stirred up, changes maybe."

"Surely that's not due to Rathbourne," Meredith said, surprised. "He only arrived last night."

Mrs. Kevern leaned forward, her brow creased with worry. "Well…"

Exasperation rippled through Meredith, but she wrestled it back. "Please, Mrs. Kevern, I implore you"—her gaze moved around the table—"all of you. I give you leave to be completely frank."

"All right," Mrs. Kevern said, slowly, hesitatingly. "Since Lord Pender's arrival…"

Mrs. Wren's eyes flashed. "We heard that Thornfield's keeping a closer eye on things—on *us*. And with the duke here, 'tis bound to get worse. The men at the mine are on edge."

Meredith was quick to defend her husband, surprising even herself. "But Pender hasn't done anything. He even went up against Thornfield after… after…"

Marigold nodded. "After little Tommy's demise. We know, milady. No offense intended, but ain't no one from the Keep's been here in years." Her fingers traced the edge of her apron. "Folk talk, and that's a fact. We all know what that means."

Sitting straighter, Meredith's mind darted like wildfire. "Yes, yes, I see what you mean, but I don't see how Rathbourne's presence should interfere with your lives." *Only mine*, she thought darkly. Her voice remained steady, but even as the words had emerged, she felt the weight of her own uncertainty.

Derwa, who'd remained silent, finally spoke, her voice low and timid. "Begging your pardon, milady, but we don't believe that. Not for a moment. Thornfield don't care about us, and that means the duke won't either. He'll have the duke's ear."

Meredith stifled a scowl. That was likely true.

The room fell silent again with a thick cloud of tension coating the air.

Any reassurances she attempted would fall on closed ears. These women were not afraid for themselves, but for their neighbors and family members, those whose livelihoods depended on the mine.

Perhaps it was time to learn just what her father's presence in Penhalwick meant, determine if his appearance was more than just a "mere" visit. She would be a fool to ignore these women, not to mention, such blatant signs. And, she was no fool.

But what of Pender? Did his presence signify something happening as well? Something beyond the villagers' control?

Meredith took a breath, giving herself a minute to think. She softened her tone. "I understand things feel uncertain right now. But you've trusted me this far. Can you trust me a little longer?"

Mrs. Kevern clenched her hands on the tabletop. "It's like they're drawing a line," she whispered. "And we don't know where we stand."

Mrs. Wren took Derwa's hand. "Mrs. Cardy already done lost her husband."

Meredith leaned in. "If there's a line being drawn, then we shall stand on the right side together. I refuse to let them control us with fear. I will not be silenced."

The women glanced at one another. Finally, Marigold met Meredith's gaze and gave a hesitant nod. "We'll try, milady. We'll try."

The tension in the room lifted slightly, but the weight of Rathbourne's presence and Thornfield's power still hung over the backroom. The entire village, actually. This was only the beginning of a larger battle and the gravity of the challenge ahead weighed on Meredith. Oh, to have Geneva, Abra, and Hannah at her side. Between the four of them, Meredith knew she stood a chance. Her friends weren't here, but she was, and she'd never forgive herself if she didn't even try.

The fact that doubts plagued her was infuriating. Her thoughts flickered to her husband. Was he truly an ally? Could she trust him? He hadn't been put off when she'd mentioned her meetings with these women. But taking the chance...

Meredith stiffened her spine then spoke encouragingly, confidently. "The important thing for us is to keep moving forward. Our task remains unchanged. Mrs. Tremayne, you will still have your haberdashery. Derwa, you'll continue sewing. Mrs. Wren's carpentry business will still operate, right?" She looked at each woman in turn, waiting until each one nodded back. Perhaps hesitantly, definitely slowly. Inhaling deeply, Meredith folded her hands on the table. "Did any of you remember to bring your contracts?"

Mrs. Kevern scowled. "I couldn't find Bart's."

For the first time, Derwa spoke up. "I-I have the one Bray was forced to sign," she whispered. "He—" She stopped and glanced around the table, then pulled a sheaf of papers from her overlarge reticule and slid them across the table. "He snuck 'em home." Tears slid silently down her cheeks. "Said he didn't know what they'd made him sign but feared it would bring me trouble. '*Take it*,' he'd said, '*find someone who can help*.'"

Meredith slid them in front of her. "Have you read through them?"

"As best I could, but I ain't no scholar, milady." Her eyes shimmered. "My Bray, he was a smart man," she said with a flash of unusual fire. "The fact that he couldn't read didn't mean he was slow-witted."

Mrs. Wren leaned over and wrapped an arm about the young woman's shoulders. "Course, he wasn't, dearie."

Sympathy swelled through Meredith as she glanced through the documents. But the more she read, the angrier she grew. This was a confession.

The Widow Elspeth's head peered around the door. "The duke's walking up," she said in a breathless rush. "The *duke*."

"Blast." Meredith stuffed the papers in her satchel. "I'll go through this with Mr. Ashcroft, if that's all right with you, Derwa."

She gave a quick nod.

"I'll head off my father. If you can sneak away without being seen, go. If not, I'll return when he's gone." She slipped out, latching the door behind her.

Spotting Mrs. Thims at her regular table with Mrs. Mordaunt and Miss Oppy took Meredith back three years to when she'd first arrived in Penhalwick. She strolled over as casually as she could manage and said hello, just as the door opened and Papa strolled in.

A collective gasp seemed to ripple through the tiny shop.

"Good morning, Papa. What brings you into the village so early?" Meredith said, her pulse pounding hard.

Elspeth carried a tray with a pot of tea and plate of scones to an empty table. "Here you are, Lady Pender."

"Thank you, Mrs. Trelawney." Relief poured through her. She took a chair at the small table near the windows and poured out a cup, surprised her hand remained so steady. She wrapped her cold fingers around the warm porcelain teacup. Though her heart raced, she kept her face calm.

Meredith couldn't afford to let him sense anything amiss, not with the women gathered in the backroom, discussing far more than household matters.

Elspeth, ever quick, moved smoothly behind the counter, her body language neutral, though Meredith sensed her tension.

"Morning, Mrs. Trelawney," Rathbourne greeted with a coolness that didn't fool Meredith. She had seen him use that same tone to dismantle men twice his size. "I hear this place is quite the gathering spot of Penhalwick."

And, where had he heard that?

Elspeth smiled, polite as ever. Meredith wanted to hug her. "Aye, Your Grace. Folks do like their tea, especially on days like this."

Rathbourne drifted toward Meredith, and she braced herself, letting out a soft, thoughtful sigh as if lost in her own musings. Before he could approach Elspeth again, Meredith shifted her chair slightly, drawing his attention.

"Mrs. Trelawney," she called out, her voice amazingly steady. "Could you bring a cup for His Grace." Meredith inclined her head, a gesture of respect tinged with cool familiarity, indicating him to join her. "How fortunate. I hardly expected to see you in the village, Papa."

His gaze sharpened, and he took a step closer to her table, clearly intrigued. "Thank you, my dear," he replied, dropping in the chair across, his tone laced with false warmth. "I find it interesting—your recent… immersion into village life."

"Recent?" She gave a tinkling little laugh no one would be fooled by. "No, Papa. I've been here for three years," she corrected him with a small, innocent smile, tilting her head slightly. "What else was I to do?" She shrugged. "Since I've taken up residence at Perlsea Keep, I've found the villagers to be quite welcoming. It's only right I do what I can to help bolster the community as mistress of Perlsea."

"Help?" He raised an eyebrow, feigning interest. "I've heard quite the opposite, actually. Some would say you're doing more than just socializing."

Meredith's heart skipped a beat, but she kept her expression serene, thanking the heavens, and her father, for her years of training. She took a sip from her cup to buy herself a moment. She set it down gently before meeting his gaze. "Goodness, Papa. I simply enjoy spending time with the women of the village— sharing recipes, mending techniques, and the like. After all, life in Cornwall is rather different than that of London."

The duke's eyes narrowed ever so slightly, as if trying to peel away the layers of her words. She knew he wasn't convinced, but she also knew that she had given him nothing substantial to grasp. "Where is your maid?" he demanded.

Blast. "Visiting her mother," she said quickly. "Her mother owns Marigold's Haberdashery."

He leaned closer, lowering his voice just enough to make it seem like an afterthought.

"Meredith, I know I needn't remind you that, indeed, this village is quite the change from London. Let us hope it doesn't lead you to misunderstanding your place… or your influence here." His smile held a hint of menace. She was his only child, but that only made things more dire. It would be expected where her loyalties lay.

Though her insides churned with the weight of what was clearly a threat, Meredith smiled politely. "I assure you, Papa, I know exactly where I stand."

The silence between them stretched and she picked up the

plate of warm delectables. "Scone, Papa?"

His cup clattered against its saucer. "No, thank you. I must be on my way. I wish to speak to Mr. Wren regarding his wood-work."

Carefully, tempering her fury, Meredith set down the plate. "Mr. Wren works for me, Papa. Certainly, you have no interest in my renovations for Perlsea?" she said mildly.

He rose from the table with a steely smile. "I trust the quality will meet the highest of standards."

"It suits my purposes."

With a sharp nod, he said, "Good day, daughter. I expect to see you and Pender for dinner tonight." Upon his exit, the collective gasp from his entrance let go with a strong exhale.

Meredith watched from the window as her father entered his own carriage, wondering how Pender would enjoy her father's edict in appearing for dinner. Seconds later, he set off…

In the direction of the mines.

Rising from the table, she slipped into the backroom, closing the door gently behind her. She leaned against it with her eyes closed, unable to shake an uneasy feeling curling in her chest. Rathbourne was no fool. He suspected something, even if he didn't know what, and it was only a matter of time before he learned exactly what she was up to. He certainly wouldn't approve of her lifting those he considered her inferiors to greater potential. To him, it was a fool's mission to give up one's power.

"It didn't go well?" Marigold's small feminine voice had Meredith's eyes opening quickly and surveying all five women still seated around the table.

"It didn't go horribly," she hedged. "But, my father…" She shook her head unable to explain. With concerted effort, she pulled herself together and straightened from the door. "It changes nothing," she said firmly, going to the table. She focused on Derwa, gentling her voice. "I'm going to go through the agreement Mr. Cardy signed before his death, dear. Do you mind if I speak with Mr. Ashcroft if I have questions?"

"N-no." Her stuttered response spoke of her innate fear.

Meredith's gaze moved about the table. "It is vital that not a word of this escapes this room. It is my fiercest belief that Mr. Thornfield does not realize this agreement is missing. Bray did a very brave thing, Derwa. I know it doesn't seem like it right now, but you have every reason to be proud of your late husband. Your daughter, too."

Derwa's eyes shimmered. "Thank you, my lady," she murmured. "That means more than I can say."

Meredith nodded. The rest of the hour, she went over budget concerns and ideas for edging prices up without alienating customers, neighbors, and mostly, friends. Because one thing was clear: Penhalwick was a tightknit community. "Let's meet next week. I daresay the duke will have taken himself back to London by that time," she said.

After the women made their way out the back door, she spoke to the room. "One could only hope."

"Pardon, milady?" Agnes said, startling Meredith.

She took in a deep breath to steady her pounding heart. "Nothing, Agnes. Next time, be sure to stay by my side."

Clearly confused, Agnes nodded.

"Come, let's go home."

LUCIUS SPENT THE morning searching Ashcroft's office, but he found nothing substantial to give him any idea of the man's motives for being in Cornwall. It was getting much too late to search the steward's cottage. The yard outside the Keep bustled with activity pertaining to more renovations and Lucius preferred maintaining a sense of autonomy for that particular task. Instead, he planned to use the rest of his time to focus on the record-keeping Ashcroft was in charge of. But that was not to be.

His wife's voice sounded in the vestibule and she did not

sound happy. It took less than a minute for the library door to crash back and for her to storm the chamber.

"How *dare* he threaten me!" she ranted.

Shock exploded through Lucius. He dropped his pen and shot to his feet, cringing at the pull in his lower back. "So, help me, I'll kill Ashcroft. With my bare hands," he said through a clenched jaw.

"Ashcroft! What are you talking about?" The door slammed hard enough behind her to flicker the gas lighting in the chandelier above.

Lucius pulled up. His teeth clenched. "*Thornfield* threatened you?"

"What? No. My father," she bit out, her hands landing at her hips.

Lucius clamped his lips tight at his stupidity. He was an idiot.

An unladylike snort of disgust sounded from her and to Lucius's surprise, she stormed to the brandy cabinet and poured out a small glass for herself.

He lowered himself back into his chair. "As bad as that, is it?" He spoke mildly now, having recouped his wits.

Slowly, Meredith turned, facing him, fury covering her lovely face. She touched the glass to her lip and tipped it back, draining it.

A sense of foreboding crept over him. "What is it?"

She turned and poured out another drink. Two this time, then strolled over and held one out to him. "My father has requested our presence at dinner tonight," she said pleasantly.

"Requested," he repeated, his tone laced with bitterness. "More like commanded."

She clinked her glass to his. "Yes. And, he expects us both to attend. And he's made it clear that we're to—er…"

"Appear properly attired," Lucius cut in. Frustration pulsed through his veins. "Who the hell does he think he is, issuing dictates in my own home."

She scowled. "Don't you mean *our* home?"

Heat crawled up his neck. "Er, yes, of course." *Hers, really.*

She stepped closer, inundating him with the scent of fresh violets… and brandy. "I advise you *not* to be late." She tossed back the second drink and slammed the glass on the hard desktop.

Lucius let out a sharp breath. "Oh, I'll be there." But he would not be playing the obedient son-in-law. No one threatened *his* wife.

He watched as she marched to the door and exited without looking back. His wife.

In name only.

Something that was becoming more and more difficult to maintain. And that was the crux of the entire matter… he wasn't certain he didn't wish to change things.

Not any longer.

CHAPTER SIXTEEN

MEREDITH STOLE UP to the hidden room, vowing to be careful, yet requiring a distraction from her father barging into *her* home and upsetting the sense of balance that had taken her three years to effect. She set her lamp on the floor near the windows where little light was able to break through the thick coat of soiled dirt. She found the old journal on the floor near where Lucius had fallen.

There was an old chair with threadbare brocade of a color so faded it was impossible to determine its origin. She tested the legs before deeming it safe enough to hold her weight, then sat. Opening the book, she settled back and lost herself in the past.

15 July 1758, "The meeting was more productive than expected. The others were in agreement—what we discussed must never leave the confines of the Keep. The implications, should the information fall into the wrong hands, could destroy not only us but the future of the Aylesbury name. My greatest fear is betrayal from within, though I have taken precautions to ensure everyone's silence."

Meredith's skin prickled at that last statement. It sounded so… prophesying. She read on.

3 August 1758, "It has been decided. The papers shall remain hidden and only those worthy shall know where to look. Marked by the mantra: The dead bear witness in silence.*

Just the thought restores my humor."

Her spine stiffened and she reread the passage. The wood legs on her chair creaked ominously. Tunnels below? The dungeons? Did Lucius know about this? She felt a little ill at the thought.

10 September 1758, "The air around Perlsea grows heavier with each passing day. I find myself pacing these halls more and more often. Our motto, once I thought so clever, now weighs upon my shoulders. The others remain steadfast, but I can't help sensing cracks in our unity. One of us has grown restless— too eager to capitalize on plans before the time is right. I fear action may be required."

1 October 1758, "The deed has been enacted. The man who would see us undone remains a threat no longer."

With a gasp, Meredith's hand flew to her chest; she forced herself to read on. As if she could have stopped. She leaned forward and, again, the chair swayed so precariously, she moved to the floor and closer to the light.

"'Tis a necessary evil. I shiver to think the earth remembers all debts. I do not write his name, for that would be foolish indeed. Guilt lies heavier than stone. Alas, in memory he shall remain. Perlsea has seen many things, but the blood on my hands may be the darkest yet."

Tears blurred her vision and she swiped them away, confused by her reaction. It made no sense. The man and the man he'd murdered were long dead. Still, she couldn't stop reading.

12 November 1758, "I have instructed my son-in-law on the importance of the family's role in these affairs. He appears to understand the gravity of our mission, and that eases my mind. Perlsea shall be his to protect, along with all it holds to his heirs. I've no option but to trust him since I've but a single daughter, but my faith is fragile. He is not of my blood. God knows I couldn't very well share such horrors with my wife and child. There are too many eyes watching now. If we are not mindful—well, the consequences would be dire."

9 January 1759, "There is talk of a fracture among us. Whispers have reached my ears, though I know not yet who dares to sow more doubt. I shall not let the situation unravel. A division would mean an end for us all—too much rests upon the success of our plans. I have already buried one secret. Alas, what is another?"

What the devil had been their plans? And, who were "they"?

"What the hell are you doing here? I thought I decreed this chamber off limits."

Meredith glanced up, blinking at the picture her husband made, stirring her pulse into an irritating flutter. His angular features appeared harsh in the oil lamp's flickering flame. The very little light coming through the dirty windows had waned considerably. His arms were folded over his broad chest and his dark hair gave him a brooding quality.

"You are disturbing the ghosts," he said.

She snapped the journal shut and dropped it to her side, scowling. "Did you just tell me you *decreed* something? The woman you abandoned for three years to her own devices? The woman who is now turning this Keep into a livable place to reside? The woman to whom you've informed you wish an annulment?" By the time Meredith had reached the end of her litany, her voice was a near shrill.

He held out his hand.

After a minute's hesitation, she grasped it and let him assist her to her feet and quashed the stab of guilt at his sharp gasp.

"My pardons, Lady Pender. You are right, of course. I did you a grave injustice. You have my abject apologies." He leaned in and touched her lips with his. They were softer than she thought they would be. His eyes closed and the tip of his tongue lined the seam of her lips.

The shocking sensation startled her and she gasped. The sharp intake left her mouth gaping, allowing the gates open for pure bliss. Without the slightest hesitation, he angled his head and slipped his tongue inside and gently lapped at the low tide of velvety warmth. Such unguarded ardor from him sent a jolt through her chest.

He drew back.

She couldn't seem to put her shock into words though her mouth still hung open.

The intensity of his eyes bore through her, and after a moment, he lifted her jaw with an index finger. "I'm, uh, here to remind you of our dinner edict." His voice came out deep and husky as if from the center of the earth's fiery core. He framed her face with his hands. "I'm not about to sit through another meal without you. And certainly not alone with only Rathbourne as company."

She blinked once, not completely comprehending until she blinked a second time. That one caught in crystallized clarity and reality reasserted itself. "Oh, blast. Dinner. Worse… Papa!" She spun on a heel and dashed from the chamber without the lamp or the journal.

WITH A WRY grin, Lucius took a moment for the cold air in the chamber to cool his nether regions to half-mast. He leaned over, wincing, and picked up the oil lamp. Then stopped, spotting the book she'd been reading. On closer inspection, it appeared to be the journal she'd shown him before. Tightening his abdomen against more pain, he managed to scoop it from the floor and open it, wondering what had captured her attention so completely she hadn't heard him enter the room.

Alas, it had grown too dark to read in the low light. Neither did he have the time if he was to make the duke's mandate. Oil lamp and journal both in hand, Lucius made his way out of the old library and carefully down the stairs.

An hour later, he entered the dining hall where a fire crackled in a hearth large enough to roast a spit pig. Long shadows danced across the floor from the flames.

Meredith stood near her father holding—gripping, her knuckles blanched white—a glass of sherry, her expression a blank mask. Quite practiced. Something worth remembering he told himself.

He strode to her and accepted his own glass from a tray Bartlett held out before leaning in and brushing her lips with his. She was so startled, her hand jerked and wine spilled over the edge of the glass on her hand.

Lucius was hard pressed to keep from laughing outright. An astonishing sensation. When was the last time he'd felt like laughing? If they'd been alone, he'd happily have licked every drop from her dainty fingertips dry. He quickly produced a handkerchief and dabbed her hand. "You must be careful, my dear. You don't wish to ruin your lovely gown." And, lovely it was. Champagne silk trimmed in gold reflected the firelight with a soft shimmering sheen.

"It's years out of date," the duke remarked with a condescending sweep of his gaze over his daughter.

Meredith's green eyes flashed then glittered like emerald shards.

"Sorry I'm late, darling," he murmured, turning into her body. "I think your gown is quite lovely."

She inclined her head but her plump lips remained compressed.

Lucius blocked the duke from seeing her reaction. He straightened and turned to the smug arse, sipping his wine.

"How nice you could join us," Rathbourne said with a cold smile. "I see your wife managed to issue my invitation."

Before Lucius could flatten his father-in-law, Verity's portly figure appeared, and he announced dinner.

Lucius took Meredith's hand and laid it on his arm. He could feel its warmth and its trembling on his arm through his frockcoat. He seated her at one end of the table then took his own seat at the far end, duke be damned. This was their home, not Rathbourne's.

Silence stretched for a time while the first course of turtle soup was delivered. A silence that didn't last long.

"It's good to see you finally returning to your rightful place, Pender. I feared you'd forgotten your family's obligations."

Lucius paused, fork half raised toward his mouth, appalled yet unsurprised at Rathbourne's insolence. The words also seemed to contradict the duke's own from that morning. He turned his own cold smile on the blackguard. "Your announcement at my father's wake of Meredith's delicate condition was quite the reminder." He lifted one shoulder. "But I'm here now."

The man did raise a point. What *were* those obligations his father had made on Lucius's behalf? Something, he decided, that needed looking into immediately. He would write the solicitor—no!—instinct told him waiting that long would be a mistake.

Rathbourne's fork clinked against his plate. "Indeed, indeed," he said in that annoyingly blustering, obnoxious way of his. "The Pender estates require a firm hand. I'm sure Perlsea Keep has missed your leadership."

Lucius bristled in Meredith's stead. "On the contrary, Your Grace. My wife has handled the Keep's affairs admirably." He flashed her a quick smile, hoping she discerned his genuine sincerity. But her attention was focused on her food. Or, rather, pushing it about her plate.

The duke's eyes flickered to his daughter then back to Lucius. "Of course she has," he said with a touch of impatience. "She is of my blood after all. But the handling of an estate of this magnitude requires a man's hand."

"I disagree," Lucius said mildly. "One of her first tasks upon arriving in Cornwall was to hire a competent steward." He shot her a smile and surprised himself by not choking on his words.

The duke frowned. "He can't be that competent," he groused. "This place needs more servants."

"That is due to the mine's needs for able-bodied workers, Papa." Meredith had finally spoken up, but her father was getting under her skin, based on the edge in her tone. "There were but four when I first arrived."

And so went the excruciating dinner... for another four courses.

$$\textbf{\textsc{Chapter Seventeen}}$$

"I FEEL A megrim coming on," Meredith told Lucius as they walked through the dimly lit corridor to their suites. "I know one is not supposed to disparage one's parent so, but…"

"Shush," Lucius whispered. At his door, he tugged her inside. "We need to talk."

"Can't it wait until tomorrow?" She pressed the heel of her hand to the bridge of her nose. The shock of that disturbing kiss when he'd *put his tongue* in *her mouth* that had dissipated through dinner came surging back. Her breasts tingled with discomfort and wanton need.

He pulled her inside. "No." The chamber was empty, and she wondered where his trusted valet was.

"Thank you for defending my abilities for putting the estate together. I know how difficult it was for you." She gave him a small smile. "Especially where Mr. Ashcroft is concerned."

"Yes, it was. You owe me a boon for that bit of balderdash."

"A boon!" What an opportunist. She narrowed her eyes on him. "What kind of boon?"

In a sudden move, she was backed against the closed door, his hands flattened on the solid oak door behind her, one at each side of her head.

"What—"

"Taking my boon." His voice, a low husky growl, sent a shiver of heated awareness over her, through her.

Her stomach dipped. Not with dread, but with anticipation.

Her lips had hardly had time to recover from that unexpected feathering he'd tortured her with just before dinner. *In front of her father.*

"What—" she started again. But, again, the chance to speak was stolen as his lips moved over hers in a caress that had her knees trembling. They didn't crash; they didn't feather. This was a firm press and a suckle of her bottom lip where he took his time. The touch of his tongue against her lips again sent a bolt of current through her, reviving her into a burning ember from the fire in the grate. The intensity was no less shocking than it had been in the hidden library. She couldn't believe her legs hadn't turned to ashes and disintegrated beneath her.

He gentled the pressure into a wisp of warm breeze that had her insides quivering with shameful desire.

Shameful? How could that be? They were wed! Her skin prickled into small bumps and her nipples pebbled. A moan rose deep within her chest, and she clutched at his frockcoat.

"Oh, Meredith." Heated breath mingled with hers in that low tone he expelled that rippled over her. "What are we to do?"

"Do?" she whispered.

He let out a sigh and stepped back, his arms falling away leaving a cool sensation.

Her skin doused in a chill that had nothing to do with the temperature. "I-I don't understand." And, she didn't. She didn't understand why she was suddenly frightened, or feared being alone, or… *feared being deserted…*

Meredith rubbed her palms over her upper arms. "I did something wrong, didn't I? You're still angry that I went into the ruin. Or, or, that I hired Mr. Ashcroft. I've already told you—" He cut her off with another kiss, but she jerked away and swept her dignity about herself in a cloak of outrage. "*You* are the one who left me here with no explanation; no 'I'm sorry this isn't for me'; no 'I will not be returning'—"

He spun around so quickly, she had no time to react. His hands gripped her upper arms and he shook her sharply. "I was wrong. I was angry. As angry as you, I expect. I… I was also an idiot."

The expression on his face stunned her. The regret. And, it stung. She tried shrugging him off, but he wouldn't let go.

"Neither of us deserved what our fathers did to us, but they did. And…" He drew in a deep breath, set his forehead against hers. "I'm sorry. I didn't give you a second thought. It was thoughtless of me."

"And selfish," she added.

"And selfish. I find myself conflicted from the inside out. I want you and that—"

"Frightens you." She nodded. "Yes, I can see how such an about face would disturb someone who came here only seeking an annulment." The bite of bitter sarcasm could not be stemmed, but she softened it with a smile.

"Not 'frightens' exactly," he hedged.

"Then what?" she demanded. She tired of these flights of fancy he tossed out at will.

His gaze moved to the ceiling as if she'd pinned him to the ground with stakes. "I'm not certain. I just know I don't want to stop kissing you." His eyes found hers and once again their intensity startled her. "We are married."

"That is not enough for me. It may have been at one time. But no longer." She huffed out her frustration and, again, tried shoving him away.

"Stop," he said, his voice fraying. "Can't you understand? I want to help. I admire what you've accomplished since you've been here."

Still, she struggled. Then froze. "What?"

He took her hand and led her to the small seating area before a less than robust fire. "Rathbourne said something intriguing tonight that requires looking into."

"My father is so full of bluster that I've learned to tune out much of what he says," she bit out.

"Understandably so," he said with a wry tip to his lips. "But, darling, I must travel to London."

"You're leaving?" Meredith's chest seemed to cave in on itself. She should have known. For half a minute, she'd believed something could be salvaged of this disastrous union.

But that, apparently, was not to be.

She was a fool. Yet again.

THE AIR IN his chamber vanished with a sudden rush. Lucius's eyes snapped to Meredith where devastation weighed five stone on her shoulders. "I'm not deserting you, love."

Her spine stiffened to that of an iron rod. She lifted her stubborn little chin. "It's not me I'm concerned for, you oaf. It's the people I thought you were attempting to help." She jerked to standing. He grabbed her hand and pulled her back down.

"I told you, damn it, I do want to help. But I need to see our original betrothal agreements. I was only thirteen when the damn things were signed and I've never thought to see exactly what they've said before," he said gruffly. "I'll only be away for a day or two."

"Oh." The word was let go with a release of her breath. Her eyes narrowed. "What is it you expect to find?"

"I don't know," he said honestly. "But the fact that Rathbourne is bringing up the commitments my family made on my behalf has me vastly curious." He shoved a hand through his hair. "I can't believe I never thought to check before, but Rathbourne's words send a chill crawling up my neck."

A solid couple of minutes crept by with Meredith's head bowed as if studying her hands. Finally, she lifted her eyes, meeting his. "Two days?"

Inside, he softened, offering her a crooked smile. "You've managed quite nicely for three years without me. Surely, you can handle two days. Can't you?" His teasing manner had an unexpected result.

"Of course." She scowled. "I just didn't have to do things with my father monitoring my every move."

A distinct disadvantage. "It will limit your activities," he admitted. He leaned in and brushed her lips with his. "I shall be as quick as I can," he promised her. He lay back against the settee. "I can't believe what I'm about to suggest, but you might consider inviting your Mr. Ashcroft to dine."

Again, her eyes narrowed on him, this time brimming with the fire he was learning gave her that glowing quality he was having great difficulty in resisting. "My—"

Lucius was tired of that persistent grievance and snagged her by the waist. Her squeal filled the chamber as she landed atop him, her legs flailing and splaying on either side of his hips. The move didn't help his back, but he didn't care. Framing her face in his hands, he brought her mouth to his and kissed that delectable plumpness he couldn't quit fixating on. A taste which exceeded that of The Copper Kettle's delectable lemon tarts.

Sharp, tangy, sweet, irresistible.

His wife.

Groaning, Lucius pulled his lips from hers and set them along her neck, then licked his way up to a soft place beneath her ear where the scent of violets was stronger, more enticing. Her fingers threaded his hair. Her lips grew more confident against his skin, leaving a blazing trail where they touched his forehead. He lifted his face and caught her lips, searing himself with a memory to carry with him on the long trek to London.

Her lips parted and he swept his tongue inside the velvet softness that dove straight for his groin. She tried to pull away, but he held her head steady, stroking her tongue until her fingers not only relaxed in his hair, but clenched, pulling him tighter, even as her tentative imitation increased in its boldness, chasing his tongue with hers. A dueling dance that set his heart ablaze with longing.

He yanked his head away and dropped his lips to an irresistibly naked shoulder. Nipped the skin with his teeth, then licked, then nipped again. The fire in the hearth was nothing compared to the inferno raging within his own body. His hands moved to her hips, and he found the edge of her gown. Fingertips tingled on the silk of her stockings that encased smooth thighs, shapely knees, and trim ankles. But he didn't linger, quickly finding bare thighs and moaning with a desire so thick and heated, his restraint would likely give him heart failure.

"Lucius."

His name on her lips sent the lust roaring through him. It pulsated the blood in his ears, until he couldn't hear anything from the rush. Burned the tips of his fingers where they glided across her silken skin. He licked the expanse of her bosom, drawing a sharp gasp from her.

If he'd ever doubted her innocence, he didn't now. Whatever Ashcroft's role, the man wasn't after his countess.

"I'm going to touch you now," he told her in a low voice that vibrated with an insatiable hunger. To his shock, his fingers trembled as they edged closer to the heart of the enchantment he craved, then brushed the curls there to a wetness he desperately thirsted for. With an index finger, he slipped between the folds.

"Oh!" Her squeal floated on the air, cascading over him, through him, seeping into his bones.

Lucius pressed against the hidden nub with the base of his thumb and her fingers dug into his shoulders. The chamber was too hot, inundating him with the spicy scent of her that mingled with the violets. He brought up his other hand and worked her breasts from her snug bodice. "Beautiful," he whispered, then took a rosy, hardened nipple into his mouth.

In rhythmic synchronization, his tongue swirled in time with his fingers working her sex. His own arousal strained against the flap of his trousers, but it was her hips gyrating against him that refused to let him stop and find a way to make her truly his.

"What—" she panted, appearing unable to form a coherent question.

"Trust me, darling. Let yourself fly. Let… go…" He took her breast back in his mouth and bit down lightly.

The most astonishing thing happened. Her squeal careened through his chamber; her sex clenched against his fingers then flooded him with that sweet nectar as she moved wildly over him.

After a time, she relaxed against him.

If only he could have done the same.

"I suppose I'm no longer a virgin," she said against his neck.

Laughter rumbled in his chest. He brought his arms up and wrapped her in them, deciding the truth could wait a little longer. Holding her firmly in his arms, Lucius clenched his teeth against the pain in his back and rose from the settee. He carried her to his large, not so comfortable bed and tossed her in the center. The twinge in his back had completely dissipated.

She gasped. "What are you doing, sir?"

"Ah, so we're back to 'sir,' are we?" He stripped off his cravat, his waistcoat, his shirt, dropping each on the floor. "I'm taking my wife to bed." He turned and sat on the edge and yanked off his shoes, then stood and unfastened the flap at his breeches, nearly laughing outright to see Meredith's hands covering her face, yet not, as she was peeking through spread fingers. "You aren't the least bit curious?"

"It's indecent," she squeaked.

"But so delightful. I'm certainly curious about you." He shucked the pants, placed a knee on the bed and lowered his voice to a purr. "For example, I wonder if the skin on your belly is as soft as that of your hands." He tugged off her slippers and threw them over his shoulder. Pushed her skirts up past her knees, baring her thighs which were indeed as silky as the skin on her hands. With deft fingers, he untied her garters and rolled down her silk stockings, then pitched them aside.

"I'm not so sure about this." Her voice wobbled.

He licked the inside of one thigh. "No? Don't worry, darling. I'm sure enough for the both of us."

She fell back against the pillows with her face still covered. "I don't think this is… is legal."

"And who shall turn us in?" He edged closer to the heart of his desire and breathed in deep.

Her fingers gripped his hair but she wasn't pushing him away. Was, in fact, pulling him in.

Definitely a sign of encouragement, he decided, licking his way to ecstasy. She writhed beneath his mouth. He was certain to lose hair before the end of this night but, oh, she tasted delicious. A minute later, her joyful cry once more careened through the chamber and his mouth was flooded with her release. He raised to his knees and gripped his arousal and placed it at her opening. "Brace yourself, darling," he whispered.

"I don't know what you mean—"

But he was more than ready to show her, and eased himself in the opening, pulling back then moving forward. Back and forth, he worked until he broke past her hymen and engulfed himself to the hilt. Her snug passage squeezed the life from him until the blood roared in his ears and drove all thought from his brain.

There was nothing strategic about this copulation. It just *was*. His skin prickled with a need he'd never before experienced. Her fingernails cut into his shoulders, and he froze. Had she gasped? Had he hurt her?

"Meredith," he croaked out.

"Why… are you… stopping?"

"I don't wish to hurt you."

"I, it—" She sucked in a deep breath. "It doesn't hurt. Not any longer."

He dropped his lips to hers. To his delight and shock, she touched the tip of her tongue to his lips, creating a sensation that shot straight to his groin. He drew her tongue into his mouth, and he moved his hips between her legs without pulling back. Just used the pressure of his groin to hers.

Her legs wrapped his hips; her arms tightened around his

neck. Her mouth broke from his. "Yes," she whispered, writhing harder against him.

The dam inside him let loose. He pulled back and surged forward. Once, twice, the third time, a brilliant spectrum of light shattered behind his closed eyes as he flooded her with his seed, his heart drumming in its wake.

It took a moment for Lucius to gather his bearings, a moment for the blood in his body to redistribute to his arms enough to gain the strength to lift himself up and fall to Meredith's side. He dragged her along, settling her head on his shoulder. Dropping a kiss on her dampened forehead, he said, "I was too rough. I'm sorry."

Meredith bolted upright. "Sorry? You're *sorry?*"

"What—"

"How dare you insult me so. It's… it's *outrageous*. Why, I still have my clothes on." Meredith threw her legs over the side of the bed, but he snagged her about the waist before she could make good her escape.

"What the devil is the matter with you?" he demanded. "I said I was sorry I hurt you. I am not sorry I took you."

The fight went out of her and she sagged against him. "Oh."

"Is this something I should prepare myself for in the future?"

"What do you mean by 'something'?" she muttered.

"This over-sensitivity, over-reaction thing."

She wriggled, outraged, in his hold. "Over-reaction!"

"See? This is exactly what I'm talking about." He yanked her up beside him in a move that reminded him of the twinge in his back. He pulled her face to his, dropped his gaze to her lips. "It appears you still require convincing that you belong in my bed," he murmured.

CHAPTER EIGHTEEN

T HE NEXT MORNING came much too soon. Meredith forced her eyes open only to see rain slashing against the windows. She glanced at the clock surprised to find it was already after eleven. Goodness, the chamber was cold. Very cold. In the three years she'd lived in Cornwall, it had never been this cold so late in the season. She snuggled deeper within the coverlets, reveling in the masculine scent that clung to the pillow before the situation hit her—she was alone.

Slowly, she rose to sitting, holding the counterpane to her nudity. After her small outburst the night before, she'd been quickly stripped of any armor. *Armor?*

A small tap sounded at the door. "Enter." Her voice cracked. She cleared her throat and tried again. "Enter."

"Lady Pender?"

"Oh, Agnes. It's you."

"I brought your wrap, my lady."

Meredith was no longer cold. Her body was one huge blush and rushed with heat. "Thank you."

"Mr. Graham informed me that Lord Pender has departed for London." She cast a side glance to Meredith. "Will he be returning?"

Irritation bristled over her. "Certainly."

"It's just that he only arrived..." Her voice trailed off.

Meredith breathed in through her nose, striving for patience then let it out slowly. "I know you are young, Agnes. And, you were not trained as a lady's maid, but speaking so is out of line."

"But Lord Pender—"

"Will only be away for a couple of days. Now, I'll hear no more about it. What is my father doing?"

"Oh, ma'am, I couldn't begin to ask about the duke. He frightens me out of my wits."

With good reason, Meredith didn't say. "All right." She snatched the wrap from Agnes and the two of them stole through the bathing chamber. She ached in unimaginable places. "Start a bath for me, Agnes. Afterward, I'd best see what havoc Papa is determined to stir up."

Thirty minutes later, Meredith eased her body into the blessed, violet scented water and thought about her husband.

Husband.

She was truly married now. She leaned her head back, smiling, and closed her eyes. Her breasts tingled where his mouth had lingered. And the insides of her thighs? Dear heavens, she'd never heard of or imagined the like. Would he like it if she put her mouth on him? On that place between his legs? Just thinking of something so indecent stirred that private part of her body to gushing hot. She pressed her fingers to her sex to stop the throbbing that pulsed there.

It only made the ache more pronounced. She pressed harder and her fingers slipped inside. Groaning, she pulled her fingers away only to repeat the motion. Until she couldn't stop. Images of his teeth grazing her nipples turned them into hard pebbles. With her other hand, she pinched her nipple. Faster and faster her fingers moved, in and out, until she couldn't catch her breath.

She pictured herself licking the length of him. Something so improper, it inflamed the inferno roaring through her until her hand ached, yet unable to stop. A peak similar to the one she'd reached the night before—thrice!—inundated her.

Despite the water's heat, another warmth flooded her fingers. Her breath caught and she couldn't seem to take in air. Her heart pounded so erratically she grasped the sides of the copper tub to steady herself lest she sink beneath the water and drown.

After a time, her senses leveled to something more normal, even if her fingers were cramped from squeezing the tub so tightly. Embarrassment rippled through her as if she'd engaged in a forbidden activity.

"Lady Pender?" Agnes peered around the door's edge. "Is all in order? I thought you were hurt with all that moaning."

Meredith didn't even have the energy to chastise her maid for her remarks. "Er, yes, thank you. A towel, please."

"Of course, my lady."

Guilt weighed her shoulders as if the heaviest rock lodged there. It was a wonder she could drag herself from the tub at all. Was touching oneself to completion considered adultery? She should tell him. No, she *shouldn't* tell him.

Agnes emitted a soft cough. "Um, the duke sent a note requesting your presence for breakfast," she whispered.

Perfect.

THIS INFERNAL RAIN would kill him or his horse, Lucius thought. But resentment pushed him onward. He was shocked at his desire to remain in bed next to his *wife*. Wife. A word he'd never believed he would utter with any sort of reverence. At least where Meredith was concerned. But, God, how he'd wished to stay abed, wake her the way he'd worn her to sleep the night before. His horse hit a slick patch, jarring his attention. Rightly so, if he didn't wish to break his stupid neck.

The dirt-packed road to the steward's cottage was steeped in muck, and as much as Lucius hated the thought of going to Ashcroft for help, the idea of leaving Meredith in Rathbourne's clutches for two whole days left his options minimal.

He rode alongside the thick copse of trees, praying the path he was on was one that led to the cottage. It was the most worn, therefore making it the most practical. One of the first tasks he planned to embark on upon his return, he promised himself, would be a thorough tour of the estate. One certainly couldn't call his visit at the age of six an official tour and definitely not one that had included the steward's cottage.

A second later, an explosion boomed through the storm. "What the hell?" Thunder that vibrated the ground beneath him. His horse reared up and Lucius attempted to grip the reins, but his fingers refused to work. He tried turning but the burning sensation in his shoulder stopped him cold. Black dots edged his vision. A gust of wind kicked up and a branch swayed, hitting him in the head, knocking him from his horse, and face down into the mud.

Meredith. He had to get to Meredith.

Blackness stole his consciousness, leaving his last impression of her horror-filled eyes.

"DAMN IT, WAKE up. Wake up, you bastard."

Lucius struggled and pushed at driving out the harsh, annoying voice, but it persisted until he'd fully, aggravatingly awakened. The pain in his shoulder gave testament to the state. Through a slanted squint, he couldn't quite believe what he was seeing. Ashcroft hovering over him, wearing his spectacles. "You tried to kill me," he croaked out.

"Wasn't me," he said. "And you could show a little more appreciation. I mustered every bit of integrity that seeped through my veins to haul you into my humble abode, when it appears I should have left you to suffocate in the muck."

Lucius could only manage a low growl and hoped it came across as a thank you. "Then who?" he gasped out.

Ashcroft's expression went grim. "I don't know. The good news, however—"

"There's good news?"

"Obviously, as your humor appears intact."

Lucius grunted.

"The shot went clean through." Ashcroft held up Lucius's fine white lawn shirt, slit down in front where, indeed, a hole showed on the front right side, through to the back when he turned it around.

"Shot?" Lucius compressed his lips, fury muting some of the pain. "Where the devil am I?"

Ashcroft dropped the shirt, went to a basin, dipped and wrung out a cloth. "My cottage. I was on my way to the Keep when I heard the shot."

Right. The humble abode. "You think Rathbourne was the culprit? It's certainly clear you have no fondness for the blackguard."

Ashcroft snorted. "Of course, not. The duke does not shoot those who oppose him. He has underlings to handle those distasteful little tasks." He came to the long wood-hewn table where Lucius lay gripping a bottle of whiskey in one hand and the damp cloth in the other. "This is going to hurt," he said.

Lucius frowned. "What?"

The man put a sneer on his face and didn't answer. Instead, he poured the whiskey on the open wound.

"What the fuck?" Lucius hissed.

"This." He pressed the cloth to his shoulder. "It needs stitching."

"From you? No thanks."

"It's me, the Penhalwick doctor, or the apothecary. The doctor or Miss Lovelock can likely help, but then the whole village is likely to know you were shot at within a matter of hours if not minutes."

Unfortunately, the man was right. "Hurry it up then," he grated out.

Ashcroft moved to a scarred counter and took down a chipped piece of crockery.

Lucius shut his eyes, dreading the oncoming event with every fiber of his being. A minute later, Ashcroft nudged Lucius's good shoulder then assisted him to sitting. He handed him the cup with more whiskey. "Drink up, soldier. The quicker the better."

Advice worth taking. Lucius tossed back the entire bitter brew and slammed the crockery down on the table, surprised it didn't shatter completely. "You laced it with laudanum. Damn you."

With a sharp nod, Ashcroft strode across the room and opened a cupboard. He took down a small tin box that looked ancient. "That I did. To help me, not you. If you jerk your arm, well… I can't bear the thought of informing Lady Pender of your untimely end, even if you were solely to blame."

"Make it quick," Lucius bit out through gritted teeth.

"Of course, your *lordship*." There was that mocking crack Lucius trusted more than the man's actual seriousness.

Lucius focused his eyes on the ceiling where years of soot marked the cottage's age. "I see my wife has yet to update your lovely accommodations."

"She's been busy setting up a school for the village children." He dabbed at the wound. "Your wound is still bleeding but thankfully looks clean. Not much debris." From the corner of Lucius's eye, he watched Ashcroft pour more spirits into a shallow bowl, then pull a set of tweezers from his box. He also took out a long, curved needle and dropped it in the bowl. He shot Lucius a quick, harsh grin.

Lucius closed his eyes, barely breathing because, blast it, his ribs hurt now.

"Stay still," Ashcroft murmured.

Lucius had no intention of moving. It hurt too much.

He had no idea how much time had passed when Ashcroft braced his arm and the sting of the needle pierced his skin. To Lucius's great relief, Ashcroft worked with surprisingly practiced efficiency. His fingers moved deftly. Of course, that didn't stop the pain. Perspiration beaded Lucius's forehead and upper lip but he stayed still.

One would think the tension between them would lessen, but

the air was drawn tight, quivering like a finely tuned string.

"Almost finished," Ashcroft muttered, more to himself it seemed. It was difficult to tell with his senses growing groggy. "On this side."

Groaning, Lucius breathed in through his nose then slowly released it, several passes until the pain ebbed to a dull throb. His thoughts grew murky, his body heavy as if a great weight pinned him to the table though he scarcely recalled lying down. He was rolled to his side and suffered a similar fate but felt more numb to the pain now.

A few minutes later, Lucius was rolled once more to his back.

"You'll have to keep an eye out for infection," Ashcroft said gruffly. He reached into the supply box and brought out a tin of salve. With a surprisingly gentle touch, he spread the ointment over the sutured gash. The faint scent of herbs filled Lucius's nostrils. It wasn't horrible. "This should help ward off trouble." Lastly, Ashcroft helped him to sitting, spread more salve, then wound a tight bandage around his shoulder enough to protect the wound.

Lucius could hardly keep his eyes open, watching as Ashcroft stepped back and stripped off his glasses.

He picked up the damp cloth and wiped his hands on it. "That should hold." Again, Ashcroft's voice held that gruffness belying his typical contempt he usually barely managed to conceal. "You were lucky."

"Aye." Lucius let out a long streaming breath. "Feels like hell." A trace of grudging appreciation filtered through him. "Thanks," he mumbled, closing his eyes again.

"Could've been worse," Ashcroft replied. It sounded as if he were repacking the small box of supplies then solidifying the fact with the soft click of the lid. "Let's get you to a bed."

Lucius groaned again.

Ashcroft assisted him from the table and steadied him before he could topple over. It was awkward, and worse, humiliating as hell.

Ashcroft guided them to a sparsely furnished room.

The only thing Lucius saw was the narrow bed and, testament to how he felt, it looked damned inviting. "I find it interesting you haven't asked who might want to kill me. It's almost as if you know the duke well." His words slurred and were barely legible to his own ears.

"I did at one time," Ashcroft allowed, but didn't elaborate, or at least so Lucius could understand it. Perhaps he'd missed his response. "What were you doing out in this weather?"

"Weather?" Lucius's stomach roiled. God, he hated laudanum. He would kill Ashcroft... *later*. Once he was home. "London," he got out. "I must get to London." He was about to lose consciousness. "You have to look after Meredith..."

"Lady Pender?" Ashcroft sounded startled. "I daresay, you can't go to London. Not in your condition. Where *is* Lady Pender? She should know about this, don't you think?"

Clarity shot through the fog. "No!" First, mauled by a bookshelf, then a bullet and a fall from his horse? No, thank you. "I have urgent business to attend to."

"I'm surprised she didn't insist on accompanying you. Unless—"

"Unless what?"

"She didn't wish to disappoint the weekly Literary Society women."

"Literary Society?" Lucius was lowered to the bed, partly due to his own knees giving out. Seconds later, his booted feet were lifted and dropped at the end. The floating sensation tempered with the sense of weightiness was odd.

"It's one of the ways she's drawn the women in. Engages their interest in politics and London society antics. She's created an interest in learning to read. It's the younger ladies who appear more eager, however."

Lucius's head seemed to detach from his body. He should be stunned. What other little meetings was she holding he didn't know about?

"Where is she now?" Ashcroft asked him again. "I can't imagine her being happy with your desire to return to London."

A grunt he intended for laughter escaped but he doubted it conveyed much as grogginess took hold, yet the words still penetrated. "I left her soundly sleeping in my bed."

"She didn't know you were going?"

"She did," he said, surprised he wasn't annoyed. Shouldn't he feel defensive? At the moment, he couldn't make himself care. Ashcroft was right. Obviously, Lucius was in no condition to make the trip to London.

Seconds later, the darkness reclaimed him.

Chapter Nineteen

T HE LONGER IT took Meredith to dress for breakfast, the more irritated she grew. Why should she be the one rushing about when it was her father who was the interloper?

It was nearly one in the afternoon when Agnes patted a strand of Meredith's hair in place and stepped back, quite pleased with herself. "There. All done, milady." And, well, she should be. It had taken two and a half years of patience to train her.

"It's perfect," she told the girl, pushing away from the vanity. The words were on the tip of her tongue—*send a note to the duke that I'll not be joining him*—but such discourse could put Agnes in danger. Her father was not above the least petty grievance. And that was the crux of it.

Bracing herself for the onslaught, Meredith threw back her shoulders and strode into the dining hall to find her father sitting at the table in Pender's designated chair at the head. She pulled up short. "What are you doing in my husband's chair?" To her knowledge, Lucius hadn't informed anyone but her of his plans for London.

He shrugged. "Pender was seen riding out this morning with an overnight bag. I sent you a note over two hours ago. If you deign to be late, you could have appeared in something other than"—he flung a hand in her direction—"another unfashionable frock gracing balls fit for '44, m'dear."

"There is no need for the latest fashion plates in this small corner of the world, Papa. I've been busy restoring this magnificent Keep. I hardly require the latest ensemble for such labor."

"Gads, how do you stand it?"

"I stand it very well, thank you." She took her place, gladly, at the other end of the table, which was as far from him as she could manage. "Coffee, please," she told Bartlett.

"My chamber is barely habitable."

"That is entirely your fault. You were not expected." A cup was set before her, and she took her time adding sugar and a dab of milk. "Why *are* you here? I haven't seen or heard from you in three years."

"Don't take that tone with me, young lady. If anything ever happens to your husband, clearly you would be returning home."

That will never happen, she vowed, even as a shiver touched the nape of her neck. "Nothing will happen to Pender, Papa. It's not like you to be away from London for days at a time. Your cronies surely miss you."

"I'm quietly handling a political matter—not that I expect you to understand such intricacies."

She sniffed her disdain. "There's no need to be condescending."

"Certain matters require a personal touch, Meredith," he said with an annoyance that abraded her skin. "Discretion was of the utmost import, and I didn't relish entrusting such a delicate situation to an agent or via post. The fewer people who know, the better for all involved."

"At the mines, no doubt." She narrowed her eyes on him. "What kind of delicate situation?"

"Nothing that concerns you." He dipped his spoon into the sugar bowl.

"You've always been a master at avoiding the truth, Papa. Pender is here and he has assured me he intends on staying. Again, I ask, why are you in Penhalwick?"

He paused, his spoon poised midair, his own gaze narrowing slightly before softening into an exasperated smile. "You do cut straight to the heart, don't you, my dear? It's a rather... vexing trait. One, I fear, you inherited from your mother." With a dramatic sigh he tipped the spoon over. The crystals streamed white into his cup. He stirred the contents, light clinking sounding loud in the hall. He lifted his cup then leaned back and stared at her. "My reasons hardly seem as urgent as the dire conditions of my chamber."

Meredith blinked, thrown by the unexpected shift of topic. "Your chamber? Certainly, if I'd learned your intentions of visiting…"

In a tone of grave injustice, as though this were the most pressing matter in the world, he said, "Have you seen the state of such disgrace? The mattress—stuffed with straw, I presume—must be as old as the castle itself. And the sheets… truly a degradation, Meredith. One might almost believe you set out to humiliate me in front of the housemaids."

"If it makes you feel any better, Pender is suffering the same fate." As the words slipped from her lips, she remembered the façade they were supposed to affect. "Um, when he sleeps in his own chamber," she finished weakly.

"If this is how you welcome your husband, it's a wonder he returned at all." He took a sip of his tea then let out a dramatic sigh. "And the, ah, draft…" Only this came out as if forcing himself to remember the current topic. "Let us not forget the draft. I vow I could feel the cold seeping into my very bones—an assault on comfort itself. One might think this house determined to drive me out."

If only it were that simple…

Meredith choked down the rest of her breakfast in silence before pushing away from the table forty minutes later. "I'm sorry, Papa. I'll let Mrs. Verity know how uncomfortable you are. In the meantime, I just recalled a promise to Pender. I must go to the village. Pender adores those lemon tarts from The Copper Kettle."

GROANING, LUCIUS PRIED his eyes open. Nausea hit him like a bullet to his gut. With slow, shallow breaths, he managed not to cast up his accounts. At least until he tried rising. He barely retrieved a chamber pot from beneath the bed before his stomach emptied. He remained on one hand and his knees, allowing the dizziness to pass before pulling himself up and sitting on the edge of the bed.

It took a moment for his vision to clear. The room was unfamiliar, and he struggled to distinguish between dream and reality as fleeting, disconnected memories slipped through his grasp. The sluggish thoughts pelting him were fragmented, as if he had emerged from beneath a cold sea trying to drag him back down. He lifted his hand to his face. Even that simple movement required immense effort.

The overwhelming desire to lie back down, slip once more into an unconscious state tempted him beyond measure, but for those fragmented thoughts persisting like bees buzzing about his head. There was a disconnect between his mind and body that frightened him, yet he couldn't get his thoughts to coalesce to anything near coherent. *Water.* He needed water. To rinse the vomit from his mouth, to dispel the cottony dryness in his throat.

Pushing through the distorted sensations, he gripped the sides of his narrow bed. Pain darted down his arm from his shoulder, finally reminding him of where he was and why. *Shot.* He'd been shot and dosed with laudanum.

Ashcroft. No. Ashcroft had saved him. Hadn't he? A flash of panic sent his pulse thrumming until the lightheadedness had white spots in his vision rendering him unable to see. He gritted his teeth and breathed through his nose. After a moment, the sensation passed, and he opened his eyes. The room was stark in its simplicity. There was no sideboard holding a pitcher and basin. Just a tall chest of drawers and a few boxes lining one wall. An unlit candle sat atop the chest of drawers, and he set his aim for that.

With caution, Lucius came to his feet, fearing a fall flat on his face. Determination, or perhaps stubbornness, definitely sheer will, kept him upright as he made his way to the chest of drawers, feeling as if he waded through a molasses-drenched undergrowth.

He knew he was forgetting something significant—Meredith. His wife. Someone had shot him. He clutched the chest of drawers to steady himself as reality knocked him in the head.

Meredith could be in danger.

Water. He needed water but with one glance at the candle, he turned away. All he'd need was to light the damn thing then collapse, setting the cottage and himself afire. Lucius glanced to the open door where firelight wavered on the hall wall with eerie shadows. The floating shapes were dizzying but if he didn't have water soon, he knew he would perish of thirst. The overdramatic thought floored him. Never would anyone have referred to him as overdramatic. Self-serving? Yes. Hard? Yes. Unemotional, stoic, unfeeling? Yes, yes, and yes.

Meredith—from all he'd ascertained—was none of those things. She certainly deserved better than him. But he was what she'd been allotted, and it was past time to do right by her.

Using the wall to balance himself, he made his way from the tiny, stark bedchamber into the great room where a low fire burned. The culprit that had been casting the shadows. In the small make-shift kitchen, steam curled from an iron kettle of water. There was a pump. He tried drawing water, but the effort left him too weak. Close at hand, he found a piece of chipped crockery on a wooden sideboard and poured hot water in the cup. It burned all the way down. He poured more, tossed that back. Twice more before he slowed enough to locate tea and a piece of bread, stuffing it in his mouth as if he hadn't eaten in days.

Immediately, Lucius felt better, more like himself. The fog in his brain cleared enough to allow him to light a couple of candles.

He sat at the table and used the solitude to gather his bearings. His shoulder pulsed, but thankfully, he didn't feel feverish. His coherence was returning as he sat there and let the thoughts roll over him.

Who shot him?

Why would someone attempt such a thing?

What was behind Rathbourne's sudden appearance?

Who the devil was Ashcroft? And, what was the man truly after?

Lucius's misgivings regarding Ashcroft and Meredith had been dispelled. *Mostly*, he inwardly clarified. On Meredith's behalf leastways. Ashcroft? No. Meredith was too attractive for Lucius to believe the man had no designs on her. Any man for that matter.

A guttural groan roared up his chest. Pangs of jealousy did not sit well. He swallowed them down and surveyed the cottage, noting the lack of personal effects, the order of the dishes in their place in the rack. No debris lying about. There was an efficiency and… disturbing *neatness* about the place. He shook his head. The man was a conundrum—

Blast. What the hell was he doing? Lucius shoved so quickly from the table, he nearly toppled with the sudden move that hit him with a bout of dizziness. Ashcroft had to have something around this hovel that gave an indication of his reasons for being in Cornwall. Quickly, steadying himself against the scarred table, he inhaled a shallow breath, letting the moment pass before taking up one of the candles and making his way through the cottage, hunting instincts sharpening his wits.

There was an office across the short hallway from the bed-chambers that showed promise.

The furniture was more formal but certainly outdated. A large wooden desk filled most of the space. Its surface was scratched but no dust covered the top. Loose papers were stacked on one corner. On the other corner were two oil lamps. Lucius raised his candle noting the soot marks on the ceiling. A massive bookshelf stood against one wall lined with old, leather-bound volumes.

He moved to the stack of papers. At first glance, nothing stood out: old lists of food stores for the Keep; wages and accounts for workers of the estate; receipts from local merchants that included the Penhalwick market and, of course, The Copper Kettle.

Lucius started to straighten the stack and put it back when something about the top paper he nearly covered jumped off the paper. Setting the one stack aside, he took up the sheet, frowning. A quick cursory glance showed what appeared to be the tin mine's shift schedule. *Recent.* He moved behind the desk and dropped into the chair. There were crossed out names and odd notations. He recognized none of the names but the hair on his neck lifted. Lucius reached across the desk for the rest of the papers, wincing at the pull in his shoulder.

The stack contained more pages that were frayed, folded, half-torn, and smudged with ink. Some looked to be unanswered notes from villagers. Written requests for repairs. For aid. And… *What the devil?* Urgent messages from Basil Thornfield.

Cold chills rippled Lucius's flesh as he took the next sheet and read.

7 Oct 1847

Mr. Ashcroft,

It has come to my attention that certain records from the mine have not been updated properly in your ledgers. I expect immediate correction of these oversights. The owners of the Penhalwick Mines demand precision in such matters, and any delays will not reflect kindly on you—or me.

Furthermore, your continued inquiries into operations that do not concern your position are ill-advised. The smooth running of Perlsea Keep relies upon each man knowing his place. If there is <u>any</u> misunderstanding about your place, let this serve as your only warning.

You are to ensure all correspondence related to the miners—most especially those tied to recent accidents—is forwarded directly to my office without delay. Any whispers, misplaced papers, or inquiries into prior incidents shall not be tolerated. I expect discretion, and I trust you do not need reminding of the consequences of failure.

Your duty, Mr. Ashcroft, is to keep your nose out of matters beyond your reach.

Yours,
B. Thornfield
Agent of the Mines

Lucius drew in a shaky breath. This very note indicated Ashcroft was indeed looking into Thornfield's misdeeds, shedding new light on Lucius's initial misgivings, leaving the question of why. What was in it for the steward? He searched his memory for answers, yet all he could come up with was that Ashcroft held some grudge against the duke. It also explained why current correspondence was on his desk at the cottage rather than the Keep.

Lucius laid the paper on the stack and drummed his fingers, thinking. Nothing made sense. He was missing something. Something critical, but what?

Everything in his mind felt muddled, impossible to pin down. After a moment when nothing jarred in his head, he went through the rest of the stack, noting other expenses and missives. He reassembled the pages and pushed them aside. Guilt never occurred to him. Not as the Earl of Pender. This was his estate, after all.

He went through the desk's drawers, finding nothing of import, yet his heart hammered against his ribs. His jaunt to London, now cut short, raised more questions. He pinched the bridge of his nose. Ignoring gentlemanly protocol no longer seemed wise. He rose from the chair and, skirting the desk, went to the last room left to search.

Ashcroft's bedchamber.

It was similar in sparsity and furnishings as the one in which

Lucius had awakened. This chamber contained a vanity where Ashcroft's shaving utensils were laid out with sharp precision. There was also a wardrobe. The narrow bed was made up with nary a crease as if Ashcroft had spent time in regimented service to the Crown. An interesting aspect to consider.

He went to the wardrobe and pulled back the door. On the floor were a spare pair of boots in perfect alignment with a pair of fur-lined house slippers. The boots were scuffed and well-worn. On a shelf over a set of pegs where trousers hung was an aged valise. He set his candle on the chest of drawers and reached for the bag. Again, he felt no compunction to conserving the man's privacy and carried it to the bed.

He pried it open.

More papers. His temples throbbed as hard as his shoulder. Likely as not, useless, yet he thumbed through them without regard…

Then stopped.

The lightheaded sensation that had assailed him before rushed forward with the force of an ocean wave in a fierce storm. He stumbled to sitting, dropping on the perfectly made bed and stared at the page he held, not quite believing what he was seeing. yet unable to tear away his gaze:

Betrothal Agreement between the Earl of Pender and the Duke of Rathbourne, 14 March 1828.

CHAPTER TWENTY

MEREDITH HURRIED DOWN the backstairs to Mr. Ashcroft's office. Gone. She spun around. "Oomph."

His hands landed on her upper arms. "Steady there, my lady." Immediately, his hands fell away and, stepping inside, he closed the door. The latch sounded loud and, after the morning she'd endured, ominous.

A frisson of fear trickled through her. "Oh, Mr. Ashcroft. You startled me. I-I was looking for you."

"I have grave news," he said. He pulled a pistol—*her* pistol—from his pocket and held it out to her, ivory grip first.

Slowly, she took the cumbersome pepperbox revolver, her insides quivering with sudden violence. She forced herself to wait to hear what he had to say. She hadn't long.

"Pender's been shot."

Black edged her vision, and she swayed. "No," she whispered.

"Where are your smelling salts?" he demanded, guiding her into the closest chair.

"No… salts," she gulped out. "How… when… who…" She couldn't seem to grapple her words into anything remotely intelligible.

"I heard the shot and found him face down in the muck. His horse remained nearby. That says a lot for a man."

She stared at him uncomprehending. "Is he…"

"He's alive," he said grimly. "The shot went clean through his shoulder. He'll live, the lucky bastard—er, pardons, my lady. He claims he didn't see anyone. But…"

Meredith blinked and looked down at the gun. It was covered with bits of mud and leaves. After a stunned moment, she pulled back the hammer to half-cocked, freeing the barrels to rotate. With a practiced twist, she gently spun the barrel cluster. The metallic sound of the rotation was soft. Then, one by one, she checked each chamber as there was no convenient loading gate like newer models.

In the fourth chamber she found a small percussion cap had fallen away. "One shot fired," she said, surprised at the steadiness of her words. She ran a fingertip over the opening at the muzzle of each barrel, feeling for residue and the absence of a ball, confirming the round spent. She lifted her eyes to his. "Did…" She swallowed. "Did you try to kill my husband?"

His lips tipped slightly. "As tempted as I might be with his arrogance, rest assured, I did not."

"Then, who?"

"It could be anyone," Mr. Ashcroft said. "The village has run rampant with tales of his confrontation with Thornfield regarding the Trenwith child's death. Usurping a man's authority before others would not go over well with someone of Thornfield's temperament. Especially one who is so accustomed to having those about him bend to his will without so much as comment or question. Your husband—and you, I might add—have done just that."

Meredith's gaze fell to the revolver again. And again, she pulled the hammer back from its half-cocked position, feeling the tension in the mechanism, then carefully guided the hammer forward, maintaining steady pressure with her thumb to prevent the weapon from firing just as she'd been taught. If done clumsily or too quickly, the hammer could snap forward and strike a loaded percussion cap, discharging it unexpectedly.

The soft click sounded, indicating the hammer had settled in place. She gave the barrel cluster one last spin to confirm everything had aligned.

"You'll need to be careful reloading that monster. It's too wet to work properly and could misfire," he told her.

Meredith rose on unsteady legs. "I remember."

"You were a good student," he said with a sharp nod.

"I'd like to see my husband as soon as possible."

"All right. I'll cart him home. I take it you would like to keep the duke from learning of these latest developments?"

"Most definitely." Slipping the gun within the thick folds of her heavy skirts, she slipped out and hurried up the servants' stairs to her bedchamber to hide her precious cargo, noting a sense of relief at being out of that stuffy office.

As much as she respected and appreciated Mr. Ashcroft's assistance over the past three years, she hated admitting that her husband's suspicions were playing havoc with her own instincts and sense of practicality.

LUCIUS TIPPED BACK the finger of whiskey he'd found in a cupboard under the chipped crockery in Ashcroft's kitchen. The blasted bottle likely belonged to Lucius anyway. He sat back with his booted feet atop a small table near the fire, though he was hot enough with the fury roaring through his veins. The door flew back with the vigor of a gusting wind and Ashcroft entered. "Ah, it's only you," he said.

Ashcroft stomped his feet on a woven rug just inside the door and glanced up. "So, you're alive."

Lucius held up his glass and wriggled it back and forth, brought it to his mouth, and took another slug.

Ashcroft's eyes held a wariness Lucius took great satisfaction in. "You sure it wasn't you who took the shot at me?"

"I'm sure."

He set aside the glass. Exhaustion hit him with the force of a hackney head on.

Lucius brought his booted feet to the wood planked floor with a heavy *thunk*.

"Are you drunk?"

"I am indeed." He stared at Ashcroft. Something vague tugged at him but the instance withered away before he could grasp it.

"Your wife is concerned for your welfare. I'm here to whisk you to safety."

Lucius rubbed his forehead. "Concerned, huh?" God knew it was more than he deserved. He came to his feet. "All right."

After Ashcroft stuffed him in a soft white shirt Lucius would never consent to being seen wearing in London, they were off.

The walk to the Keep was brutal. Ashcroft guided them through the trees to the cliffs where the wind blew in great bursts, nearly knocking him off his feet. If not for Ashcroft's quick reflexes, he likely would have been tossed over the cliff and out to sea.

"Why are we going this way?" Lucius shouted.

"It's a shortcut to the steward's office," Ashcroft shouted back.

They reached the door and Ashcroft leaned Lucius against the castle wall like a broom. "Wait here." He slipped inside but was back within an instant with Bartlett.

"Evenin', milord. I'll have you right as rain before you know it."

"I would appreciate you not mentioning rain."

Bartlett's teeth flashed in a quick grin as he went to Lucius's good side.

"God, I'm starved," he muttered.

"A good sign, I assure you." Ashcroft poked his head in the door again, then back out, nodding at Bartlett.

They entered the Keep and Lucius gripped the railing, pushing Bartlett aside then made his way slowly up the stairs with the footman right at his side.

"I'll wait in my office," Ashcroft said in a low voice at the first level.

Another one and a half levels up, and Lucius sweating profusely, he and Bartlett entered the family floor. Perspiration lined Lucius's forehead and left him feeling clammy. "Help me to my wife's chamber," he growled. Sheer determination and Bartlett's grip were the only things holding him up.

"Yes, my lord."

Outrage stole through Lucius's blood by the time the master chambers came into sight. Graham stood in Lucius's doorway. "My lord," he said softly, then glanced over his shoulder and back. "It's Lady Pender—"

"I'm on my way to see her now."

"She's here, my lord, in your chamber." Graham stepped aside so they could enter.

The chamber was hot and stuffy. "I need food."

Meredith hurried to him, clutching his black silk banyan to her chest. "I'll help his lordship," she told Graham. "Make certain no one knows Lord Pender has returned." She stopped and faced his valet directly. "Am I clear on this?"

"Yes, my lady." Graham disappeared, leaving Bartlett behind.

She turned back to Lucius and worked the button at the top of his shirt. "Assist Graham, Bartlett. Bring hot tea with lots of sugar. If anyone asks, inform them that Agnes is not feeling well and that I'm with her. Oh, and go to my chamber and let Agnes know her role in this fiasco."

With an incline of his head, Bartlett, too, disappeared.

"Oh, dear. I fear you may be feverish," she murmured.

The attention was… unexpected, and… nice.

"Mr. Ashcroft says you don't know who did this abhorrent act."

"No. The shot knocked me clean off my horse."

"I suspect it was that horrid Basil Thornfield."

"Just tear the shirt." He spoke sharply.

"Oh, yes. Of course."

"I have scissors in my sewing basket. I'll hurry." She dashed to the door and was gone.

But Lucius wasn't ready to let her out of his sight. For some unfathomable reason, he needed her and followed more slowly. He reached the arch of her sitting room door.

She spun around with the scissors in her hand. "Oh! You startled me."

"I'm standing right here, there's no need to run. You're likely to trip and stab yourself in the chest. Then where would we be?" He tried lightening his tone to teasing, but it still sounded much too harsh.

Meredith scowled in that adorable way she had. "That's a perfectly morbid thing to say. Come this way, near the light."

He did as she bade, stopping before her. He closed his eyes and drew in the fresh scent of violets. The scissors snipped, and the shirt loosened from his shoulders. His eyes snapped open to see her dainty fingers clasping the parted cut as she ripped it apart. The action sent an oddly erotic thrill rippling through him.

Her eyes widened. "Oh, goodness." Hot breath feathered his bare chest where the bandage didn't cover. She pulled soft lawn— *lawn?*—from his free arm. His other arm remained folded against his body.

"I fear your shirt is beyond repair." She set the scissors on the table next to the lamp.

Fire surged through his blood, keeping the words from penetrating his brain. Then they did. "The shirt belongs to your Mr. Ashcroft. How much are you paying the man?"

"The regular amount," she said frowning. "I sent a note to Mr. Oshea asking for the recommended wages. *He* actually responded to my missive," she chastised smartly.

"You sent me a letter?"

"I did. Only one. What are you holding?"

He'd almost forgotten. "A copy of our betrothal agreement."

Her head whipped up. "I thought you didn't make it to London."

"I didn't." His voice dipped, bound by the menace that gripped him. "I found it in Ashcroft's cottage."

"Surely they were left there by your father. In the care of the previous steward?"

"No," he said softly. "They were in Ashcroft's valise."

"His *valise*? You went through his *valise*?"

"You are missing the point, Meredith." He spoke through a clenched jaw. "Ashcroft. Had. A. Copy. Of our *Betrothal Agreement*."

"But why?"

Dear God. If he'd had use of both arms, he would shake her to within an inch of her life. Instead, he grabbed the papers and slammed them in her hand and pushed her into the chair at the table. "Read the section on Perlsea Keep. Number five, if you please," he bit out.

"All right." She pulled the oil lamp closer.

The ebony sky coming through the windows reflected the flickering light of the glass panes behind her, deepening the streaks in her hair that ranged from flaxen to wheat to soft chestnut.

"This says that should I predecease you, ownership of Perlsea shall revert back to the Pender estate, ensuring the property remains under Pender control."

"Read on."

She lowered her head and continued aloud. "Should Lucius Oshea predecease Meredith Jephson after the marriage is consummated—" Her face turned a becoming shade of pink. "—*Perlsea Keep* shall remain in her sole ownership, independent of the Pender estate..." She lifted her face. "Oh."

"Someone tried to kill me," he said. "If I die, *you* retain ownership of the Keep. And, in the event you've forgotten, our marriage was consummated. Granted, it was years late, but no one can deny the fact now. Especially, if you are with child."

"With child!"

"That is the usual method for bringing a child into the world."

He swooped the scissors from the table and strolled over to

her open sewing basket. Dropped them in where they landed with a clunk.

Metal on metal?

Frowning, Lucius glanced down and froze. The lightheaded sensation returned with a vengeance. He lowered to one knee for two reasons. One, fainting was unacceptable. Two, this find required an immediate explanation. He reached in and pulled out a pepperbox revolver. Flecks of dried mud dulled the barrel and ivory handle. He held it in an open palm, his insides quivering with fury, while black dots scudded his vision. "Would you care to explain this?" he rasped.

MEREDITH DREW IN a sharp breath. "It's my pistol," she said softly. "Do you think you ought to sit down? Your complexion is green. Or gray. I can't quite decide."

"Never mind my *complexion*," he bit out. "Why do *you* have a pistol, and why is it muddy?" His anger was palpable.

The shock of the moment passed. Bristling, she came to her feet and moved to his side. He needed to lie down, and not on the floor. She'd never be able to get him to a bed without help, which would require explanation. "Don't take that condescending tone with me, my lord." She gently removed the gun from his hand and set it on the floor then guided him to his feet with difficulty.

"What sort of tone should I take, pray tell? Do you even know how to use that thing?" His tone was near breathless, and she worried over his ability in making the short trek to the bed.

"I do indeed. Mr. Ashcroft gave it to me three years ago after a confrontation with Basil Thornfield. He taught me how to use it to protect myself." That statement quieted him momentarily. As it should have. She'd been terrified at the time. They reached the bed, and he nearly collapsed. She stood back, studying him intently.

His brows furrowed appearing so sinister in the low light, it sent shivers up her spine.

"Stop it. Stop looking at me as if I planned to smother you with a pillow." Meredith frowned. "I believe it was used to shoot you."

A slow hiss escaped through his pursed lips. "So, you don't deny it?"

"Deny what?" Exasperation hit her with a vengeance. "That you were shot with my gun? Of course I don't deny it. What I want to know is who took it and tried to kill you."

"Where did you find it?"

"Mr. Ashcroft found it in the mud close to where you had fallen from your horse."

"Ashcroft seems to be everywhere all at once," he remarked, his irritation flooding the atmosphere. His pallor appeared almost chalky.

"Thank heavens for that, leastways," she muttered. "Lie back, sir, before you lose consciousness." A second later the outrage hit her. "You can't possibly believe that Mr. Ashcroft or I attempted to murder you. Next you'll be accusing us of conspiring to do you in."

"Need I remind you that if I predecease you, *you* retain Perlsea Keep?"

"Have you looked about lately?" she snapped. "Perlsea Keep is hardly a jewel. Besides, I—"

Lucius fell onto his back, rubbing his forehead with the heel of his hand. "That's true, but you are forgetting something even more lucrative."

She strolled back to the table and looked at the document. "The mine."

"Yes. Upon our nuptials, your father was awarded thirty percent ownership of the mineral rights with profits split in accordance with his shares."

"That doesn't sound like all that much, considering his current wealth," she pointed out.

He tried spearing her with a look she was certain was designed to quell, as if she were some uneducated nitwit. It fell short. "Do you know the status of his current wealth?"

"Of course not." A man like her father would never consider his *daughter*, or any woman, privilege of such information.

"Men have lost entire fortunes in the space of a night spent at a gaming hell." His irritation was vastly amusing.

She snorted. "*My* father? Why he's as tight fisted as a spinster with her dowry."

"Or a widow," he retorted, falling back and folding his arm over his eyes.

"A widow…"

"A widow. If I die, all rights—one hundred percent—revert to you. He will no longer receive his thirty percent. Which, incidentally, could be a substantial amount. We don't know because we have no idea of the mine's actual output—ore and monetary. Do you think Rathbourne prone to letting *you* run things? And, if there's no child, who do you suppose steps in to assist you, the grieving countess?"

"Grieving?" she said with a bite to her tone. After a moment, her shoulders fell. "You think my father tried to kill you."

"No, as I was politely but firmly informed earlier, those are the sort of pesky tasks a man in a duke's position doles out."

Meredith fell into a chair at the table. "Dear heavens. I hate admitting it, but you could be right."

"Ashcroft has a history with the duke. We need to learn the nature of that history."

Stubborn resolve goaded her. "I refuse to concede that Mr. Ashcroft stole my gun."

"Someone… did." His voice grew concerningly more breathless with each uttered word. "And… Ashcroft… works at… the Keep. How… the devil… can you… be… so blind?"

"Yes. Someone did," she repeated softly, rising from the table and hurrying to him. She poured out a small glass of water. "Drink this." She needed to think.

Meredith believed Mr. Ashcroft when he said he hadn't tried to kill Lucius. But there was also no discounting the tremor of fear she'd felt when he'd shut his office door, trapping her inside. *Trapping her.* Still, she shook off the notion. She couldn't fathom it. She just couldn't. He'd been too instrumental in assisting her since coming to Penhalwick.

The school.

The Keep.

His help with her Literary Society.

In teaching her how to defend herself against the likes of Basil Thornfield.

Meredith lifted her gaze to find Lucius staring at her through the lamp's soft light. The intimacy of the situation struck her in the chest. She wanted to dive into his arms—*arm*—but that wasn't possible for several reasons, the first being she might hurt him further. Setting the glass on the bedside table, she leaned in to help him sit then took the glass and set it to his lips. She cleared her throat. "What of Mr. Thornfield?"

"Do you really believe Thornfield snuck into your bedchamber to pilfer your revolver? For one, he'd have to know where to look."

Letting out a frustrated sigh, she set the glass back on the table and stared at it. He hadn't even taken a sip. She shook her head. "There must be some explanation. I don't see Papa doing so either."

"On that we're agreed. Which brings us back to Ashcroft. We need to learn more of his background. There's something familiar about him I can't put my finger on. Could I have that water?"

Heat infused her cheeks. How could she be so disconcerted. "Of course."

A tap sounded at the door.

"Enter," Lucius said.

Meredith shot him a stern, exasperated glare. "This is *my* chamber, sir. Not yours. In point of fact—" She angled her head to the paper on the tabletop. "According to that, *you* are trespassing on *my* property."

A wolfish grin curved his firm lips despite his eyes drooping and him clearly straining to remain upright. "Only if I'm dead."

She opened her mouth to blast him, but Graham's face peered around the door. "Your food awaits, my lord."

"Bring it in here," Meredith said before her husband could. She was still mistress of this Keep.

CHAPTER TWENTY-ONE

MEREDITH WENT TO the door and pulled it back. "Come in, Graham. I believe the earl requires your assistance in, er, in being made more comfortable." She flung a hand indicating his boots.

Graham moved in the direction of the table and Meredith hurried over to take up the betrothal agreement that was spread out for all and sundry to see. Quickly, she gathered up the documents and took them to the escritoire and set them atop with a quick glance to her husband.

He watched her with a small tip of his lips. She suspected he wanted to roll his eyes but was too exhausted or weak to do so.

"I'll just retrieve a wrap for him," she told Graham.

He offered her a respectful bow. She quite liked him. "Thank you, my lady."

Meredith stole back through the bathing chamber, through her sitting room, and into Pender's chamber. The space was a stark reflection of neglect and disuse. She'd quashed her guilt before, but it hit her now in full force, seeing the lack of warmth and vitality. Especially in light of her goals toward that of a well-tended estate.

The heavy four-poster bed dominated the space and was draped with faded damask curtains that were once richly colored but now hung limp with age and dust. The mattress and linens were serviceable but clearly not of the quality befitting an earl, hastily arranged after years of disuse.

The chamber was lit by the fire, casting long shadows across the walls, which were adorned with outdated tapestries and a large, once-ornate mirror that had long-ago tarnished along its edges. She made her way across the cold floor partially covered by an antique rug that had grown threadbare in places to a massive wardrobe carved with intricate but worn designs. She pulled the door back, its hinges creaking ominously.

The air carried a faint mustiness, and she wrinkled her nose. She was a horrid person, forcing him to stay in such abhorrent conditions. She reached inside and drew out his black silk banyan and pushed it shut. She strolled back to the adjourning door and stopped, catching sight of a familiar pamphlet, *Women and the Need for Economic Equality: A Plan for England's Future*, and picked it up. The sight of it startled a laugh out of her. "Ah, well, sir. I hope you were suitably enlightened," she whispered.

Beneath that was Aylesbury's journal. She started to set the pamphlet back down only to see another set of tri-folded papers. She laid the pamphlet aside and, hesitating only briefly—long enough to justify how he'd found her pamphlet as he had to have gone through her escritoire to find it, hadn't he? "Yes. Why, yes he had," she murmured. She swooped up the folded papers and moved to the fire and unfolded them.

> *To the Most Reverend Official of the Ecclesiastical Court,*
>
> *I, Lucius Oshea, Earl of Pender, write to formally seek counsel regarding the annulment of my marriage to Lady Meredith Jephson, daughter of His Grace, the Duke of Rathbourne.*

Meredith's heart stopped, her breath constricted. Difficult with her vision blurring so. She yanked a handkerchief from her pocket, wiped her eyes and blew her nose and forced herself to read on.

> *This union, entered with solemn intent, has not fulfilled the conditions necessary for its continuance. Chief among these is the absence of consummation, which renders the marriage, by*

the laws of our Church and state, invalid in practice if not in form. Additionally, circumstances of misunderstanding and mistrust have arisen, leading me to question the foundation of our union.

In keeping with propriety and the dictates of conscience, I have enclosed herewith a preliminary draft of the petition for annulment. It is my understanding that Lady Meredith must also affix her acknowledgment to this petition, thereby consenting to the dissolution of our bond and facilitating the proceedings.

The further she read, the hotter her blood roiled. And, yes, there was a little line for her signature to *serve as confirmation of her agreement* to pursue *this course with dignity and discretion.* The blank signature line below her name reeled through her as if her gun had fired haphazardly and she hadn't time to set her stance.

"It is my sincere hope that this matter be resolved without undue delay or hardship," she read aloud, bitterness pulsing through her. "I await your guidance on the next steps." How *dare* he! "I remain, Your humble servant, Lucius Oshea, Earl of Pender."

Disbelief curdled her stomach. Her knees gave way as shock, betrayal, and self-loathing congealed her blood and her bum hit the horribly uncomfortable settee. That cur! He could stay in this hovel for the rest of his days for all she cared.

More tears blinded her. She swallowed the rising lump in her throat and forced herself to read the document through a second time, all her thoughts clashing. How could he draft such a letter *after* they'd been together? Was she nothing but an obligation to him, even now? Hands trembling, she gripped the arm rest for support, her chest tightening.

Well, he wasn't worth her tears. Her fury fed into humiliation. How could she have been so… so *foolish* for believing they'd turned a corner.

She came to her feet, strode to the bed, and snatched his banyan off the floor where it had fallen. Then stormed her way back to her chamber fully prepared to demand answers.

"Ah, you've returned, my lady," Graham said. "His lordship is sleeping. Would you, er, should I…"

His face turned scarlet.

"I'll stay with his lordship. If there is a need, I shall summon you." *Like murdering him in his sleep.* Meredith closed her eyes against the hurt and fury thrumming through her.

Graham nodded and slipped out, without even taking Lucius's silk wrap from her.

And she still clutched the damning draft.

Meredith's gaze went to Lucius. The coverlet was pulled to his chest though his shoulders were exposed.

After all the recent events, it was difficult to imagine him wanting to go down a path of ruin, destruction, not to mention public humiliation. She drew in a deep breath. The air flowed through her veins and the rage inside gave way to reason. She glanced down at the document again. There was no indication of who'd assisted him in drafting it.

Realization dawned as her thoughts swirled and settled into common sense. He'd told her the moment he'd arrived his intentions of petitioning for an annulment. At the time, they hadn't even consummated their marriage. That had since changed. Not since he'd learned she hadn't disavowed him.

With another deep breath, she moved to the bedside and looked at him. Really looked.

His slumber was restless, his face pale and shadowed, making the sharp contours of his cheekbones and jawline more pronounced against his ashen complexion.

Something inside Meredith cracked. A faint sheen of sweat glistened on his forehead. His dark lashes rested against his cheeks, giving an illusion of peace that belied the tension visible in the furrow of his brows and the faint tremor of his lips.

Thankfully, the bandage over his shoulder showed no discoloration.

His breathing was shallow but steady. She watched the faint

rise and fall of his chest.

Meredith moved to the table by the window where the other documents were and laid the agreement on top of the small stack and stared out at the night. Except it wasn't the night she saw. It was her own reflection. She rubbed her arms and looked about her comfortable chamber with a new sense of resolve.

Three years of running things at the Keep to her own specifications had allotted her an independence she didn't relish relinquishing. From hiring Mr. Ashcroft to seeing to other servants, and even to the restoration process.

Perhaps it was time to own up to her duty to her marriage. It had since been consummated. She looked down at the tri-folded agreement. Signing a document that stated she'd been unfaithful was ludicrous. Lucius's only other recourse would be to admit to impotence. The thought touched her with a sense of hysteria—he wasn't, and she couldn't see him submitting to such a farcical claim.

He stirred drawing her attention back to him. He'd kicked the coverlets sending them askew.

Meredith hurried over and tugged them back in place, but he remained restless. She set her hand on his forehead—burning up. "Shush," she soothed.

His hand shot out, claiming her wrist. She met his unfocused eyes. "Don't," he croaked out. "Don't leave me."

Again, she was blinded by a sudden welling. "It's all right, darling. I-I won't. You aren't alone."

It took a moment, but he calmed and his slumber grew more restful. His hand relaxed but she found she couldn't convince herself to move. Eventually, she crawled up on the bed, clothes and all to stretch out beside him—just in case he woke—and let sleep take her too.

THAT CARRIAGE THAT Lucius felt had run over him the day before seemed to have made a return trip to finish the task of grinding him into pulp. Not the pulp of wood, but one of lavender or violets. Soothing, clean, herbaceous fragrance filled with a sweetness that should have refreshed and calmed. The images of sun-drenched fields and gentle breezes assailed his nostrils even as rain pelted the windows.

He had no desire to open his eyes, wanting to drown in the unfamiliar sensation of... hope... filling him from the inside out. Yes, his body felt like a week-old corpse but a corpse didn't experience warmth along one's side. Did it? He turned the only part of his body that didn't ache to the source of heat and that invigorating aroma, soaked in its tranquility.

Soft hair tickled his nose. He sneezed, a mechanism that jarred his wrapped shoulder and had him gasping. His other arm was trapped beneath the source and started to tingle. He forced his eyes open.

Meredith's head lay on his good shoulder. Dark lashes veiled her closed eyes in a peaceful sleep. His sneeze hadn't even disturbed her. He closed his eyes again and laid his lips against the petal-soft skin of her forehead. Breathed her into his soul.

This.

Her.

It—*she*—felt... right.

Seconds later, she stirred. Her head fell back and sleepy moss-green eyes lifted, meeting his. "Oh." There was something a little distant about her as her gaze gained focus. She scrambled back nearly smacking his nose with her head. "I thought only to close my eyes for a minute." The husky tone her voice took on stiffened his morning erection to painful intensity. She moved off his arm, sitting up in the massive bed and shoving her disheveled hair from her face. The tingling in his arm intensified as the blood rushed in. Alas, it took his mind off the other aching parts of him...

He flexed his fingers. "Yet, it's morning," he groused with a wry turn of his lips.

Her legs fell over the side of the bed, but he snatched her hand before she could move out of his reach.

"What is it?"

She didn't meet his eyes. "Nothing." Her back straightened with the deep breath she took in then she turned to him with an overbright smile. "Tea? I think we could do with some tea."

He didn't buy it for a moment and tugged her back to him. She landed with a *thunk* against his side, her face near his. Better than that, her lips within reaching distance. "You are truly the most stubborn woman I've ever encountered."

"Entirely a product of your own making, my lord," she said on a breathless huff. "For three years, I've had naught but my own assurances to see me through. Of course, I did have Mr. Ashcroft's assistance."

"I've heard just about enough of Ashcroft's exemplary virtues."

Mischief sparkled in her eyes. "Oh?" she challenged.

"You minx," he growled, taking her mouth, leaving nothing behind.

She froze but he didn't relent. He brushed her lips with his, until the battle catapulted in his favor—as he knew it would—and he slid into the velvet confines of her mouth and her tongue danced with his.

This old Keep, his young bride, the low lighting of the early morn, the storm outside raging, all components weaving him into a spell nothing short of black magic.

Good ol' Cornwall. He stroked; she reciprocated. She suckled; he returned the favor. Her fingers tangled in the hair at his nape. His erection grew tighter, harder.

Lucius licked her lips and dove back inside for more, his good arm tightening her to his torso. There was no pain in his shoulder. Or if there was, it was muted by the pleasure of having her close.

She drew back. "All right, I promise not to extoll another

single noble trait of Mr. Ashcroft's sterling character."

"Is that so?"

"I solemnly vow."

A single noble trait… The words struck Lucius with the tines of a sharply pointed fork.

"Lucius?"

He blinked, bringing him back as quickly as his mind had departed. The concern in her eyes clawed at his heart. "I'm good." His voice came out a low gravel he barely recognized.

She moved carefully. "Shouldn't we rise?"

He raked a gaze over her then at the tented coverlet. "I find I require a bit more time in bed."

"Is that so?" she whispered.

It was the loveliest sound in the world. "I'll let you rest."

"I don't need rest, love. Just you." God, for the use of both arms. He shifted slightly, watching her, knowing his gaze lingered too long, but he couldn't tear his eyes away from her upturned face.

She bit her lip.

He groaned and pulled her back in for more. The softness of her lips, her upper arm, the subtle fragrance of lavender—mingling with the violet she usually wore. If ever there was a moment he could consider heavenly for the least heavenly person ever, this was it. "Meredith," he whispered. He leaned away and looked into eyes filled with a sense of guarded… dare he say—hope?

The fire in the grate was too low to disguise the high points of color in her cheeks. And it certainly failed hiding the erection still swelling beneath the coverlet.

Her fingers grazed his waist where the edge of the linen bedsheet had slid and flattened against the blazing heat of his flesh. He clenched his jaw. Hot breath against his cheek ignited his groin and he couldn't hold back a hiss.

Her head snapped back, her eyes wide, dark and unfathomable, within the confines of an intimacy he couldn't remember ever experiencing. She licked her lips and lowered her gaze to his straining arousal.

In a brazen move that left him speechless, she lifted the cover away. "I, um, don't suppose I could touch it…" The husky tonality prickled his flesh.

Truly? "At will," he gritted out.

Again, she licked her lips, and he could almost feel them on the inferno of his skin. With the tip of one finger, she traced the length of him, back and forth until he thought he would go mad, but he allowed her to play. He could endure anything but her turning away at this moment.

"How do you live with this thing in your breeches? Or ride a horse? It seems quite impractical," she said softly.

"Admittedly, it can be most inconvenient," he growled. "But you are in the unique position to do something about it."

"Me?" Her low tone almost undid him.

"Yes," he croaked out.

Her eyes took on that mischievous glint he was beginning to recognize. One she was mastering with diabolical precision and designed—in his estimation—to cause him much suffering. That traveling finger found its way to the tender skin at the base of his staff and he quivered beneath the touch.

But he had his own brand of daring and couldn't resist seeing if she was up for the challenge. "Your breath is so hot, I'm likely to melt beneath any touch."

She froze. Then her head tilted. "Touch?" The wisp of breath went straight to his blood.

"Touch," he confirmed in a whisper.

"You mean like this?" Her tongue lashed against his length. Molten lava. This was how Pompeii had disintegrated under the blast of Mt. Vesuvius. He knew because he'd toured the ruins.

A low moan escaped him.

"You appear to be holding up," she said.

"Do I?" He pushed his fingers through her hair, sending pins flying, then cupped her head with his palm. The effort to keep from pulling her face into his groin had sweat popping out along the hairline. "Meredith."

Her lips touched the tip of his cock and his head fell back against the pillow.

Lucius laid his good arm over his eyes and listened to the clothes she'd slept in rustling. He pictured her throwing one leg over his hips and riding him into oblivion.

The mattress shifted and her finger traced his bottom lip.

"If this is all it takes to kill you…" she said softly. The melodic tone of her voice was velvet on his skin. Her fingers delivered their feathered touch along his jawline and down the column of his neck. She traced the edge of his bandage. "Are you in pain? It's obvious any extraneous activity is beyond your capability."

Lucius removed his arm, wrapping it around her waist and pulling her on top of him. "You really think so?"

"Mr. Ashcroft had to stitch you up, sir. It would be beyond bad etiquette to undo his handiwork."

"Take off your clothes and I'll show you just how *polite* we can be to your Mr. Ashcroft."

"Lucius—"

"More so when you say my name so breathlessly and tenderly like that."

Her lips formed a moue, but curiosity sparkled in her eyes. Slowly, she moved from the bed to stand beside it. To his shock and delight—watching her through a slitted gaze—she worked the buttons from the modest scooped neck of that horrid wool dress.

"What the devil are you wearing, anyway?"

Her eyes flashed. "Don't you start. I've already been chastised for not donning the latest Paris fashions from my father. I'll not hear it from you as well."

"By all means," he said quickly, through a muffled laugh. "As long as you continue on your current path, my lips are sealed."

"Yet I still hear you talking."

He didn't bother responding, just gave a small smile, awaiting the rest of the show of which she might generously grace him.

The wool frock loosened, hiding her luscious shape as she worked the buttons free, then parted, exposing an older style corset. An abomination of which he'd never seen. It was grayish in color, and the only frills it sported was a tiny black bow near the crevice of her breasts. He swallowed hard.

Two petticoats fell away next. She shimmied out of the mounds of fabric. Then, with an exaggerated flourish, she released the ribbon of her corset. Dear God, though impossible to fathom, he grew even harder.

"Do you require assistance?" he growled.

She smiled. It resembled a knowing feline who'd lapped up all the cream. "I do not." The corset fell away, leaving her sheer chemise teasing him with the shadow of dusty nipples.

"You are killing me," he said. "Come here."

"But my stockings…"

"Leave them. I can't wait. Not any longer."

She crawled on the bed.

"Straddle me."

She threw one leg over his hips. "Like this?"

"Exactly like this," he murmured. He set his palm on the top of her thigh. The ties of her garters tickled his legs. "Pull off your chemise."

Her eyes narrowed on him. "Are you certain this is wise?"

"Oh, yes." The guttural sound rumbled up his chest.

She clutched the soft material between her fingers and slowly tugged it over her head.

Small, rounded breasts beckoned for his taste. His mouth watered.

"Lean forward," he whispered. "I can't reach you from here."

Blood pummeled his body that had several places on his person painfully throbbing. She set her hands on the bed, one at each side of his head, bringing one luscious orb within suckling distance. He grasped her nipple with his mouth and smoothed his good hand down her backside to her buttock and squeezed.

The fleshy part of her sex pulsed against his cock. His lips plopped from her breast. "Lift up."

She did, leaving a sheen of dampness on his skin. He adjusted himself to the heart of what he craved most. Her body, a magnet to his, knew its purpose, drawing him inside her snug passage.

"Kiss me," she whispered, dropping her mouth to his.

Fool that he wasn't—he didn't need to be told twice—he swept his tongue into the heat of her mouth. His hand flattened on the silky skin of her lower back and down. He pressed his hand against her and, following his silent guidance, she ground herself against him. Dear God, he wouldn't survive the precious torture.

"Harder," he murmured.

She licked his lips while grinding herself against him, panting in his ear.

"Yes," he growled. "Yes, darling. Harder." If only he could flip her to her back. But it was too late. The pressure hit the point of no return and he roared, surely rendering her deaf.

Her own scream plowed through him as she pulsated against him. He lifted his hips for a last grind and felt the tear in his shoulder. *Damn it.*

She froze. "What happened?" The breathless rush hit his cheek.

Lucius gritted his teeth, hating to tell her, knowing he had no choice.

She pushed against the mattress, straightening her elbows. "Oh, no. There's blood." She moved off him, his still-hard cock plopping against his abdomen. "There's blood seeping through your bandage. If you weren't hurt, I'd... I'd..."

"Kiss me again?"

She snorted yet her face expressed her mortification. "I can't believe you are so careless. I must send for the doctor."

"What? And have your father realize I'm not dead? Absolutely not." He worked himself to sitting, wincing as he dropped his legs over the edge of the bed.

"The apothecary then. Mrs. Lovelace won't say anything."

Meredith came to her feet and dashed across the chamber. She turned a knob he hadn't noticed and an overhead chandelier lit the room, showcasing just how industrialized and inventive his wife truly was. "Let me see it."

"That's all I need. For you to faint dead away."

"I'm not the fainting sort," she said in a breathless huff.

An image of her in the mud with the Trenwith child speared him, backing that fact. "All right."

She snatched up a wrap and tucked those lovely breasts from sight, then moved between his knees. Once more he was inundated with the breath of spring while the storm outside raged, mirroring the turmoil swirling within him. With dainty fingers, she unwrapped the bandages and drew in a sharp gasp.

"What?"

"It's red. Inflamed. There's blood too. And bruising."

Her breath tickled his skin. Frankly, he couldn't feel a thing. Not with the crevice of her breasts still enticing him.

"The stitch is definitely torn." She moved back then pierced him with stern but concerned eyes. "I fear that if left alone, infection could set in."

"Fine. If you must send for someone, send for Ashcroft. He's proved capable enough thus far." He closed his eyes and pinched the bridge of his nose. "But put some blasted clothes on."

FACE WARM, IF not outright flaming, Meredith scooped their clothes off the floor and dumped them on the settee with the exception of her own frock. She glanced down. She still wore her stockings and it took a moment to locate her missing chemise. She found it on the cushioned bench at the foot of the bed, then pulled it over her head. Her corset and stays were on the floor near where Lucius sat on the edge of the bed. Right where she'd dropped them like the wanton she apparently was.

Did she regret it?

Not if her still humming body was any indication.

The low fire in the grate, hopefully, kept him from seeing just how red her face was. Avoiding his eyes, she slipped into her corset and quickly laced it up. Stays next. She stalked to the settee, snatched up her dress, and drew it over her head.

Once she was certain she had herself under control, she went to the fire and stoked it, though it clearly needed more fuel. She glanced at her husband to find him watching her with a bemused half-smile, clutching the bandages in one hand.

Her insides melted. "Does it hurt?" she asked softly.

"Does what hurt?"

"Your shoulder. What else?"

His lip kicked up a notch, filled with innuendo.

Her face definitely flamed. She went to the door.

Lucius stood from the bed, and she was outraged.

"What do you think you're doing?"

"I can't very well cover myself up, sitting on the counter-pane."

Her eyes, of course, went straight for his… his nether regions. *Mercy.* "Oh. Of course." She found his silk banyan at the foot of the bed and held it out. "I brought this for you last night. Mr. Ashcroft likely hasn't arrived yet this morning. I'll leave a note for him. And request breakfast… Are you hungry?" she asked as an afterthought.

"Starved."

With a quick nod, she slipped from her chamber and ran for the main staircase without thinking.

"What the devil is going on around here?" Papa bellowed from the bottom of the stairs. "Where were you last night? I should not have to dine alone."

"Time escaped me, Papa. My maid provided me a tray."

"Well, I wish to speak with you." He strode to the library, then turned back. "Immediately."

Blast it. What was she to do now? And, what the devil was he doing up and about so early?

Bartlett peered around the edge of the staircase. "Coming, Papa." She inclined her eyes to the floor above, hoping he could read minds. He gave her a minute nod and disappeared again with Papa none the wiser.

Meredith entered the library. Her father paced before the fire with his hands clasped at his lower back, and based on history, she prepared herself for a long lecture.

He speared her with an aggravated look. "There are some disturbing revelations regarding your behavior."

She pulled up stunned. His audacity sent a surge of raw fury through her. "My behavior?"

"You are rarely home. You are often spotted at The Copper Kettle and cavorting with the villagers much too often."

"I live *here*, Papa. And, it's hardly mattered in the past three years with whom I've associated," she ground out through a clenched jaw edged with an impatience of her own.

"I also understand that steward you've engaged is a total incompetent."

"My husband has made Mr. Ashcroft's acquaintance. He is still earl in these parts and has approved my choice." She crossed her fingers at her lower back for that little stretch of truth. "Again, not your concern." A sudden thought flashed through her and she frowned. "I take it Mr. Thornfield is the source of your information?"

"As a matter of fact, he is. I approved the steward he originally recommended. Apparently, you turned your nose up to his suggestion."

"First of all, Mr. Thornfield has no notion of Mr. Ashcroft's competence. Secondly, Mr. Thornfield's recommendation was unavailable and Mr. Ashcroft was."

"Thornfield told me he offered to assist you until Underhill made it to Cornwall."

"And, *I* made the decision to turn down his offer."

"Well, now that I'm here, we can send for Underhill." He

spoke as if his word settled the matter.

"That's very generous of you, Papa, but I'm perfectly satisfied with Mr. Ashcroft. I have no intention of retaining this Underhill."

"I have a reputation to maintain, young lady. Meddling in village matters does not look good. Your position requires dignity. You have a duty to me—er, the earl."

His displeasure had her grinding her teeth. How was one supposed to respond to such blatant... manipulation. He *was* trying to manipulate her. There was also an undercurrent of something else. Fear of losing control. Yes. Her father was obsessive when it came to loyalty.

"Secure an introduction with your Mr. Ashcroft. I wish to make his acquaintance."

"What!" His arrogance floored her. Meredith snapped her fallen jaw shut and breathed in through her nose, striving to remain calm. Yet, defying him outright was dangerous. "It occurs to me you have lost track of your own entailments, Papa," she said mildly. "Perlsea belongs to Pender not Rathbourne."

The surprise on his face shifted to mottled fury. "You forget to whom you are speaking, my daughter." A sudden blast of ice rent the air. She glanced around, surprised the room hadn't been encased in a sudden freeze, complete with icicles and snow-covered tundra, due to his voice alone.

An image of his hand squeezing her throat had her splaying a hand on her sternum. Fear, a ripple of glacial waves, pebbled her skin. But there was no turning back. From the corner of her eye, she attempted to assess the library for a weapon of some sort. *He blocked the fireplace poker.*

Wits. She had wits. A small thread dangled before her, she tugged. "Ah, are you... are you threatened by my independence, Papa?" she asked with a small smile she prayed conveyed a confidence that was as flimsy as an ocean wave.

His lips tightened and he started in her direction.

A fissure of panic fluttered in her stomach.

The door opened and help entered in the form of Mrs. Verity rolling in a cart with the tea service.

"Mornin', Yer Grace. Milady." Her hawklike gaze flickered between Meredith and her father. "Beggin' yer pardon, milady, there's been an accident. It's Agnes."

Meredith's head whipped around. "Heavens."

"Who's Agnes?" the duke demanded.

"My maid. Enjoy your tea, Papa. I must see to her." She strode to the door.

"Now, just one damned minute," he thundered.

"Later, Papa. And do not bother engaging your Mr. Underhill. It will be all for naught." She stole from the library into the large entry hall and, for the first time since she'd been accosted by the duke, pulled in a breath. She inhaled deeply and speared Mrs. Verity with a sharp look. "What happened? Where is she?"

Mrs. Verity glanced over her shoulder where she'd closed the door behind her own exit. "She's fine. I feared fer yer safety. The steward's made his way to the master suites."

Meredith let out her breath. "That was quite risky of you, Mrs. Verity. If my father gets wind—"

"Bah. He don't scare me none. Ye best see wot that Mr. Ashcroft is up to, milady."

"Oh, right." Meredith ran for the stairs. She also glanced at the library door then to Mrs. Verity. "Thank you," she said softly. But the housekeeper was already bustling away.

CHAPTER TWENTY-TWO

THE STING OF alcohol burned sharply, and Lucius sucked in a harsh breath. Ashcroft's spectacles reflected the light, and his hand was surprisingly steady as he applied his large, curved needle to Lucius's still tender skin. He held back grunts of pain, unable to regret the reasons behind this little setback.

"Your wife's chamber is quite comfortable," he said, his fingers working deftly. "I suppose you wouldn't care to expound on how you've managed to undo some of my best crafted needlework?"

"I would not," Lucius said through gritted teeth.

The lighting of Meredith's chamber highlighted Ashcroft's smirk. Especially, looming over Lucius so closely as he worked. "Where is Lady Pender?"

"Bartlett said Rathbourne demanded her presence."

"She shouldn't be alone with him," Ashcroft said softly, never lifting his eyes.

Fear curdled low in his gut. "Explain. What do you know of the duke?"

"Plenty," he bit out. "Don't *ever* underestimate him."

The warning made Lucius's shoulder throb. "Like what?" The needle jabbed sharply and Lucius winced.

"A short temper, for one."

"I need to get down there," he said, coming to his feet. "We can finish this later."

"Calm yourself. I informed Bartlett to send Mrs. Verity in

with tea and an excuse to extract her."

Lucius slowly lowered himself back to the bed. He grasped for a subject to suppress the worry. "What were the marks on the drawing you made of the estate I found on your desk?"

Again, Ashcroft's needle jerked.

Lucius bit out an oath. "Watch it, man. I'm not allowed to kill you."

"Hmm."

"Yet," Lucius clarified.

"Apologies," Ashcroft's hand steadied and he continued with his task. It was a couple of minutes before he answered. "I believe it's possible those missing stewards on that list are buried on the estate."

"You think they were murdered?" The pain in his shoulder faded with Ashcroft's stunning declaration.

"Yes." He straightened and dug through his tin box for the salve, his face averted from Lucius's.

Lucius's pulse took an erratic leap. "And you believe the duke is responsible," he stated in a low voice.

Tension bracketed Ashcroft's mouth. "I do." He spread the medicine on the wound, then picked up the bandages.

"But?"

Ashcroft straightened, removing his spectacles and eyeing Lucius with an inscrutable gaze.

Lucius let out a frustrated sigh. "Look. I have my doubts about you, to be sure. But, I rather suspect we find ourselves aligned in our interests here."

Without a word, Ashcroft returned to the methodical task of re-bandaging Lucius's shoulder.

The door opened and a breathless Meredith entered. "Heavens." She spoke in a gasped rush.

The steward lifted his eyes to her where the gas lighting illuminated his face, the softening of his expression. The sight sent a jolt of harsh green envy pounding Lucius's blood. Something else too.

The green shifted to a haze of red and Lucius's fists clenched at his sides. With unerring patience, he waited for his vision to clear and the ebb of fury to subside.

Ashcroft completed the bandaging and took a step back to eye his handiwork. Again, he speared Lucius with a considering look. "You should be more careful," he murmured. His insolence was galling.

The pain in his shoulder pulsed with nagging intensity. Sometimes such pain was welcome, and it was now. He quickly reminded himself that letting his guard down, even if Ashcroft had proven himself capable in his wife's eyes, was not an absolution. There were far too many questions surrounding the man.

Meredith's pink cheeks heightened. She aimed a pointed look at Lucius. "He'll be careful," she promised.

Lucius bristled, his gaze boring through Ashcroft. In that brief span, he was hit with a blinding light of recognition. "You were one of the reporters outside St. George's at our wedding," Lucius accused him. "By God, it was you who purchased an illustration of us from that caricaturist."

Meredith's brows furrowed. "What?" She turned a condemning spear on her pet steward.

Ashcroft's body stilled, his face hewed into carved marble.

"Is this true, Mr. Ashcroft?" she demanded softly.

His mouth firmed.

She stormed to Lucius's side and, to his astonishment, she shoved Ashcroft's six foot plus frame aside, turned and placed herself in front of Lucius as if to *protect him.* "Meredith..." he started.

It was as if she hadn't heard and poked Ashcroft in the chest. "You tried to kill my husband! You *knew* I had a gun—you *gave* it to me. Showed me how to use it."

Lucius, despite the pain, leaned forward and grabbed her with his good hand. He was now convinced it hadn't been Ashcroft who'd made the attempt on his life. "What do you have against

Rathbourne?" he directed at Ashcroft.

That stopped his wife from struggling to free herself.

"He murdered my mother," he said, his voice low and guttural. He speared Meredith with a gaze glittering with shards of emeralds. "I suspect he murdered yours as well."

The words echoed against the newly plastered ceiling.

Meredith paled and her hand splayed the throat of her unbecoming frock. "Murdered," she whispered. "But... but..."

Lucius came to his feet and guided her to a chair at the table near the window. Taking her by one shoulder, he turned her to him and pushed her gently into a pulled-out chair. A tri-folded document atop some other papers brought him to an abrupt halt. His gaze flew to her accusing one.

Well, that explained her distance when she'd woken.

"I..."

Her mouth tightened, and he realized there was nothing he could say in this moment to excuse himself. Especially with Ashcroft's annoying presence invading the chamber. Lucius was an utter cad who deserved to be flogged to within an inch of his life.

Time enough for that later.

Without taking his eyes from her, Lucius spoke over his shoulder. "We shall talk later, Ashcroft."

The next sound in the room was the door latching softly on his exit.

LUCIUS SHOVED HIS hand through his hair, but Meredith had no inclination to set him at ease, despite her reasonings the night before—she'd had a weak moment—and another this morning—also weak—he should have told her about the agreement.

She swiveled in her chair and stared out at another wet, gloomy day. A sudden melancholy blanketing her had her tempted to crawl in her bed and pull the covers over her head. Instead, she spun back facing him with an unwavering stare. "Why?"

He lowered to his haunches before her. "In all fairness, I had every intention of giving that blasted agreement to you the instant you stormed the library that day looking like a drowned rat."

"A drowned rat…" she said slowly.

His palm flattened on her thigh. "But I'd never seen anything so magnificent as all your muddied glory. And, sad. You'd carried that boy from the mine without a thought for yourself. You confronted Thornfield on behalf of the child's family." His hand squeezed her thigh. "That is still something I'm still recovering from, however."

He came to his feet, took her hand, and pulled her up to his chest. "In any event, darling. There's no putting the hymen back in place. I fear you are stuck with me."

Heat infused her face. She leaned in and laid her cheek against the steady thump of his heart. Such a reassuring sound, filled with life and warmth. It seemed to seep beneath her skin. "Stuck with you?"

"If you'll have me. Of course, only you and I know about your broken hymen."

"Could you stop talking about… about…"

"Your hymen?"

"Yes, you cur."

"How else am I supposed to let you know—oh." He stepped back and snapped his fingers. "This should prove I'm serious like nothing else." He lifted her chin. "Your Mr. Ashcroft is growing on me. Some," he clarified. "A little. Let's just say, I don't feel an urge to murder him. For now."

Meredith's heart pounded against her ribs. She went up on her toes and touched his lips with hers. "You're impossible," she whispered.

"I'm but a simple man. Now, could you send for tea? And

eggs. Perhaps some bacon, kippers, scones. Or toast if you don't care for scones."

Melancholy dispersed, shaking her head and laughter taking over, Meredith took up a pen and jotted a list to hand off to Agnes. The girl was completely scattered. "If you have no wish for anyone to know you're not dead, I recommend you confine yourself to my chamber," she told him.

"Brandy."

She turned to him, jaw dropped. "It's barely eight in the morning, sir. Is there anything else you require? Reading perhaps. Something along the lines of *Women and the Need for Economic Equality: A Plan for England's Future?*"

Lucius shot her a sheepish grin. "I found it excellent reading."

Again, that shot of warmth billowed through her from the depths of her abdomen and spread to the tips of her fingers and toes.

A few minutes later, on her task for grabbing a bottle of brandy, Meredith tiptoed down the stairs every sense attuned and ever vigilant for her father. She had no desire for another unexpected audience. His presence at Perlsea still made no sense. Not with Lucius home, er, in house.

Home. With Lucius. Sudden lightness had her nearly floating down the stairs. She wasn't certain her feet even touched the carpets.

At the base of the stairs, she reached the library but something to her left caught her attention. Down the short hall a light flickered against the newly varnished wood-planked floors from beneath the study door. The servants weren't supposed to clean in there. First of all, it was unnecessary. The ceiling was in worse repair than Pender's bedchamber. The furniture was draped in sheets for protection against the dust and elements in preparation for another phase of her plans for turning the Keep into the grand castle it deserved. Besides, it was too dangerous. She stalked down the hall, pressed the handle, and silently entered.

The faint glow of a single candle illuminated the dust-choked room, its flickering light casting eerie shadows across the faded wallpaper, sagging bookshelves, and draping cloths. Her father was hunched behind the desk and appeared weary. A figure of decay among the rest of the desolation. A small shudder rippled over her body.

His coat, usually a pristine sign of his status, was now a part of the dust-covered furnishings, his cravat, rumpled, his hair askew. A shocking sight, to be sure. The sheet covering the desk had been pushed back and he was rummaging through a stack of papers. She had never seen him like this—so diminished, so… human.

"Papa?"

His body jerked as if she'd poked him with a hairpin which did not sound like an entirely horrible idea. "What are you doing?"

His spine stiffened, before he turned toward her, his features etched with a mix of annoyance and surprise. His eyes, bloodshot and shadowed, locked onto hers, and for a fleeting moment, she thought she saw a flicker of something unspoken—fear, perhaps, or guilt.

"Meredith," he said, his voice rough and low. "What are you doing skulking about at this hour?"

"I might ask the same of you." She moved farther into the room though cautiously, cognizant of her one escape route. The air was thick with disuse, the scent of damp and neglect mingling with the acrid tang of old papers. "What are you looking for?"

The tension in his frame was palpable. "Tying up loose ends," he said gruffly. "Nothing that should trouble you."

Aggravation pierced her, pushing out any tender thoughts that had sprouted. "This is my home," she reminded him crisply, taking a step closer. "Anything that happens at Perlsea Keep concerns me."

His jaw tightened and the flicker of guilt was replaced by his steely resolve. "Then I trust you'll respect my judgment," he replied, his tone even but pointed. "Some things are better left to experience, Meredith. You've done well here, but this… this is a matter of history."

"History," she said, startled. The deliberate way he avoided answering her directly was as condescending as it was typical. "I insist on knowing what you're hiding, Papa."

He exhaled sharply, running a hand through his hair—something of which she'd never witnessed of him. "If I told you, what then? Would you fix what cannot be undone? Or would you carry a burden you shouldn't have to bear?" He turned his back on her, moving to the window. "It's best you leave it be."

Something in her father's tone—regret?—tugged at her. But this was Rathbourne. "That sounds almost as if you care," she said.

"Of course, I care, Meredith. You are my only offspring. My legacy goes through you." Bitterness emanated from him, coating her skin. "Now that your husband has deserted you… once again."

"How touching," she bit out, the dig sharp as a dagger in her heart being twisted. She closed her eyes, drew in deeply and released her breath in a slow stream. "Papa, my husband has not deserted me. He is, er, due home today. Besides that, I am not a child." Keeping her voice firm but not unkind was one of life's most important lessons taught by the duke himself. "If there's a burden to carry, I'd rather know the weight of it than stumble beneath it in ignorance."

For a moment, he looked as though he might relent. His shoulders sagged slightly, and his lips parted as if to speak. But it must have been an illusion as the familiar mask of utter disdain returned. He straightened and his voice cooled. "Leave it be, Meredith. This is for your sake, not mine."

Such a statement was so out of character, she opened her mouth to refute him—

"Lady Pender?"

She spun around and found Mr. Verity in the arch of the door.

"You've a visitor, my lady. I've placed her in the library." He hesitated, then appeared to think better of saying more, inclining his head instead.

"Bring tea, please. I'll be there momentarily."

"Now you're entertaining the villagers?" her father said, disgust coloring his tone.

"I'm not expecting anyone, Papa," she said with a resigned sigh. "You'd best remove yourself from this chamber, Papa. It's a hazard." She turned on her heel, escaped the cold to the library which seemed a tropic in comparison, and stopped.

"Miss Hale?" Meredith's surprise bounded against the walls. "What are *you* doing here?"

"It's nice to see you, too," she said with a barely disguised smirk. Her gown of soft yellow suited her complexion.

Miss Docia Hale hadn't changed in the five or so years since Meredith had last seen her. At her friend Abra's come-out ball where Miss Hale had behaved abominably toward Abra. The blonde curls still framed her elfin face and now, like then, her blue eyes flashed their irritation. Needless to say, Miss Hale and she were not the closest of friends. She was much older than those of Meredith's set. Though now that Meredith peered closer, there did appear something... hmm, *softer* about her.

A moment of self-gratitude, and vain-ness truth be told, touched Meredith that the library's renovation had been completed. Watching Miss Hale survey the gleaming wood, the warming fire, the gentle glow of the gas lighting in the overhead chandelier was highly gratifying. Mostly, it was the surprise on her face. "Ah, Lady Perlsea—" she started.

Meredith cut her off. "Pender."

Miss Hale's eyes flew to her looking somewhat—*and no surprise*—puzzled. "Pardon?"

"It's Lady Pender now," she corrected her mildly. "My husband is now the Earl of Pender." If memory served, Miss Hale had greatly resented Abra's higher station as a marquess's daughter and address as "Lady" compared to that of her own address of "Miss" being the daughter of a missing viscount. Apparently, it still grated.

"Oh, ah, yes. Forgive me." The overly sweet smile with which Miss Hale graced Meredith made her teeth ache. "*Lady* Pender," Miss Hale said with an incline of her perfectly coiffed head. "I was hoping to speak with Lord Pender."

"Pender was on his way to London yesterday," the duke said in all his haughty arrogance, appearance notwithstanding.

Meredith bit back the sharp laugh that threatened to erupt at Miss Hale's widened eyes, watching her father stroll in as if he owned the place.

"How lovely to see you again so soon, Miss Hale." Papa speared Meredith with a sharp look. "When is Pender due to return?"

"Today," she murmured and restrained the impulse to roll her eyes as if she hadn't told him that very thing not five minutes ago.

Papa turned to Miss Hale. "Meredith is thrilled to have you, my dear. She's been out of society much too long. It appears she's forgotten how to issue an invitation."

With no other option, Meredith tipped her head, concurring. "Of course, Miss Hale, you are most welcome." She went to the bell chord and tugged. "I'll inform my housekeeper to set up the—" She smiled at her father. "—Green Room for your stay." The Green Room was a neighboring chamber to her father's. "Though a word of caution. The Keep is still under construction and, I regret to inform you, most of the chambers have yet to be modernized."

"I'm sure I will be more than comfortable," Miss Hale demurred.

"One could hope," the duke muttered.

CHAPTER TWENTY-THREE

L UCIUS PRIED HIS eyes open. They went straight to the mantel clock. Nearly noon! Stretching, he came up on the bed and found a tray had been placed on the table. His body ached but the sleep had been restorative. He moved from the bed to pour out a cup of tea. Cold. He set the cup down and went to the fire and stoked the embers back to life.

One thing Lucius was learning of himself, he didn't care much for being alone. He especially didn't care for being confined to his wife's suite of rooms—but for the bathing chamber. He did so *love* the bathing chamber. Unfortunately for him, due to his wound he couldn't very well make use of it. The feeling that he was hiding out did not sit well at all.

Oddly, for the first time in his life, a sense of belonging— usefulness—had begun to fill him. Was it Perlsea? Meredith? Whatever or whomever, the feelings were accompanied with a million unnamable emotions. Like… missing his mother. He'd never considered himself sentimental, but being at Perlsea seemed to bring her closer. Brought on memories of her kindness, her joy, her generosity, for the love which she had heaped on Noah and Lucius.

He picked up a cold scone and took a bite, chewed slowly, thinking how brilliantly Meredith was doing in bringing the castle into a modern era. It had been neglectful of him—his entire treatment of her, placed in a situation not of her choosing any more than it had been of his own.

Frowning, he dropped the half-eaten scone as a new sense of purpose enveloped him. Well, he was lord and master of this ancient Keep and it was time to start acting the part.

The door opened and his wife entered. Her expression dissipated the sense of purpose, replacing it with a wary thrumming that pulsed through his veins. "What is it?"

"You've a visitor," she said with a sweetness that clearly meant something entirely opposite. "Miss Hale has graced us with her presence."

"Docia?" His voice echoed against the walls and into his ears deafening him. Or perhaps it was the rush of blood pommeling him. There was no hiding his shock.

"You can't hide in my chamber forever, my lord."

He narrowed his gaze on her. "Hide?" The accusation stung. His fury was swift. "I believe it was *your* suggestion I remain in *your* chamber."

Her lips tightened. "Just how well do you know this paragon?"

Nothing like cutting to the chase. Lucius stalked to the door but stalked back and taking her by the shoulders, gave her a swift, hard kiss, unwilling to tackle that particular subject. He strode back to the door then looked at her over his shoulder. "Where is the duke?"

"How should I know?" Her mulish tone was encouraging. "I think he's gone. Meeting with that horrid Mr. Thornfield, I suspect." She frowned as if just recalling something. "I caught him in the study—"

"That deathtrap?"

"Yes," she said on an expelled breath. A crease appeared between her brows. "He was searching for something."

"What the devil could he be looking for in the study? Everything is covered in sheets." He grabbed the door's handle. "Never mind. His being out should work to our advantage."

"Advantage?"

He shot her a quick grin. "I was due back today, was I not? I'll speak with Miss Hale. Where did you stash her?"

"The Green Room."

He did not have a good feeling about that. "And where might the Green Room be?"

"Near the Rose Room."

Lucius groaned. "And its condition?"

"Much like the master suite." Her smugness did not escape him.

"Good God," he breathed. "Let her know I'll see her in the library." Lucius stormed through the door to his own suite. Why hadn't he written Docia? Told her of the change in his situation? Because he was an idiot, that's why.

Graham strolled in. "I hear we've a new visitor."

Lucius turned a scowl on him. "Yes." He scrubbed at the scruff on his face. "I need a shave."

"You need more than that. You smell quite ripe, and not in a good way. Don't know how the countess has put up with you thus far."

"True enough." Meredith would be tearing his head off before long. "You think Docia has heard I'm truly married now? Wouldn't put it past her for taking a shot at me."

"She's got the head and the aim for it, for certain," Graham agreed.

That she did. And Lucius needed to speak with Docia before she took it upon herself to enlighten his wife to the real reason he'd been so determined for that annulment.

With one arm bandaged and the other behind attempting to disengage his blasted banyan, there was no slapping his forehead in frustration. Because the more his thoughts catapulted skyward, the more likely the chance of knocking himself unconscious.

And yet, the idea held merit.

MEREDITH TOOK A long steamy bath, filled the tub with her favorite scent of violets and donned her most attractive muslin day dress even though it was three years out of date, all the while telling herself it was not due to Miss Hale's sudden presence at Perlsea. It was her most flattering color—emerald—with ivory stripes, each stripe trimmed in gold thread. Why shouldn't she look her best?

"Cor, milady. You look brilliant," Agnes breathed. Her awe was gratifying.

"Agnes, we do not say 'cor.' It's most unladylike." With a grimace at her reflection, Meredith shook out her skirts.

"Apologies, ma'am," she demurred, though Meredith suspected it was without an ounce of remorse.

Blast it, she forgot the brandy. "All right. I'm as ready as I'll ever be," she said.

"That Miss Hale has nothing on you, milady," Agnes said with staunch loyalty.

Meredith blinked quickly. "Thank you, dear."

Papa was likely still out. Perhaps she should search *his* chamber. In any event, she should speak to Mrs. Verity regarding Miss Hale and took the servant stairs for that very thing. The kitchens were blessedly warm, and the fragrance of fresh bread reminded her she hadn't eaten much.

Mrs. Verity bundled over, wiping her hands on a towel. "Your ladyship? Is aught amiss?"

"I wanted to make certain there were no issues regarding Miss Hale and her accommodations."

"Nah. Installed her in the Green Room like ye asked. Linens are clean. Privy's rushed an' so on."

"Thank you. I take it she's still in her chamber then?"

"No, milady." Her lips compressed into a snarl. "His lordship requested tea in the library."

"I'll find them."

"With the door closed," the older woman added pointedly.

Meredith shook her head. "Thank you, Mrs. Verity. I'm sure

everything is fine." They were, she silently insisted to herself as she moved confidently to said closed door. She pushed down the lever and quietly peered inside.

The scene before her unfolded like a punishing tableau, her breath caught in her throat. Miss Hale's hands locked behind Lucius's neck. His one hand smoothed up her arm and covered her interlocking fingers. His expression was unreadable—no… tender—

"Darling, please. There are no words," he said.

"Oh, Lucius," she cried.

Before Meredith could process what was right before her eyes, Miss Hale went up on her toes and pressed her lips to his. Time stuttered, stretched, each second elongating with unbearable cruelty. The air grew thick, suffocating, as though the walls of the library had folded inward to trap Meredith in this moment.

Forever.

It was as though she had stumbled into someone else's dream—a warped and grotesque facsimile of reality. An iron band tightened about her chest. Her pulse roared in her ears, but her feet remained rooted to the spot. As if the ground had turned to quicksand right there in her beautifully refurbished library. The edges of her world blurred, the sounds dimmed, and for one fleeting, absurd second, she thought perhaps she wasn't truly there at all—that this scene was just a trick of her mind, a shadow of some long-buried fear brought to life.

But the sharp ache of betrayal pierced her through the haze, slamming her back to reality. The fragile threads tethering her heart unraveled.

Meredith stepped back, the latching of the door breaking the fragile spell and her heart. She couldn't seem to breathe properly. She dashed up the main stairs, brandy forgotten. Everything forgotten but one tiny item lying on the table in her bedchamber. Tri-folded.

Throwing the door back, she stumbled inside but managed to choke back any tears, letting fury take the lead. She snatched up the annulment agreement then dropped the shelf of the escritoire open. She fumbled with the top on the inkwell but finally got it open. Her fingers shook so violently that when she dipped the nib of her pen, a blob of black ink pooled and smeared just above the line for her signature. But she was past caring and scrawled her name with a fiery flourish. Without bothering to sand the ink, she refolded the agreement and stormed into her husband's bed-chamber and tossed the offending document in the middle of his sagging bed where he was certain to see it.

She hoped he choked on it. Instead, it was she... choking on tears she could no longer withhold.

At the adjourning door, she stopped. Wiped the tears from her eyes, spotting the journal he'd pilfered from the hidden library. That was *her* find, she raged in silence.

Hers.

She swiped it from the bedside table and stormed out.

CHAPTER TWENTY-FOUR

Lucius gripped Docia's hands and disengaged them from behind his neck. "Docia!" he barked. "Please. This is unseemly."

Time seemed to move in a vat of molasses. A second later, she jerked away from him, her expression stung with rejection. "So, Rathbourne was right. She *is* with child."

"No," he said startled. He'd forgotten Rathbourne's lying announcement to all and sundry. "But…" Lucius passed his palm over his face. "Things have… have changed."

"Changed how?" she demanded.

He had no words.

Slowly, realization seemed to take hold and her eyes filled with tears. "But, us," she whispered.

"There can be no us. Not any longer. I'm sorry, darling. I should have written you." Turning to the windows, Lucius was surprised to find the rain had stopped, if only momentarily. He pushed his hand through his hair, staring out at the lush landscape due to all the moisture. "Hell, the first day I arrived, I found Meredith in the mud."

"The mud!"

"There'd been a cave-in at the mines. She'd dashed in with no thought to her own safety and carried a small child from the rubble. Then Rathbourne appeared, up to no good from what I can gather. Then the shooting—"

"Someone *shot* you?" Her eyes flew to his arm folded against his body. "I didn't shoot you." Her voice touched the C on the soprano end of a pianoforte.

Resisting the urge to cover his ears and another to run from the room, he recognized the importance of the moment, surprising even himself. "Calm down, Docia. I'm not suggesting anything of the sort. I'm trying to tell you… I'm married. I should have owned up to the fact three years ago whatever the circumstances."

"Calm down. *Calm down.*"

"All right," he snapped. "Don't calm down. Weren't you to marry my brother?"

"Yes, but he married my sister instead," she shouted. Docia paced the length of the library like a caged tiger, nostrils flaring in her uniquely feminine features.

Lucius's mouth opened then shut. Opened again. Shut. He swallowed. "Sister? What sister?"

Pulling to an abrupt stop, she glared at him. Then, all the air deflated from her body where she seemed to fold in on herself. "I guess you hadn't heard. Since your departure from Stonemare, I've acquired a sister. One Geneva Wimbley, now Oshea."

Shock pierced with regret pricked his chest. "Noah… Miss Wimbley… My brother's married?" He couldn't fathom what had brought that about. "But… how is Miss Wimbley *your* sister?"

She lifted one shoulder. "My father, her mother. How else? As I understand it, she's one of your wife's closest friends."

A pattern began to converge in his head. One suspiciously related to the Clandestine Sapphire Society pamphlets. Lucius went to the corner cabinet and poured out two brandies, strolled back over, and held one out to her—a peace offering of sorts.

Docia accepted the glass and stared down into the amber contents. After a long moment, she raised her eyes. The blue depths held resignation, not vengefulness or hate. His heart softened.

"You are welcome to stay at Perlsea in light of the horrible weather, but we've enough trouble with Rathbourne in house, so you'll mind your manners. Respect my wishes. More importantly, you'll respect my wife."

"Thank you. I would… like that," she said on a sigh. "What is there to do in the wilds of Cornwall?"

"Not much," he conceded with a small smile.

"Is the Green Room the best I can hope for?" she asked with a narrowing of her eyes.

He gave her a small smile. "I'm afraid so. Lady Pender had not been expecting any of us."

"The library is quite nice," she conceded.

Lucius nodded and took his leave of Docia, anxious to let Meredith know she had nothing to fear from their new guest but she wasn't in her chamber. The bed was nicely made. No clothes were strewn about. The pitcher held fresh water. Even the sun looked to be fighting its way through a haze of thinning clouds.

Disappointment flitted through him, and he ducked through her sitting room and the bathing chamber to his own bedroom. Graham stood beside the bed holding a document, familiar by its creases alone.

Lucius pulled up, unease trickling through him. "Did my wife leave a note?"

"Not exactly." His perfectly formed brows furrowed. "'Tis more like the dropping of a boulder." He held out the offending document. "I found it in the center of the bed."

Signifying unwelcome news Lucius wagered. Hesitating for a second only, he reached for the papers as if they were doused with poison. His imagination had truly run amok. He snatched them from his valet. The first thing that jumped out was the huge black smear of ink near the bottom. The second, was Meredith's harsh, *angry* signature.

His arm fell to his side, his gut coiling with something indefinable. Fury? Fear? The easing storm outside had migrated inside, to just below his skin in a mix of raw uncertainty and relentless anguish. His gaze floated about his chamber. But everything appeared normal.

Normal. What an odd, unassuming word. It may have looked normal, but it felt anything but… until his eyes came to rest on the bedside table.

The journal was missing. Damn it. Damn her! He'd told her that hidden chamber was dangerous. He tossed the annulment agreement into the fire then slammed out of his chamber and crossed the portrait gallery to the tower then took the stairs up by two.

MEREDITH'S FURY—NO, HER *hurt*—took her straight back to her chamber, and swiping the tears from her face. She entered her sitting room quickly only to find Agnes sitting in her usual spot reading.

She jumped to her feet. "Oh, milady. I didn't expect you back so soon. Is aught amiss?"

"Everything is fine, dear. Why don't you take the day to visit your mother. It appears the sun is attempting to break through the clouds for the first time in days."

Her smile grew brighter than the sun. "Oh, thank you, ma'am. I should love that."

"Of course. Have Bartlett drive you. I'll see you in the morning."

"Aye, thank you, ma'am." She hurried out of the sitting room, leaving Meredith alone and at a loss.

Minutes later, she took to the unused portion of the castle. But she found no comfort in going to her hidden library. It would be the first place Lucius would think to look for her, should he bother. In any event, she wasn't up to facing him. Hearing whatever excuses, or fabrications, he thought she'd swallow.

Still, the unused tower was the quietest part of the castle. Something of which she was in desperate need of at the moment.

Donning an apron to cover her day dress, she stuffed the

journal into a deep pocket, took up a warm shawl and an oil lamp, and made her way to the remotest portion she could find. Anything to overtake the image of her husband kissing Docia Hale.

She blinked back more tears as she wandered the ruin. The quiet was unnerving without the rain pounding against panes and rattling them from their frames. The long hallway was lined by tall windows that let in natural light. She followed one corridor to an old sitting chamber. Portraits and landscape paintings still hung on faded papered walls of an indiscriminate color. There were bookcases here, too, but the shelves appeared intact. Most of the furnishings were sturdy—French—if she were to guess.

A good polishing of the wood and perhaps updated upholstery and the pieces would fit right in with her plans—

Plans. She might not last the summer in Penhalwick. All her work… the Literary Society, the women who needed and respected her business sense. The children's school. None of that would survive her desertion. But how could she bear to stay if Lucius remained?

Meredith set her lamp on a low table next to the settee, spun about, and plopped down, stirring up a cloud of dust, and sneezed. Thus was her life, she thought with a not so normal bleakness. She tugged the journal from her pocket, determined to lose herself in the mysterious past she was certain had much to do with the present.

CHAPTER TWENTY-FIVE

L UCIUS LET OUT an oath that stirred the moth-eaten drapes. There was no sign that Meredith had entered the chamber. Everything was just as they'd left it a few nights ago. A few nights. It seemed months, not days. He stormed down the stairs, determination a driving force to speak with Ashcroft.

Mrs. Verity stepped into the hall, frowning. Her expression, one of disapproval. "Mr. Ashcroft 'ad the school children today."

"I'm looking for Lady Pender. Did she accompany Ashcroft to the village?" Drawing on all the noble blood in his body, he managed to keep his tone inquiring, not demanding, despite the underlying fear that he'd lost something truly dear.

Her gaze narrowed on him to an uncomfortably intense degree, and damned if he wasn't glad to know Meredith had this shrewd and sharp-tongued housekeeper watching after her. "Aye, I saw 'er ladyship. On her way to the library door. It was closed," she said with a disdainful, accusing sniff.

Christ. Had she witnessed Docia kissing him? Guilt pricked him. It was almost a certainty. Swallowing the groan that crawled up his chest, he inclined his head though his fist clenched at his side. "Thank you, Mrs. Verity. You've been most helpful."

The rain had kept them housebound in what seemed forever. Perhaps she desired getting out and was meeting with the women at The Copper Kettle. He couldn't very well blame her. But her signing the annulment agreement after they'd spoken about it didn't bode well. Every sense he possessed was on alert. And, the longer he failed in locating her, the more frantic his heart pounded.

Staying to the shadows, Lucius went out the servant's entrance. As he'd mentioned to Meredith, this was one way to play his "return" from London.

He stalked to the stables, surprising Prys. His heavy gray eyebrows shot to the heavens. "Yer lordship. Ye're back."

"I am indeed," Lucius gritted out. "Did Lady Pender request the carriage?"

"Aye, milord. I'm preparing it now. Without delay." Prys's hunched wiry frame hurried away.

He walked outside to wait. The rain had softened the ground, and his boots sank slightly in the muck. True to his word, Prys brought the carriage around. Bartlett sat atop the box.

The carriage rolled to a stop at the door and relief hit Lucius's chest seeing his wife bundled up, hood on her head. He hurried to the carriage and assisted her up. She settled across from him and lowered the hood.

"Agnes?" The carriage jerked into motion.

"Oh, milord. Lady Pender gave me the day off."

"She's not coming?"

"No, milord."

He stifled another groan as the carriage took the path leading to Penhalwick, leaving Lucius alone with his wife's lady's maid and his own thoughts, and an inability to unsee the annulment agreement with her furious signature, the ink of her rage etched across the page. Frustration pounded his blood, knowing she would do everything she could to avoid him if she'd indeed seen Docia kissing him. A kiss that had left him shockingly unmoved.

The village loomed ahead, its narrow, cobbled streets emptying into the square. Lanterns flickered dimly in windows, casting a faint glow against the muted sunlight. Lucius tugged his coat tighter against the cool wind, his thoughts a storm of confusion and anger. She must have seen. What else could have driven her to such madness?

As the carriage descended into the square, Lucius forced himself to adopt the guise of a man freshly returned from London, a neutral expression masking his inner turmoil. Villagers passed him with guarded nods, then averted their eyes. Apparently, his reputation still hung in heavy tatters over the town. The weight of their suspicions pressed down on him.

Ahead, The Copper Kettle stood, its wooden sign swinging gently in the breeze.

"Where shall I drop you, Agnes?" he asked her.

"The Kettle works for me, sir. Me mum will be over for luncheon soon. She owns the haberdashery, you know."

Lucius smiled. "I didn't know. Shall I wait to return you?"

"Oh, no, sir. Bartlett will pick me up tomorrow morning."

The carriage stopped and Lucius stepped out and assisted Agnes down. The door to the tea shop opened, and the faint hum of voices spilled into the street. He ushered Agnes inside and the low chatter slowed to silence as all eyes turned on him. Squaring his shoulders, he surveyed the crowded room.

No Meredith, and of course, he now knew she was likely hiding out in the Keep somewhere. Hopefully, she and Docia would not come to blows before his return.

The Widow Elspeth flashed him a sharp smile and he moved in her direction. "Would you care for a lemon tart, my lord?"

"I would indeed," he said slowly. Carefully. "Two, thank you. Lady Pender seems quite fond of them."

After a beat, the surrounding conversations resumed, as if the interruption had never occurred. The widow handed him a small box and he stepped back outside. He reached the carriage, but heavy boots sounded against the cobblestones. He thrust the box at Bartlett as some instinct had him stepping back to the shadows next to The Copper Kettle.

Near the entrance of the square two figures appeared—one stocky and deliberate, the other tall and sharp—Thornfield and another man Lucius didn't recognize. Neither had yet noticed him. They spoke in low tones, and Thornfield gestured toward the path to the mine that cut through the far end of the village.

Lucius froze. If Thornfield spotted him, the pretense of his absence would be shattered. He ducked into a darkened alcove, his pulse quickening.

Thornfield's gruff voice carried over the wind. "Are you sure he's not there?"

"No one has seen him," the other man said with a glance over his shoulder. "The carriage is just across the street. The shot hit him. There ain't no way it didn't, sir."

Thornfield muttered an oath, his hand tightening around his cane. "We should have heard something by now. Rathbourne will be furious. This is not the time for games. It's that blasted steward the countess hired. There's something off about…"

The rest of the sentence was lost to the wind, but the intent behind his words was unmistakable. Lucius's jaw tightened. That certainly answered one question. Were they searching for him, or Ashcroft, as well?

He stepped farther into the shadows, watching as Thornfield motioned toward the far end of the square. The duo moved with renewed purpose, disappearing down the path that led to the mine. Lucius hesitated only a moment before following at a distance, ducking through alleys, his steps silent as he kept them within sight. The hike was short.

Thornfield paused briefly near the entrance to the mine office, conferring with his companion before continuing toward the old smelting works.

Lucius watched from behind a stack of barrels, his thoughts turning over the pieces of the puzzle. Meredith's fury, her disappearance, Thornfield's involvement—what was she tangled in now? And why did he feel as though everyone in this cursed village was hiding something?

The sound of footsteps echoed from the opposite direction, and Lucius spun to see another figure approaching—a man cloaked and hooded, carrying a lantern. For a fleeting moment, he thought it might be Meredith and his heart stopped, but as the figure drew closer, the light revealed another familiar face: the duke.

Lucius's breath caught. He flattened himself against the barrels as the duke strode past, his presence as commanding and sinister as ever. What was *he* doing, skulking around the village, and in broad daylight?

The pieces were falling into place, but the picture they formed was still incomplete. Lucius clenched his fist, his gaze trailing the duke as he strode down the same path as Thornfield and his friend.

Unease wound its way through his thoughts. The mines were dangerous enough without adding Rathbourne's scheming to the mix. Whatever their purpose, their task left Thornfield's office unattended, an opportunity Lucius had no intention of squandering.

This was Perlsea's operation and if Lucius chose to search the mine's office, then by God, it was his prerogative. Tugging his hat down to obscure his features, Lucius waited until the trio moved past yard workers and disappeared inside the mine entrance. Without hesitation, Lucius moved with a confidence he didn't quite feel through that same milling crowd to the stone building's entrance.

More men inside, just like the previous time he'd visited, lined the walls. The same clerk manned the desk outside Thornfield's office. The clerk's eyes shot to Lucius and his mouth opened.

Lucius snatched off his hat and waited until recognition set in. "What is your name?" Lucius asked him.

"Anson… Anson Rigg, yer lordship," he stuttered. He appeared a diligent, quiet man in his mid- to late-thirties, with ink-stained fingers and an air of nervous efficiency.

"Mr. Rigg, I'm going to wait for Thornfield in his office. See that I'm not disturbed." He leaned in. "I would also appreciate your keeping this to yourself for the time being. If at some point, Thornfield or the duke return, please drop a drawer or slam a heavy book on your desk. Your future at Penhalwick mines rides solely on your response. Am I clear on this, sir?"

"Y-yessir." His steady gaze back was most reassuring.

With a sharp smile of approval, Lucius entered Thornfield's office, latching the door softly behind him.

The room was as unwelcoming as Lucius remembered. Reminiscent of its main occupant, dark and oppressively tidy. The battered oak desk was still cluttered with ledgers and the scattering of loose papers. The map of the mine on the wall held more annotations with crabbed handwriting. The air smelled faintly of damp stone and stale ink.

Lucius crossed to the desk, his pulse quickening. This was madness, he thought, his fingers hovering over the first ledger. But Thornfield was hiding something—and the duke appeared to be in on it up to his neck. No way in hell would he let them pull Meredith down with them.

He opened the ledger. The numbers swam before his eyes at first glance, but as he flipped through the pages, the irregularities began to emerge. Large payments to unnamed contractors, odd notations in the margins—details Thornfield had either failed to obscure or didn't care to disguise for whatever reason. One entry in particular caught his attention: "Expenses—Special Handling," followed by an exorbitant sum. *Special handling? Of what?*

His jaw tightened. He set the ledger aside and reached for a stack of letters pinned under a large bronze paperweight in the shape of a hawk. A predatory bird that symbolized cunning and dominance. *Fitting.* Its bluish oxidation gave credence to the length of Thornfield's position. Likely gifted by Rathbourne and his own father for a job well done. Taking it by its head, Lucius set it aside and lifted the stack of correspondence.

One, written in elegant but hurried script, bore the seal of a prominent member of Parliament.

Thornfield—

The proposed revisions to the Mine Acts could spell trouble for your operation. I trust you'll ensure compliance is not required, by whatever means necessary. The consequences of failure are yours to bear.

Lucius read the letter twice, the weight of its implications settling over him like a leaden cloak. He folded the paper and slipped it into his coat pocket, determined to examine it further later. Just as he began to replace the stack of missives, another caught his eye.

The familiar handwriting jarred him. What the devil was Noah writing to Thornfield about? He swept it up, started to open it but his gaze stopped, falling on a locked cabinet tucked against the far wall he hadn't noticed on his previous visit. Lucius stuffed his brother's letter in his coat pocket alongside the other note then strode quickly to the cabinet.

Locked.

The key was easy enough to find—in the top drawer of the desk, lying in plain sight. Seconds later, the lock gave way with a faint click, and Lucius pulled the cabinet door back to reveal another small journal bound in cracked leather. He flipped it open and skimmed the pages. The handwriting varied, as if multiple authors had made entries over the course of many years, but the contents sent a chill down his spine.

Names. Dozens of names. Many he didn't recognize, of course, but a few were undeniably familiar—former stewards of Perlsea, crossed out with curt notations:

A. Featherstone – resolved

J. Bancroft – relocated

C. Whittingham – relocated

F. Aldridge – removed

At the back of the journal, he found a crude map of the mine, marked with what appeared to be routes and locations. One area was circled, unmarked by any label. Lucius stared at it, unease pooling in his gut. He thought of the map he'd found on

Ashcroft's desk.

A crash outside the office startled him to his current circumstance.

Heart pounding, Lucius stuffed the journal in the pocket of his greatcoat and relocked the cabinet. He arranged the desk as he'd found it and hurried to the windows. Voices sounded outside the door. Anson had stopped Thornfield and Rathbourne though Lucius couldn't make out what was being said. But time had run out. He unlatched the window and jumped to the ground below, quickly pulling the window to but not quite shut.

Unable to resist the opportunity, he crouched and listened. The conversation was grim. Low and urgent. He strained to catch their words, snippets drifting through the crack in the window.

"The Mine Acts will ruin us if they take it upon themselves to enforce their ridiculous rules," Rathbourne said, his voice tight with anger. "Ensure that doesn't happen, Thornfield. No mistakes. And find Pender."

Thornfield was silent, but Lucius pictured him nodding, his jaw clenched, his face pale, his hands twitching as he adjusted his coat. Then he said, "I'll find him. Harper said he was hit. He should have been found by now."

"If he had, the news would have been all over the village." Something crashed against the wall. Perhaps it was one of those ridiculous, uncomfortable chairs, he thought with a bite of sarcasm that would do his wife justice. Rathbourne went on. "It's obvious he was found, you fool, and that someone assisted him."

If they spoke more, Lucius couldn't have repeated what they'd said for the blood rushing in his ears. Ashcroft had been right. The duke doled out those pesky tasks he didn't wish to dirty his own hands with.

Whatever was afoot, it was worse than Lucius had imagined. Yet, his worst fear was Meredith being caught in the middle of whatever nefarious machinations were in the works.

He leaned against the building, the cold stone seeping through his coat, chagrined to admit, needing to speak with

Ashcroft now more than ever. With a shaky exhale and the weight of not only the journal but Noah's letter. Both burned in his pocket as he made his way around the back of the property and onto the path toward town, keeping from sight, his thoughts churning.

There was more to uncover, and he'd need to tread carefully if he hoped to untangle the web of deceit without ensnaring himself—or Meredith—in its traps.

MEREDITH'S ANGER NO longer flared as if stoked by the fiercest midsummer heat. It only simmered now after losing herself the last couple of hours through the words of a man who'd belonged in Bedlam. She leaned back in her chair with the open journal on her lap.

Truly, Aylesbury was an interesting character. Almost fiction-like. Especially having written lines like *"In shadowed halls where vintages sleep, truths long buried whisper their secrets to those who seek."* Such passages had sounded introspective at times, sensitive. Other times, so ruthless her skin raised in prickles.

The August passage kept drawing her back. There was something poignant about its phrasing. *"The dead bear witness in silence,"* and *"Guilt lies heavier than stone."*

She flexed her fingers, numb from the room's chill, thinking. A mantra. From all accounts, Aylesbury spoke of hiding something under said mantra. Yet, what? And, where?

The most logical and the worst logical place was the hidden room she and Lucius had inadvertently exposed. It was also the most dangerous. It struck her as the most—too—obvious place to hide something of import.

Wherever the aging marquess had chosen to "hide" whatever "items" he referred to, Meredith was certain she would find those words hanging over said location. A yearning to share her thoughts with Lucius swelled within her until extinguished in a surge of resentment as a vision rose unbidden of Miss Hale's arms clasped around his neck.

Meredith had a vision of her own—one of her hands squeezing the breath from him. She blinked away the hurt and came to her feet. "I wish you every delight," she said to the cold room. Bitterness compressed her chest. Stewing over the images would do her no good. This quest she was on belonged to her, didn't it? What need had she of a husband who showed her such lack of respect? She'd signed the annulment agreement. He could have his precious Docia.

Her stomach emitted an unladylike growl but she ignored it, snapping the journal shut and tossing it on the table. She stretched her limbs and rubbed her hands over her arms then spent the next hour touring the forgotten tower. An unfruitful endeavor. There was no going around it; the hidden library required searching. Lamp in hand, she stalked down the hall and around the corner to the old library where the dust and dampness hit her with a bitter cold.

She steered clear of the fallen bookcase and poked at papers that had scattered to the edges of the table and onto the floor. There was nothing of interest at first glance, only a collection of faded folios and crumbling tomes. But no arch separated the two chambers and no inscription appeared painted or imprinted on the beams overhead.

Finally, the hunger gnawed at her, leaving her too lightheaded to linger over the ancient scripts and take the time to decipher their timeworn glosses. Perhaps a search would fare better on a full belly. Just the thought of eating sounded like a better plan at the moment. And with no desire to see her husband—she was still too angry—she would have plenty of time on her hands, as sleep was likely to elude her in the coming nights.

Meredith took the lamp. In the hall she turned in the opposite direction from which she'd originally entered the tower to the servant's stairwell. Three flights down and she exited near Mr. Ashcroft's office. It was dark, indicating he was still in the village teaching the children. Truly, he'd been her best find since arriving in Cornwall.

"Ah. Lady Pender, ye look famished," Mrs. Verity said.

"How did you know?"

The question was rhetorical since her stomach let out another growl of protest.

Grinning, Mrs. Verity didn't respond to that, only saying, "Take a seat in the dining room, milady. I'm just waitin' on a maid to return from the wine cellar." She scowled. "The duke's quite particular in his choice of spirits."

"Yes." Meredith peered at the door, her mind a chaotic storm. "Yes, Papa has always been most particular." She spoke slowly as Aylesbury's words, indelibly seared in her brain, flashed like lighting… *shadowed halls where vintages sleep, truths long buried.* "I'll be in the dining hall," she said slowly, even as the hair at her nape lifted and the flesh on her arms raised in prognostic bumps.

Setting the lamp on a table in the empty dining hall, Meredith took her chair, surprised at her outward self-possession when all she wished was to dash straight to the wine cellar to see if her instincts held merit. The spike in her pulse refused to slow, however. She folded her hands in her lap, but her foot tapped with an unfamiliar impatience that was far more fitting to that of her friend Geneva's restless nature.

Mrs. Verity entered with two maids. One carried a plate of small sandwiches, the other a tray of steam rising from a pot of tea.

Meredith stilled her foot that seemed determined to thwart her. "Bartlett?"

"He drove Agnes to the village."

"Oh, right." She'd forgotten.

Mrs. Verity turned a sharp-eyed gaze on her. "I believe his lordship accompanied her."

Excellent, as she had no desire to see her *husband*. She took up one of the tiny cucumber sandwiches and nibbled on it. "Miss Hale too, I assume?"

"Nay, she did not." Mrs. Verity's indignation touched her.

"Agnes will return tomorrow," she said gently to say *something*. "By the bye, these are delicious." The housekeeper poured her a cup of tea with a nod and shooed the maids out, then followed them.

Meredith devoured two more sandwiches, gulped more tea, then quietly stole from the dining hall—taking the lamp—hoping she would find the wine cellar unlocked.

Thankfully, the hall leading to the dungeons was vacant. She paused at the top of the stairs. A cold chill drifted up, raising bumps on her skin. The flame in her lamp flickered, its dim light barely piercing the gloom below. It was enough to highlight the treacherous descent of steep, uneven stone steps, while she gripped the rudimentary handrail. She lifted the lamp, exposing stones worn smooth and tilted from centuries of use. Her slippered foot hovered over the first step, and she tightened her grip on the lantern and the rail.

The farther she descended the colder the temperature and heavier the scent of mildew hung in the air. Each step required careful footing. She had to catch herself more than once. Halfway down, her lantern illuminated a streak of dark moss clinging to the steps. She stopped, her pulse quickening. One slip, and anyone could easily tumble to the bottom.

She reached the floor of the cellar, exhaling in relief.

"This will never do," Meredith murmured, her breath visible in the chilled air.

Her mind turned over possibilities as she inspected the space. Aylesbury's ancestors hadn't concerned themselves with comfort or safety—this staircase was a means to an end, not a thoroughfare for the living. But now, it was necessary, not just for the servants to access the wine but for herself as she combed through the keep's forgotten spaces.

It needed a sturdier handrail—wood and polished to resist the dampness. No one should have to risk their neck every time they came down here. She pressed the handle of the closed door and pushed.

Unlocked.

Meredith stepped through an arch into a shadowy, stone-walled room and shivered in the damp air. The faint aroma of old oak and earthen floors blended with the slightly sour scent of aged wine. She lifted her lamp and glanced around. Narrow barred windows high on the walls appeared as black endless hollows. The flame cast eerie shadows across the stone surfaces. Low-lit sconces lining the walls revealed the cellar's age and long history.

Another arch separated the space into a second chamber. She ventured slowly in that direction, but it was almost too dark to discern details other than massive oaken barrels. She backed away from the second chamber and studied the thick wooden racks, heavy and darkened with age. They stacked against the walls like wooden soldiers and were laden with dusty bottles.

A quick perusal of the labels amid bouts of sneezes found many of the bottles were decades old, hinting at Perlsea's wealth and its history of collecting fine vintages. Among the racks were massive oaken barrels, some branded with the Aylesbury family crest. A couple of tables were pushed against the walls for practical purposes. She set the lamp on one and continued her perusal.

There was a gothic essence to the cellar that was fascinating. It reminded her of her days at Miss Greensley's School of Comportment for Young Ladies of Quality and all those nights she, Geneva, Hannah, and Abra had spent reading and romanticizing their favorite horrid novels. One thing Meredith could gladly claim, she didn't fear ghosts.

The thought brought a smile to her lips before a gust of wind whistled from one of the narrow windows. She stopped as another shiver rattled her spine. Breathing in through her nose and letting it out through her mouth calmed the edge of her nerves. She closed her eyes, called herself silly, then reopened them, focusing on the toes of her slippers.

The uneven stone floors were worn by generations of footsteps… footsteps that angled to a corner in a shallow depression. For drainage, she supposed, noting a stained trail that trickled to the area. But anticipation rippled through her that spoke of a more sinister past.

Too many of Aylesbury's words were sending her imagination into wild contemplations, she thought wryly. She raised her eyes to the wide arch that separated the two chambers and picked out one of the dusty bottles and carried it to the light. Brandy.

"Lady Pender?"

The bottle slipped from her startled grasp, crashing to the floor as she spun, nearly slipping on the now aromatic floor. "Oh," Her hand flattened at her throat. "Mr. Verity, you gave me quite the fright."

"May I assist you with something, milady?"

"I-I was looking for brandy." Her voice faltered, but she flung a hand toward the shattered bottle.

"I would have gladly retrieved it for you." His portly chin doubled as he looked down at the amber pool swirling her feet. He raised a neutral look, meeting her eyes. "There is brandy in the library, milady."

His insolence set her teeth on edge. In fact, wasn't *she* mistress, no—*countess*—of this castle—of this *Keep*?

She drew herself up and adopted Papa's most daunting superiority. "Mr. Verity, I trust my status is not lost on you. If I choose to select a bottle of brandy from my own cellar, that should hardly concern you." That sounded horribly smug. But she suppressed her cringe.

An unflattering scarlet crawled into his florid cheeks that went to the tips of his ears.

His blank expression failed in suppressing the sudden hostility that seemed to saturate the atmosphere along with the spilled brandy. Stiffly, inclining his head, he moved to the wooden rack she'd confiscated the first bottle from and selected another, then wiped it down. He returned and held it out to her with a respectful incline of his head.

Meredith accepted the bottle, feeling horrid for wearing her father's skin. It didn't fit well. "Thank you, Mr. Verity," she said flustered. *Guilt lies heavier than stone.* She blinked. Where had that thought come from?

The portly butler went to the arch. "Shall we, milady?"

"Er, yes, of course." She turned about, took in the vast number of dusty bottles, the wood racks, the large beam that separated the chambers—stopped. "Is that an inscription?"

"Aye, madam."

She grabbed her lamp from the table. Edging forward, she held the light up, squinting. *"The Dead Bear Witness in Silence."* Her words barely whispered from her lips and an odd chill stole up her spine.

Ghostly fingers seemed to feather her nape.

From the corner of her eye, where the floor sloped, nearly hidden from view by one of the casks, she took in the drain a second time.

Again, she spun. It was a wonder she hadn't fallen on her backside, dizzy, where she would have landed in a field of shard glass. "I should like another moment or two." She faced the butler, speaking with a confidence that had served her well over the years.

His bushy brows rose, and she was quite certain he'd never been so surprised.

Meredith widened her eyes and waited for her intention to sink in.

And, waited.

"But the lights, milady," he rasped.

She waved out a hand. "You may return in a bit to extinguish them," she said with a smile she hoped was as guileless as she strived for.

An awkward moment passed before the butler moved to the door. "Of course, madam. Mind where you step."

The flames flickering upon his exit seemed to pound against the stone walls. Or, perhaps it was the pulse pounding in her ears.

She waited an entire two minutes before daring to move. Her gaze went back to that downward trek in the floor. She set the brandy and the lamp back on the table and considered her next course of action. The cask didn't sit level on the floor. She moved to it, reached out and tested its sturdiness. To her surprise, it appeared empty and rocked fairly easily.

With a rush of excitement, Meredith tugged on the cask, using more force. Setting her teeth, she moved to its other side and put all of her weight behind her shove, nearly felling her to her knees. The entirety of a small compartment crafted of heavy oak was set flush with the stone floor. The wood was weathered and had darkened over the years. It blended almost seamlessly with the surrounding stone floor. Reinforced iron bands with adorning rings lay flat on its surface that were similar to that of the Keep's entry door.

But… no handle. A burst of frustration flooded her.

How the devil was she supposed to remove the top?

Uncaring of the spilled brandy or her best green and cream striped frock, she went on her knees to examine the trapdoor—for that was exactly what it was—straight out of one of those gothic tales she'd so adored as a girl. Perhaps a hidey-hole used to hide Catholics from the seventeenth century? A small laugh escaped her, though it edged on the side of hysterical.

Meredith ran a fingertip over the wood. So worn, any splinters had been smoothed into submission.

She came to her feet and grabbed the lamp for better light. On the far edge of the hidden compartment door, she found a small, nearly invisible catch embedded into one corner. Again, she smoothed a fingertip over it and pressed. She felt, rather than heard the latch's release. Still, it did not rise enough for her to grasp.

The rings?

Rising, Meredith once more set the lamp aside, her heart thumping erratically. Sliding her fingers into the two prominent iron rings, she attempted to lift. They proved difficult and stiff from disuse. She couldn't give up now! Going up on her knees, she tugged again, excitement tearing through her with sheer will as it gave way.

The trapdoor was heavy. It creaked and resisted her efforts, but she was strong, and in the end triumph was hers. She could scarcely believe it.

With a rush, she snatched up the lamp again and peered inside the compartment. *Too small to hide an entire person.*

Several objects appeared to have been hidden with purpose. She knew it through to her soul. She reached in and pulled out the items, each wrapped in faded, oil-stained burlap cloth that shockingly looked to have been protected from the damp and dust.

Carefully, she pulled back the frayed and brittle edges of the coverings of one item. Beneath an outer layer she found papers wrapped in aged leather—cracked but still mostly intact—with faint remnants of wax seals that had long since chipped away. It was impossible to tell if the wrappings had preserved any valuable or incriminating information but she had to think, and quickly before Verity ignored her instruction and returned. Even if he didn't, if Lucius returned, she was certain the butler would inform him.

She gathered her treasures, five in all, placing them on the table with the lamp and the brandy. The pockets on her apron held all but the brandy. She'd have to leave it behind. She went back to the compartment and folded the lid back into place with a resounding thud. Then she considered the cask she'd shoved aside. With nothing left in the compartment, it wouldn't hurt for anyone to see it, she decided.

Unwilling to linger, Meredith took the lamp and the brandy and hurried—waddled, more like—to the door.

Chapter Twenty-Six

Lucius crashed through the entryway door of Perlsea, frantic to find Meredith. "Verity."

The portly butler hurried into the vestibule. "Oh, sir. Your wife—"

"My wife—"

Their simultaneous words echoed in the vast hall. Lucius inhaled a harsh breath and let it out slowly. "Go on, Verity."

The butler drew in his own breath. "Lady Pender is visiting the wine cellar, my lord."

"What the devil? Where *is* the wine cellar?" he asked appalled that he had no idea where his own cellar was.

"A part of the old dungeons was converted many years ago. The stairwell leading down is near the steward's office, m-my lord. It's quite hazardous."

Lucius tore off his greatcoat and tossed it to him.

"Lucius?" Docia was halfway down the grand staircase. "What's going on?"

He strode past her without answering and took a short path through the dining hall.

Verity's heels clicked on the polished planks hurrying behind him. "I tried discouraging her, sir, b-but she insisted on my l-leaving."

"Unless she is lying dead. Verity, you are hereby excused of any wrongdoing. I know how elusive and stubborn my wife is. Find Ashcroft and send him to her sitting chamber," he threw over his shoulder.

Lucius reached Ashcroft's office but the stairwell door to the dungeons stood open. A deep black hole beckoning—or repelling—one to unspeakable emotion. A faint flicker of light danced from the depths below, a tremulous glow barely holding back the oppressive darkness. His pulse quickened, unease pooling low in his stomach.

"Meredith?" His voice carried, harsh and sharp, into the still air.

No answer came, but the faint scuff of a footstep on stone drifted upward, easing his fear. The light grew stronger, its source drawing closer, until she emerged from the shadows.

Relief mixed with a jagged stab of frustration pierced him. He couldn't decide whether to hurry down to kiss her or shake her.

She climbed the steps carefully, her head bowed as if the task required her full attention. The oil lamp in her hand cast a wavering halo of light, illuminating her pale face. Dust streaked her cheeks, and her other hand gripped her skirts tightly, keeping them from snagging on the rough stone.

"Meredith," Lucius said, his voice tight, harder than he'd intended. "What in the devil's name are you doing down there?"

She paused mid-step, lifting her chin, meeting his gaze. The faint sheen of sweat on her brow, the faint tremor in her fingers were details only someone watching closely would notice. Someone, being him.

"Thank God," he breathed, and stepped down.

"Oh, Lucius." Her words soft, almost fragile, pierced the fear encasing his heart. She hurried up. Nearly reached him when she lost her footing or tripped on her skirts, the lamp flying from her hold as she tried to save herself with nothing to grasp onto. The lamp crashed below and the oil caught fire lighting the stone stairwell.

His free hand shot out, catching her hand just as she lost the war with her balance. "I've got you, darling." Fear trembled in his voice, but he managed to keep her steady until she regained her footing.

He dashed back down the stairs with his right hand on the wall. At the bottom, he tore off his frockcoat and threw it over the flames, then stomped on top of it. There was no telling how far a fire could spread even surrounded with stone steps and walls. The door to the cellar wasn't stone.

Satisfied he'd averted disaster, he made his way back to the top, somehow having kept his temper in check.

By the time he reached the top his temper sharpened into something closer to rage. He spun her about, facing him. "Are you out of your senses?" The pain in his shoulder fled beneath his fury.

The hall's low light revealed smudges of grime on her hands and the appalling apron she wore. The moss green of her eyes glittered with fury, excitement, uncertainty. "Oh, Lucius," she whispered, and launched herself at him.

Instinctively, his one arm flew up and wrapped her. Two things hit him at once. His front side was besieged by bulges that did not belong and... He winced. "Not again."

She slid down his body and his cock took on its own bulge.

Her spine straightened, her expression puzzled. "Oh, no. Your shoulder."

His lips compressed.

"What were you doing down there? Alone."

"I-I wasn't alone," she said softly, gesturing vaguely to the void behind her. "The ghosts of this place... they're everywhere."

Lucius clenched his jaw, resisting the urge to shake her in truth. "Ghosts don't leave footprints," he said tersely, his gaze flicking to the damp trail her shoes had left on the stones. "What did you find?"

Her hesitation was brief but telling. "A hidden compartment," she said. "Hidden beneath an empty cask."

A cold knot formed in his chest. "Compartment?" His voice dropped, his anger shifting to wary curiosity, his eyes going to the bulky pockets of her apron. "What did you find?"

Her eyes met his briefly before darting to the darkened stairwell. "I don't know yet," she admitted, her voice low. "I haven't had a chance to look yet."

He stepped closer, towering over her as his eyes bore into hers. "You shouldn't have gone alone, Meredith," he said, his voice tight with suppressed fury. "That was very dangerous."

"I had to," she said quietly, her arms hugging her waist. "Someone has to uncover what's been hidden."

The quiet conviction in her tone left him momentarily speechless. He could hardly argue her point in light of what he'd learned himself that day.

He glanced down the dark stairwell, the faint glow from the open door below barely touching the endless black. The air seemed heavier now, colder, as though the very stones were holding their breath.

"Verity," he shouted.

The man stepped from around a corner. "Sir?"

"The oil lamp broke. Get someone to tend to it."

"The broken brandy bottle too," Meredith added. "And don't forget to douse the sconces."

"Broken brandy bottle?" Lucius inquired a little too calmly for the riotous emotions roiling through him.

Her skill at ignoring him was growing legendary, he decided, stuck between irritation and admiration.

"We best see to that shoulder."

Whatever secrets the dungeons held, Lucius felt a grim certainty that they would not let go easily.

CHAPTER TWENTY-SEVEN

With a wary eye, Lucius watched Ashcroft wander about his bedchamber. He stopped at the bedside table where the pamphlet on *Women and the Need for Economic Equality: A Plan for England's Future* lay in full view. He picked it up and turned to Lucius with a lifted brow.

Frustration gripped Lucius by the throat but he had one weapon at his disposal. "Don't change the subject. If you don't wish to discuss our mutual beneficial partnership, as my wife so delicately intimated, I can apprise the duke of your presence in a matter of minutes."

Ashcroft's mouth tightened and he dropped the booklet back on the table.

It was amazing how much satisfaction Lucius gleaned at setting the man back on his heels. "Now, would you like to tell me what it is you have on the duke thus far?"

"As I said, he killed my mother. I had returned home from school and saw him."

"Home from school," Lucius repeated. Little pieces of a large puzzle started clicking into place. "So, that would make you…"

"Rathbourne's son and heir. Lady Pender's brother. If he'd seen me that day, I suspect it would have been worse for me."

Lucius shoved a hand through his hair, stunned on more than one front. "Jesus, how could it have been worse?"

"Oh, I don't know." Another sardonic lift of his brow. "Beat me to a bloody pulp, imprison me in my own home? One scenario. Facing my own death as a second. I was thirteen. Rathbourne's a powerful man."

"But what reason would he have for murdering his own wife?"

"I think she opposed his father's dealings in Cornwall."

"His father's!" Lucius straightened. "Your grandfather?"

Ashcroft raised a shoulder and let it fall. "Once the former duke expired, my father was there to take up the reins."

"The reins of what?"

"You found the list of former stewards," he reminded Lucius.

"Yes, but you said he didn't handle such pesky..." Lucius slapped his forehead. "Right. So, you're looking for evidence?"

His lips curved into a grim, humorless smile. "Yes."

"Have you found any?"

"Not yet," he bit out. "It's not as if it will be written out with arrows leading me down a clear and merry path."

Lucius pinched the bridge of his nose, recognizing the truth of that statement. "You think Thornfield is carrying out Rathbourne's agenda?"

"Yes. But I have yet to learn what that agenda is."

"Why do you believe he killed Meredith's mother?"

Ashcroft shrugged. "If he killed one, why not another?"

"Yes. Why not?" Lucius glanced at the clock on the mantelpiece over the hearth. "And Meredith?"

His lip curved in a grim smile. "Someone had to look after her."

There was nothing Lucius could say to that. "Yes, well. I'm here now," he said gruffly. "Where the devil is the brandy?"

But even as the words escaped him, unease slithered over his skin. "Help me with a shirt, would you?"

With a grim set of his mouth, Ashcroft stepped forward and helped Lucius out of his shirt. "You can't go traipsing about the Keep and expect no one to notice."

That uneasiness banded his chest with iron until Lucius could barely draw in a breath. "The cat has been let out of the bag. The whole village is quite aware I've returned," he said, thinking of those gazes who'd dropped or turned from him.

A light tap sounded. "Enter," Lucius barked.

Ashcroft turned and opened the door.

"What is it?" The anxiousness, reminiscent of a dive off the cliffs into a glacial sea, iced his veins.

Bartlett held up the brandy.

"Finally," Ashcroft breathed. "Where is Lady Pender?"

The pipes clanged loudly. "In the bathing chamber," Lucius said. "She was acting oddly. Said she wished to be alone."

Ashcroft's eyes flicked to the pamphlet and back to Lucius fraught with meaning. "Seems to be plenty of that going on around here," he muttered.

"Thank you, Bartlett. You may go." Lucius prowled the chamber for a shirt then snatched up the closest thing at hand, his black silk banyan. "Out. Both of you."

He went through the adjourning door to the bathing chamber.

Meredith was reclining in her nice comfortable tub, her plump lips firmed with a stubbornness he was beginning to recognize. Regularly. "Hand me that towel."

"Ah, ah, ah. Is that anyway to speak to your lord and master?" He spoke mildly but did as she… demanded.

She sat forward, the globes of her breasts—nipples rather— were still concealed by foamy water. She lifted one arm, and he snatched the towel out of her reach.

"What are you hiding? Besides your nipples," he added.

The steamy bathing chamber could have been the culprit behind the sudden rosy cheeks, but he decided to claim credit for the lovely phenomenon.

He threw the towel over his shoulder. "Give me your hand."

After a long moment, she lifted one elegant, dripping hand. He gripped her fingers and tugged her to her feet. Water sluiced over her perfectly proportioned curves. Unable to help himself, he leaned in and licked the dampness from one nipple.

She gasped and her hand tightened in his.

He moved to the other then slowly drew back. His hands tingled as if he held warm apples within his palms; his lips sizzled for want of trailing them over the supple planes of her belly.

"Plenty."

His eyes flew open. "Plenty of what?" he croaked out, meeting her puzzled gaze.

The rosy flush of her damp face deepened. "I believe I've found what Aylesbury referred to in his journal."

The words he understood, but their meaning escaped him. She seemed to be speaking in tongues or Hebrew or some sort of gibberish.

She tugged the towel from his shoulder. "I should dress," she said softly. The low husky vibrance of her voice went straight south.

"Er, yes, of course." Lucius watched as she wrapped herself in the large strip of linen, then he took her hand again, helping her from the copper tub. "There will come a time," he said. "Where we shall share this decadent bath." Where he would lather her lovely body with the scented soaps she seemed to adore.

With one foot out of the tub, the other still in, she stopped. "Share?"

"Oh, yes," he growled, retrieving her wrap for her. "Share. I'll send your maid in with clean garments."

"She is in the village with her mother. I gave her the day off. You accompanied her. Do you not recall?"

"I can't recall anything but your delectable breasts." Lucius took on the task himself and went into Meredith's bedchamber and to her wardrobe. He found a silk chemise and a drab gray dress then hurried back through her sitting room and pulled up. Ashcroft and Docia were eyeing one another warily, each on opposite sides of the room. "What the devil?"

"I wish to speak with Meredith," Docia said.

"I need to check your stitches," Ashcroft said.

Lucius shook his head and hurried into the bathing chamber.

"Prepare yourself. We've company in your sitting room."

"But, I've no shoes. Or stays. Or petticoats," she said aghast. "My *corset!*"

"Your dress should cover your feet. We are among friends."

"Friends? Your ex-lover is not my friend."

"She's not my ex-lover—"

"Current then—"

"Don't be daft, Lady Pender. You're wasting time." He slipped out of the bathing chamber, grinning. Because the situation was fraught with the ridiculous.

CHAPTER TWENTY-EIGHT

MEREDITH STRODE INTO her sitting room ahead of her husband and came to an abrupt stop, surprised. "What are you doing here?" she said to Mr. Ashcroft.

A small smile touched his lips. His fist came up with a thumb aimed in Lucius's direction. "Your husband sent for me."

"I believe I said, 'Get out,' didn't I?"

Ashcroft held up a tin box. "'Tis fortunate I brought my supplies. Don't you think so, *my lord?*"

"You'll show my husband his due respect," she snapped, sounding quite like her father. Slowly, her head turned to her other uninvited guest. "And you, Miss Hale?"

"I was coming down the stairs when Lucius issued his order. It was all quite curious and thrilling," she said without an ounce of decorum, her bright smile as inappropriate as the casual way she perched on the armrest of Meredith's favorite chair.

Meredith's jaw tightened, but she kept her composure, refusing to give Miss Hale the satisfaction of rattling her. What a fool she'd been, almost believing that scene in the library had been manufactured by Miss Hale herself. Meredith's gaze flicked to Lucius, sharp and questioning. "You invited them? Her too?"

Lucius closed the door behind him with a measured deliberateness that sent a ripple of unease through the space, through Meredith with the precision of a stiletto-point knife. His expression was unreadable, his gaze fixed on Ashcroft as though weighing the man's very existence. "Ashcroft has information you may be interested in," he said, his tone clipped. "Miss Hale's presence is… was incidental."

"I see," Meredith said coolly, folding her hands before her to keep from strangling someone, anyone. "And what answers are so urgent that they must be addressed here, in *my* sitting room?"

Ashcroft straightened and adjusted his cravat with a casual air that grated against the tension, thickening the atmosphere. "I believe your husband wishes to discuss certain… irregularities I've uncovered," he said, his gaze darting to Lucius, then back to Meredith. "Though I'm not sure Miss Hale is an appropriate audience."

"Oh, nonsense," Docia interjected with a laugh, waving a hand as though brushing away a bothersome fly. "I'm sure whatever clandestine topic—"

Meredith's gaze shot to her, the blood rushing her ears. Questions pelted her insides. Why would she have used *that* word? Did she know Geneva? Had Geneva shared their secret society with her?

She was still speaking in that annoying way Meredith so despised of young women who aimed for the highest dregs of society. "—is far less shocking than what I've already heard today. Besides, I'm here for… moral… support." She turned a coy smile on Lucius. "Aren't I, Lucius?"

Meredith's heart clenched at the easy familiarity in Docia's tone, at the way she said his name as if she had every right to claim a place in his—*their* lives. Her gaze flicked to Lucius again, searching for some sign of his intentions.

He sighed, a long-suffering sound, and pinched the bridge of his nose. "Docia," he said, his voice weary. "Perhaps you should leave us."

Docia blinked, clearly unprepared for the suggestion. "Leave? But I—"

"Now," Lucius said firmly, his tone stern and leaving no room for argument. He turned and opened the door.

Miss Hale's disbelief was palpable. Her heart-shaped face and upturned nose struck Meredith, again, as innately familiar, reminding her of Geneva of all people. Not the familiarity of having met her all those years ago at Abra's season debut. How… odd.

For a moment, the room hung in a taut silence as Lucius's edict sank in.

Horrible of Meredith, and not her proudest moment, as a surge of perverse satisfaction rippled through her.

With a huff of indignation, Miss Hale rose from the chair, smoothing her golden-colored skirts with exaggerated precision. "Well," she gasped, tossing her perfectly coiffed head. "If you insist, my lord. But do remember, I'm only here because *you* asked me to stay."

"I believe it was my father who issued the invitation," Meredith said with the politeness that was inbred to her bones. Oh, how she wanted to rail at the woman even as nagging sensations pricked at her. More importantly, she had questions. Many questions.

As Miss Hale swept past her, her perfume permeating the air, Meredith snagged her arm. "Wait."

Miss Hale turned dark blue, again familiar, eyes on her, filled with a depth of loneliness Meredith recognized within her own soul and those of her closest friends. "Your point has been made, Lady Pender. I shall endeavor to maintain my visit to Rathbourne's company."

Meredith, still holding her wrist, was quiet for a long moment. Then, softly, "Did you try to kill my husband?"

The shock on Miss Hale's face was all Meredith needed even as the atmosphere in the chamber grew suffocating.

"No. I. You…" The galling smugness Miss Hale wore like armor crumbled. She stared at Lucius, her countenance dangerously pale. "Someone *shot* at you?"

"And met their mark."

"You were almost *murdered*?" Miss Hale's voice was so shrill, Meredith nearly put hands up to cover her ears. Her slight body swayed. In an instant, Mr. Ashcroft, nearly pushing Meredith aside, caught Miss Hale just as her legs buckled beneath her in a swoon that appeared genuine.

Lucius dashed from the sitting room but returned just as quickly with a half-filled bottle of brandy and a teacup.

Mr. Ashcroft carried Docia to the settee, then took the brandy and cup from Lucius and poured out a measure.

The whole scene was surreal as Meredith wouldn't have pegged Miss Hale as the swooning sort. "What am I missing?" she asked her husband in a low voice.

"She and my aunt stumbled upon a dead body some years ago. Docia was just a girl at the time," he returned softly.

Meredith gasped. "How utterly horrifying." She drew in a deep breath, her heart going out to her. It was no secret that Miss Hale had been deserted by her father. It had been the talk in all the ballrooms for years and still believed in some circles the viscount had merely left the country. Of course, that was many years before Meredith's own come-out. But it still hadn't stopped her governess from relaying all the latest gossip every time some tidbit kindled the fires. "You may remain, Miss Hale. I retract my question. I don't believe you shot Lucius."

RELIEF, SURPRISE, AND hope sprang through Lucius. Relief that Meredith was wise beyond her years. Surprised at her quick defense of him. Hope in the belief that she was willing to give their unorthodox relationship the chance it deserved. *Deserved.* He'd truly lost his mind.

His gaze went to Meredith. The concern in her eyes for the woman he'd intended on marrying but for his and her fathers' agreement once again stirred his admiration. The smudges on her upturned face failed in detracting from her beauty. He leaned in and touched her lips with his. Slowly pulling away, he met the question in her eyes.

Why did you kiss her?

I didn't. But how was he supposed to convince her? If he'd walked in on the same scenario, he wouldn't have believed her. He'd already accused her of carrying Ashcroft's child. Lucius took her hand and brought it to his lips.

"Enough! I am not a child to be coddled over."

Lucius and Meredith turned as one to the Docia he was more familiar with. The forceful personality unchagrined and demanding. She'd regained her poise and eyed Ashcroft as if he'd wandered in from Bethnal Green or St. Giles.

Ashcroft came to his feet, his jaw tightening and letting out a harsh scoff, not bothering to disguise his disgust.

Stifling a grin, Lucius went to the door and closed it. The latch sounded through the chamber.

Meredith turned back to her husband. "Well?"

Lucius hesitated, his gaze flickering to Docia, then Ashcroft. "Are you certain about Docia remaining?"

Meredith glanced at Docia then turned back to him. "She's quite exhausting, but, yes. I'm sure."

"Thank you," Docia muttered, throwing her legs over the settee, sitting up, and smoothing her hands over her yellow dress.

"All right," he said on an exhaled breath, his voice low.

The faintest gleam of satisfaction glinted in Ashcroft's eyes. "By the way, Pender, you were spotted in the village."

"Of course I was, you dimwit. I walked straight into the village's gossip hub."

"You went to town?" Meredith demanded. "*Into* The Copper Kettle?"

Lucius's smile turned grim. "I did indeed. And it was most enlightening," he said.

The tension in the room seemed to settle on Meredith's shoulders. "It was Papa, wasn't it? He's the one who shot you." It wasn't a question.

"I overheard Thornfield and your father speaking." He took

her hand again. "I'm sorry, darling. I'm afraid he instructed Thornfield with the task."

Meredith pulled her hand from his, her brows furrowed, her face pale. Not as pale as Docia's minutes earlier, nor did it appear as if his wife was ready to swoon. She moved to the settee and dropped beside Docia, pressing the heel of her hand to her forehead. "I knew he was... was... awful, but murder?" She looked up at him, her eyes glistening with unshed tears. "It wasn't some passionate temper-led fit, was it? It was deliberate," she whispered.

"Bastard," Ashcroft bit out.

Docia's lips compressed, but she remained mute during this exchange.

Lucius crouched in front of Meredith. He wanted to comfort her, but what could he say?

Her hand flattened over his heart. "There's blood." Her voice barely rose above a whisper. "You best let Mr. Ashcroft tend to your stitches." She glanced at Docia then back to him. "We'll be fine. I've things to tell her."

With a sharp nod, he came to his feet and exited the sitting chamber with Ashcroft behind him.

Once inside Lucius's bedchamber via the bathing chamber, Ashcroft set his tin box on the bedside table. He pulled his spectacles from his waistcoat pocket and slipped them on. "Don't know why we're bothering to doctor you up."

"Because my wife demands it," he said wryly.

The late afternoon sun struggled to pierce the heavy drapes, casting long, somber shadows across the chamber. Lucius moved next to the bed, discarded his banyan, and stood wordlessly watching Ashcroft situate his tin box.

Ashcroft gently tugged at the bandages. "Why didn't you tell Meredith who I am?"

"Frankly, I forgot. But I think I will leave that to you. Should be quite the awkward conversation."

"Something you take great pleasure in, I take it?"

"I don't want her angry at me. I've done enough damage," he said with a quick grin. It just as quickly disappeared. "Rathbourne fears Parliament is going to enforce the laws passed in the Mines Act, isn't he? But I fear my knowledge on it is limited."

"1842."

"What?"

"The Mines and Collieries Act of 1842. Basically, it prohibits women and girls from working underground in the mines. Too dangerous. The act also bans boys under the age of ten. Before that, boys from the age of five were put to work."

The bandages came away without Lucius even feeling them. "Good God," he breathed. No wonder Meredith was so angry. "So if there are inspections…"

"They would have to comply with the laws." Ashcroft straightened and stood back. "And here is the real kicker, my friend."

Lucius lifted a brow at this familiarity.

Ashcroft folded his arms over his chest and rocked back on his heels. No apology forthcoming. And why should there be? He was Rathbourne's heir after all. "The fact that you are not dead means you could be charged with the same crimes. *You* are the Earl of Pender."

"Christ." Lucius shoved his hand through his hair. "You're right. Meredith, too, could be charged."

"Unless we learn exactly why Rathbourne is so determined to keep the inspectors at bay. He owns thirty percent of the mineral rights, I believe."

"You don't remember? It was in the betrothal agreement you had in your possession—in case you've forgotten," he added, his voice coated with irony.

Ashcroft disregarded his jibe, his thoughts already whirring with something Lucius couldn't read. He dug around in his tin and pulled out the salve then applied it. "The stitch is torn just a little. If you can restrain yourself from overzealous activity for another few days, you'll likely be fine."

"The mineral rights?" Lucius prodded him.

"Right." Ashcroft tugged off his glasses and slid them back where he'd retrieved them, speaking absently, as if his thoughts were already miles beyond the current track. "I haven't observed children working the mines. Not under the age of twelve at any rate." His eyes blinked and his focus was back. "It was your wife who was instrumental in keeping the really young children from the mines due to the school she introduced." He sounded proud, admiring. "She literally pays families to keep their children in school."

And, damn if Lucius could fault him. The same sense of appreciative gratification filled him at what she'd accomplished over the past three years. On. Her. Own. "Tommy Trenwith?"

"Yes. There's also talk in Parliament of another inquiry. The Mines Act of '42 was just the start. They're looking for heads to put on pikes," Ashcroft said, his voice low but firm. "I suspect he and Thornfield are hiding something even more nefarious."

Lucius pinned Ashcroft, his eyes narrowing.

Again, the man ignored him. "My mind keeps going back to those missing stewards."

"Hell." Lucius flew off the bed and snatched his banyan. "My coat."

Ashcroft's brows beetled.

"I searched Thornfield's office and found a book. A ledger of sorts. Some of those missing stewards' names were listed. Beside their names were notations of 'removed' and 'relocated' and 'resolved.'" Silence filled the room after this little revelation. "Not very encouraging, is it?" Lucius said.

Ashcroft paced the room, again with that closed yet thoughtful look on his face. "Rathbourne's not wrong to worry. The employment of children younger than ten working the mines is quite specific and a direct violation of the law. Hell, the Trenwith child was ten. And though he snuck inside, his age alone doesn't break the law. Indeed, it speaks volumes that Thornfield offered no protest when Meredith fixed the age limit to twelve."

Lucius frowned. "And the women?"

"As long as they are not working below ground… again, not illegal. Which tells me…"

"That if inspectors come sniffing about, they'll find more than enough to hang him," Lucius finished for him.

"—and you." Ashcroft's lips compressed.

The possibility infuriated Lucius. He crossed the room in a few long strides to the fire. "And me. This is Rathbourne's and my father's doing. Their mines, their overseer, their orders. Neither Meredith nor I had anything to do with any of it."

Ashcroft's tone was sharp. "True. Unless we can learn what they are hiding. I suspect your death not only gives my father control of everything through Lady Pender, but also a place to lay blame. Your name is still tied to the estate, and these are your lands. Do you think Parliament or the broadsheet dwellers will care to untangle the nuances? You'll both be condemned."

Lucius ran a hand through his hair, pacing the room. "So, what then? Do I march into Thornfield's and demand to know what he's hiding?" He stopped. The ledgers he'd received from Thornfield. The numbers hadn't added up. "Thornfield's likely skimming profits."

"Probably not enough for Rathbourne to care. No. There has to be something else."

Something hit Lucius like a kick in his chest. "Meredith caught Rathbourne searching the study. It didn't make sense because the room is unusable and being readied for renovation."

"Apparently, he's desperate enough to silence anyone who threatens his control," Ashcroft said, his voice taking on a darker edge. His hand squeezed into a fist at his side. "He knows the tide is turning. He's scared." His lips curled in a cutting smile sharp as a dagger's edge glinting in candlelight. Again, his eyes focused. "We need that book you took from Thornfield."

"Yes. Yes, we do." Lucius stormed from his chamber prepared to shock anyone who crossed his path.

CHAPTER TWENTY-NINE

"WHERE'S YOUR MAID?" Miss Hale's pretentious tone returned with a vengeance.

"I granted her leave for the day." Meredith strode across her bedchamber and splashed her face with the cold water in the basin and shivered. She took up a scrap of linen and patted her face dry.

"What the devil are you wearing?"

Meredith glanced down at the serviceable gray dress Lucius had appropriated for her. The lovely, out-of-date green-and-white striped silk lay across the bed alongside the apron she'd worn to cover the gown. The apron was smudged with dirt and the pockets still bulged with the treasures she'd yet to unwrap, quickening her pulse with anticipation.

"You aren't with child, are you?"

Surprised she'd nearly forgotten her presence, Meredith's gaze shot to Miss Hale. Miss Hale's question had been delivered more as a sullen statement of disappointment. What Meredith saw shocked her. Hurt, despair, and a flicker of envy, all poorly masked behind Miss Hale's what Meredith was starting to recognize as an armor as dense as Perlsea Keep's stone façade.

Meredith's breath hitched, the weight of the unspoken tension settling between them. "No," she said gently. "I understand my father announced the fabrication at the late Lord Pender's memorial gathering." Her own confidence faltered and her voice trembled at the edges. "That's what sent my husband flying to my side, I suppose. And now you—"

Miss Hale averted her eyes, twisting a delicate handkerchief in her hands she'd tugged from her sleeve. "Yes," she murmured, almost to herself. "It's why he's here. But…"

Meredith's chest tightened. "But?"

Miss Hale's gaze snapped back to hers, her voice sad, resigned. "But he suddenly seems… interested. In you. It's because you are a duke's daughter."

"I have my doubts on that score." A wryness accompanied the words. "If it makes you feel any better, it didn't start out that way," Meredith said, thinking back to that first night. "He arrived with an annulment agreement."

Miss Hale's face lit up with a flash of hope that quickly dimmed.

Meredith felt so badly for Miss Hale, she would gladly have turned her husband over to the poor woman if Meredith hadn't fallen so deeply in love—*love?* She swallowed and grew a little lightheaded.

"But?" Miss Hale's soft voice pierced the sudden jumble of her mind.

Meredith reached over and touched her hand. "But no longer. I'm sorry, Miss Hale. Our marriage has since been consummated. He… belongs here. With me."

"Yes." She sighed. "I-I can see that."

"What will you do now?" Meredith asked her, curiosity nipping.

"Return home, I suppose. Become the doting aunt to my sister's children."

"Sister?" Meredith frowned, thinking back to Abra's come-out ball. "I don't recall you having siblings."

"I had an older sister who died when at sixteen. But recently it's come to light that my father…" She hauled in a deep breath and let it out. "My father had another child. Turns out her mother married a horrid man to keep my sister from being born out of wedlock. She was raised…" Her face turned an unbecoming shade of red that clashed with her goldish frock of the latest French plates.

The back of Meredith's neck prickled. "Raised where?" she asked lightly.

Miss Hale's nose wrinkled. "On Berwick Street."

Meredith's mouth dropped opened, the muscles so slack she couldn't seem to snap it shut. "Geneva?" That's who Docia Hale reminded her of. It was all so clear now. Everything fell into place. Her friend's upbringing. Her speech.

"Yes, Geneva Wimbley. Now, Geneva Oshea. She married Lucius's younger brother, Noah. I suppose you know him."

The shocking news brought forth a bark of laughter that mutated into something more hysterical that brought tears to Meredith's eyes. "Er, yes. I'm familiar with Mr. Noah Oshea. I send the bills to him for the Keep's renovation."

"Geneva is quite forthright," Miss Hale said defensively, "in an endearing sort of way."

Meredith wiped the tears from her eyes. "Please, do forgive me, Miss Hale. I'm not laughing at you or Geneva. She happens to be one of my dearest friends. We attended school together, you know. Her mother sent her to Miss Greensley's School of Comportment for Young Ladies of Quality."

In an instant, Miss Hale's shoulders relaxed. "Oh." Then she smiled. A genuine smile that was certainly reminiscent of Geneva's. "You may as well call me Docia." She stood and moved about Meredith's chamber, running her finger along some of the furniture.

"Thank you, Docia. You are welcome at Perlsea Keep for as long as you like. Frankly, we could use the help diverting my father."

She spun around, her eyes narrowed. "Diverting him from what?"

"There's something afoot. We aren't quite sure what nefarious deeds he is up to. But," she finished grimly, "it isn't good."

"Oh, of course." Docia continued her perusal, reaching the

vanity, picking up and sniffing bottles of perfume and pots of cream. She moved to the bed and fingered the apron. "What do you know of your Mr. Ashcroft?" Her attempt at nonchalance fell way short.

Meredith leaned against the table, her hands planted at her sides and watched her, touched with bemusement and still astonished that this woman was her friend's half-sister. "He was a traveling scholar when I hired him," she said. "He now acts as my—our—steward. He teaches at the village school we created in Penhalwick."

Again, Docia's shoulders fell, this time in defeat. "How wasteful," she said on an expelled breath.

"Wasteful in what matter?" Meredith asked her.

"Attractive—but for that awful beard. Untitled." She picked up the apron, sagging heavily with the items still in the pockets. "What's this?"

"Oh." Meredith hurried over and took possession of the garment. "I'd nearly forgotten." She spread it out on the bed and pulled each item from its location. "I found a hidden compartment in the wine cellar." She glanced up at this unlikely companion, grinning.

"How on earth did that come about?" The pretentiousness seemed to have completely dissipated.

"I found an old journal that belonged to the Marquess of Aylesbury. Apparently, Lucius's mother lived here as a child. Aylesbury was her father or grandfather. I've forgotten which. In any event, reading it was quite enlightening."

"Sounds like something one might read in a horrid novel."

"Abra, Geneva, Hannah, and I found such novels all fun when we were younger," she said, a delicious shiver going down her spine. "Aylesbury had some intriguing passages." She selected the papers she'd seen earlier.

Docia picked up a much smaller item, unwrapping it to reveal a small vial. "What on earth?" She started to uncork it but Meredith stopped her.

"Wait," she said quickly. "The things I read in the journal spoke of doing someone in. That could be poison."

"Oh, dear." Docia set it aside and picked up another token and unwrapped it. "A key." She held out an ornate key of heavy crafted, now tarnished, silver with unusual markings that resembled old family crests. The letter "A" was distinct and prominently engraved in the handle.

"This proves the items belonged to Lucius's grandfather." Her own voice was hardly above a whisper. "As I said, the castle came to the Pender estates through his mother."

"It's lovely," Docia whispered in the same barely audible tone. "What do you suppose it opens?"

Meredith shook her head. "Perhaps a safe or drawer in the hidden library."

Docia's eyes gleamed. "Hidden library?"

"Yes, but we are forbidden to enter. It's too dangerous. What else have we?"

The next token Docia selected and unwrapped was a signet ring. "The tarnished silver matches that of the key. Though it bears an emblem of an owl with a dagger—" It was a crest Meredith didn't recognize. "Do you think this was Aylesbury's?"

She took the ring from Docia, lifted and studied it. "I don't know. The face of Papa's bears our family crest and is gold."

"Look! On the inside. There's a 'P'…" Her voice trailed and she slowly met Meredith's eyes, her dark-blue eyes so like Geneva's were huge in her heart-shaped face.

"Pender?" Meredith's voice cracked, knowing the possibility was real.

Docia dropped the ring on the bed and took Meredith by the arms. "Dear heavens. You are white as an ocean's foam." She spun her quickly and pushed Meredith to sitting on the edge of the bed before her legs gave out beneath her, her stomach threatening to recoil.

"How could it not be? One… one of the passages Aylesbury wrote was how he had to include his daughter's husband into his scheme because he couldn't very well tell his daughter and wife."

"What scheme?"

"That's what we are trying to learn." A glass of water was placed in her hand.

"Drink."

Meredith gulped the contents. "It must belong to one of the families involved with the marquess's scheme." She retrieved the ring. "Its weight and the intricate detailing suggest it a prized possession of someone influential." She looked up at Docia, this unlikely and unexpected friend. "Lord Pender married Aylesbury's wife. We have to talk to Lucius."

DRESSED FOR DINNER—TO alleviate speculation of course—Lucius left Ashcroft in his bedchamber and stole down a different back stairwell, one the servants rarely used. The faint tap of his boots echoed in the stillness as he emerged in a hall that brought him past the old study and the renovated library.

The scent of varnished oak lingered, mingling with the faint musk of the stone walls. He paused, surveying the vestibule ahead, where the gas lights in the chandelier above reflected off the polished wood floors.

This section of the Keep was a far cry from his memories as a small child. Gone were the faded tapestries and peeling paint. In their place stood walls painted in soft cream with delicate moldings and sconces that cast a warm glow over the space. It was tasteful, efficient, and all Meredith's touch.

Still, for all its improvements, the Keep remained an irritating maze. Especially at urgent moments like this one.

He reached the vestibule that was, thankfully, devoid of occupants. Then he realized… he had *no idea where Verity stashed greatcoats, pelisses, bonnets, and such.* Turning, he squinted at the paneling to his right. "Where in blazes is the cloakroom?" he muttered.

His gaze fell upon a section of paneling along the entryway wall. It seemed to ripple subtly in the gaslight, the grain of the oak slightly off kilter from the rest. He frowned and stepped closer, running his fingers along one edge.

"Ah." A quiet click and the panel gave way, revealing the hidden door set almost seamlessly in the wall. "Clever." More of his wife's ingenuity, he'd wager.

A disguised door. Perfect for appearances and thoroughly maddening for practicality. He gave a rueful shake of his head and with a tug, the door creaked open, revealing a modest cloakroom lined with hooks, shelves, and the faintly musty smell of wool and damp leather. His coat was there, slung haphazardly over a hook as though mocking him for his struggle. He released a relieved breath, straightened his coat on the peg then checked the pocket—

Gone. The book from Thornfield's office safe was... gone. Thankfully, however, the missive and the ledger papers were still there. He moved into the light and opened the letter from Noah. It was addressed to Meredith. He read through it quickly.

Stonemare Castle, Northumberland
5 April 1847

To the Right Honourable Meredith, Countess of Pender
Perlsea Keep, Cornwall

My dear sister-in-law,

I trust this letter finds you in good health and spirits, though I imagine the news I bring may come as something of a surprise. It is with a heavy heart that I inform you of mine and Lucius's father's passing on 29 March. The Earl of Pender has left us, his burdens and duties now falling to Lucius, of course, who has inherited both the title and the responsibilities that accompany it.

As the wife of the new earl, your status has accordingly ris-

en from Viscountess of Perlsea to Countess of Pender. While I regret that such news must be delivered under such somber circumstances, I hope you will take solace in the opportunities this transition may bring to influence and assist those under your care at Perlsea.

I must also extend my personal thanks for the efforts I hear you have undertaken to manage the estate in Cornwall. It is no small task to restore and maintain such a property, and your diligence speaks volumes of your character.

My brother has been deeply preoccupied with the affairs left in Father's wake, but I trust he will join you in Cornwall soon to discuss the path forward. Until then, if there is any assistance I might offer, you need only write.

Please convey my regards to those at Perlsea Keep and know that you have my heartfelt condolences in this time of change and reflection.

Yours faithfully,
Noah Oshea

So... Meredith had never received the notice regarding Father's demise. What need had Thornfield to keep the information from her? He glanced back to the hidden door. And, who had stolen the journal from Lucius's greatcoat? Nothing made the slightest bit of sense.

His whole world wavered before him. Lucius raced up the grand stairs by two, stormed his bedchamber and found it— *empty.*

He bent over with one hand on his knee to catch his breath and gather his bearings. Ashcroft was in on it. Why else would the man have disappeared? He knew everything, could have Lucius transported. Just the bit he'd shared with Ashcroft could be construed as Lucius having prior knowledge of those missing stewards.

And, perhaps most important of all? Why hide his identity from Meredith the last three years?

Goddamn. The bastard had him by his nether regions.

Chapter Thirty

MEREDITH PEELED BACK the burlap coverings, revealing a bundle of letters, yellowed with age, held together with a piece of twine. She tugged at the twine even as fear prickled her skin. Taking the top missive, her fingers shaking, she carefully unfolded it from a seal that had long since cracked.

To Lord Aylesbury
14 November 1762

My Esteemed Lord Aylesbury,

Matters proceed as anticipated, though our recent discovery in the lower mine shaft presents a complication. The laborers' superstitions are easily stoked, and the sight of so many re-mains has created an uneasiness even of the most hearty overseers. This grave, though unexpected, may serve as an opportunity if managed correctly.

I propose the following: the bodies shall remain undis-turbed. Any attempts to relocate them risk exposure. 'Tis imperative the miners believe nothing more than an unfortunate relic of our forebears' folly was the unfortunate outcome.

Perhaps the spreading of a rumor of an ancient collapse—a cautionary tale for the weak-minded is in order. If we encourage the notion the Keep's foundations are cursed, it will go far in quelling curiosity.

I've enclosed a diagram carefully marked with points of concern. These locations are where the operations must remain shrouded. Should we be forced to expand further, ensure that no laborer is allowed near the marked shafts without proper supervision.

I implore you to burn this diagram once you've memorized its contents. Should this information fall into the wrong hands, the consequences would be... catastrophic.

As for the safety measures, Parliament prattles on about your man in the Commons. He must move swiftly. The prospect of enforced standards would bankrupt all six of us needlessly. Personally I will not see my investment squandered by fools and bleeding hearts. We must ensure that key votes are swayed. My contributions to the cause will follow upon confirmation of success.

Thornfield has proven himself a capable fixer, though I remind you, his loyalty hinges on continued payments. The man knows enough to be a threat should he turn on The Order. Watch him closely, Aylesbury. Ensure he feels indispensable but never untouchable.

Our collaborators grow restless, and I note hesitation among some of our circle. Weakness in any form should not be tolerated. Should dissent arise, you know what must be done. The future of our endeavors depends on unity, and I will not see us undone by sentiment or cowardice.

My son's inheritance depends upon the secrecy of these arrangements, as does the prosperity of your own line. Should this knowledge surface, it would end us both.

Yrs. R

Meredith refolded the missive with violently trembling fingers, swallowing back bile. Her head spun at the implications. R. *Rathbourne?* Surely not. But who else could it be? A letter of this significance would explain her father's appearance at Perlsea Keep, his nosing about in chambers that should not concern him, and worst of all, the attempt on Lucius's life. To the depths of her soul, she felt the letter had been authored by her grandfather. And somehow Grandpapa had coerced her father into cooperating.

"Lucius needs to know about these," she said, urgency surging through her.

"Dear heavens, you are white as chalk." Docia took the letter from her tenuous hold and set it atop the others, then retied the twine. "What do you wish to do?"

Meredith gathered up the key, the signet ring, took the bundle of letters from Docia, and the other pages she was suddenly too frightened to look at. "Speak to Lucius. Right away." With difficulty, she grappled with her composure but managed to lead Docia back through the sitting room, to the bathing chamber that led to Lucius's chamber.

"My heavens," Docia breathed from behind, her voice filled with unexpected awe. Meredith turned to see her spin in a slow circle. "Why, this isn't a sitting room at all."

"It was at one time," Meredith murmured relieved to find her voice more steady. "It's a bath—"

"A bathing chamber. In the wilds of Cornwall." Docia turned, her eyes wide with incredulous delight. "More like your own bathing palace! How perfectly decadent."

Docia picked up a neatly folded towel and pressed it to her nose, inhaling deeply. "Meredith, this must have cost a fortune. Lucius outdid him—"

Meredith snorted. "Stop right there, Miss Hale. I hadn't seen him in three years as you are well aware," she muttered, surveying the luxury about her. Her gaze landed on the small collection of grooming tools set precisely on the vanity amid bottles of scented oils and a bowl filled with salt crystals. When had he done that?

Docia's gleeful exploration was interrupted by a soft click of the adjourning door of Lucius's bedchamber.

Mr. Ashcroft stepped through.

"God's teeth," Mr. Ashcroft huffed out. "I thought half of today's students had somehow found their way to the Keep without my knowing." He paused, taking in the room with a shock similar to that of Docia's. His gaze flickered from Docia whose expression hovered between shock and indignation, clutching the violet-scented towel like a prize to her chest.

"Mr. Ashcroft," Meredith said, her voice clipped. "Where is Lucius?"

"Retrieving something from his greatcoat. The work here is impressive," he said with mild surprise. He'd been aware of the work of course, since he'd dealt with the bills: handling the correspondence and sending the requests for payments to Mr. Oshea in Northumberland.

"It's not every day one finds a bathing chamber in such a gloomy castle—" Docia shook her head. "And, in Cornwall of all places." She spun to Meredith. "You must allow me to try it out."

Meredith doubted Docia was one for begging, but...

"Indeed," Mr. Ashcroft said, his tone maddeningly neutral. "Though I must warn you, Miss Hale, Lord Pender values his privacy."

Docia's eyes widened then narrowed. "How dare you, sir!" She looked to Meredith for rescue, but Meredith merely pinched the bridge of her nose.

"Come along, Docia. Mr. Ashcroft, it is imperative I speak with Lucius as soon—"

The door widened behind him and her husband filled the doorway. Fury mottled his expression then landed on Ashcroft. His expression cleared though his brows met in a puzzled frown.

"Are we holding a meeting in the bathing chamber for any particular reason? Has Rathbourne uncovered *all* our sanctuaries?"

Meredith clutched the items she held to her breast, unsure of divulging their contents in present company.

"Meredith read a letter that nearly had her swooning," Docia informed him.

She bit back a groan, darting a glare at Docia—her back rather since she stood in front of Meredith. *Truly?* Spinning on her slippered heel, Meredith strode into her sitting room, to the table near the windows, and set down the articles. The noise behind indicated the others had followed.

Again, with fingers less than steady, she drew in a deep breath. She grasped the twine on the bundled letters and tugged. She took the top one and held it out to her husband much preferring to warn him of the contents, but Docia had stolen that opportunity.

Lucius's gaze swept the page, his demeanor darkening incrementally, his silent fury expanding like a mist until it consumed her sitting room—tangible and throbbing—with each passing moment. He lifted his eyes, meeting hers. "You believe Rathbourne penned this?"

"My grandfather," she whispered. "I cannot fathom Papa…" Her vision blurred with welled tears.

Her husband clasped her hand and squeezed, then let go and set the letter aside, going through the rest of the bundle. A task that didn't appear to satisfy him. Seconds later, his fingers rested on the other stack of pages. The air grew palpable until Meredith could hardly breathe.

It seemed as if he gathered a cloak of inner force before picking up and glancing over the aged papers with their frayed edges, perusing each one quickly, then again, setting them aside. The fourth or fifth one down, she'd lost count, he lifted his eyes to hers again. What she saw in their stormy gray depths chilled her blood to black ice.

Slowly, she lifted her hand. It felt as if she were reaching for a viper, its venom promising an agony and an end she could not escape. She lowered her eyes to the parchment.

At the top, a heading in bold, formal script read:

Registry of Interest: Aylesbury Compact, 1758
Hereby referred to as The Order

Just below, several names appeared with brief, vague titles and an identifier spelling out their supposed roles. The audacity was astonishing.

The Most Honourable Marquess of Aylesbury
Custodian of Holdings and Keeper of Records
The Right Honourable Earl of Pender
Chief Overseer of Operations, Western Veins
His Grace The Duke of Rathbourne
Patron of Governance and Protector of Secrets
~~Baronet Greaves, Baronet of Windbrook Abbey~~
The Most Honourable Marquess Blackstone
Heir Apparent to Rathbourne
Arbiter of Continuity and Logistics Overseer.
Sir Edgar Hollingbrook, MP
Advocate of Parliamentary Interests
Mr. Oswald Vayne
Custodian of Funds and Facilitator of Transfers

She read through the list to the bottom of the page to the most sinister line of all:

"Bound by blood and silence. Betrayal warrants swift reprisal."

The handwriting was neat but varied, suggesting parts may have been amended, even added later.

The small wax seal in the lower right corner gave the menacing document a sense of authenticity. All sealed, rather, stamped with a crest that matched that of the signet ring. Not Aylesbury's—she'd seen his enough to realize that—perhaps one had been created to represent the compact.

Swallowing hard, Meredith found she couldn't speak, the words stuck in her throat. She opened her palm, now indented from clutching the ring and key so tightly.

Lucius took the items, then her arm, and guided her to the settee before the fire. "Where's the damn brandy when one is in need?" he demanded to no one in particular. He dropped beside her and studied the crest.

"They match the one on the document," she whispered.

Mr. Ashcroft padded across the carpet with hardly a sound. Yet each step seemed to pound in rhythm with Meredith's blood. He picked up the damning paper with its yellowed age and brittle edges. She felt ill in the passing seconds.

His own countenance seemed to go pale as he read. "Jesus." The whisper echoed about her skull with the force of an ancient anvil.

"How informative," Ashcroft bit out. The bitterness in his tone was as mysterious as it was, also, telling.

Lucius leaned in and brushed his lips over Meredith's. "We'll get things sorted out, darling." He stood and moved back to the table beside Ashcroft. Lucius sorted through the other papers Meredith had found, marveling at how she'd found that compartment.

In a wine cellar.

In the floor.

It boggled one's mind at her deductive reasoning. Lucius possessed no such intelligence. But rather than resenting her superiority in that particular area, he found his chest welling with an unspeakable pride. It stunned him to the bottom of his soul. His fingers stopped at a familiar page that was years old. One he'd seen before yet… hadn't.

"What is it?" Ashcroft said softly.

"A map. There's a similar one in Thornfield's office."

Ashcroft took the delicate sheet and stared down at it.

Lucius leaned forward. "I believe it's a layout of the mine."

The map was brittle with age, its edges curling inward as though reluctant to reveal its secrets. Ashcroft laid it on the table and smoothed it flat as carefully as he'd applied the salve to Lucius's shoulder. Ink lines, faded yet precise, were sprawled across the surface, delineating the mine's complex layout with an unsettling exactness to the one on Thornfield's office wall.

The top was marked by a bold "X" that appeared to mark the mine's entrance. The mark helped in orienting one's position. Just beyond a large open area, two main tunnels diverged, fanning out like tributaries from the Thames. The passage to the left ended abruptly in chaotic scrawls and jagged lines, annotated with a single, ominous word: "Danger."

Ashcroft set a blunted fingertip to that area. "This here is where the most recent cave-in happened. Where Tommy Trenwith died."

Where rubble and sorrow coalesced Lucius didn't say. Didn't need to say.

The tunnel to the right twisted with meandering lines that grew thinner and more intricate—as if the cartographer had hesitated to commit to the certainty of what lay beyond. Numerous smaller veins appeared to splinter off, labeled with unfamiliar names—"Polmear Seam," "St. Eustace," "Silver-hope"—indicating sections already mined and were perhaps abandoned, their riches long since extracted beyond usefulness.

The central shaft was marked with a thick, almost gouged circle. The mine's fulcrum? Notes in cramped, spidery handwriting surrounded it: "Ore pulleys," "Staging grounds," "Rest house." It was clear this area served as the bustling hub, the heartbeat of its operation. From there, tracks snaked outward, annotated with precise measurements, revealing a well-organized network for transporting the tin to the surface.

Near the bottom-right corner, the map shifted. The lines were darker, more deliberate, unlabeled, indicating the deep recesses. A cavern was sketched in unnerving detail that raised the hair on Lucius's neck.

Unlike the rest of the map, this section projected a fervent intensity that seemed to leap from the parchment. The shading was more intricate, the dimensions painstakingly noted and marked by an enigmatic phrase: "Sanctum Inviolatum." *Sacred and unviolated.*

His breath hitched. He traced the area with an index finger. Surrounding the cavern, faint marks suggested barriers or collapses, intentionally or naturally sealing it from view. "No opening is indicated," he said grimly. Scrawled next to the cavern was: "Chamber of Rest." How easy it would be to dismiss this as a romanticized euphemism, but the ominous undertones were difficult to ignore especially in light of the note Meredith had discovered.

The far edges of the map showed more winding tunnels, their paths looping and doubling back, as if the mine itself did its best to confound intruders—at the least, one attempting to decipher the map. Several other paths were annotated with warnings: "Flood risk," "Unstable rock," and "No entry."

Ashcroft tapped the map with one finger. "These notes seem to serve as genuine precautions."

"Or serve as a clever misdirection," Lucius returned.

"Yes," Ashcroft returned softly. "My exact sentiment."

Lucius glanced up at his unlikely partner in crime. "I do believe a visit is required."

"Tonight?"

"Of course—"

"Absolutely not." Meredith had moved quietly and disturbingly close. She shoved between them. "No. I won't have it."

Lucius caught her by her one upper arm, planted a kiss on her full lips. "We've no option, darling. We'll be careful. Don't—"

Her finger landed gently across his lips. "Don't tell me to not worry. I have a horrible feeling." A single tear spilled over her bottom lash. "I will not be placated."

"All right," he said in a low voice. "Can't you see? We have to go. We'll return as soon as we can. With no one the wiser."

She dropped her hand and escaped into her bedchamber.

Lucius stared at the closed door. He was torn between haring after her and setting plans in motion with Ashcroft. He glanced at Docia. "Stay with her."

Her blonde curls bobbed with her agreement, and she hurried after Meredith. The door latching behind her was as final as the sealing of a tomb.

"Back to the business at hand," Lucius said gruffly. "We'll go on foot. If we arrive after the third shift settles in, there's less chance of drawing notice…"

Ashcroft's head dipped a sharp nod. "Horses would be too noticeable." He turned back to the map, then tapped a spot in that far left corner. "Look here."

Lucius pushed Meredith from his mind. Concentrating on her fear was too detrimental for a task fraught with so much at risk. He focused on the practicalities required. He leaned in attempting to dissect what he was looking at. "I'll be damned…"

Ashcroft's eyes took on a menacing glint. "Suppose it's another entrance?"

Lucius grinned. "Only one way to find out."

CHAPTER THIRTY-ONE

THE WORLD HAD fallen into uneasy silence by the time Lucius and Ashcroft left the Keep from a door as far from Rathbourne's chambers as Lucius could locate. The change of workers was marked by a low, distant toll of the bell—the night shift had begun at the mine.

With the Keep's staff and the duke long abed, Lucius risked only a brief glance at the darkened windows of the old castle before tugging his coat tighter and pulling down his hat. He nodded to Ashcroft.

Ashcroft carried a satchel under one arm and a lantern in his other hand. He masterfully kept its glass shielded so that only a faint gleam of light spilled onto the narrow path ahead.

Lucius kept his hand on the hilt of a sword cane, the blade hidden within its polished shaft. Old habits from London died hard. Especially when skulking about like thieves in the night.

Skirting Penhalwick's main thoroughfare took them along a barely discernable path and up a slight hill that ran behind The Copper Kettle. It took a good half hour to reach the old mining path that was as treacherous as it had been forgotten. Thick mud from the earlier rains clung to his boots, and the occasional gnarled root and jagged rock caught his steps.

By mutual and silent agreement, they paused now and then to wait out some drunkard belting out a bawdy tune that echoed through the hills. The narrow, winding trail cut through overgrown edges before curving to the backside of the mine's office. Mother Nature had been generous enough to provide sporadic moonlight with the passing of dark clouds moving amid a brisk breeze in the cool summer night.

Ashcroft stopped behind a copse of trees and pointed up another incline to a structure overlooking the expanse of the Perlsea Mine in the brief spill of moonlight. "That's Thornfield's house," he murmured.

Lucius followed the direction he indicated. The house appeared as a silhouette against the glowing backdrop of the moon's beam. No candles from the windows illuminated its stark gloom. The clouds did another pass, effectively rendering it nearly invisible.

In the quiet, they could have been the only two people alive. Lucius shuddered.

Ashcroft lowered to one knee.

The trees rustled and they froze.

Waited.

"It's nothing," Ashcroft whispered. He set the lantern on the ground and pulled the map from his satchel. The flickering light cast strange, fleeting shadows over Ashcroft's sharp features, lending the man the air of a specter.

Already brimming with suspicion, Lucius surveyed the darkness crowding them and found his unease growing. The breeze faded to a deadened hush that was near suffocating.

Ashcroft tapped the map against the flattened side of his satchel, then traced a line. "This path should lead us on around toward the water. If there is another entrance as we suspect, the opening will be on that side." Ashcroft's voice was barely audible.

After an interminable amount of time that seemed hours of strained silence, Lucius said, "All right. Let's go." Even whispering, his voice sounded too loud against the hushed backdrop of the night.

Ashcroft replaced the map, came to his feet, and grabbed the lantern.

Lucius took the lead on a steepened path as the mine came

into view. Its towering shape rose against the clouds, its beams stark and angular exposed by another bout of moonlight. From the distance, the faint clatter of carts and muffled voices of miners at work sounded.

Avoiding the main entrance, they kept low, rounding the backside of the mine property until the distant roar of waves crashing against the cliffs below echoed faintly. It was a stark reminder of how perilous the edges of the Cornish coast were.

Ashcroft moved alongside Lucius and gestured toward a narrow fissure in the hillside, half-hidden behind a thicket of brambles. Lucius recognized its location from the map. From all accounts, it looked like a forgotten side shaft, long disused. But the hair at his neck raised along with chilled bumps on his skin that hinted at something infinitely more sinister.

"This must be it," Ashcroft whispered.

"All right." Lucius began pulling aside branches then eyed the narrow opening with another sense of foreboding. "These are just sitting here."

"To hide the entrance." Ashcroft set his satchel on the ground and pulled out a torch. He lit it with quick efficiency, then handed it to Lucius before retrieving his satchel once more. The small flame flared to life and cast flickering shadows as they crossed the threshold of the rough stone entryway.

The walls were rough-hewn, marked by the toil of countless hands. Water dripped from above, the sound irregular and echoing in the confined space.

"This shaft hasn't been used in decades," Lucius murmured, holding the torch high. The light caught on a faded sign near the entrance—half-rotted wood scrawled with warnings in Cornish. He frowned. "Does that say what I think it says?"

Ashcroft gave him a tight smile. "That we shouldn't be here? I expect so."

Lucius let out a low snort. "Encouraging."

The passageway narrowed as they pressed deeper within. Loose stones crunched and echoed beneath their boots, and the air felt colder with each step. Something about the stillness of the mine—untouched by human hands for so long—felt wrong. Ominous.

"Here," Ashcroft said, pausing at a fork in the tunnel. He consulted the map again, his brow furrowed. "The back portion we're looking for is farther ahead. But the layout isn't consistent with the rest of the mine. It's almost as if—" A faint sound interrupted him.

Lucius stiffened, his hurt arm twinging as his hand went to the hilt of his cane sword. It was distant, but unmistakable: the scuff of a footstep on loose stone.

"We're not alone," Lucius murmured, his voice low. For a moment, only the sound of their breathing filled the space. Then, from somewhere deeper in the mine, came a barely discernable creak—the groan of shifting timber.

Lucius's grip tightened. He had the distinct feeling they were walking into more than just a forgotten part of the mine. Seconds later, the narrow passageway opened into a cavernous room.

Slowly, Lucius and Ashcroft edged toward an open pit in the old mine shaft and held up their lights—Lucius the torch, Ashcroft the lantern. The ebony gloom seemed to swallow much of the illumination.

The metallic tang of tin and damp earth hit his nostrils. And something else.

Something unspeakable.

Rot. Sour and cloying, it seeped into the lungs, choking his every breath. The kind of smell that stuck to the back of one's throat.

The smell of... death.

THE FIRE CRACKLED faintly in the hearth, its warmth doing little to soothe Meredith's frayed nerves. She paced the length of her sitting room, her hands twisting the lace handkerchief she held until it threatened to tear with her intermittent stops at the window. Once the lantern had disappeared completely from view, sporadic moonlight filtered through the thin drapes, casting silvery patterns over the thick rug. Docia was splashing about, moaning with aggravating delight from Meredith's bathing chamber.

"I don't know how you keep from spending every spare moment in here," she called out. "I vow, you'll wear a path into the floorboards if you don't stop your pacing."

"And if you utter another single word, I vow I shall hold you under the water," Meredith muttered.

"I heard that." Docia's voice was light, amused, as though Meredith's unease were an overreaction to some minor inconvenience.

Meredith shot the door a glare. "Lucius and Ashcroft could be in danger this very moment, and you think I should sit down and read? Embroider?"

The door from the bathing chamber opened and Docia stood in the arch, her blonde hair darker from its dampness. She hugged a wrap about her. "They're grown men, Meredith. They can manage a walk in the dark without you hovering. Besides, I hardly see how working yourself into a frenzy will help anyone."

A faint noise reached Meredith—a dull thud, coming from *her* bedchamber. The scathing retort she was set to deliver died in her throat. "Did you hear that?" she whispered, turning toward her bedchamber.

"Hear what? The sound of your overactive imagination?"

Unease roiled in Meredith's stomach. She dashed to the adjoining door and pushed it open, her gaze sweeping the dimly lit room.

Her heart stopped.

Agnes lay sprawled on the floor near the bed. Her face was pale and contorted with pain. The vial of hemlock lay beside her, its stopper rolling slowly to a stop against the edge of the rug.

"Agnes!" Meredith rushed to her maid's side, dropping to her knees. She shook the girl gently. "What have you done?"

Agnes moaned, her eyes fluttering open. Tears streaked her cheeks, and her lips moved as though she were trying to speak but couldn't form the words.

"Good heavens, what happened?" For the first time, Docia's voice sounded with concern.

"She's taken something—" Meredith's voice broke as she reached for the vial. "The hemlock! She must have—"

Docia, still wearing her dressing gown and clutching a towel, appeared in the doorway, her earlier languor replaced by genuine alarm. "Fetch the cook or the housekeeper! Isn't there a remedy for such things? Charcoal, or—"

"She didn't drink it," Meredith said, her voice trembling. She held up the vial, noting that most of the liquid remained inside. "She must have only tasted it. But she's unwell all the same."

Agnes began to sob, her hand clutching at Meredith's sleeve. "I didn't mean to, milady—I swear I didn't mean to—"

"Didn't mean to what?" Meredith demanded, her voice both soft and urgent. "When did you return? You were supposed to be with your mother."

"I overheard them—" Agnes coughed violently, curling in on herself.

Meredith adjusted her position, propping Agnes against her knees to keep her from choking. "Mr. Thornfield, and... and Harper. Or maybe the duke. They're going to kill 'im. They're going to kill Lord Pender!"

Meredith's blood ran cold. "What? What did you hear?"

"They said it would look like an accident," Agnes sobbed. "Something in the mine—they're planning it tonight."

Docia gasped and Meredith glanced over her shoulder to see Docia clutching the doorframe. "An accident? In the mine?"

Meredith's thoughts raced. Lucius and Mr. Ashcroft were on their way to the mine that very moment, unaware of the danger that lay in wait. She tightened her grip on Agnes's hand.

"Agnes, are you certain? What exactly did they say?"

Agnes nodded weakly, her face pale as wax. "Yes, milady. Mr. Thornfield said the timbers were… were weak. Harper laughed and said no one would question it—just another collapse, like before…" her voice trailed to a whisper that weaved Meredith's spine with icicles.

Meredith's chest tightened. She turned to Docia, her voice sharp. "Send for Mrs. Verity—now." She came to her feet.

Docia hesitated, her usual poise cracking under the weight of the moment. "But what if they're already—"

Meredith leaned her maid against the bed and raced to the wardrobe then yanked the door back. "Don't even say it. Don't even *think* it."

"What are you planning on doing?"

Meredith grabbed a dark riding habit. "I'm going after them. Help me with this dress."

Docia hurried forward and together Meredith was changed in no time. "You can't possibly go alone."

"No. I'll get Bartlett." She went back to Agnes and went down to her knees. "Docia is going for Mrs. Verity. Agnes, did you give Mr. Harper my pistol?"

"Aye," she cried in harsh gulping sobs that Meredith had no time in which to deal with.

"Agnes, listen to me. I must reach Lord Pender and Mr. Ashcroft before they… before they…" Merdith swallowed her fear and gripped Agnes's hand.

"It was all my fault," she cried again.

"We can sort that out later." Meredith did her best to quell her frustration, her irritation, her rising anxiety, her panic. "I-I must go."

She pierced Docia with a hard stare. "Do as I said. Get Mrs. Verity. If you happen into my father, do not—I repeat—*do not* tell him anything of this. Then you shall remain with my maid. I've no time to waste."

Docia fled, her footsteps echoing down the hall.

Meredith turned back to Agnes, brushing damp hair from her forehead. "You've done the right thing, Agnes," she murmured, though her heart pounded wildly. "Can you make it to the settee?"

"I-I don't know."

"All right. Docia and Mrs. Verity will be back soon. Don't tell anyone where I've gone. Rest now. I'll return as quickly as possible." Meredith hurried down the servants' stairs then crept to the foyer. Her kid-leather half boots made virtually no sound on the polished floor. She didn't need Verity hurrying forward in his nightshirt and cap, leveling any disapproving stares. Not that he would. To her face. But she would not think him above alerting her father of her doings. No matter that the duke was not Perlsea's lord and master.

Sconces provided low lighting, and she slipped out the door. She didn't see Bartlett, but waiting was out of the question. Time was her adversary.

She hurried in the direction of the stables; rounding the corner—"Oof."

"Steady there, milady."

Her hand flew to her chest. "Oh, Bartlett, you gave me a fright. I need a horse."

"I'm way ahead of you, milady." He led her to two horses already saddled.

"You are a godsend, Bartlett." Meredith accepted his boost up. "We must make haste. I fear for Lord Pender's safety."

"Yes, milady."

"We'll stop just inside the copse of trees, then approach the mines on foot."

She felt rather than saw his look of surprise. "My lady?"

"Trust me," she said.

"Of course." Bartlett took the lead down the path. The way was treacherous with the moon hidden behind moving clouds, but with their periodically shifting, it allowed some visibility.

They rode in silence, and with each passing minute, Meredith forced herself at a steady pace. Not kicking her mount into a headlong run thus killing herself in the process.

Ten minutes later, they reached the copse of trees and dismounted. She tried picturing the map, but all she could recall was faded squiggly lines. "We'll have to go in through the front," she said.

His response was but a grunt and a stomp on the ground—

"I have another way to enter."

Meredith's stomach dropped at the sound of a voice she didn't recognize. "Bartlett?" Just as she said his name, she saw him lying on the ground, unmoving. Her eyes moved to the other booted feet and, slowly, she raised her gaze. "Harper?" she whispered.

"Mornin', milady. Aren't ye an unexpected surprise. I see Agnes couldn't contain her sweet trap shut." In the moonlight, his face took on a spectral quality. Sharp angles of his cheekbones and jawline cast shadows that deepened the hollows of his face. A jagged scar cut from his temple to his cheekbone and gleamed faintly silver as the clouds shifted and caught on the uneven edges that made the hollows appear even more prominent. Like cracks in weathered stone.

Meredith opened her mouth to scream but the burly man had hands that matched, and one instantly covered her face, squeezing her cheeks.

"Now, now, none o' that. Yer papa wouldn't like it." His low growl held a hint of sinister amusement that churned her stomach into a cramp.

She started to bend over, but he clamped his hand around her upper arm and dragged her along a path that ran behind the mine, then curved toward the cliffs. Harper didn't slow his steps, dragging her when she stumbled until they reached a twisted tangle of vines he kicked away. He entered the yawning blackness first and stopped so quickly, she ran into him.

"Not a sound, milady, iff'n ye know what's good for ye." The growl seemed a permanent aspect of his voice. He pushed her in front of him, blocking the entrance.

Meredith recoiled. "I-I can't…"

He rustled about but she couldn't see a thing. "Ye can, and ye will," he said from the dark. Flint struck against steel and seconds later he held up a lighted torch. His hand clamped her arm again. "Let's go."

CHAPTER THIRTY-TWO

THE OPPRESSIVE WEIGHT of the earth above pressed down on Lucius as he stepped deeper into the cavernous mine, the faint light of his lantern casting long shadows over the jagged rock walls. Beside him, Ashcroft moved with the precision of a man driven, the map they'd followed clutched tightly in his hand. Lucius's stomach churned with unease. They were too close to something—something foul.

"What do you expect to find here?" Lucius murmured, his voice low.

Ashcroft didn't answer immediately. His gaze flicked to a patch of disturbed earth ahead, then to a pit. A gaping maw carved into the mine's floor. The stench grew stronger, sour and metallic, turning Lucius's stomach. Ashcroft kneeled by the edge of the pit and pointed silently.

Lucius approached with a wary step. Light from his lantern fell over bodies piled within. His breath caught. Skeletal remains interspersed with fresher corpses. The sight of a man's lifeless face, even in its decayed state, sent a jolt through him. "Who is it?" Lucius whispered.

"I suspect it's Derwa Cardy's husband."

The name echoed in his mind, and with it, the weight of countless injustices. "How long ago?" he whispered.

Ashcroft's voice was flat, devoid of emotion. "Three years. Soon after your wife arrived and hired me. I-I suspected, but—" His voice broke.

Inside, guilt squeezed Lucius's chest like a vise. "Any idea how many?"

"Too many. I believe some of those missing stewards might have found a new home here. Other miners. Anyone who threatened to talk."

Lucius's chest tightened. "What is Thornfield hiding?"

"The same thing Rathbourne is," Ashcroft bit out.

Heavy footsteps echoed from the mine's entrance. Lucius turned sharply, his hand instinctively going for his cane, again, sending a sharp pain through his shoulder. He ignored it.

Ashcroft lifted his torch.

The flame revealed Rathbourne and Thornfield descending an incline toward them, their expressions dark and foreboding.

"Couldn't keep your nose out of it, could you, Pender?" Rathbourne's commanding and resonant tone bounded against the stone. The sound carried the smooth authority of an orator. He held his own lantern that made his eyes appear as empty sockets in the inadequate lighting. "What you've uncovered here will do no one the least amount of good." His conversational rhythm failed to disguise an almost indiscernible tremor.

"This is *my* land, Rathbourne. Admittedly, I've been as neglectful as was my father, but I'm here now. My wife has grown fond of Perlsea. And, I've grown fond of my wife."

Thornfield stepped into the light, closer to the pit as if daring Lucius to challenge him. "Have you any idea what you've stumbled upon?"

Lucius squared his shoulders, his fury boiling over. "This is murder, Thornfield. These people didn't just disappear—they were buried here like refuse because of your greed. I want to know why?"

"Tell them," Rathbourne instructed Thornfield. "They shan't be leaving here alive."

"Have you forgotten the terms of the betrothal agreement, Your Grace? If I die before my wife, she retains full ownership. Not you."

Rathbourne's harsh laughter echoed in the chamber as he backed away. "I can handle my daughter, Pender. I find her quite manageable." He lifted his other hand, exposing a pistol, aiming for the rafters above the entrance from which Lucius and Ashcroft had emerged.

"Good God. He's planning to bury us alive," Ashcroft bit out.

"You're quite right—" Rathbourne stopped, froze in place. "Dorian," he breathed. "Impossible."

"At your service, Your Grace." Ashcroft stepped forward and whipped off his hat.

The duke clutched at his chest. "But... you... you ran."

"I saw what you did. I watched you murder my mother," Ashcroft snarled. The weight of years of pain seeped into his words. "I've spent every day since ensuring you'd pay for it."

Dorian. The name echoed in Lucius's mind. "The Marquess of Blackstone," Lucius said, remembering.

Ashcroft, rather Blackstone, flashed a quick smile, his teeth gleaming against the torch he held. "At your service, *my lord.*"

Before Lucius could respond, more footsteps whispered on the stone floors, lighter but frantic. Lucius spun to see Harper emerge from the shadows, hauling—*dear God*—a struggling Meredith by the arm.

"It's a trap, Lucius! It's a trap—" she screamed.

A blast cut her words short and the low ceiling crumbled like wadded up foolscap and rained on her and her captor's heads.

Terror like he'd never known spiraled through Lucius. He dropped his torch and sprang forward, his world narrowed to the frantic beat of his heart and the suffocating dust filling his lungs. His fingers tore at the rubble, rough rocks cutting into his skin as he dug desperately. Each movement sent searing pain through his shoulder, but he didn't care. He couldn't care.

"Meredith!" he choked, his voice raw with fear. Images of her still form beneath the debris flashed through his mind, just like the child he'd witnessed her carrying, threatening to paralyze him. No. She had to be alive. She had to be. He would know if she...

He cleared his mind and felt Blackstone beside him, digging just as frantically.

The weight of the collapsing mine pressed down on him, both physically and mentally. Sweat mixed with the smell of blood assaulted him. His muscles screamed in protest. His shoulder felt as if it might tear apart, but he pushed through, his nails scraping raw against unyielding stone. The thought of losing her, of her being swallowed by this darkness, drove him to the edge of madness.

"Hold on," he whispered, his voice cracking. The words were as much for him as for her. He refused to let her slip away. Not like this. Not here.

It seemed hours, but couldn't have been but seconds, before his fingers brushed against fabric. Relief surged through him, numbing the pain in his shoulder. With a surge of renewed vigor, he dug faster uncovering her face as the dust settled. Her features were pale, streaked with grime, but there was a faint rise and fall of her chest.

Alive. She was alive.

"Meredith," he breathed, his voice trembling. His hands cradled her face, desperate to assure himself she was real. "Stay with me. Please."

Blackstone's voice rang out. "Harper—he's dead."

Lucius turned briefly, his gaze falling on Harper's lifeless form, blood pooling from a gaping wound at his temple.

"We'll have to leave by the main entrance," Blackstone said. "Hurry, the whole place could collapse."

Without time to waste, Lucius lifted Meredith and followed Blackstone's lead. The late shift miners had gathered, mouths gaping.

"Get me a conveyance! And the doctor." Lucius barked.

At the end of the line, a man he remembered as Trevorrow held Thornfield by the neck in an iron grip.

"Hang onto him, Trevorrow," Lucius said. "He's out and we'll need a new Mine Agent."

"You can count on me, milord." Trevorrow spoke with great relish.

With a quick glance to Meredith, Lucius murmured, "Hang on, darling. We'll be home in a thrice. You'll live to give me hell." His voice was a promise he had every intention of seeing through. He strode through the cavernous opening where it seemed the fresh air rushed in. His steps grew more frantic for need until he burst outside.

"Bartlett?"

The footman looked dazed and was rubbing his head. He held two horses by their reins. His eyes dropped to Meredith. "Sorry, milord. 'Tis my fault. The man caught me unawares…"

"He was a sneaky bastard, Bartlett. Where's the duke?"

"Ashcroft's got 'em." He pointed to a cart hitched to an old nag.

"Blackstone," Lucius bit out. "He's the Marquess of Blackstone."

The duke stood hunched next to Blackstone, who had a grip on him similar to that Trevorrow had on Thornfield.

"I'll walk him back to the Keep," Blackstone said with a menacing smile. "We have much to discuss."

Lucius gave a sharp nod then turned to Bartlett. "Tie the horses to the cart. Can you drive?"

"Aye, milord."

Lucius laid Meredith gently in the back on blankets someone had generously provided and crawled in beside her. He rested her head in his lap to protect it from the bumpy ride home. "Let's go."

CHAPTER THIRTY-THREE

L UCIUS CARRIED HIS unconscious wife up the stairs, his prayers for her a silent murmur with each step. He hurried through her sitting room into her bedchamber and to the bed—the occupied bed.

Docia rose to sitting. "What—" She threw her legs over the side of the bed nearly leaping up. "Oh, dear."

Carefully, Lucius laid Meredith in the spot Docia had just vacated and smoothed the tangled burnished strands from her too-white face. He placed his fingers to her neck, searched, then found the faint pulse. Her bloodless lips iced his own blood. She couldn't die. Not like this. Not ever. "Put some clothes on," he told Docia without taking his eyes from his wife, as if he could will her to wake and berate him to oblivion. "The doctor should be here soon. I-I don't know what to do…" he finished on a whisper. "Why? Why did she follow us?"

"Her maid—I forget her name—told her she overheard some men talking. The plan was to lure you and Mr. Ashcroft… to kill you. She—" Her voice cracked.

He looked over his shoulder and was stunned to see tears glistening in Docia's eyes.

"She… she loves you. You belong together. You were never mine." She went to the door. "I'll bring the doctor as soon as he arrives."

He turned back to Meredith. "Thank you," he whispered. But the door had already latched. Gently, he intertwined their fingers, urged his warmth into her, and bowed his head over their joined hands. The profound rush of emotion was too vast for mere words. Anguish swelled in his chest, threatening to consume him, leaving him gasping for breath. "Please," he whispered. *"Please."*

The soft crackle of the fire in the hearth was the only sound filling the silence. Her hand vibrated, trembled within his. It was so slight, he was certain he'd imagined it. His eyes raised quickly to her face just as her eyelids fluttered open. "Lucius?"

An illusion, he told himself, but his heart raced, relentless, frantic, loud. "You're awake."

"You're not dead."

They spoke simultaneously. Both their voices, a tremor of sound.

He brought her hand to his lips. "Thank God… you're awake." He closed his eyes against a sudden sting. His voice shook with choked violence.

"What… what happened?" She attempted to rise.

"No. Lie back. The doctor should be here any moment." He brushed his hand instinctively over her forehead where a bump protruded. "The mine collapsed. You were struck by falling rubble. I thought—" He swallowed hard, unable to finish.

Her forehead creased. "I remember a shot."

"Thornfield. He thought to have the entire place bury us all."

"My… my father?"

"Is being dealt with. Harper is… was the only loss." *And not a great one at that*, he didn't say.

"I don't understand." Her eyes fluttered shut. "How long have I been out?"

"Not long. That's a good sign, I think. How does your head feel?"

A small smile curved her lips. "Like I've survived the collapse of a mine. You've been here the entire time?"

"Where else would I be? I—I couldn't bear leaving you."

"That doesn't sound like the Earl of Pender I know." Her voice had adopted his previous lightness and swamped him with guilt.

"I deserve that. Worse, I suppose. But… darling, when I thought—" His voice faltered. He dropped his head briefly to compose himself. "Nothing matters more than your life. Not Perlsea, not my pride. Just you. You're my wife."

"I-I didn't think you cared. Not truly. Not after… everything," she finished on a whisper.

He gently squeezed her hand. "I've been a fool—a blind, selfish fool. Docia…"

Meredith's fingers tensed in his. "Docia?"

"She's wiser than I've ever given her credit for. She said you love me."

Her lips firmed, her cheeks flushed despite her pallor, her eyes darting away. "Docia talks too much. She had no right to declare my feelings to you."

Lucius leaned in, his voice soft but insistent. "Is it true, then? Tell me, Meredith. Do you—could you—love me, after everything I've done? Leaving you to flounder on your own for three years."

She met his gaze, her eyes glistening. "It's true, blast it. Even when I wanted nothing more than to see you to oblivion. I found you to be a hero to the nth degree."

His hand tightened around hers, his voice thickened with emotion. "I know very well I don't deserve you. I never did. But if you're willing to suffer through to give me another chance, I swear, I'll spend the rest of my life trying to be worthy of your love."

She blinked and a lone tear escaped from the corner of her eye. He brushed it from her cheek. "Then don't leave me again, Lucius. That's all I ask."

Lucius cupped her face. "I won't, darling. I swear it." He pressed a soft kiss to her forehead avoiding the lump, letting his lips linger, closing his eyes. "Never again."

CHAPTER THIRTY-FOUR

The next day

"ARE YOU CERTAIN you're up for this?" Lucius paced the chamber, stopping and spinning to Meredith until she thought she would keel over from dizziness.

Meredith let out a frustrated sigh. "Absolutely." She came to her feet and went to the mirror. She adjusted the square modest bodice of her deep sapphire-blue gown, smoothed her hands over the long tapered sleeves that ended in a subtle point just past her wrists.

"You looked as grand as Victoria," he murmured, lifting her chin with a forefinger for a brush of her lips.

These tiny touches he showered her with seeped under her skin, turned her insides to a quagmire of mush. It was messy and not so easy to sort out... except... she adored him. She wrapped her arms about his neck. "And she would happily trade Albert for you."

The sharply tailored coat he wore was of the finest wool—not three years out of date like that of her own gown. His charcoal gray trousers were cut straight to fall cleanly over black leather shoes.

"We shall outshine even Docia," he said.

Her fingers touched her forehead. "But for my bumps and bruises," she said with a wry smile.

"You've never been so beautiful." His lips turned down and his expression grew serious. "You must be prepared for the worst, darling. Your father is in a world of trouble."

"It would be infinitely worse not knowing the extent of his misdeeds. Especially in light of the contract we uncovered. We both have much to learn regarding our fathers. I would ask you the same. Are you sure you are up to this?"

He laid his cheek against her temple. "With you at my side, I can face anything." His breath stirred her hair.

"Thank you," she whispered.

Meredith took his arm, and they descended the stairs after a quick stop for the journals and documents to lay out their case. He led her to the grand dining hall. At the door, she hesitated. His patience warmed her, gave her the courage she required. He looked askance at her. Meeting his eyes, she inhaled a deep breath then nodded. He patted the starched cravat at his chest as if to shore up his own resolve then threw open the doors and strode in with a confidence she latched on to.

The sight of her father hunched in on himself stunned her, looking every year of his fifty-eight. Thornfield's wrists were tied to the arms of his chair though armed men were stationed at the various entry points of the room. Their attire blended military precision with a sense of gravitas: coats of dark navy, sharply tailored, and high collars. Polished brass buttons gleamed from the gas-lit chandeliers overhead and both sported epaulettes of gold fringe on their shoulders indicating their higher rank.

The most disturbing aspect, she found, were the pistols holstered at their waists and the sabers sheathed to their sides. On the other hand, the most comforting aspect was their imposing stance with an alertness that remained at the ready. The tension was palpable, and Meredith's heart thumped loudly.

At the head of the table was a man she didn't recognize. He came to his feet when she entered.

"Lady Pender," Lucius said. "May I present Mr. Albert Forsythe and Mr. Oswald Vayne—"

"Oswald Vayne?" Meredith turned quickly to Mr. Forsythe. "Mr. Vayne's name is most familiar," she said.

Mr. Vayne bowed deeply. He was younger than she'd

thought he should be. Considerably so. He was polished and somewhat unassuming in appearance, with sharp, intelligent eyes that suggested ambition. His neatly combed hair was dark and brushed from his face, and he sported a lean, refined build. He projected a professional demeanor, in his understated elegant clothing. "You must be thinking of my father, or perhaps my grandfather," he said. "I regret to say, my father met his demise some two years past."

"I-I see," she said softly almost faintly. "My condolences on your loss."

He responded with a sharp smile and incline of his head, then stepped back.

"Mr. Forsythe is a senior member of Parliament and is known for his unflinching investigations," Lucius said with a light squeeze of her hand.

Mr. Forsythe's lips turned down at her presence, but she lifted her chin. She inclined her head. "Mr. Forsythe. Welcome to Perlsea Keep." Slowly, she surveyed the rest of the occupants—the clerk from the mine office and Mr. Ashcroft—

She tilted her head to one side. "Good afternoon, sir." She was startled to find him so well-dressed, a stark departure from the unassuming practicality she had come to associate with him. Though his outfit lacked the precise polish of a nobleman's wardrobe it was clear he had made an effort to appear dignified and composed. Most shocking was the absence of his beard, cleanly shaven that revealed a strong jaw amid a fierce demeanor.

His coat, though slightly worn at the seams, fit him well, and the waistcoat, while not overly ornate, hinted at a sophistication she hadn't realized he possessed. Even his boots, polished to a shine, seemed to speak of a man stepping into a role far removed from the one he had carefully displayed until now. The transformation unsettled her.

"Meredith."

With a sharp gasp, her eyes shot to Lucius.

He winced. "I, er, forgot to mention…"

"I'm Rathbourne's heir." Mr. Ashcroft stepped forward, took her clenched hand, and bowed over it. "The Marquess of Blackstone."

"Your… mother…"

His lips tightened and his eyes flashed to Papa. "We shall speak of it later," he said softly.

"Gentlemen and, er, my lady. If we may get started?" Mr. Forsythe moved to the head of the table.

Lucius took the journals and documents—the letters and maps she'd unearthed in the wine cellar's compartment—and set them on the table before him.

"Come, my dear." Lucius escorted her to the far end of the room to observe without drawing too much attention.

She lowered onto a winged-back chair near the fire, her nerves shattered. *Mr. Ashcroft was her brother?* She gripped the armrest, her mind racing. The men sitting around the table were an imposing group with their dark coats and serious expressions. Meredith forced herself to concentrate.

Mr. Forsythe stepped forward. He glanced toward her dark corner frowning again—still—but then seemed to pull himself up. His voice cut through the room. "Your Grace, my lords, gentlemen. We are here on behalf of the Crown and Parliament to investigate allegations of corruption, unsafe working conditions, and the mishandling of funds tied to the Penhalwick mine. There is damning evidence that implicates members of this estate."

He'd forgotten murder. Meredith's gaze went to Lucius. His face was as unreadable as her recollections of the falling debris she couldn't remember.

Her father shot to his feet. "This is an outrage! I demand to know the source of these so-called allegations."

Mr. Forsythe's lips curled into a thin smile. He shuffled through another stack of papers. "The Marquess of Blackstone, Your Grace."

The inspector pulled over the familiar aged, yellowing papers.

Papa lowered back to his chair, his expression faltering, his face darkening.

Mr. Forsythe slid a paper in his direction. "Do you recognize this signature, Your Grace?"

Her father's lips tightened in a compressed line.

Mr. Forsythe held up another paper. "This correspondence, dated 1828," he went on, "details bribes paid to members of Parliament to stall safety regulations. The signatories include the late Earl of Pender… and you, sir, the Duke of Rathbourne."

Meredith kept her gaze steady, though her pulse quickened. Lucius leaned forward, his brows furrowed. She wondered if he was realizing for the first time, as was she, the depth of their fathers' betrayals.

"These are fabrications," her father blustered with the disdain and disgust that only a man of his station could effect. "Forgeries! I'll not stand for such baseless accusations."

Before Forsythe could respond, Meredith spoke up, her voice clear but firm. "The papers are genuine, Your Grace. I found them myself, hidden in a secret compartment in the wine cellar. They are a record of decades of deceit."

The room fell silent. All eyes turned to her in various degrees of surprise. As if they'd forgotten her presence altogether. Lucius's gaze was a mix of surprise and something deeper— admiration? She wanted to bask within the warmth she found there, but Papa's face had twisted into fury.

"You dare accuse me, girl?" he snarled.

"I speak the truth," Meredith said evenly. "You have exploited the people of Penhalwick for years and tarnished the name of this estate. The inspectors are here to see justice done."

Lucius cleared his throat. "In addition to my wife's finds, I also recovered detailed payout information from a safe in Thornfield's office."

Mr. Forsythe's eyes narrowed on Lucius. "I see." He drummed his fingers on the polished wood. "Lord Pender, there are questions regarding your involvement. These papers suggest your late father and the duke orchestrated these schemes. Even so far back as the Marquess of Aylesbury. Did you have knowledge of these actions?"

Lucius shook his head, his voice steady but tinged with anger. "None. I have spent years away from this estate, ignorant of the treachery my father and…" He leveled his gaze on Thornfield then Papa. "…others committed. There is also a compact agreement my wife found that indicates the duke's father. And," he flicked his gaze on Mr. Vayne, "a Mr. Oswald Vayne."

The room stilled where it seemed all eyes moved to Mr. Vayne in varying degrees of accusation.

The blood drained from his face. "I beg your pardon, sir."

Lucius retrieved a tri-folded missive from an inside pocket of his waistcoat. He held it out to Mr. Forsythe. "This is a letter we believe was penned by the former Duke of Rathbourne. He speaks of a member of Parliament assisting them."

Mr. Forsythe accepted the letter and quickly read through it.

"In the stack of documents my wife recovered, there is the 'Compact of The Order' I spoke of. It contains a list of the original members and is signed by each. I believe Mr. Vayne's grandfather was instrumental in assisting The Order with their nefarious deeds."

Mr. Forsythe thumbed through that stack and found the paper Lucius indicated. He then handed it to Mr. Vayne who looked near to fainting. Mr. Forsythe gave a sharp nod. "I believe the evidence supports your claims, Lord Pender. The duke and Mr. Thornfield shall accompany us to London and appear before Parliament for further action."

A relief so profound hit Meredith in the chest, she had to bite her lip from crying out. Her hands clenched in her lap. She couldn't pull her eyes from Lucius. How could she not love him?

LUCIUS LET OUT a long-held breath as Forsythe outlined the next steps—placing the mine under government oversight and preparing formal charges against Rathbourne and Thornfield. Watching Rathbourne's mask of arrogance crumble should have given him greater satisfaction, but it didn't. The man had no care for anyone other than himself, but he was Meredith's father.

He swung his gaze to Thornfield's pale face where defeat beaded his brow and upper lip. Ah, he'd realized his protector was losing his grip.

"You can't do this," Papa hissed. "The mine is my legacy!"

"No, Papa. It's mine. The betrothal agreements prove that so." Meredith had stood and moved into the light. "You and Mr. Thornfield succeeded in making it a graveyard." Her voice carried the weight of all the lives lost due to her father's greed and neglect. She locked eyes with him. Hers, unflinching. "And now, it's your reckoning."

Lucius couldn't have been more proud of her. He rose from the table and moved to her side, entwined his fingers with hers.

Forsythe swiveled a cold glare on Thornfield. "And you, sir. Did you use a pistol with the intent of forcing a collapse?"

Thornfield's beady eyes narrowed and his pointed chin lifted, though he refrained from speaking. The man reeked of venom.

Forsythe was unmoved, however, and directed his attention to one of the guards. "Arrest him. He killed a man by the name of—" He glanced down at the tabletop and pulled a document toward himself. "He killed a man by the name of Harper." He looked back up. "Lord Pender, I wish to thank you for your cooperation. We'll take our leave at this time to begin the formal interrogation." He gathered the incriminating documents and withdrew from the dining hall.

Tension lingered after their departure.

Rathbourne stormed out, but not before casting a venomous glare at Meredith.

Lucius squeezed her hand. "You sent the documents to Forsythe?"

"Yes," she admitted. "Also the document Bray Cardy was forced to sign the day before he died. It was the only way."

His exhale was fierce and sharp. "You've done more for this estate—and these people—than I ever have."

"It's not about me," Meredith replied. "It's about justice. For all of them." She turned to Blackstone. "A word, with you, my lord?"

Lucius caught Blackstone's eye, and a grin erupted from Lucius watching the two depart. There was a similarity between them he hadn't noticed before. Something in the way they held their heads, perhaps the stubborn look about their mouths. A flicker of something unfamiliar fluttered in his chest. He wasn't certain what it was.

Hope? Yes, that felt right. Hope—and for the first time in his life… a brighter future.

He saw to the guards leading Thornfield and Rathbourne out then made his way to the library to witness Blackstone's fallout.

CHAPTER THIRTY-FIVE

MEREDITH ENTERED THE library quite aware of Mr. Ashcroft—no! Lord Blackstone. A marquess. She spun around and poked him in the chest. "I cannot believe you have been employed by me for three years and not once have you indicated our relation."

He grabbed her by the fist, wincing.

"How did he not declare you dead after all these years? Answer me that! This is outrageous." She fairly growled.

"Do I receive no credit for the work we've accomplished here?"

She jerked her fist from him. "Don't you dare make light of this," she snapped. "You led me to believe I was alone, left to deal with *him*—my father." Her voice cracked, but she refused to falter. "And all the while, you were here. Laughing behind my back, no doubt, at the foolish little countess playing at being a schoolteacher. Running an estate."

His smirk faded, and his brow furrowed. "Meredith—"

"No! You don't get to say my name as if we are… close." Her voice shook, and she hated the tears threatening to fall. "You don't get to act like any of this is normal. Do you know what I've endured because of him? Because of *them*?" She waved her hand, encompassing not just the duke but every man who had betrayed her trust. "And all the while, you—my *brother*—hiding behind a false name."

He stepped closer, his expression softening, though his eyes gleamed with a mix of regret and something deeper. "It was never about hiding from you, Meredith."

"Oh, wasn't it?" She crossed her arms, her voice low and sharp. "Then what was it about, pray tell?"

He hesitated, and for the first time, she saw the vulnerable man that lay beneath the surface. "It was about surviving. Staying one step ahead of *him*. Yet making sure there was doubt of my death. If he had known that I was alive—"

"You could have come to me," she interrupted, her anger flaring anew. "You could have told me the truth, Mr. Ashcroft—Lord Blackstone—whoever the devil you are. We could have faced him together."

"And gotten you killed?" His voice rose, and his hand clenched at his side. "Do you have any idea what he's capable of? He killed my mother. I *saw* him."

Her breath hitched at the raw emotion in his tone. "Then tell me," she demanded, softer this time. "If you're truly my brother, tell me."

For a long moment, he said nothing, his jaw working as if struggling with the weight of his words. "I will," he said finally, his voice hoarse. "I still have work to do. He can't be allowed to threaten and murder people."

She turned away, needing the distance. "You don't get to decide if or when I'm worthy of the truth."

"Meredith," he said again, almost pleading now. "I didn't wish to hurt you."

She laughed bitterly, running a hand over her face. "Well, congratulations, Blackstone. What is your actual *Christian* name, if you please?"

"Dorian. Dorian Jephson."

"Well, Dorian Jephson, you failed."

A small choked sounded from the corner of the room. Meredith stiffened, spinning toward the source. There, half-hidden behind the shadow of a bookshelf, sat Docia Hale. She had been so still, so silent, Meredith hadn't even noticed her presence.

Docia stood, her face a portrait of astonishment and… something else. "You're the Marquess of Blackstone?" she asked, her voice breathy with wonder. "Truly?"

Meredith groaned. Of all the people to overhear this revelation, it had to be *her.* She opened her mouth to respond, but Blackstone beat her to it.

"Yes," he said, his tone cool and practiced now, the mask slipping back into place. He bowed slightly. "At your service."

Docia's eyes sparkled as she stepped closer, as though drawn by some invisible force. "I had no idea."

Meredith closed her eyes and pinched the bridge of her nose. This day could not possibly grow any worse.

The door opened and Lucius entered. "Rathbourne's been taken into custody. Forsythe spoke of his title being stripped." He looked at Blackstone. "I suggest you speak with him if you have inklings of maintaining your heritage."

"Blast," he muttered, storming out.

Docia hurried after him. Meredith rolled her eyes.

"Are you truly that angry with him?" Lucius asked her.

"Yes." She stomped her foot. "No. I-I don't know."

"Come along. I know something that will do wonders in making you feel better."

Meredith leaned her back against her husband's chest, the scented hot water seeping through her skin. "Thank you for the lemon tart, my lord. How did you know it was my favorite?"

"A ridiculous question, my lady. The question is how could I not know?" he breathed against her neck, sending a delicious shiver through her.

"This was an excellent remedy to my shattered nerves," she told him.

"I'm the one with shattered nerves." His arm tightened across her abdomen with his words. "I mean it, Meredith, don't you ever run headlong into those mines again. I vow, I'll shut them down."

"I wonder what Papa was looking for in the old study."

"I venture to guess it was the journal. He had to know his signature as Marquess Blackstone would come back to haunt him," he said thoughtfully.

"That makes perfect sense, I suppose. How long have you known that Mr. Ashcroft—I mean Lord Blackstone—was my father's heir?"

"Don't you mean your brother?"

She wrinkled her nose unable to address that particular subject. Why ruin a perfectly good bath in a perfectly good bathing chamber with a perfectly good husband? "That's too difficult a concept to think about right now. Do you think Thornfield will be hung?"

"At the very least, transported." Lucius's hands caressed her ribs then came up to smooth over her shoulders. An oil extract released the pleasant fragrance of violets.

"Who will you designate to run the mine?" Her voice came out breathy while her body tingled beneath such tender ministrations.

His hands moved over her breasts and her breath hitched. She closed her eyes and covered his hands with hers, letting out a long, satisfied sigh.

"Trevorrow," he murmured against her neck. "He was pushing back at Thornfield's utter lack of safety measures. Trevorrow shall do admirably. Especially with Samuel Trenwith's assistance."

She turned her head sharply, meeting his eyes. "Samuel Trenwith?"

"I think he would be especially cognizant of safety, don't you?" His fingers slid between her legs and pressed her sex.

Meredith gasped and her head fell back to his shoulder—the good one, she hoped. Her fingers grasped his adding her own pressure to ease that climatic ache. "Yes. Most… definitely."

He bit then licked her neck, suckled lightly while his fingers worked their magic between her legs. He started slowly. But that didn't last. Soon his hands were working furiously until she couldn't catch her breath.

"That's it, love. Let… go. I've got you. I've got you."

The words. The freedom. The validation blasted through her. The light struck with such fierce intensity that it seemed to sear the air itself. As though the world behind her eyes had been dipped in molten gold, every detail washed in a white-hot brilliance so sharp it etched its presence to the backs of her eyelids. It wasn't simply the brightness—it was an assault, a flood of radiance, that overwhelmed her with blazing magnitude.

Her breaths came in harsh, rapid intakes.

"Turn around," he panted against her neck. "Straddle me."

A pleasant shiver in the water's warmth stole through her. "I'm not certain I have the ability." But she did as he asked. Her eyes went to his shoulder then to the bandages floating in the bath. "Oh, no, your wound." Bruising in dark purples, greens, and fading to yellow bloomed around his puckered skin.

He acted as if she hadn't spoken, pulling her over him and guiding the stiff rod of his erection into her, then groaning.

She leaned forward and his lips grasped one nipple, then grazed it with his teeth. White-hot fervor coursed through her like a stream of raw energy, ravaging her every nerve ending. "Lucius." She hauled in a deep breath. "Lucius. I… I…"

"I love you, Meredith. *Marry*… me." His hips surged up, sending water sloshing over the sides of the tub. Then a second time. A third time as another climax pinpointed and claimed her senses, stealing any ability to comprehend his words.

"Marry?" Her backside burned where his hands imprinted her body, pressing her closer.

He took her mouth in a torrid kiss that robbed her of further words. Tongues dueled for dominance but there were no losers in this contest.

With a last surge up, his roar bellowed against the bathing chamber's steamy walls. All she could do was hold on for dear life. "God, Meredith. Oh, God."

She fell against his chest, her heart and sex pounding in perfect synchronization with his while attempting to draw breath into her lungs. It took a moment for her sensations to return though her pulse still beat with erratic thumps. Slowly, she pushed from his chest. "Did you say marry? Lucius, we're alre—"

"I mean truly marry, darling. Nothing held back. I wish to pledge my commitment to you for all to see."

A blast of emotion had Meredith blinking quickly. She was touched as never before.

"Don't cry, darling. Please. I didn't wish to upset you…"

"I-I'm not upset," she hiccupped. She cupped his face with both hands. "I love you, too." Raising her voice above a whisper was an impossible feat.

His breath seemed to release in a huge sigh of relief. "Help me out of here," he said smiling slightly. "Your breasts are too enticing and distracting for me to think properly."

Closing her eyes, Meredith felt the track of a tear trailing down her cheek as she leaned in and brushed his lips with hers. "All right." With him steadying her, she stood in the tub and stepped over the edge onto the sopping wet floor. She wrapped herself in a large linen towel then assisted Lucius up, grasping his hand tightly. Once he'd gained his footing, she took up another towel and set about patting his backside dry, his lovely buttocks, the backs of his legs, before straightening up before she did something truly embarrassing like licking his softening manhood. She searched for a topic to quell more thoughts of satisfying her curiosity when it came to his body. "What do you suppose will happen to my father?"

"That will be up to Parliament. Blackstone, too, I suspect. It's possible the duke could be stripped of his title." His arm draped her shoulders, and he pulled her into him. His chin rested atop her head. "Do you worry that you will no longer be the daughter of a duke?"

She coughed out a choked laugh. "No. I've always envied Geneva, you know. She never suffered the constraints of Society I and our other friends suffered."

"You say that now, darling, but the name Pender isn't exactly unscathed, and I've done little to bolster its reputation."

She heard the smile in his voice. "Papa's crimes are too egregious to ignore. He *should* have to pay consequences for his actions."

"The scandal will be far-reaching."

"I can withstand any scandal," she said against his dampened chest. "As long as I'm with you."

He pulled away and framed her face with both hands. Looked deep into her eyes. She was caught momentarily by the stilled storms missing in his gray ones. "The people of Penhalwick are lucky to have you, my love."

"Us," she returned, going on her toes and feathering his lips. "They are lucky to have *us*."

One week later

THE LIBRARY DOOR swung back, hitting the wall behind with a decisive crash. Startled, Lucius glanced up from his place before the fire expecting to see his wife. Instead, Mrs. Geneva Oshea— his recent sister-in-law—entered, followed by Lady Abra Washington and Miss Hannah Williams—sister of his friend Baron Ruskin—marched in, forming a wall of indomitable feminine determination.

Lucius groaned, already knowing this would not end well. "Oh, splendid. The Fates themselves, come to pass judgment."

"Don't flatter yourself, my lord." Geneva Oshea spoke with a cheerfulness that offered no reassurance. "We're more like the Eumenides, here to ensure justice is served."

Lady Abra arched a brow. "He won't know what that means, Gen. Look at him—he's clearly never picked up a book unless it was to bludgeon someone."

"Charming as ever, Lady Abra," he said dryly. "To what do I owe the pleasure?"

Miss Williams, ever the polite and poised one of the trio, clasped her hands before her and stepped forward. "Meredith."

Lucius stiffened but remained quiet. He, more than anyone, knew he didn't deserve his wife's generosity, her love.

"Your wife should be treated as a queen. But for her horrible father, she would be the pinnacle of Society." Geneva's hands clenched at her sides.

"We're here to ensure you treat her as she deserves," Lady Abra cut in. "Or else."

Lucius was amused in spite of himself. "Or else what? You'll glare at me harder? Attempt to outwit me with your vast collection of insults? You might find I've an incredibly thick skin."

Lady Abra leaned forward and poked her finger in his chest. "Oh no, my lord. The Clandestine Sapphire Society is not heralded for wasting our breath. We look after one another. You are an earl but sacrificial in our estimation. We'd simply toss you into the Chamber of Rest."

Lucius blinked, his mouth gaped then snapped shut. He stared at them, stunned, for a moment. "Where—How—"

"We have ears, my lord," Geneva said as if he were an imbecile. "It's all the talk at The Copper Kettle. Although, to be fair, Hannah did volunteer to push you into the mine herself. Abra and I thought that a bit unseemly, but..." She trailed off with an innocent shrug.

A grin started deep in his chest, and he let out a small cough to cover a laugh. "Er, it's comforting to know Meredith is surrounded with such... benevolent friends."

"Sarcasm will not fly with us, my lord." Lady Abra strode to the fire and spun about, piercing him with her hazel eyes so unique to her mother's Jamaican heritage. "We're immune. I should like to discuss your, shall we say, abysmal performance on your wedding day three years ago. I was there, you know."

Groaning, Lucius slumped in his chair. "I suspected. You have the look of someone who enjoys witnessing misery."

"Quite right," Lady Abra said smartly. "And I don't mind saying, your misery was most entertaining. I've never seen a groom look more like he wished to face a firing squad than a bishop. The bishop had to remind you to say your vows! Twice!"

"Admittedly, not my proudest moment," he said with a sheepish smile. "It was a rather… overwhelming day."

Geneva snorted. "Overwhelming? Oh, my lord, I believe the word you're looking for is 'cowardly.'"

Miss Williams gave a solemn nod. "Tragic, really. But now you're lucky enough for a second chance, which is more than most men are afforded. What of Meredith's other efforts, my lord? Her Literary Society, the school for the children?"

Lucius leaned back in his chair, scrutinizing them. He quashed any irritation, scrubbing a hand over his face. He deserved this set down. And if it squared things with Meredith's dearest friends, then so be it. "My wife's good works are safe from my nefarious hands, I assure you. I know I made a hash of things. But I'm here now and I shall assist her in any way possible."

He stared into the three fierce faces for a long moment before breaking into a rueful smile. "I take it I'm under the full attack of the Clandestine Sapphire Society?"

Geneva didn't hesitate. "You are indeed, my lord. The four of us made a pact years ago. We have every intention of following through on those endeavors."

"Well. It seems my fate is sealed then. Either I prove myself worthy of my wife, or I get tossed into the mines by three very determined women." He stood, offering a bow. "Challenge accepted."

Geneva grinned. "Good. Now, off you go. Groveling takes time, and you're years behind schedule."

They marched to the door just as they had marched in, Miss

Williams bringing up the rear, but short of disappearing through, she turned. "By the bye, Lord Pender, we are quite looking forward to the renewal of your vows tomorrow."

They swept out as quickly as they entered, leaving Lucius standing in the library, bemused but oddly invigorated.

"Three harpies I may never survive," he muttered. But that wasn't true. He'd survive anything with Meredith at his side.

CHAPTER THIRTY-SIX

11:00 A.M. Monday, 16 August 1847
Penhalwick, St. Petroc's Church

THE CURRENT EARL of Pender, Lucius Oshea was past caring what anyone thought save for one person—Lady Meredith Jephson-Oshea, the current Countess of Pender. No longer did he consider his bride at four and twenty to his four and thirty obscene. There was no one more perfect for him in every sense of the word.

St. Petroc's church was a humble yet striking example of Cornish ecclesiastical architecture, blending medieval heritage with the rugged character of the land itself. Inside, he found an air of quiet resilience, much like the people of Penhalwick themselves. The scent of stone and wood lingered in the cool air and mingled with flowers and the wax of the many candles burning. Though humble, the church held a sense of sacredness—a solace and unity—that touched him.

Lucius thought of the last time he'd entered a church, remembered how tempted he'd been to knock over one to two of those candles to set St. George's ablaze with his fury.

An entirely different feeling engulfed him now. Last time, he couldn't recall his bride's name. Today, he wanted to shout her name to the rafters. Make certain the church—full to bursting with villagers, family, and friends—knew that he not only recalled his wife's name this time around but realized exactly how much he adored and cherished her. Hence, the recent interrogation from her three closest friends.

All of whom seated prominently in the first two pews of the church along with Lucius's own brothers, Noah and Julius, his cousin Isabelle, his Aunt Verda and Uncle Sander. Baron Ruskin, now betrothed to Lady Abra, was also in attendance.

Lord Blackstone sat in the back row, determined to keep a low profile for the time being and for reasons unknown to Lucius.

The gown Meredith wore, if he wasn't mistaken, was the same ice-blue gown she'd donned the first time they'd wed. Three years ago, the blood had congealed in his veins. Now, his blood ran hot as an Italian's and matching depth of passion.

The same veil of stark white lace covered her face. The Queen's trend in covering the bride's face he'd gladly approved of at the time. He now abhorred it with his every breath. His fingers itched to see her lovely face. To see her eyes shining with her love he vowed to bask in for the remainder of his life.

Vicar Bosworth's deep voice jarred Lucius from his radiant and hope-filled reflections. *"Wilt thou have this Woman to thy wedded wife, to live together after God's ordinance in the holy estate of Matrimony? Wilt thou love her—"*

Yes! He *would* love her. He *would* comfort her. He absolutely *would* keep her in sickness and in health.

"Lord Pender?"

Lucius flinched.

"Your vow, sir." The vicar's low timbre caught him unawares. The stab of Lady Abra's stare pierced the skin between his shoulders. Surely, he was bleeding profusely.

Lucius cleared his throat and spoke loudly, proudly. He wanted no doubts of his intentions this time around. "I absolutely will." His voice bounded with renewed confidence through the ancient church.

His wife's fingers shook just as they had three years before. But this time it was with excitement and anticipation. Insides smiling, Lucius steadied her hand and slid the gold band in place then brought her hand to his lips and kissed the ring and finger he'd placed it on.

"You may lift her veil, my lord."

The Brussels' exquisite lace was soft within his fingers. His heart pounded, and it was a wonder it didn't drum against the stone walls. With a shallow breath, he forced himself to calm, then lifted.

The streaks of chestnut in her blonde, goldish hair was in keeping of their reenacting that day three years ago—swept from her face in a bun that set at the crown of her head just like before, encircled with that same diamond-studded tiara—the promise of starting anew from that moment.

Her moss-green eyes stared up at him, twinkling with mirth, joy, contentment. God, she was so beautiful, so lovely. For a long moment he was caught in the exhilaration he saw there. Her plump pink lips curved, revealing her true desire. *Him.* This journey they were on, destined to one another for the remainder of their lives.

"I now pronounce you Lord and Lady Pender of Penhalwick. Kiss your bride, my lord."

With great enthusiasm, Lucius did as the vicar commanded.

The congregation broke out into deafening cheers. He was almost certain Lady Abra and Geneva's were among the loudest.

Lucius took Meredith's arm and faced the standing assembly. "Please join my new wife and me at Perlsea Keep for the traditional wedding breakfast. All are welcome."

More rousing cheers greeted this announcement and together, he and Meredith took the long walk to the open doors at the back of St. Petroc's. On the church steps, no raindrops splattered the cobblestones. It was pure bright, cleansing sunlight.

The gaze of the crowd didn't judge or dissect or wait for cracks to appear. These people, his people, were here to celebrate; they were here to witness and share the new beginning Meredith and he had chosen.

As before, Bartlett stood beside the carriage and swung the door back as they approached. Lucius assisted Meredith up and leaped in after her, grinning. He settled across from her and met her… worried eyes.

Lucius took her hands in his. "What is it?"

She lowered her eyes and shook her head, her lips trembling.

He lifted her chin, stunned to find tears shimmering. "Darling, tell me. It can't be that bad."

"It's terrible," she whispered. After a moment, she breathed in through her nose and seemed to stiffen her spine. "I-I have a confession to make."

Lucius's stomach dropped like a dive from the cliffs and hit the depths of the underworld where Poseidon ruled. He was being fanciful, ridiculous. "Whatever it is, my love, we shall weather it together."

"I've been… unfaithful," she whispered again.

His grip on her fingers tightened but he waited. Jumping to conclusions was the old Lucius. The scared child Lucius. He meant it. They could, would weather this *together*.

"I… I used my fingers to… to pleasure myself. In the bath. I'm sorry."

He barely kept from gasping, or his laughter from erupting. "And, er, were you thinking of someone in particular when you embarked upon this heinous crime of… passion?" he asked softly.

"Yes," she whispered, dropping her gaze. "I was thinking of you."

"I… see." Lucius pushed a hand through his hair, trying to decide how to handle this miscarriage of justice—the fact that he hadn't been there. "Well," he said briskly. "There is only one punishment for such a flagrant infraction."

Her eyes quickly lifted to his.

His lips twisted at the earnestness in her expression, but he met it with mock disapproval. "I believe I shall be required to witness this transgression firsthand."

Meredith's mouth parted in an 'O' before her gaze narrowed on him. Wisely so. "Firsthand," she repeated slowly.

"Definitely. Firsthand." He tugged her onto his lap. "I must ensure you are doing it correctly, of course. At the first opportunity. Right now, however, I just wish to kiss you."

Her arms weaved their way about his neck. "All right," she breathed hotly against his cheek. "I suppose I can agree to your decreed punishment. And, perhaps, other edicts as long as such 'transgressions' as you call them are reciprocal." This was said with a coy smile, because, by God, his wife was quick on the uptake. She then locked her lips to his that lasted all the way up the hill to the Keep that overlooked—oversaw—their commitment to this land, these people of Penhalwick. Perhaps his reputation as *The Shadow* could finally be laid to rest.

Thus, began the Earl and Countess of Penders' marriage in earnest.

About the Author

Kathy L Wheeler writes historical and contemporary romance and has hit the Amazon Best Seller list several times over. In the face of danger, her heroines save themselves, their heroes just need to be there to catch them… after the fact.

Her many joys include the NFL, Musical Theater, travel (for example: she once spent twenty-one days going from Oklahoma City to San Francisco and back through Utah to Colorado. When her husband called to ask if she was coming home anytime soon, she then headed back home), and … karaoke.

Main sources of inspiration? Yes, well, they come mostly from an over-active imagination. She currently resides in the Pacific Northwest with her musically talented husband, Al, and their adorable dog, Angel who lives up to her name—*mostly*.

kathylwheeler.com
facebook.com/kathylwheeler
Instagram.com/kathylwheeler
TikTok.com/@kathylwheeler
YouTube.com/@kathylwheeler-author